ONE
MADDER
WOMAN

ONE MADDER WOMAN

DEDE CRANE

Freehand Books acknowledges the financial support for its publishing program provided by the Canada Council for the Arts and the Alberta Media Fund, and by the Government of Canada through the Canada Book Fund.

Canada Council for the Arts Conseil des Arts du Canada Alberta Government Canada

Freehand Books
515–815 1st Street SW Calgary, Alberta T2P 1N3
www.freehand-books.com

Book orders: UTP Distribution
5201 Dufferin Street Toronto, Ontario M3H 5T8
Telephone: 1-800-565-9523 Fax: 1-800-221-9985
utpbooks@utpress.utoronto.ca utpdistribution.com

Library and Archives Canada Cataloguing in Publication
Title: One madder woman : a novel / Dede Crane.
Names: Crane, Dede, author.
Identifiers: Canadiana (print) 20200220039 | Canadiana (ebook) 20200220055
ISBN 9781988298689 (softcover) | ISBN 9781988298696 (EPUB) |
ISBN 9781988298702 (PDF)
Subjects: LCSH: Morisot, Berthe, 1841-1895—Fiction. | LCGFT: Novels.
Classification: LCC PS8605.R35 O54 2020 | DDC C813/.6—DC23

Edited by Deborah Willis
Book design by Natalie Olsen, Kisscut Design
Cover photo © Artokoloro / Alamy Stock Photo
Author photo by Josh Davidson
Printed on FSC®-certified paper and bound in Canada by Marquis book printing

Though based on actual people and events, this book is a work of imagination. The dates of the Exposition Universalle and the appearance of certain works at the Paris Salon have been changed for the sake of the narrative. Any misrepresentations are mine alone.

FOR BILL,

FOR EVERYTHING

ARTWORK MENTIONED

PARIS

1895

I RESOAK THE CLOTHS around your wrists and ankles, inside the burning hollows of your knees and behind your ears—the perfume points, as Grand-mère Manet called them. Finally the one across your brow. Fear makes me superstitious and I perform this ritual always in the same order, back and forth, on the stations of your body's cross.

A spoonful of beef broth. I know it hurts to swallow but you must. Lips pressed tight, you turn your face away too slowly, as though your neck has stiffened. I can't look. Beyond the window, the lamps along rue de Villejust extinguish, one after another, in sombre rhythm. Is it so late?

As I replace your quilts, you kick them off with a fierceness which floods me with hope. How right that you, my child, have not only the features but the character of a Manet. Knowing your wants as well as your needs.

In the amber lamplight your sunken cheeks look bruised. Your chest pumps breath out and out in a kind of race. Are you dreaming? Of Cousin Jeannie and the orchard in Bougival seeing who will be the first to reach the fence? Always it is you. You must be first. It is a greed I love in you.

Please, I pray—to what I don't know, as the great name God means nothing to me—let us trade places. At seventeen you are scarcely in your bloom. At fifty-four my life is lived, my hair is white, my hands unsteady. I have lost the two men who share my soul but I will die first before I lose you. This I promise.

The cloth across your brow is already hot. Your damp hair is hard under my lips and smells of fruit gone sour. Why? What does it mean?

There are so many things I haven't told you, believing you too young to understand and not wanting to burden your spirit. No doubt I underestimate you, fixed as I am in seeing you as a child. But after I am dead and buried, people will consider it their right and duty to speak of me in their spewed stew of gossip and guesswork, their half-digested facts. You will hear hurtful rumours not only about me but about your father and even more so your uncle. And, therefore, about you. When that time comes you, Julie, deserve to be armed with the truth.

Here at your writing desk, the night makes a mirror of the window and returns my stare. I will not make excuses for the choices I've made. Life is not a painting whose misguided pigment you can scrape off and do over, and if it were, where would I begin? For even a single brushstroke alters a painting entirely.

1858

THE SUN REFLECTED off newly fallen snow to whiten the air and cause the dining room of our little mansion to set everything and everyone afloat. Reading the final letter on his tray, Papa huffed with amusement then peered over his glasses at me. That peer held a familiar distance as if he sat upon a hill and I at its foot, small and unremarkable. I wanted to fling my arms about and shout my presence, but already he'd turned to the other side of the table and Edma.

"What is it, Papa?" she asked.

I tried on her calm inquisitive smile as if that might draw him back. Every morning of our privileged youth our butler, Thin Louis, set the silver mail tray at Papa's left elbow alongside his carafe of coffee, buttered toast and egg cup painted with the bowed heads of bluebells. Maman, my three siblings and I, long trained, ate in silence until he had finished reading the mail. Thin Louis then gathered the opened mail and brought Papa the day's newspapers. I was sixteen that year, my dearest Edma two years older. Our sister Yves was a distant twenty-one with interests all her own and our brother Tibby a sparking, self-absorbed ten-year-old.

The district of Passy, still two years from being swept into Paris's whorl of *arrondissements*, was more country than city. Our home in rue Franklin perched on a hill which overlooked the river at the Pont d'Iena and our stables abutted the Trocadero. The cook's garden, coops and orchard sloped gently down toward the *quai*. Unlike the pavements of today, earth was our common ground.

That morning, Maman set down her coffee spoon and leveled her gaze at Papa. "Will you share what's so amusing, Tiburce, dear?"

"Monsieur Guichard."

I looked to Edma, whose shrug only I could detect. M. Guichard was Edma's and my painting teacher. Papa cleared his throat with dramatic purpose and read the letter aloud.

Dear Monsieur Morisot,

As you have entrusted your daughters' instruction to my care, I feel I must speak frankly and bring to your attention what has become increasingly evident to me. If your daughters are to continue under my tutelage, they will be in serious danger of becoming real artists. And in your social circle, as you may well appreciate, this path would be catastrophic. I trust you understand my words and intention and will heed this warning.

Sincerely, Joseph Guichard

Tossing the page aside, Papa picked up his newspaper. "Apparently, girls, your lessons have come to an end."

Never in doubt that her daughters' desire for husbands and children would override any other erstwhile obsession, Maman was likewise unconcerned and urged on Tibby another piece of toast. "You girls can always paint on your own."

Yves stared at us, her younger sisters, eager for our reactions and something she might lord over us or use to pit one against the other, jealous as she was of our intimacy. Edma's small devastated smile tore at my heart as, following Papa's lead, she returned to her egg.

It was Edma who had requested lessons. It was she who had aspired, above all else, to be a painter. I merely aspired to be Edma. And though my sister's abilities were obvious, I was astonished to have been included in said catastrophe. Edma absorbed each lesson with an ease that impressed, if not alarmed M. Guichard while I alarmed in less charming ways. Each line or dab of colour I dared commit to paper became not a solution but a fresh and insoluble question for in the next instant it became untrue and a mistake. As light through Monsieur's studio windows brightened or faded, the flowers, fruit or plaster cast became less a solid object than a stream rushing under clouds and sun. Edma once made me a gift of brushes whose ends were blunted so that in my blind frustration I could not as easily stab through the heart of another canvas.

Barred from the Académie des Beaux-Arts and the life drawing studios, as females we'd had no choice but to take our lessons privately. Until today, M. Guichard had never taken our interest in painting seriously. In fact, he seemed surprised if not disappointed to see us continue to appear at his door.

I picked up my butter knife and held it in my fist. So… our teacher was telling us that we could succeed as painters yet mustn't—I severed the top of my egg—while our parents believed such success impossible and, besides which, why would anyone care? The orange yolk was undercooked and garish. Any hunger I might have had gone, I vowed to plague Maman, for Edma's sake, to find us another teacher and not stop until she did.

EDMA AND I, trailed by Maman, trudged behind M. Corot through the mist, paint boxes and easels strapped to our backs, tripping over roots in our effort to keep up and having to stop every few minutes to untangle our skirts from brambles and hold away the branches that clawed our cheeks. We were accustomed to the groomed walkways and swept gravel paths of the Tuileries and Le Jardin des Plantes, not this narrow, ragged, animal course in the woods in the near dark. I'd little doubt this first lesson would be our last.

Finally emerging onto a grassy bank, we followed M. Corot's mute lead and set up our easels on either side of his. The whistling laugh of a hidden thrush drilled the air. The sun was not yet high or warm enough to part the haze and I could see no further than six feet in any direction. Somewhere below us, the river Oise was a muffled wet tumble and without any explanation, M. Corot walked toward the watery sounds and was swallowed up by the mist.

Why insist on such a toneless hour? It would be like painting while wearing a veil. The glowing rectangle of my canvas, previously prepared to M. Corot's instructions, not with the normal bitumen underpainting but with a strangely reflective pale grey, mirrored well this shapeless landscape. Done. Captured. May we return to our beds?

Maman unfolded her stool where she could use a large evergreen as a backrest only to discover its sap ruining her good velvet cape. Rustlings erupted from the bush behind us. I imagined a boar's ruby eyes, its knifing tusks, and shrieked as a squirrel scratched its way up the trunk of Maman's tree, embarrassing myself but arousing no apparent concern from M. Corot, who failed to reappear.

"Where has he gone?" I whispered. I was growing chilled, my stockings inside my boots soaked with dew.

"A little patience, Berthe," whispered Edma as she arranged her paint tubes from dark to light. I followed her lead and did the same.

Earlier, when we had picked up Monsieur, an unlit pipe hooked into a corner of his frown, he had greeted Maman with few words. The landscapist was nearly as wide as he was tall, his ruddy face pared with magnificent lines under a startled mess of hair white as birch bark. His clothes stank of sweet tobacco and fish, his boots of manure. On the drive, Maman attempted conversation but he rode with eyes closed, pipe in place, catching a few more notes of sleep. Since female students would never bring a teacher recognition, he likely regarded Edma and me as spoiled young ladies whose father afforded us an expensive pastime. How I wanted to prove him wrong.

"Is he hoping to scare us off?" I didn't bother to whisper this time and Maman shushed me.

"He'll return," said Edma.

It had been Edma's express wish for a teacher of the new Barbizon school, one who painted *en plein air* in natural light. Yet this was no light at all, nor shape nor colour.

We waited and waited some more. Had he forgotten us entirely? I was about to suggest we leave him to find his own way home when the mist grew transparent and there he was, standing on the riverbank, in profile, his squat figure now dressed in a knee-length white painting smock to resemble an old washer woman, or a sorcerer. His arms were raised as if to embrace or to be embraced by someone celestially tall. Maman turned her head aside to give him privacy in his bizarre ritual. I loudly blew the dust from my canvas then took up my knife to sharpen my pencil to a fatal point when Edma's hand touched my sleeve.

I looked up. Blades of sun parted the haze. Like a sword slid from its scabbard, the river was revealed, the water an unexpected whitish pink with blinking silver eyes. On the far bank trees, not the usual brownish grey but a chaste and humble black, their shimmering leaves lavender mirrors. The horizon's white glow rose into a wash of deepening blues. As the sun touched the grass at our feet, tiny wildflowers bloomed like stars in a green sky.

"Listen."

It took a moment to know it was not a voice inside my own head but M. Corot's. He stood facing downriver, an apparition bathed in light.

"Can you feel them?"

These were my teacher's first words. The question less jarring than the fact that I *could* feel them, the colours, of course—because what else could be meant?

1863

I WAS TWENTY-ONE that spring when I first learned the name Édouard Manet. It happened at Le Salon des Refusés, the first Salon of its kind and, as far as Edma and I were concerned, the most enticing event of the year.

For an entire fortnight before the opening, it rained without reprieve. Braided streams ran from the corners of the roof and the streets were a maze of soupy ruts etched by hooves and carriage wheels. The planks we precariously trod to bridge them had sunk out of sight and our hems soaked up the water to whip about our feet like some dead yet clinging animal.

As Chief Advisor in the Finance Ministry, our father was away these long weeks on government business. Or so we believed. Maman, our constant chaperone, had mysteriously and uncharacteristically taken to her bed. Therefore, like pigeons in their coop, Yves, Edma and I were trapped in our house on rue Franklin, receiving no one and allowed nowhere. Our brother, Tibby, now fifteen, was free to roam the city alone. Other than when he was in school, we had no idea of his whereabouts.

In our upstairs sitting room that doubled as our studio, Edma passed the time trying her hand at portraiture with me playing her model. Because a week had passed and still Maman had not left her room, Yves sat at the desk by the window and sealed a summons for Dr. Rafinesque. She rang for Pauline, our lady's maid.

Pauline stood there on her sturdy posts, one slow finger tracing the red wax seal of Maman's initials, CMM—Cornélie Marie Morisot.

She turned the letter over and blinked at the words, somehow guessing their meaning.

"Madame does not need a doctor," she said. "Madame is in good health."

Yves had begun a new letter, one to a particular gentleman, a tax administrator she had been introduced to in Ville d'Avray where we'd gone last summer to be near M. Corot. "If her health were fine"—Yves didn't look up—"she wouldn't be in bed with the draperies pulled. See that it's delivered within the hour."

Pauline sighed a protest. "Madame needs no doctor."

"Pauline, don't question my—"

"Madame is sick at heart."

Yves turned in her chair, Edma stopped painting and I dropped my pose.

Pleased to have our undivided attention, Pauline hesitated, drawing out the moment.

"Pauline?" demanded Yves.

"It is Monsieur, Mademoiselle. He has a new *lorette*." Her hand stirred above her head, performing a twirl her body couldn't. "The ballet dancer he sponsors."

The notion shocked the room to stillness. That ballet dancer was sixteen at best. And what did she mean new? There'd been others? Yves snatched back the letter, startling us all, and Pauline scurried away.

Having married at fifteen, our maman was but forty-one and still lively and beautiful. Our father was entering his sixtieth year. The notion of him taking a mistress had simply never occurred to us and I felt as dirtied and mean as if I was that young girl.

Yves' eyes flashed around the room looking desperate to return to the moment before this one. Adept at ignoring what displeased her, she set her jaw, mumbled something about dinner and monkfish and left us staring after her.

"Poor Maman," I said. "How could he?"

"The needs of men are different from those of women." Edma's way was refuge in logic. "We cannot judge what we know nothing about."

"We know enough."

She laid a hand along my arm. "We don't, Berthe."

"How can you defend him?"

"Because how do we know if what Pauline said is even true? Think about it. How would she have such information?" She picked up her palette. I raised my dry brush toward the canvas. "It's not our business, Berthe. And apparently they've worked it out before."

I dropped my arm. "What could he gain from having a child as his mis–"

"Don't, Berthe." Any answer was too lurid and ugly to consider.

"Are we, his family, not enough? Have we somehow failed him?"

"We have not failed anyone. He is his own person."

I raised my brush.

"An inch lower," she added, gently.

I lowered it. "That poor girl."

"To dwell on it won't change it."

"You're right." Edma was always right. But try as I did, I could neither ignore nor rationalize my feelings. Nor could I forgive. Despite my best interest, I would gather like kindling the pent-up jealousy of my mother, the hurt and shame of my sisters, the blithe bullying that surrounded us, to fuel a rage that cleared my vision in ways I'd yet to understand.

When her portrait of me, playing the artist, was complete, Edma had caught my inner torture and disquiet. That is how talented she was.

ON THE OPENING DAY of Le Salon des Refusés, the sky was the transparent blue of a candle's flame and beneath the Pont d'Iena, the river rolled like a bolt of silver satin. The plank bridges had vanished, the mock-orange blossoms in the courtyard dry and sweetly fragrant. The flower seller in her muslin headscarf was again at her corner, cart hilled with violets, and our elderly neighbour, Mme. Higgonet, her fur stole done tightly beneath her double chin, haggled over some white hydrangeas that she poked at with her parasol.

As we headed down to breakfast, Papa's exasperation could be heard from the dining room. "This business in Mexico. It's costing the government a fortune." He must have returned late the previous night.

"Why colonize such a distant land?" said Maman. "They don't even speak French."

"Mines in the north. Silver."

"Of course. Please pass the butter, dear."

How nonchalant she sounded. Had his betrayal been forgotten like the shift in the weather? My feet halted on the landing, unwilling to take another step.

"Come on, Berthe." Eager for a return to peace, to normalcy, Edma wanted to join them.

"I can't pretend," I whispered. "I just can't.

"For Maman's sake?" she said.

I pleaded, "Not yet."

Edma was the unspoken peacekeeper of the family. Knowing my stubborn nature, she sighed and asked Pauline to bring our breakfast upstairs along with *Le Figaro* if Papa was through with it, and to tell them, please, that we needed the extra time to get ready for the Salon.

IN OUR HOUSECOATS, no one to impress, no hoops and crinolines to enforce the proper distance, I brushed Edma's hair as she scanned *Le Figaro.* The least vain of the three of us sisters, Edma was the only one who could be considered beautiful. Yves' face was lean and pale, too long in the jaw and pinched in the eye, her hair thin and dun-coloured. I had Papa's broad-cheeked face and narrow brow. My right eye drifted off-centre when I was tired and my large ears splayed like a bat's. My hair, thick and easily knotted, was a loamy brown. But Edma's face had faultless symmetry and was always accepting of the light, which is why I came to love painting her. Her hair was the lustrous brown of cooked meringue, and fell across my fingers in soft even curls.

Between sips of coffee and bites of tartine, Edma read aloud about a new law banning women from riding on top of the omnibus. "For fear of showing an ankle while climbing the stairs."

In the corner sewing stays, Pauline gave a grunt then muttered that she preferred "the high ride."

With the comb, I parted Edma's hair into sections. "Whose fear? A woman's or the lawmakers? And if the latter, what is so fearsome about an ankle?"

"My ankles are nothing to look at," said Pauline.

Edma read about Tom Thumb. We'd seen the midget paraded about at the American circus. The size of a five-year-old, yet mustached and weary-eyed, he was marrying another midget named Mercy. In New York City. Tom and Mercy Thumb.

"Their babies will be small as kittens," said Pauline and we laughed nervously.

I began braiding as Edma folded the paper to read the latest installment of M. Baudelaire's *Paintings of Modern Life*. Something we looked forward to each week.

"*The commission of the modern artist is to give beauty to sights that do not possess beauty in themselves*—is that not wonderful?—*not by making them romantically picturesque but by bringing to light the sublime human soul within.*"

"Yes, and daunting."

"Perhaps today at this new Salon we'll see such a—"

Yves burst into the room, pressing a letter to her breast. With no concern for what she may have interrupted, she caught us up on her quality of sleep and her dream of the river overflowing Passy's streets. "Our neighbours were swimming along in their evening clothes, the women's skirts surrounding them like the whites of eggs." Judging by her merry demeanor she, like Maman, had also managed to submerge yesterday's revelation. For no reason other than to create division, she had singled me out to address and now fanned herself ostentatiously with the letter, begging the question though Edma and I both knew who it was from.

"Read please, Edma." I tied off one braid and she found her place again.

"No matter the subject, be it—"

"He didn't even wait until I'd responded to his last letter," Yves said, drawing the letter from its envelope as Maman bustled in complaining anew about our linseed oil giving her a sinus ache. Even Yves didn't dare speak as Maman circled the room, ran a hand across the polished wood of the dressing table, shook out a curtain and smoothed the bed linens. She picked up the gloves, pale as the inside of a lemon, that I had lain along my chosen skirt and replaced them with the cream ones I had decided against. She didn't see how the yellow deepened the skirt's apricot tones and I would switch them back as soon as she left.

"Théo," said Yves, breaking the silence, "has responded to every topic in my last letter without a hint of condescension."

"A thoughtful man." Maman clasped her hands together as if in prayer. Having borne three children by the time she was Yves' age, no one was more keen to remedy her daughters' unmarried condition than she.

"I like his honest eyes," said Edma. "You can tell what he's thinking."

"Very honest eyes," said Maman.

I remembered his eyes a transparent grey, the colour of rain, thoughtful, but lacking in vigour. Théodore Gobillard also lacked a left arm, from the elbow down, and his jacket sleeve was kept folded in the neat triangles of a retired flag and sewn into place.

I shivered to think of that stunted arm unsheathed. Was the skin folded too? Or thick with watery-pink scars that hugged the bone beneath? Could I love such a man? Whether I was too sensitive, or not sensitive enough, I didn't know. Yves chose to view it as a badge of honour for he had lost the arm in the Mexican campaign and I admired her for it. But could he row a boat? Cut his own meat?

Maman held up two wallpaper samples and laid them against the wall. "William Morris," she said. "The English are coming out with rather attractive florals." Redecorating was how Maman cheered herself and I was glad to see it.

She had ordered both carriages readied. "I will ride with Yves in the coupé. Edma and you, Berthe, with Papa in the landau. Tibby will take a horse. He's become a fine rider, your brother." This was Maman's way of informing us she knew that we knew and would be getting back at Papa in these small ways.

I wondered why Papa was even bothering to come. He'd called the rejected paintings "all monsters, no masters," and himself a "*patron qui refuse*, who will leave his purse at home."

Edma and I had breathlessly awaited this day which he could too easily ruin. We'd already attended the Paris Salon, only to come away feeling we had seen it all before. Walls awash in the same meat-and-gravy tones under the same glassy finish and on the same perennial subjects: saints pierced by wounds, hovering cherubs, naked goddesses, battle heroes upon mildly sweating horses. This year there had been so many nudes of Venus that the critics rechristened it Le Salon de Venus.

Today, though, we anticipated the new, the modern, by those artists who dared to push back. Artists who, last winter, took to the streets in protest after the Salon Jury rejected 2800 paintings, over three-quarters of the submissions. A petition too, signed by Ernest Meissonier himself, had been sent to Emperor Louis—this is what we called Napoleon III to distinguish him from his uncle, one being the conqueror of the known world, the other a politician anxious for re-election. As a result, the Emperor called for this separate exhibition of the rejected works, the disallowed, to take place upstairs from the official Salon. "The jury had their turn," he'd pronounced, "and now the people of France will judge."

Born not for the sake of art but for politics, the exhibition's official name was the Emperor's Salon, but the critics were quick to call it what it was—Le Salon des Refusés.

Maman plucked at the hem of Edma's zaffre-blue satin. "*Le Moniteur* says today's opening will be *an experience of zest and stimulation.*"

"*Le Moniteur* is composed at the Emperor's office," Edma reminded her and turned the pages of *Le Figaro*. "Monsieur Gautier here is encouraging viewers to *prepare to be shocked if not scandalized by the works of dilettantes, democrats, and the deluded.*"

My pulse quickened. The *rejected*. Why did I feel in league with them? What right did I have?

Over the course of the morning, we donned our armour: garters and stockings, corsets and crinoline cages, camisoles, two petticoats, the latest in bodices and skirts. We finalized gloves and bonnets, and also shawls, because the Palais de l'Industrie was cold no matter the weather. Just the right neck band and arrangement of hair—Pauline, as usual, did her best to hold in my ears. Twice-polished boots. A touch of scented water. Reticules into which we put our embroidered handkerchiefs, small mirrors, fans and vials of scent. Beauty, Grand-mère Morisot had been fond of saying, was not merely an aesthetic. Beauty was morality itself.

THE MAHOGANY of the carriage gleamed in the sun like a fresh coat of bitumen. The horses' black manes were braided with gold ribbon and between their ears sprang a tiny feathered fountain that quivered when they moved their heads.

Thin Louis handed Papa his top hat and cane. Tall and elegantly slender for his age save for the small paunch swelling his vest, his plum-coloured cravat only half-hiding the sagging cords of his neck, Papa appeared well rested, even jaunty, showing not a hint of remorse. I was determined to not exchange a single word with him.

"Off we go." Papa offered his hand to Edma.

Edma and her mountainous skirt climbed the stair block into the landau. Since I could see nothing of the block or my feet and didn't dare lift my skirt for, I realized, fear of an ankle showing, I'd little choice but to take his hand too.

"You're looking very well today, Berthe," he said.

The compliment sounded sincere. Perhaps my face was thinner, the bones more evident? I had cut back on butter in that hope. I settled myself beside Edma, opened my parasol against the sun and angled away from him.

He took the seat opposite and repeated himself in the same cadence and volume. "You're looking very well today, Berthe."

Like a line of captive slaves, neighbourhood children were playing in the street, a length of rope tied around their waists.

"Wax in your ears?" Rather than raising his voice, he dropped it. "I'm speaking to you, Berthe."

Hidden by our skirts, Edma's boot pressed alongside mine. I squinted as if mesmerized by the children, now shuffling along. The smallest, tied at the back end, fell and was dragged on his belly several feet before he screamed out and the others stopped.

"I will not signal the driver to depart, Berthe," he said patiently, almost carelessly, "until you can respond."

My first thought was how long it would take to walk to the exhibit. My second raised a blush of hatred at my father's power over me and the confusing fact that I respected him for it.

One of the horses whinnied and tossed its head. If I held out much longer, I would be denied this day. And possibly Edma too, who now sharply turned her face from me. Her resentment was unbearable to me and I turned to him, blinked hard once as though coming out of a daydream. "I'm sorry, Papa, were you speaking to me?"

He repeated his original compliment as if carving the words from stone.

"Thank you." How I despised that he held the reins to my life.

He signaled the driver with a rap of his cane on the floor and Edma slipped her warm hand into mine. After these impotent battles of mine, her sympathy was my consolation prize.

The carriage lurched forward to bounce across the newly dried crests of mud. We rolled onto the cobblestones that encircled the Trocadero, the horses' shoes loud and clattering, and were rattled like dice in a cup. The sun flashed knives off the river, the *quai* crowded with pedestrians remembering the sun. Cargo boats, their flags limp in the tranquil air, lined up for their turn at the delivery docks. Across the river the excavations on the Champ de Mars had already begun for the Exposition Universalle, still years away. In behind, another near-completed block of Haussmann's limestone *appartements*. A destruction-in-progress, the landscape fluid and unreliable, Paris was then more a question than a city. I remembered waking one March morning to a grey sun and smoke searing my nostrils. Overnight the entire Quartier d'Arcis had been burned to embers. Having declared the old city a breeding ground for cholera and plague, the government forced its tens of thousands to relocate near the new factories on the city's outskirts. Not long after, along with its narrow snaking roads where we had fretted over our carriage squeezing successfully around the next corner, the Île de la Cité vanished. Gone forever the squat medieval churches perched like gargoyles atop their stone steps, the little arched bridges over the river Biere whose water was the colour of pumpkin rind from tannery waste. How do you pave over a river?

We bumped along, passing a mountain range of dirt, displaced for another section of Haussmann's new sewer.

I used to beg to accompany Maman on her errands to the old city despite a stench so pervasive the government once lobbied to deny meat to the inhabitants so their gutter mess would be as inoffensive as that of horses. Unlike quiet Passy, their crowded streets were a continuous festival—drying undergarments criss-crossed overhead like pennants, chickens exploded out of the way of our horses' hooves, heavy-headed pigs wandered out of doorways and children perched on rooftops like watchful cats. Once I saw four women in coarse dresses each holding a corner of a grey blanket which they heaved upward as if to shake free the dust when up flew a girl my size, all thrashing limbs and screaming laughter. I had been taught by the nuns at school to pity the poor, but could only envy such abandon.

The carriage wheels stopped bouncing and rolled on to the macadam of the Champs-Elysée, the smooth and quiet contrast as if we'd lifted off the earth. Along the promenade fountains like watery sheaves flashed between rows of young chestnut trees whose panicles bloomed a wounded pink. People streamed toward the soaring arches of the Palais de l'Industrie, wearing top hats—taller than last year's style—and bell-shaped skirts which rang soundless in the sun while scattering pigeons and their filth. Stick-legged urchins, cap brims pulled low, wandered among the throng to plead for coin.

Maman's cab sat parked and waiting for us as Tibby, still in his saddle, entertained by forcing his mare to dance a sideways trot, rear up and then turn in a tight circle. Ignoring our arrival, meaning Papa's, Maman gleefully applauded her son. The horse jerked at the bit, her eyes bulging.

LES RÉFUSES proved so popular that we were forced to wait in line in the Palais' grand foyer. Despite the immense fireplace where whole trees blazed, the foyer was cold as a root cellar, its tiles moist and slick underfoot.

Finally we were allowed upstairs where the sun through the glass dome melted off our wraps. Filtering the light, a bolt of white cotton stretched overhead like the wingspan of an endless bird.

Unlike the staid, watchful atmosphere of the Salon below, these halls were boisterous with debate. Groups of self-conscious Académie students in turbans and linen suits glanced suspiciously at their bohemian counterparts shrouded in smoke from their cigarettes. I was trying to decide which group of young men I envied more when Edma grasped my elbow and pulled me into Room A, Maman calling after us.

Like the Paris Salon, each room was arranged according to the artists' surnames and the paintings mounted respectfully in the same gold frames. Filling the walls floor to ceiling, some paintings were high enough to require opera glasses, others so low as to demand kneeling. Emperor Louie had his say in the staging and every painting at eye level was a tribute to his uncle, Napoleon, mounted on the famous white steed. If the subject was neither Bonaparte or his mount, it was Venus or Daphne or Madame Liberty. No matter how poorly executed, any paintings with all three—Bonaparte, horse and a half-clothed woman—took the centre spot on each wall.

As we moved through Room A, Edma, as was her wont, stepped in close to analyze a painter's technique. I stood back and appraised a painting by how it made me feel. Only if it made me feel something, anything, would I be compelled to examine its finer points.

Some had experimented with a slightly brighter palette, and others dared paint the secular subject: Paris neighbourhoods, rural landscapes and villages, ordinary people at work and at rest. Raising the mundane to the level of art was sacrilege and, no matter how well executed, this alone would have warranted their rejection.

In Room C a group of grown men bent nearly in half, hands on bellies, had laughed themselves breathless. Beside them two women pressed down on each other's arm to lift their gasping lungs free of their corsets. I'd never seen such a display in a public gallery. Spurned by the connoisseurs, these paintings were now fair game, tethered targets that even the most ignorant spectator was free to mock.

We had to wait our turn to understand the source of the hilarity: a triptych of oil paintings hung in a row. With the linear sensibility of a frieze, the works resembled a child's gentle attempt at figures and landscape; all foreground, no perspective, blob-like people, while fat unblended strokes ran across the canvas to represent the sky and water. The execution was indeed laughable, yet I had the disquieting feeling that the painter had been deliberate, as if loathe to spoil his peculiar vision by adding detail.

"My blind niece paints better," snorted someone behind us.

His companion noted that the women didn't have faces.

"Why not just leave out the hard parts," said another, which set off more merriment.

Edma whispered, "If this painter was brave enough, maybe we *should* submit next year." We had debated if our work was ready.

She opened the program. "The triptych is called *The Judgement of Paris*." Though the title referred to the myth, we joined in the laughter. This prescient fellow, Paul Cézanne, was indeed being judged by Paris. Having caught up, Maman admonished us to calm ourselves.

Whenever we encountered friends and acquaintances, it was as though the freer expression on the wall had freed up tongues.

"A bit like framing one's meat scraps," said our neighbour, Mme. Higgonet, a stiff satin bow beneath her chin twice the width of her head.

"There are some livelier colours," noted my former piano teacher, the kindly Mme. Tesseyre. "Makes the heart beat a little faster."

"Room S has a country woman hanging out her laundry," our pharmacist, M. Gourot, informed us. "I grew up in the country and my mother hung ours in the very same order."

"Why," said his wife, clearly mortified and fearing our opinion, "would anyone paint their undergarments?"

We had viewed through to Room L, but because a shoving match was going on in Room M between the stylish Académie students and the smoking bohemians, Papa announced it time for lunch.

We dined in the Palais garden under the clock tower where Salon sculptures watched us partake of the *garde manger.*

"There's a bone in my terrine," said Yves, making a face.

I looked across the table to see a pair of bronze breasts, slightly wall-eyed and sloping cheerfully upward, protruding from Yves' ears like ornaments. I nudged Edma beside me and we convulsed with laughter.

"You are a gang of two." Yves touched her hat, her latest fashion creation. "Apologize."

Edma explained about the sculpture behind her. Yves' eyes narrowed, not wholly believing her.

Our grand expectations of the exhibit had been dulled. Yes, there were more landscapes—our particular interest—but they had the dead look of having been painted in studio. And most of the experiments in colour were timid deviations from the same biblical browns, russets and ochres.

Uncle Octave, who'd joined us for lunch and rarely expressed an artistic opinion, couldn't say enough about the exhibit's profanity and ugliness. "Room M is the most offensive. Vile really." My aunt stroked the back of his head as one might soothe a cat. "I suggest skipping the room altogether. It's hardly appropriate for young ladies."

Edma and I exchanged looks, our expectations revived. Room M, then.

ROOM M was empty except for a large grousing crowd at one end, people straining to see over or around those in front. Papa had gone ahead of us and I located his grey nest of hair and egg-shaped bald spot. The taller head of Tibby perched over him, rocking side to side. Pretending I needed to reach my father, I wove through the grumbling commentary in order to get an up close view.

"He's left it unfinished."

"She's horrid."

"A shaved rodent."

I could see only the painting's top half—the blackish-green feathery tops of pines, hints of a lavender sky.

"Le Déjeuner des Dégénérés."

Despite the violent critiques, no one moved. Rather, more people pushed in from behind. I slipped in behind Tibby, just as Papa whispered into his ear, "Look, son, at the way she holds your gaze. Splendid."

Papa saw me and his cheeks darkened before his face closed down. What did he mean, splendid?

The crowd shifted, and I eased past Tibby to stand in front of the three-by-five-metre canvas. The objects in the picture appeared to be tumbling toward me and I scrambled to find the horizon line. Up there? Was that even allowed?

"Not worth our time," said Papa.

The painting's lights and darks were in such severe contrast I was unsure where to look.

"Where are your sisters and mother? Let's go." Stepping in front of my brother, Papa took me by the elbow. I snatched it back without thinking. His nostrils flared but too proud to make a scene in public, he merely turned and left, with Tibby mindlessly following. The sudden sense of control over my own life was breathtaking, though I well knew it was short-lived and would come with a cost.

Slowly the painting's composition came clear: a picnic in the woods, two young gentlemen and one young woman lounging on the grass. The men were dressed in Left-Bank style while the woman was a pale blaze of nakedness. You couldn't call her a nude. There was no pretense of mythology or divinity. She was a naked woman, fleshy and real and no different than if I, in this gallery, shed my clothes for all to gawk. In the background a second woman wore a see-through chemise and crouched in a pool in the wood. Curled around herself like a cat grooming itself, she was… bathing? The artist had painted a woman at her toilette with men nearby?

Like my uncle, I could think of nothing more boorish. Yet the painting didn't *feel* vulgar. Neither the men nor women in the painting showed any hint of embarrassment or hesitation, making the nakedness and the bathing appear natural, even wholesome. More like Eve in the garden, without the shameful leaf.

The arrangement of the foreground figures was familiar yet I couldn't place it. Was the painter paying homage to a Master or making a mockery of one?

"He should be locked up," someone bellowed and a roar of agreement rose from the crowd, whose press forced me sideways. The naked woman was now directly in my gaze. Elbow to drawn-up knee and casually resting her chin on her hand, she stared out from the painting and held my gaze just as my father had said. For I had to admit, I found her splendid too. In contrast to the inanimate faces of the other models, hers was alive, expressive of an actual person with thoughts, feelings, likes and dislikes. I could know her, could have passed her on the street.

A man's nasal voice spoke over the din. "Nothing better for keeping you in trim than the insults of the herd." In the sudden hush, came a whispered "Monsieur Baudelaire," and I caught the briefest waft of ecstatic perfume. But again, shouts were traded, and in the jostle Edma appeared. She grasped my hand, her keen eye racing around the canvas as if it were the best of riddles. What had I missed? The still life in the foreground: a spilled basket of fruit, a *boule de pain*, and a pile of women's clothes. Those discarded clothes made keen the weight of my own. Of my skin beneath those layers, the mean cinch of my ribs, the small weights of my breasts, the garter straps denting my thighs. Not only had the painter liberated the women from the pounds of fabric that kept us moving at an invalid's elegant pace, he had liberated them from the ideal of beauty. The woman looking out at me was no Venus.

She had rolls of flesh, large feet, a plain face, her hair pulled into a simple knot.

"Who's responsible for this profanity?" someone called.

"A visionary." The nasal voice again, to even louder jeers.

The crowd's bile was understandable. The painting made them feel stupid. As it did me. The contrasts of dark and light, clothed and unclothed, urbane and natural, classical and modern, demanded something no other painting did: confusion. People remained in front of it to get past this discomfort and it took the form of ridicule. My skirt was knocked from behind and I bumped against Edma.

"He has juxtaposed the bourgeoisie and their *prostitués*," she whispered, steadying me, "within a respectable family activity. A picnic."

What?

"Men of class lounging on the river bank with their paramours," she continued, "their wives safely tucked up at home. It's shocking really. An exposé."

"Of men's dual lives," I said and suddenly understood my father's words to my brother. There are two types of women: domesticated and wild. Men were free to indulge in both worlds, even encouraged to. "The painter is not decrying the practice."

"Nor is he supporting it." She'd caught the edge in my tone. "He is simply displaying reality, no?"

That art could be a social exposé overstepped my knowledge of what a painting could do. To see a rendition of my father's indiscretion made public, even ordinary, justified and somehow eased my fury toward him. As for the painter of this piece, I felt he knew everything about me. How proscribed my life. How it felt to wear my clothes. How I secretly believed myself equal to any man. How my body had nothing to do with Venus or Virgin. How I longed for independence and the freedom to express my deepest truest self in both art and in life. Though I had no idea how to achieve such a feat or if I was remotely capable.

"He's not attempting to hide his brushstrokes or even blend the paint." Edma put a hand on her heart. "It's as though he's deliberately exposing his process and, in that way, putting himself into the picture!" She shook her head yet was smiling. "The whole thing's a mess."

"Edma, it makes me want to paint."

"I know. I know."

Maman and Yves had found us.

"This room is madness," said Yves, clutching her hat. "Let's go."

"And this awful painting," said Maman, closing her program, "is by one Édouard Manet. My sympathies to his family." But as though searching for answers of some kind, her gaze never once left that canvas.

BACK HOME and alone in our room, Edma and I couldn't stop talking about the painting.

"What could be more satisfying"—Edma paced between the windows where I lay on the divan—"or bring more happiness than painting?"

Though my obstacles were many, and my joys while painting few, I knew what paint could do. How, as M. Baudelaire wrote, it could bring to light the sublime human soul within. My body ached with the knowledge, and in wanting to taste its achievement. It was a hunger almost sexual. "Nothing can," I said.

Edma took up my hands with uncharacteristic urgency. "Do you think, Berthe, that you could forego marriage and children? That you could make such a sacrifice?"

"Are you asking yourself? I have no desire to have my life further circumscribed by another man. To suffer Maman's humiliation."

"I have concluded that it's not possible to do both in any satisfying way. Not if we want to be real painters and not mere copyists or wallpaper artists." Edma bit back her lip. "Maman will be disappointed to say the least."

"She won't believe us anyway."

"Neighbours and friends will be scandalized. That will be hard for her." She returned to pacing. "And we may well be rejected from society altogether."

"Then we will find new society."

"Papa will be concerned about our future finances." This seemed the obstacle that gave her the most pause. "So... we must reassure him and present the notion with confidence in our ability to make a living from painting."

"We'll pool our inheritance." I was not as confident as Edma. "And live humbly."

"Do portraits on the side. The occasional copy but only if we must." Edma came and kissed my cheeks, her eyes brightening as if feverish. "It is a terrible sacrifice," she said but her expression said otherwise.

"Not for me. Not for me." I'd only ever wanted what Edma wanted and it was a joy to think that we'd never be parted by marriage. That we could continue to live and paint side by side. As for the inappropriate nature of a woman of our class daring original work, that only made the notion more enticing.

Our pledge was sealed with a hug, fierce and lingering, as we held fast to a future we could not begin to predict.

THE NEXT MORNING all of Paris knew the name Édouard Manet. Every last paper had singled him out to summarize the horror that was Le Salon des Refusés.

Le Déjeuner sur l'herbe *looks to be painted with a floor mop.*

This crude work is a shameful open sore. A young man's practical joke.

Le Déjeuner sur l'herbe *is the artistic ideal of ugliness.*

Never had such venom been directed at a painter. Édouard Manet had swung open a door in the walls of the Académie where there had never before been a door. In their terror, the custodians of convention scrambled to close it again.

1864

THE WEEK BEFORE the Salon cart was to arrive, as if both paintings I'd chosen to submit were living creatures in need of food and light, I repeatedly dragged them back to the easel to help or harm them in some new way. Since Edma and I painted side by side and I invariably copied her choice of landscape as well as palette, our submissions were similar. After Edma worried aloud if this might harm our chances, in my guilt, I tried to distinguish my *Old Path at Auvers* from her *Abandoned Orchard* and added figures: a boy in a black coat, a black kitten. One minute the additions seemed clever, the next I was convinced they gave away my youth. I rubbed out the boy's facial features, thinking myself very modern. Worried it looked unfinished, I filled them in again. Then rubbed out his face again. Repeating the process until both choices seemed equally terrible and I moved onto our similar views of the Oise. Here I altered the time of day by adding dramatic reds and pinks. The next time I dared look, it was a baroque caricature of a sky at dusk.

By the week's end, defeated and exhausted I confessed to Edma that my work simply wasn't ready, wasn't nearly good enough. "I want to delay until next year." She nodded as if she understood.

"Then I too, will delay. I have no intention of entering the lion's den alone."

Her work was ready, she was ready and had anticipated submitting. My beloved sister was willing to put my vanity before her desires. But that same vanity couldn't allow her to do that.

When the collection cart arrived the following morning, I distracted myself on the piano with a challenging scherzo and pretended to ignore Thin Louis carrying our four canvases through the front door, out the gate and into the world.

WE WAITED TWO MONTHS to hear our fates, during which time I rehearsed for the humiliation of my paintings being returned stamped on the back with a fat red R. In front of the glass, with an expression of elegant disappointment, I practised the word aloud to denude it of its meaning. "Rejected. Rejected. Rejected."

My dread was nearly forgotten when one soggy day in early March Pauline informed us, with a glee that bordered on scorn, that letters from the Paris Salon had come for us in the morning post. Without a word and before Thin Louis carried the mail tray into breakfast, we threw on our housecoats and hurried downstairs, my stomach sick with hope.

Two letters of identical thickness lay on the silver tray in the foyer.

"We will open each other's," said Edma. "It's more sympathetic that way." She handed me her letter and the letter opener. I slit open her envelope and handed back the knife. She slit open mine. It felt like a ritual. At what point did I stab the knife through my heart?

"I'll go first." Afraid of being incapable of reading Edma's acceptances after my rejections, I was determined to be able to express genuine happiness for her.

There was no Dear Mademoiselle, only the name of her two paintings and a line beside them. On top of each line sat an elongated black check mark.

"Both paintings accepted! *Je le savais.* How could it be otherwise?" My nerves kept me speaking. "I'm so proud of you and not at all surprised… Oh, it's wonderful. I'm so pleased. I am."

Edma showed not a hint of pleasure but immediately unsheathed my letter. My body tried to faint to head off the agony.

"Both accepted."

I stared at her, certain I'd misheard.

"Both accepted!"

"No!"

"Yes!" She thrust the paper at me, kissed my cheek. "We did it."

I burst into loud sobs. Edma laughed and hugged me, and Maman rushed from the kitchen.

"What's happened? Berthe, dear, are you hurt?"

"Maman, here." Edma showed her the letters.

"Oh my. That's something to show for my efforts." She regarded my weeping quizzically before her gaze roamed the foyer. "Well done, well done." Stepping up to the front door, she furiously polished the brass doorknob with a corner of her skirt. "Have two ducks killed," she instructed herself. "Invite their aunt and uncle and open the good Bordeaux. No, three ducks. And a dozen of their eggs. Well done indeed."

On our way upstairs, we ran in to Yves and announced our news. She kissed us both in congratulations. "I am not surprised at your acceptances," she said to Edma. "And how lucky for you, Berthe."

PAPA SAT UNRESPONSIVE at one end of the table as Maman, her ears turning the same noble red as the wine, summarized for her brother and sister-in-law the parade of lessons over the years, her patience in the face of stuffy studios, the noisy halls of the Louvre, frosty dawns, of arranging the summer season to be near M. Corot.

I hardly needed wine, giddy as I was. Yves had developed an attention-getting cough and Auntie kept rubbing her back.

Uncle Octave kindly asked us about our paintings: how long they took to complete, their most challenging aspects and if we had plans for our next projects. Edma spoke briefly and then it was my turn. Having never before been the object of a dinner conversation, I eagerly described my struggles with the boy's face in *Old Path at*

Auvers when Papa interrupted. "What's next? Cigars in the library? Sheep in the drawing room, and worse in the bedroom?"

Most everyone laughed. The joke was in reference to Rosa Bonheur, the single renowned female artist of our time. Mlle. Bonheur once applied for a police permit to wear pants, in order not to be bothered when sketching at the Paris horse market. Rumour was she kept a pet sheep in her third-floor *appartement* where she lived with another woman who was not her sister.

"Her horses are said to rival the great Meissonier's," I said.

"Perhaps, but I believe Monsieur Meissonier would look better in a dress."

More laughter.

"I can assure you, Papa," said Edma with a laugh, "we've no desire to trade our skirts for trousers."

"I'd like to see a woman in trousers," mused Tibby.

"She's to be decorated with the Legion of Honour," I said, "the first woman to receive it."

"I trust she will shave for the occasion." In position behind Papa's chair, even Thin Louis snorted laughter. Maman might have come to our defence, but she had drunk too much wine and, head thrown back, laughed the loudest.

Yves stared at me, eager-eyed, her coughing magically having stopped while Edma remained majestically calm, her eyes encouraging me to do the same. She was only trying to protect me, yet the very fact of her equilibrium was perhaps what afforded me my temper.

"Is it an embarrassment, when we have worked hard and have not one but each two acceptances to the Salon?"

Papa let my coarse bragging hang amplified in the quiet. Now I *was* embarrassed.

"How my daughters pursue and handle their success will decide that." He trimmed the fat off his pork chop and speared a bite-sized piece. "I expect you not to speak of your accomplishments in public like shop girls. Nor use them as an excuse to escape your obligations." As he did when displeased, he changed subjects. "An estimated 600,000 men dead thus far in Lincoln's war. If and when it ends, do you think, Octave, that America can ever become a true union?"

"Brothers killing brothers. How can that ever be forgotten much less forgiven?"

The celebration was over.

BECAUSE OF MY OUTBURST, Edma and I were denied Varnishing Day. Once devoted to finishing touches, the day before opening day of the Paris Salon was now a grand social event attended by critics, celebrities, even the royal family. Artists held parties beneath their paintings and the elite had opportunity to greet the artists and have first chance at purchase. Promising to control my temper in the future, I apologized to Edma at every turn, knowing how much she'd anticipated catching a glimpse of the artists we admired and in particular Édouard Manet. Together we had fantasized of his appearance and social standing—a black-haired bohemian of the merchant class; his age—twenty-four, the age dividing hers and mine; and his character—unable to afford art lessons, he was self-trained and therefore freely painted his disdain for the privileged classes.

Nor did Papa allow us to attend Opening Day. An entire fortnight would pass before we attended our own Salon debut, our initial excitement all but withered and dead. By then we had read our meagre reviews which were littered with terms such as youthful, feminine and delicate-of-hand. Our landscapes were called loyal copies of our teacher's style, crediting our hard work to M. Corot, and each commented on our "sisterly similarity." To no one's surprise, Edma's were deemed the more accomplished.

Édouard Manet's new works were as crucified as his subject matter; the corpse of Christ in *Dead Christ with Angels* and a skewered matador in *The Bullfight*. Critics suggested his paintings had only been accepted as spectacle to attract more paying viewers. There wasn't a single review that didn't pillory him. How he'd be able to continue to paint in the face of it, I didn't know.

Whether the scandal that was Manet did succeed in attracting viewers we didn't learn, but we did see his work for ourselves, on the same grim wet day we were finally allowed to see our own. Again, the thrill of coming face-to-face with our new fame had dampened and almost died, and our stroll through Room M was leisurely. In fact, we encountered and stopped in front of Manet's paintings first.

Again his work was akin to fresh air in a stale room. Yes, *The Bullfight* suffered a dilemma of perspective, but the bright colours of its matadors thrilled. The black of the dead toreador's costume was alive with the fluctuating tones the eye registers when adjusting to pitch dark. As for painting Christ's sword wound on the wrong side of his body? That was indeed a careless mistake—unless, that is, he was suggesting a mirror image? And though one critic claimed Manet "had made ugly the most beautiful of men," for the first time I felt sympathy for Christ's ubiquitous figure whose ears fanned outwards not unlike mine.

As for my canvases that I had fretted and wept over, they hung in a darkened corner of Room M and up so high that Papa couldn't view them without suffering a dizzy spell. Edma's hung at a more advantageous height and, as fate would have it, alongside the deplored work of Édouard Manet.

"Nearly touching," said Edma, and she swallowed as though to keep her next thought to herself.

1867

IT WAS COPYING DAY at the Louvre. Edma was replicating a Veronese—*The Wedding Feast at Cana*—hoping to decipher how he had achieved the intensity of his colours. Because I had forgotten how to paint hands, in the same way one forgets how to spell the simplest of words, I was attempting Titian's *Man with a Glove.* Hands had become elusive leggy creatures with too many joints, angles and confounding shadows.

Suppressing any preconceived image of a hand and any notions of what a hand did, along with the fact that it was a hand, my hand, that wielded the brush attempting to paint a hand, I let my brush begin. With the simple-mindedness of an idiot, I was not going to *paint* anything, only replicate the lines and tones in front of my bare eyes.

Yves had married her one-armed administrator by this time and was living in the south. We'd learned in her most recent letter, in which she'd scolded Edma and me once again for burdening the family with our decision not to marry, that she was several months gone with child. Tibby, having turned eighteen, had his own *appartement* in the 5th, where neighbours complained of the noise of his gatherings. Twenty-eight and twenty-six respectively, Edma and I still shared a bed in our parents' house, dutifully visited and received neighbours and relatives and the one schoolmate whose marriage had not removed her from Paris. We delivered baskets of stale bread to the Women's Asylum each Saturday for their *pain perdu*, and in fine weather took the air in the Bois de Boulogne or along the *quai*. We attended concerts and the opera and avoided the ballet. We endured Tuesday dinners where Maman, as resolute as we, always had a suitor or two on the menu. Any that piqued my blood predictably took an interest in Edma, yet those who believed Edma's kind attentions suggested something deeper came away disappointed.

Painting was our escape, then our *raison d'être*. We summered in the countryside seeking inspiration, and refined our work in the fall before submitting to the Paris Salon. For three years running our work had made it past the jury. Though our reviews remained tepid and sales nonexistent, acceptance to the Salon was encouragement enough. Despite having to be chaperoned everywhere by our mother and ruled by Papa, despite days pocked with self-doubt, I had painting and I had Edma—I could not separate the two—and our shared life was enough for me. I had no doubt she felt the same.

There in the Louvre, Titian's gloved hand was the colour of sun-dried mud so I squeezed burnt umber onto my palette, then a touch more lead white. The little finger angled... the glove puckered at the joint... tip curling into shadow... the next finger... longer, more tapered. Before reaching the index finger, I saw that I had caught the corrugated light at the bend of the knuckles, the hollow of air under the palm... and... well... it was looking just like a hand! As the triumphant voice rang in my head, my own hand froze, mystified as to how to proceed. I slammed down my brush and Edma jumped. "I detest hands."

"Useful, though, to a painter," came a stranger's voice.

Henri Fantin-Latour, whom we'd been introduced to, had appeared out of nowhere with a companion who grinned at me as if I was his day's entertainment. The companion waggled his gloved finger in the air. "I think of what a hand is about to do. If I can capture that intention"—he observed his waggling finger then lowered it—"it tends to behave itself."

"I didn't ask for a lesson."

His eyes widened but I didn't care. Now his hand became a snapping jaw which turned to his face and attacked his beard. He bravely held it off at the wrist. Henri spit with laughter.

"Henri, so nice to see you," said Edma while peering past Henri at his friend, whose gloves were a surprising aubergine and matched his silk vest, and whose pants were the tan of a deer's spring coat.

"Édouard Manet," said Henri, "I'd like to introduce les Demoiselles Morisot. Edma and Berthe."

Edma stood abruptly, knocking her easel and nearly upsetting her paints. This was the infamous painter? Our fantasies about him had become so real that this flesh and blood man seemed an imposter. I didn't know what to do or where to look so remained seated in hopes of being forgotten altogether. Quick to regain her composure, Edma put down her palette and brush and offered her hand. When he pressed it to his lips, his eyes drifted closed.

"My sister and I are admirers"—Edma glanced at me—"and have followed your experiments with eagerness."

"Experiments." He stood straighter.

I slouched on my stool, but Edma, who could summon ease in awkward situations, laughed. "I'm referring to your bracing originality."

"You flatter me"—he was all smiles again—"and really life should be lived like an experiment, no?"

His voice was high-pitched and struck a clear singular note like that of certain querulous women. He was not black-haired; rather, copper curls tangled in light framed a high, intelligent forehead. A shade darker, his beard was a burnished red. And he was older than we'd guessed, even ten years my senior.

"Édouard's a painter's painter," said Henri, ready, as always, to agree with Edma. Hoping a shared interest in painting might turn her daughter's head, Maman had twice invited Henri to her suitor dinners.

M. Manet now turned to me. A thin band of gold circled his russet eyes as if something burned in behind. I held out my hand. To mock me further, he left it dangling in the air.

"Hands reveal a lot about a person," he said, and I grew conscious of my chewed and chipped nails, the paint crowning my middle knuckle. I lowered my hand but he caught it, lifted it to his lips and kissed the paint spot. The softness of his beard was unexpected. I could relax only when he turned back to Edma, saying something about having seen our work at the Salon.

Judging from his clothes, he was not of the imagined merchant class, or even the *petit bourgeois*. He was one of us. Yet despite his fine clothes there was a chaos about his manner, unpredictable and loose. Whereas Henri, in his billowing sleeves and scarf and long hair, looked every inch the bohemian, Édouard Manet seemed to possess the soul of one.

Edma wasted no time introducing him to Maman, who sat absorbed in her Dumas.

"Thank you for introducing us," I told Henri as I found my voice again. "We've been very eager to meet Monsieur Manet."

He looked glumly after Edma. "You'll be glad of it. He is both charmed and charming."

As if to prove his point, something Édouard said made Maman laugh the head-tossing laugh that normally took several glasses of claret.

When the two men finally wandered off down the hall, I watched Édouard clap his hands on the shoulders of another painter, jarring his brush. The man's anger turned to merriment when he saw who had disturbed him. Edma returned to her stool, erect and pleased. "That was thrilling." She was breathless.

"I guess." I asked what it was M. Manet said to make Maman laugh so.

She hiccupped a laugh. "Maman, in her forthright way, said she had been shocked by *Le Déjeuner sur l'herbe*. And he said: 'Some say a good shock cleans the palate.' He then invited her and us to attend his mother's Thursday soirées and assured her that 'everyone would be fully clothed. Except perhaps an older gentleman or two.'" She laughed again.

"Soirée?"

We had attended luncheons and dinners, and the occasional ball at the house of Papa's patron, Deputy Minister Thiers. After Maman's weekly dinners, we played Écarté or I performed my limited repertoire on the pianoforte. We did not attend soirées.

"This Thursday. And the next if we like. And the one after that." Edma could hardly contain her pleasure.

"He seemed awfully enamoured with himself."

"Insisted I call him Édouard," she said.

"What kind of man wears purple gloves?"

"I didn't expect him to be that handsome."

"I didn't expect him to be that old."

"Oh, it's exciting, isn't it?" She took up her palette. "I bet he keeps a whole company of artist friends."

"Perhaps."

She returned to her Veronese. No matter how hard I tried, for the rest of the morning, Titian's hand proved a demon and the day a waste.

IN THE FRONT HALL of Mme. Manet's *appartement*, I was greeted by my own uncertain image in the enormous mirrored armoire. I was leery of seeing M. Manet again, while Edma had been counting the days—six, to be precise.

Pushed up against the armoire was a First Empire console on top of which sat crystal bowls of potpourri whose dusty perfume overwhelmed the nose. On the wall behind, a train of portraits in charcoal and red chalk hung too close together, all bearing the signature *Édouard Manet.* Weaving through the distant hum of conversation, a Chopin *étude* was being played with intimidating accomplishment.

In the room at the hall's end a raging fire filled a black marbled fireplace. A hidden pocket of sap exploded upon our approach, raining orange sparks onto the parquet already pocked with burns. It looked as though we were entering the mouth of a dragon. In retrospect, it was true.

We stepped into the drawing room and a seated gentleman, whom at first glimpse I dreaded was Édouard, sprang to his feet. Edma greatly enjoyed meeting strangers. Ironically, meeting new people made me feel lonely, my shyness a battle between the pride of wanting to be well thought of and a childish craving for attention of any kind.

The gentleman's hair bore the same reddish tones as Édouard's. His face was similar in shape, as was the cut of his beard. But where Édouard's features were defined, his were rounded, smoothed of their edges, his skin more translucent. His clothes looked a size too big, as if he used to be a heavier man, and gave off a chalky smell like plaster.

"Eugène Manet," he said by way of introduction. "I'm Édouard's brother?"

Was he not sure?

Maman came right to life, offered her hand and introduced her daughters as if she were a proud butcher and we superior cuts of meat. In her zeal she failed to introduce herself. But she had done her homework. The rogue painter who piqued the establishment was the thirty-seven-year-old son of the Chief Advisor to the Judiciary, now deceased, while his mother had ties to Swedish aristocracy. Most pertinent, Édouard was the eldest of three brothers, all of independent means.

Without any of his brother's bold grace, Eugène kissed each of our hands. He then stuffed his into the pockets of his jacket, leaving his elbows akimbo, useless little wings. He glanced over his shoulder. "Édouard is here somewhere."

The drawing room was crowded with people and music and furniture that must once have belonged to a larger home. Paintings, great and small, in ornate gilt frames, smothered the walls. The pianoforte was set squarely in the drawing room's centre, forcing people to pass in single file on its either side. The piano's final sustain faded and the background conversation came to the fore. I estimated sixty-and-some guests, though perhaps more swarmed the dining room. Behind the pianist a short black-haired woman warmed up her violin and when her sliding bow stabbed a man in the back, she did not apologize. She looked familiar though I couldn't recall from where.

"Eugène, *chéri*" – a commandeering voice cut through the noise – "please bring our guests over and introduce them."

Small yet imperious, her feet propped on a pillowed footstool, the matriarch sat in a green velvet armchair whose back rose well about her head. She spoke to the woman occupying the smaller chair beside her and the woman immediately rose and left. She instructed Maman with a stab of her finger, to "Sit." Nesting in the folds of her hem and sharing her foot pillow, a copper-and-white King Charles spaniel stared out at us.

Eugène made introductions then positioned himself behind his mother's chair as if using it as a shield. Music began, a mazurka for piano and violin.

"Monsieur Morisot works in the Ministry of Finance," Mme. Manet informed my mother. She raised her hand and the music magically became quieter. "Very well thought of." She didn't seek confirmation. "Édouard has told me what talented painters your daughters are. A shame they're not men."

Maman thanked her for the mixed compliment. "And you've three sons."

"Yes. No daughters to share the feminine burden. All three of my sons are idealists and have their heads in the clouds." This statement was not without pride. I expected a rebuttal from Eugène, but as if to prove his mother's words, he stared sideways out the window.

"Gustave is my youngest, and fiercely opinionated like his late father. He's not here, he's not fond of merrymaking"—she swept a lacey arm through the air—"but you might have seen him in one of Édouard's paintings? *Le Déjeuner sur l'herbe?* He wears the turban." She didn't wait for a reply. "Anti-Bonaparte, he wants nothing less than to see a working-class government." A snort escaped her nose. "What does he know of the working class? His hands are as smooth as mine. Writes pejorative articles against the government, holds secret meetings, carries a pistol and wonders why he's questioned by police."

"I'm sorry. That sounds—"

"My Eugène"—she reached blindly over her shoulder and he hurried to unfold one wing and grasp her hand—"is a great support to his brothers and to me. He does very pleasing watercolours, you know, a little writing for Gustave about his own particular concern—education—though I've asked him to keep his name out of it. Reads novels in hopes of writing his own someday. Has an *appartement* in the 8th."

"In the 8th," repeated Maman with a glance at Edma.

There came the distinct sound of passing gas from Mme. Manet.

Eugène turned toward the direction of the kitchen. "The cassoulet is ready?"

Madame continued without embarrassment. "Since my husband died, Eugène has taken over our finances. He understands numbers." Her aggressive forthrightness was the kind that hid rather than bared secrets.

She released Eugène's hand, which slipped back to its pocket. The air stank of the corpse of food.

"You've met my Édouard." She squinted to locate him. Edma, too, craned her neck. "We thought he'd make a fine lawyer but he didn't pass his exams." Her forefinger shot up like an exclamation point. "Because from a very young age, that boy was enamoured with painting. We lived across the street from the Académie des

Beaux-Arts, you see, and my brother would take him to view the student work. He liked the nude models is what I think." She lifted a corner of her lip as if to signal we were to smile or laugh. Eugène snickered, demonstrating the correct response.

Gracious Maman snickered too. "He's an inspiration for the younger painters. My daughters are positively bewitched by his—"

"All the girls are in love with Édouard for he's in love with them. He has married a Dutch girl, a Leenoff." She nodded towards the piano. "Musically inclined. An uncomplicated woman, she suits Édouard's genius."

I caught the bewilderment on Edma's face. Apparently her fantasies had outpaced mine. I gave her a questioning look but she was eyeing the pianist, a matronly figure clearly older than Édouard, whose fleshy arm showed through her chiffon sleeve. Her nose was reddened at the nostrils as if she'd a cold and her mouth sat slightly open. This was his wife?

"The boy turning the sheet music is her young brother, Léon. He has lived with Suzanne and Édouard since he was an infant. His mother too frail to care for him, you see."

As if sensing he was being spoken of, Édouard came striding toward us, his approach as palpable as a swell of water. Beside me Edma inhaled sharply. Tonight his vest was a rusty gold. Were the matching gloves in a drawer somewhere? As if we were the oldest of friends, he kissed first Maman on both cheeks then Edma and, taking my hand in his, pulled me into him with surprising force. His kisses were so close to my ears that I felt the moisture of his breath. Did the term flirt apply to a man?

"You've met my intrepid mother, I see."

"We've had the good fortune," said Maman.

"Now I will steal away Mademoiselle Edma Morisot and Mademoiselle..." he hesitated, then peered at me as if to see how I would respond.

"Berthe." My cheeks grew warm.

"Berthe. And introduce them around."

"He's teasing," said Mme. Manet, delighted.

"Ignore him," said Eugène, roused to speaking. "It's the only way he'll behave."

"See how my family gangs up on me," said Édouard. "In my own home."

He lived with his mother?

"And try the *gougeres*," Mme. Manet called after us, "my cook makes excellent pastry."

Édouard led us, single file, past his wife at the piano without so much as a glance her way. I recognized two of the guests: Henri Fantin-Latour in the far corner, whose eyes fixed on Edma, and a young friend of M. Corot, the Barbizon painter Antoine Guillemont.

Édouard steered us to a group of men and one very beautiful auburn-haired woman. "This is Mademoiselle Morisot, Edma, and her sister Mademoiselle..." He snapped his fingers, one, two, three times.

Everyone waited with polite smiles, eyes darting my way. How dare he?

He triumphantly grabbed my name from the air. "*Berthe*."

The way Edma smiled at his antics felt like betrayal.

"Students of Corot." He whispered loudly behind his hand, "They paint *en plein air*. But we won't mention it." Edma's smile broke into a laugh. I was ready to leave.

He turned to a straight-backed young man with a mouth reminding me of a monkey's muzzle which sported a dripping moustache frayed at its ends. Wire spectacles hung on a leather cord around his neck. "This here is the merciless critic Émile Zola." He slapped his hand onto the man's shoulder. "Be nice to him and he might not belittle your work in the press."

"We follow your articles in *l'Evenement*," said Edma. "It's heartening to have a defender of modernism speaking for us."

I pictured him writing furiously while sucking on the ends of his moustache for courage. In my shyness and admiration, I could only nod and smile.

"Thank you," he began. "I wholeheartedly believe—"

"That an artist be of his own time and place and paint the truth of what he sees," finished Édouard. "See, I know how he thinks. And why does he think such thoughts? Because all else has been done to death." He gestured as to hang himself, tongue lolling.

"Art is not what *you* see," muttered a man behind me, "but what you make others see." As no one else seemed to have heard his remark, I turned to acknowledge him but his hooded gaze remained pinned on M. Zola.

"Yes," said M. Zola, "Académie recipes no longer satisfy. Let's see more of the natural world, of real people—"

"Oh, he's a dangerous man." Édouard wagged a finger. "And soon his scandalous novel shall be unleashed upon us. *Confessions of Émile*"—he winked at M. Zola, who blushed. "I mean *Confessions of Paul?*" He clapped a hand over his mouth. "I'm mistaken, that is not the title. Claude it is, *Confessions of Claude*." He turned to Edma. "Disgraceful reading for proper young ladies. A must-read."

"I'll look for it in the shops." Her smile was coquettish. My sister was never coquettish.

Zola ran a hand through his hair. "It's my first novel and I hope to improve on—"

"You may have trouble finding it," said Édouard. "The Justice Minister ordered our friend's rooms searched and is now examining the book to make sure it doesn't pose a moral danger to the public."

"Outrageous!" said the beautiful woman. "Censorship in the hands of Luddites."

Édouard ruffed M. Zola's hair. "This helmet is filled with novels, each more vulgar than the next."

M. Zola gently lifted Édouard's hand away. "I've been inspired by this man's shocking brush."

Despite my discomfort, the conversation was like drinking cold water. I realized only now that I was parched for it.

"Enough of you, Zola the Great," said Édouard. "Let me introduce the impeccable Alfred Stevens, and his wife, Marie."

Édouard toured us through his friends as if they were paintings. "You may have seen his *Still-lifes* and *Parisiennes* at Oubliot's gallery, where every last picture had a sold tag on it."

"Yes, I have," said Edma. Had she forgotten we had seen them together? "It's easy to understand why your work is so popular."

"Stevens makes his models more lovely than they are is why," said Édouard, "and yet he thinks himself a modern painter." It was hard to tell if he was being serious, funny or both. No matter, Stevens and his beautiful wife appeared charmed.

Édouard now put his arm around the brown-suited man behind me who had kept slightly back from the group. "I must introduce this depressing fellow here. Ladies, meet Monsieur Edgar Degas, son of a banker, which we do not hold against him, and former student of the Académie des Beaux-Arts, which we do. He has not done much worthwhile to date, I'm sorry to say, but is now painting a portrait of my wife and me."

"Two separate portraits?" asked Zola.

"Two in one"—Degas spoke in a monotone—"the piano player and the listener." The thinnest patchwork of a beard grazed his chin, his cheeks smooth as a boy's. His knit suit was too warm for the weather while his lidded eyes made him appear world-weary, even bored. I had the feeling it was an act. That he was, perhaps, as shy as me. "But one of my models"—he stared at Édouard who, no longer listening, gazed about the room—"cannot keep still and the work is taking longer than I had expected."

"Very good." Édouard announced that he must attend to his other guests and with a grand gesture of his arm said, "Do make yourselves at home." He sidled away and into another clutch of guests to interrupt whatever conversation was in progress.

Because I admired his work I wanted to admire the man, but was wholly relieved to see him go.

THE SPACE Édouard had occupied now seemed cavernous, and the group began to break into disparate parts. M. Zola leaned in to ask something of Edma that I couldn't hear over the violin's crescendo. An older woman, her waving hands bejeweled and jingling, pulled away the Stevens, and Degas mumbled something to me.

"Pardon?"

"Fanny Claus," he said, "on the violin."

"Claus? Of the Claus quartet?'

"The sisters, yes."

"Oh, yes, we saw them in the Tuileries. Fanny had stood out among her very blonde sisters."

"I heard"—he made a soft fist and held it to his mouth—"that her mother had an affair with the Asian zookeeper."

Was he joking?

"Your Cuban slipper"—he pointed—"it has a pink rose."

I looked to Edma to come to my rescue but her ear was inclined to M. Zola as her gaze followed Édouard across the room.

Degas' finger now tapped the pearl enclosure on the wrist of my glove. "I am writing a treatise on woman's fashions, and more specifically, on ornaments worn by women. Beauty's condiments."

How to respond?

"I'm fascinated by the whole *mundus muliebris*, the meaning of these ornaments and how a woman uses them to define herself?"

I had never heard of a man interested in dressing women. Only undressing them. The grounding notes of the piano had stopped as those of the violin whined overhead. I saw Édouard's wife kneeling beside Mme. Manet's velvet chair as though she were a servant.

"Why flowers instead of bows?" asked Degas.

"I just prefer flowers." Edma walked off without even a glance my way.

"Preference is never without meaning." His tone insinuated that I was holding something back, not from him but from myself. It was time to change subjects.

"The Stevens make a handsome couple."

Degas sniffed. "Marie Stevens is too beautiful to be beautiful."

I knew exactly what he meant. "Because beauty calls out for contrast. To set it off, propel the eye around the subject. A lean in the nose. A melancholy."

Degas considered me with new interest. "Beauty is imperfection. Imperfection, beauty."

"If one has the eye."

"Yes."

My hand went instinctively to my chin. We said nothing for a moment, content in our mutual understanding. The Stevens were now caught up in a knot of admirers. "Perhaps we're simply consumed with jealousy," I said.

The smallest and wryest of smiles bent his lips. I felt proud to have been the cause, for it was clear he was not a smiler. In fact, there seemed a sorrow behind his cynical mien, as if for a soft second his guard had dropped and a private sadness revealed.

He sighed. "It's a beautiful thing, jealousy."

It was my turn to smile. I felt not the least bit shy around this man whose lonely demeanor asked nothing of me and promised nothing in return.

"So you're painting Édouard and his wife?"

"The piano teacher."

"Piano teacher?" I waited for him to go on.

"Did you notice that young man turning the sheet music?"

"Madame Manet said he is Suzanne's brother. Édouard's nephew?"

"Did she now?"

What was he implying?

"I must meet my cousin at the train station." He said he had enjoyed our conversation and excused himself with a bow of his head. Making his way through the gathering, he thinned himself sideways to prevent his body from touching another's and thus being acknowledged. What a terrible gossip, I thought, sorry to see him leave.

The talk and the music flowed around me like a river. On the far side of the piano in front of an enormous standing clock, Edma spoke to Édouard's cocked ear as he stared, so it seemed, directly at me, his expression concerned. That I was now unengaged? Any gentleman would come introduce me into another group or wave me over but he turned his back and said something to Edma that made her cover her opened mouth. From the other side of the room, his brother Eugène was looking my way yet he too stayed put. Had their mother taught them no manners?

I walked to the near window which overlooked the boulevard and its line of waiting carriages, among them our four-in-hand and Levin, our driver, who attached feedbags to the horses' rankle while a family of rats made a meal of a manure pile. Another driver, missing his top hat, tossed bread bits to the ground, causing pigeons to swarm and fight.

"DID YOU NOT THINK it strange we weren't introduced to Édouard's wife?" Edma asked as we prepared for bed.

"Very."

"What was it, I wonder, that brought them together?"

As I climbed into bed I shared my encounter with Edgar Degas and his enigmatic comment referring to Suzanne as the piano teacher. "Her playing *was* highly accomplished."

"Édouard claimed the colour black as his favourite to paint. Imagine having a conversation about that colour. He's been trying to find the bottom of it and can't." Her voice thinned as if drifting into daydream. "The bottom of it. Says he's fascinated by black skin and is seeking a negress to model for him. Berthe, I couldn't begin to predict what would come out his mouth."

"You didn't find his behaviour overbearing?" Had she been at all aware of how I was made to feel? "If not outright rude?"

"Or is he forthright and exuberant? I don't think we've ever met someone who embraces life like he does. And therefore life seems to embrace him."

My throat stiffened. "You're clearly enamoured."

Edma pulled back the quilts on her side the bed. "I'm just as enamoured about the friends he keeps. Aren't you?"

"I like Monsieur Degas."

"He seemed quiet and gentle."

"Not so when you speak to him. You wouldn't know, though, as you spoke only to Édouard."

Edma sighed. "I'm inspired by his work. I thought you were too."

"Of course I am."

She climbed in beside me and, as always, the bed grew warmer and the darkness beyond the lamp less threatening. She blew out her lamp. I blew out mine. Whatever it was that fueled her attraction to Édouard, I didn't like how completely he stole her attention. Or was it how completely she stole his?

THE NIGHT HAD IMPRESSED Maman too. Shortly thereafter, she changed her regular Tuesday dinners to soirées with an open invitation, believing it a more expedient way for Edma and I to meet eligible young men.

Our lives suddenly revolved around these evenings. We obsessed over what to wear, copied Mme. Stevens' hairstyles, read Zola's skewering articles and informed ourselves of the issues of the day. We made moneyless bets on what garish colour Édouard's gloves and vest might be, ensured the cooks knew about Degas' penchant for hot milk with honey at an evening's end and Édouard's love of pickled white asparagus. His wife, Suzanne, did not accompany him. When Maman asked after her, he simply said she preferred the quiet and must be home to care for her brother Léon.

As though Édouard were an illusionist able to make me disappear, whenever Edma was in his presence, I ceased to exist. Or matter. I wondered if this was a relief to her. Was it possible she had tired of my company?

Édouard charmed everyone he met with the exception of Papa, who called him "the kind of man who receives too much encouragement from a mother." Was he also jealous of Edma's enchantment?

Édouard invariably left our soirée early to journey to infamous Montmartre and his reserved table at the Café Guerbois. Zola, Henri, Antoine and Stevens left with him, and only on occasion Degas, who considered himself above mixing with "the rabble."

Édouard went from drinking sweet claret from stemmed crystal in the *haute arrondissement* of Passy to swilling beer from ceramic mugs in a noisy, smoke-filled bar in Montmartre. From admiring proper young women to appraising barmaids. From tempered intellectual discussion to drunken bellowing. Oh, how I envied his liberty to move between worlds and be more than one kind of person. Genius, as far as I could tell, was another word for freedom.

OUR TEACHER, M. COROT, had recommended the Norman coast for its "drame and light" and that summer Maman managed to rent a converted mill in Beuzeval, on a property owned by the artist and first cousin of Delacroix himself, Léon Reisener.

Straight out of a German fairy tale, our cottage mill had a thatched roof of dense straw, diamond-shaped windows of leaded glass and heavy wooden doors that groaned on their iron hinges. Inside, exposed beams of charred wood bore the concave scales of the adze, and the staircase spiraled round itself. A stream ran along the cottage's side, its current no longer turning the half-rotten wheel. The surrounding woods were alive with birdsong in the day, and tree frogs at night, their *chanson* that of a thousand creaking doors being opened but never closed.

The property's small beachfront was certainly bright and dramatic, with cliffs behind, barnacle-covered rocks that sliced through gloves and endless rotting seaweed that gave off the air of a vast cadaver. A constant wind sent seabirds careening sideways while threatening to lift our skirts and us with them. On my first visit a gust tore off my brand-new hat, which was lost to the churning surf. Edma was less than charmed by the beach and had little desire to revisit. This was fine with me, though my reluctance arose more from my bewilderment. Simply, it seemed impossible to paint such constant motion and endlessly fracturing light.

The Reiseners' summer home was near our mill house and as soon as we were settled Léon, or Leo as he was called by his family, and his wife, Laure, kindly invited us to dinner. Joining us were Leo's mother, a rigid antiquated figure swathed in black lace and a sleeve collar at the table's far end; his plain-faced daughter, Rosalie, the same age as Edma; and a sculptor—a year older than Edma—who went by the name Marcello. No Madame or Mademoiselle, no last name, just Marcello.

"Marcello's a pseudonym"—her smile carved dimples into her ivory cheeks—"as a precaution against the chauvinism of the Salon jury. Art is considered a man's business."

I sat up straighter.

Of Danish aristocracy, Marcello was educated and worldly. She was also exquisitely feminine and beautiful, and these qualities alone won my father's admiration. Notwithstanding her pedigree, or perhaps because of it, she was disarmingly frank. When Maman asked if she didn't care for marriage, Marcello told her story without sentiment or self-pity. Formerly Mme. Adele Colonna, she had fallen in love with a Roman nobleman and married at age twenty-two. Six months into what sounded like the most passionate of unions, her husband died.

"We were on horseback," she told us, clear-eyed, between the soup and the fish, "on our estate in Grenoble when, as if struck by lightning, he stiffened in his saddle beside me. His boots still in the stirrups he fell unnaturally backwards, slipped down one side and"—she paused, as though to focus the memory as vividly as she could—"dangled there. The horse shimmied away from the strange weight of him. His arms were loose as ribbons, his eyes wide with what felt like my own astonishment."

Our wide eyes begged the question.

"A seizure to the brain," she said.

Her grief forced her to leave Grenoble and spend six months in a monastery, "in hopes of a rebirth. I took to clay like a dumb animal. I shaped it into everything and nothing, into things holy and unholy." Her hands, muscular and expressive, kneaded the air as she spoke. "It was the forgiveness of clay under my hand that began my healing."

Marcello rented a studio from the Reiseners in Paris and was here renting the small cottage in the woods between our place and theirs. Not only did her beauty impress Papa but her society, whose names were revealed innocently through the evening's conversation: Empress Eugénie, George Sand, Charles Garnier, and Deputy Minister Thiers. At the mention of Thiers, Papa boasted of his twenty-year acquaintance with the man, leaving out the fact that Thiers was more patron than friend, having helped secure him various posts, including his present one in the Finance Ministry.

Upon learning that Marcello had exhibited in London that fall, at the Kensington, and had had sculptures accepted into four Paris Salons, I nudged Edma under the table. She understood immediately. Here at last was an example for our father of a successful female artist who, unlike Rosa Bonheur, was making her own way without a husband while having retained her feminine charms.

Edma asked Leo if he was familiar with the work of Édouard Manet. Was that colour rising to her cheeks? By just saying his name? She began to list off his Salon paintings but our host raised a hand to stop her.

"Of course, I'm aware of him."

"*L'enfant terrible,*" said Marcello with a crooked smile.

"I see Velázquez in his purity of colour," said Leo, "but judging from his preponderance of homages, he struggles with composition."

"Could it not be deliberate?" defended Edma.

"Take his *Duchess of Alba,*" Leo continued. "It's Velázquez's *Lola de Valence.* And his *Déjeuner sur l'herbe?* Raphael's *Judgement of Paris.*"

"That's it," I said. "I knew I had seen it before."

"Most of his figures' expressions, I'm afraid"—Leo raised his finger—"are stiff as still lifes. But look, here he is now, far from Paris, at our dinner table. Like a man falling into snow, he has made an impression on the public."

"He has two younger brothers," said Maman, looking at everyone but Edma. "We've not yet met Gustave, the youngest."

"The artist's job"—hands pressed palm to palm, Leo made slow chopping gestures as he spoke—"is to translate the human need for beauty and clarity. And this is a need as basic as any. But the translation requires a poetic exaggeration, one that captures the effect light imposes on visible nature."

Papa bristled at our host's didactic tone, as though only he should have the prerogative to adopt it. He reached for his wine and swirled the ruby liquid. "Is it only the artist who sees nature in its correct light? I assure you," he laughed, "if the Finance Office did not see things clearly, Paris would quickly fall to disarray and there would be neither beauty nor contentment."

"Disarray is a great inspiration to artists," said Marcello, who had kept pace with the men when it came to the wine.

"Then I apologize for attempting to prevent it, Madame." Papa lifted his glass to her. She didn't lift hers.

"I understand that a great portion of Monsieur Haussmann's sewer system lacks the slope to effectively flush away our ordure." She waved a hand in front of her nose. "And I've been a guest at the

Tuileries and seen firsthand the royal spending of our tax dollars. Pun intended. So I wonder if your office is not also inspired by disarray."

I had a new hero.

Two beats behind the conversation, Leo said to Papa, "No, no. The artists are not 'correct.' They are above or below such relative truths. People who see things for what they are, no doubt, are superior in intellect, but they are not artists."

"Here, here." Now Marcello raised her glass.

Kept busy assisting her ancient grand-mère, who was incapable of following the conversation or balancing soup on a spoon, Rosalie, we learned, was also an aspiring painter. She generously offered to lend Edma and me any supplies we might have left behind.

Edma spent much of the evening befriending the humble Rosalie, while my attention remained riveted on the widow with the man's name.

ON OUR FIRST MORNING in Buezeval, Edma gently suggested that she and I find separate landscapes to paint.

"You don't have to tread so lightly with me," I said, embarrassed. Salon critics had never failed to remark on our *sisterly* landscapes, which Edma found patronizing. I was being pushed out of the nest and had no one to blame but myself for overstaying.

"Without even consulting, or revealing where." She said it as though cajoling a child with a game. "That way we can surprise each other."

"I completely agree." I didn't but, of course, she was right. So that morning and each morning after, easels on our backs, we set out in opposing directions.

For weeks I wandered around the Reiseners' property, literally in circles, seeking inspiration and the numinous light described by M. Corot. The light did possess a diffusing aura, as though the ocean rose to stain the very air, yet every perspective seemed equal in value to the next and mocked my inability to make decisions. Each day I began any number of despairing sketches that by evening I rubbed out.

Not meaning to spy, I nonetheless noticed during my wanderings that every afternoon at 2:30, wearing her sculptor's smock, her blonde hair drawn into a simple ponytail, Marcello retired to her terrace. One afternoon she caught me staring from between two trees like some stricken deer and invited me to join her. To save face, I demurred, said I was expected home.

"Expected home?"

How childish that sounded. "But it's hardly pressing. I'd be pleased to join you."

"Brilliant." She asked what beverage I preferred.

"Whatever you're having will do."

Marcello fetched two glasses and a pitcher full of a reddish-brown drink that looked like tea.

"You don't have help?"

"No. No." She waved away the thought. "I leave my servants behind so they can gossip about me, try on my hairpieces and gowns. Test out my bed."

"Are you serious?"

"Oh, they're quite careful and everyone needs an alternate life, don't you think? It's freeing all around and keeps us on good terms."

Maman had brought along our first cook, one lady's maid and hired out locally for a housekeeper.

"Who cooks your meals?"

"I prefer cold food in summer. Weak cheese, radishes, cherries. The Reiseners' man brings over bread and eggs. I have a pot of chives"—she pointed to the kitchen window—"and make a fine omelette." She twirled the liquid in her glass. "And I drink this throughout the day. To sustain the spirit."

We clinked our glasses. The tea seared a path down my throat and my nostrils flared at the medicinal taste.

"Claret mixed with English bitters. An Italian invention, but I call it my London tea."

A taste to get used to, the effects not unpleasant. In no time, my body felt wrapped in a woolen cloak, my thinking lively.

Marcello urged me on with questions about my life in Paris, my art, my plans for the future. Unaccustomed to such directness I was stingy with my answers so she filled in with her own.

"Paris is exciting but demanding of its women, no?" she said. "We must be beautiful, elegant, conversive, in command of our servants, all while doting on our men. Not to mention witty whores in the bedroom."

Beyond Marcello's shoulder a brown squirrel scratched its way up the trunk of a pine and froze. Could I imagine a whore's wit?

"I love the city but find it exhausting and take regular holidays. Here I need please no one but myself." She tipped her glass to the forest. "Nature is the greatest of respites. In the fall I'll travel to Florence to study. A woman can relax in Italy. Italian men are misogynists and have wonderfully low expectations of us."

With a sopranic chirring, the squirrel disappeared into the leaves. Mute with my inexperience, I scrambled to piece together a response, witty or otherwise, but again Marcello spoke for both of us.

"Food and sex. Sex and food. That's all Italian men want. Italian women are the most beautiful in Europe but end up unfulfilled in love and then angry and finally fat on their own wonderful cooking."

"I've not yet been to Italy."

"You will. You will." She refilled my glass.

For a long moment, I pretended to admire the trees but had the prickly feeling that she was studying me.

"I believe that all creative acts," she said, her voice gentler, "be it love-making or art, depend on the surrender of the rational self. That it's through the animal that we experience the spiritual. What do you think?"

I knew of no woman who thought such things, much less said them aloud. "Yes, of course."

After a second London tea, my tongue loosened and I found myself speaking freely of my father's infidelities, my mother's preoccupation with marrying off her children, and my sister's obsession with Édouard Manet. I lamented how we were not spending the entire season in Normandy but the second half in Louveciennes.

"Near the fashionable Île de Chatou?"

"A favoured watering hole of our Emperor."

"Edma claims an interest in the area's rolling hills but I know the real reason is its proximity to Paris and to host our new friends, Édouard Manet in particular." It felt disloyal to be talking about Edma behind her back but also liberating. "I voted against it, insisting our work would be compromised, but Maman decided it a wonderful idea."

"Well, many things that inspire one's art," she said, diplomatically. "Men being one."

MY VISITS TO Marcello's cottage and "teatime" became a near daily event. One muggy afternoon, I arrived to find the door to the kitchen flung open. Flies buzzed over the leftovers of an omelette on the kitchen block, underclothes hung on a rack beside the stove and an opened letter lay on the kitchen table. Had she received bad news? I knocked on the doorframe and, without asking whom it was, Marcello called for me to come in. I found her sitting in the drawing room in front of a propped-up mirror, naked to the waist, sketchbook in hand.

I blushed and apologized, told her I would come back. What if it hadn't been me but Leo's man?

"I'm almost done. Please have a seat."

Oh. I took the nearest chair, which happened to face the glaring white of her breasts, picked up a copy of *La Vie Parisienne* and attempted to read.

"I wanted to sketch myself while the moon is near full because, as you know, our figures are also at their fullest. We must study the nude if we are serious about art, yes? Or so the men say while denying us that opportunity. But how many men know about the moon?"

"I imagine none." Was it true about the moon?

"Lucky for us, we can pose as our own goddesses." Then she swore me to secrecy about the fact that the breasts on her sculptures "are modeled on my own."

There was only one acceptable breast in sculpture as well as in painting. Modest in size, symmetrical, buoyant as a soap bubble and with pale nipples no larger than a centime. Any deviation constituted realism and was therefore considered indecent.

I realized I had seen Marcello's breasts before. These same triangular, wall-eyed breasts with the smiling curve had once straddled the ears of my sister Yves in the Salon garden. As I told Marcello, she said, "My Pythia," and laughed, her breasts jiggling happily.

She put down her pencil, pulled on her chemise but left the buttons undone, her cleavage exposed. "I would love to sculpt you. Your shoulders are perfection. Your arms thin and threatening. Your knees I'm guessing are almost points." She ran her hand along my skirt and a chill shook my spine.

"There are my ears to consider," I said, reclothing the subject when she leaned in and cupped my chin. Just before her lips met mine, I turned my face away. She kissed my cheek with a loud smack.

"Well, then." She began to button her chemise. Try as I might, I'm not sure I hid my shock. "Let's not dwell. A waste of life shame."

I'd disappointed her, but what could I do?

"Now if I were to sculpt you, I would make you into Bia, the daughter of Pallas. She represents force, compulsion."

"Forgive me, Marcello..."

"Oh, no apologies. No. No." She waved a hand. "Your lips made me curious and I became absorbed in thoughts of my own making.

Please, pay it no mind." Her eyes roamed my face. "Berthe and Bia. Brilliant. Shall we, my friend, have some tea?"

"Yes, let's." She disappeared into the kitchen. Did female attraction arise naturally in unmarried women artists? With time, might it happen to me too?

"MAMAN RECEIVED a letter today," said Edma brightly. "Both Édouard and Degas have accepted her invitation to visit us in Louveciennes."

I had returned home from a shopping trip with Marcello, whose overtures of friendship hadn't waned as I'd feared, to find Edma and Rosalie on the terrace with Maman.

"The Stevens, however, sent their regrets," said Maman. "They are summering in Venice."

"Will Suzanne be accompanying Édouard?" I asked to temper Edma's enthusiasm.

"He didn't say who would accompany him."

Quiet Rosalie watched our exchange.

"Yves and the baby will join us for ten days," continued Maman. "And your aunt and cousins for a week. Tibby also with friends."

"So much for working," I said.

"Well, you're working now," said Maman.

"We'll find time," said Edma, without conviction.

"So tell me"—Maman clapped her hands onto her lap—"what exactly are you three working at?"

Edma had completed two landscape studies and had begun to put one to oil. Which perspective? Where? Three weeks had wafted by and I had nothing to show for myself but two insipid watercolours of the mill.

Rosalie was doing a portrait of her *grand-mére*. How conventional, I thought, not surprised.

I confessed to have been unable to settle on any one perspective and feared wasting my summer entirely. Edma looked contrite but said nothing.

"It helps me," said Rosalie, "to have someone in mind when I'm painting. And what it is I'd like to show them."

"One paints for the sake of painting itself, no?" I said, quoting something I had read but not understood.

Rosalie, who wouldn't force her opinion on a flea, nodded in agreement. In contrast to my Marcello, Rosalie was unsophisticated and dull and I hoped Edma was envious. It was her turn to know what it felt like to be abandoned by her sister.

"HOW FREEING TO BE out in the world without one's mother." Standing at the vanity, I removed Edma's hairpins. "Marcello engages shopkeepers and lackeys as though they are her equals. Asks them personal questions and reveals personal stories." These exchanges had made me feel less special in Marcello's company but I didn't tell Edma this. "I wonder if her ease with the lower classes comes from the fact that bloodlines cannot be contested and the aristocracy have nothing to prove. Whereas we haute bourgeoisie, forever scaling the social ladder, need people to look down upon."

Edma enjoyed debating such ideas but all she said was, "I can see your logic."

"I haven't told you, Edma"—I lowered my voice—"what happened at Marcello's cottage." I had saved telling her of the kiss but now wanted to impress her. But as if my life held no interest for her, she said, "I too received a letter from Édouard today."

Even here, a hundred miles apart, he stole her attention from me?

"Why? Had you written him?" I tugged apart her braid.

She looked up at me in the mirror. I was expecting a look of guilt but her eyes were stained with happiness. "He had requested that I write and tell him about Normandy and its landscape. He's not been, you see."

"No, I don't see."

She ignored my tone. “He was very impressed to hear that we were dining with Leo Reisener. Besides being what he considers a brilliant colourist, Leo, he says, is a Communard sympathizer.”

“Edma.”

“What?” She gathered the hairpins into a straight pile. “We're friends and fellow painters. His brother Gustave is a staunch –”

“Communard, I know.”

“He has found a negress to model for him. Says he's been inspired by Titian's *Venus of Urbino* and is doing an homage.”

“With a negress?”

“It seems so.” Though her face was not, her voice was smiling. “So he is furiously at work with high hopes of winning over the critics.”

I brushed the bent angles of her hair.

“You're pressing too hard.”

“Sorry.”

We said nothing for a moment. She was being dishonest with me or perhaps only with herself. Either way I couldn't bear it.

“My sister is flirting with a married man. And worse, he's flirting back.”

Her dampened smile finally broke loose.

“See, I'm right.”

“It is completely innocent.”

“It doesn't sound innocent.” She was still holding back.

Edma sighed. “Oh, Berthe, we might as well flirt a little, no? When nothing can come of it, what's the harm? We are women after all.”

Édouard brought out a side of my sister I didn't trust but needed to. “Being married, as we know, is no great obstacle for men.”

“I'm not mad, Berthe, nor am I a fool. Yes, I find him handsome and exciting, but you know me. I'm a realist. Besides, he's a gentleman.”

“Like Papa?”

“That's different.”

I didn't think it was.

"He sends his regards, by the way."

"To me?"

"Yes, to you. He's your friend too, is he not?"

"He can't even remember my name."

"Regards to your sister were his words." She sounded as though she had the letter memorized.

"As I said."

THE FOLLOWING DAY I set up my easel at the narrow end of the pond in the woods behind our cottage. The day was uncomfortably hot and windless; even in a loose cotton dress and smock my skin was slick with sweat. I picked up my pencil then slammed it down. Where was the meaning in a weedy pond and green trees? I held my hands to my face and stretched flat my palms and fingers to watch the creases grow red with blood. Since meeting that pompous man, Edma no longer cared to paint together. Nor was she the least envious of my time with Marcello. Would she soon be joining him in spirit and forget my name too? I pressed my hands against the mounds of my breasts. Could I imagine painting my own nude figure to hang in the Salon for all of Paris to ogle and judge? I closed my eyes. Were they at their fullest? For a moment my hands seemed other than my own and my spine radiated a nervous light. I opened my eyes and there, reflected upside down in the water, were the dark green shapes of Édouard Manet's forest and lavender sky from *Le Déjeuner sur l'herbe*. As though the sun rose for a second time that day, the pond and forest, like Dante's multi-foliate rose, flowered before me in heightened clarity. Foreground and background and middle distance. Grasses, waterstriders on thread-thin legs, the hover and chase of turquoise dragonflies. Browns, greens, blues and yellows, shadows and light, textures I could somehow taste as if I'd run my tongue along their surface. Every object so singularly defined that the air between them punched forward to assume its own vitality. The pond was at once reflective and transparent, seen and hidden. Without hesitation, I began. I knew exactly what I would paint because, as Rosalie had suggested, I knew for whom I was painting—Édouard—and why—revenge.

I sketched right onto the canvas, anticipating my next line, and my next, and a dozen more to come, hardly able to keep up. The light was new and even the darkest of shadows seemed lit from within. The hours passed without my notice. At some point Pauline appeared bearing soup and bread. She had the sense not to disturb me and left the tray on the ground, the bread taken bit by bit by triumphant field mice.

HAVING FOUND MY landscape, I now desired a model. Maman let me borrow a maid, a young girl from Caen called Sidonie. She was a homely thing with coarse manners—Tibby, when he visited, referred to her as "*la cretine*"—yet her figure was plump and pleasing, her skin thick as cream, and her abundant hair a satisfying cast-iron black, shiny with its own grease.

But what drew me to Sidonie was how at home she was in her body. She inhabited her flesh like dumplings ride in soup, buoyantly displacing the space around them. Even the way her hands hung loose and heavy by her side made me aware of how little comfort I had in my own flesh. While hers appeared a single settled whole, mine was a complication of parts to be tended and bargained with and then forgotten altogether. Tibby's cruel name-calling, I imagined, arose from denial. Despite Sidonie's manners, one wanted to embrace her or be embraced by her, to bury oneself in the soft earth of her.

To mirror the bather in Édouard's *Le Déjeuner,* I draped Sidonie in one of Maman's cotton nightdresses then arranged her sitting on the bank, her bare feet in the water. I asked her to lean forward and look down at her reflection when she announced she was "tired as night." Before I could insist otherwise, she made herself comfortable on the grass, stretching and groaning with the pleasure of it. Though displeased by her insolence, I felt that pleasure in my own limbs.

She lay on her side, her figure falling into the most natural of poses: head along her outstretched arm, her torso and legs a gently rolling landscape. The sun made her skin glow a little.

"Perfect, beautiful. Might you move a little closer to the pond and peer into it." I wanted only her profile.

She sighed but edged closer.

"Can you see your reflection?"

"No, Mademoiselle."

"Can you try for me?"

She propped her head up on one elbow, tipped her head forward.

"Thank you. That's it. Can you hold that?"

"I suppose."

"You are a female Narcissus."

She glanced up at me, frowning.

"I meant that your figure will be that of a woman pondering her reflection."

Sidonie gave a small snort.

As soon as I began drawing, she shifted, complaining of the cold ground. I reset her former pose. She batted at her bare foot. "There are ticks in these grasses."

I arranged her again, tucking the nightdress around her legs. I asked about her family and made murmurs of interest as I listened to what sounded like the happiest of childhoods. Her moving mouth magically stilled her body so whenever the flow of words slowed I asked another question. A born storyteller, Sidonie had finally been invited to speak.

As she paused for air, I asked her to slip the nightdress off one shoulder, and then the other. She did so without thinking as she described another brother, the third sibling in a line of eight, who "never grew any hair. No eyebrows, no lashes, not a stick on his head."

I sketched the roundness of her shoulder. "Smooth as a pebble. We used to take char from a cold fire and draw hair on him." I asked her to place one hand between her legs. She went quiet.

"On your knee."

Unlike Édouard's model in *Le Déjeuner*, my Sidonie would not look out at the viewer. I was not that bold, nor did I care to be. My gaze would remain inward for now.

In the end I copied Édouard's forest, his bather's dress, his fragment of sky and distant water, his shame-free, large-footed woman. His classical air. I would use his innovations and ideas but improve upon them. I realized that from the moment we met, I felt in fierce competition with him. And not just for Edma's attention. I wanted his respect. I wanted him not only to learn my name but need to say it.

EDMA, ROSALIE AND I convened in the garden to discuss our paintings, taking turns displaying them on an easel. I had invited Marcello to join us but she had gone to town to meet with a fellow sculptor, M. Carpeaux. She was to be gone for three nights so I presumed that they were lovers and her tastes variable. Such daring and freedom as I could only imagine. I wondered if I had returned her advances, would she be here now?

Edma went first. Of muted tones under a misted sky, her painting depicted two cows in a field, a stone wall and distant farmhouse. Harmonious colours flowed from earth to sky and back again, her loaded brush bringing texture and richness to the animal's coat.

"Perfectly rendered," I told her, "a marriage of Bonheur and Corot. The spaciousness of the field and sky produce a wonderful calming effect."

Neither Rosalie nor I had any suggestions because the painting was technically perfect and complete in itself. My single reserve was that the painting did not make me feel a new feeling or think a new thought. But to say so would sound arrogant.

Generous Rosalie was not generous when it came to her portrait of her grand-mère. The old woman's sagging cheeks were cracked with lines, her eyelids veined, her lips bloodless and drooped on one side. In fact, she had exaggerated these, her perception clearly tinted by something beyond the keenness of her eye. I wondered how Rosalie felt about the old woman. Was this what Zola had meant by interpreting through one's own temperament?

"You have a deft and honest hand," said Edma. "Your grand-mère's white hair against her black sleeve-collar is striking and the silver pendant harmonious. But, Rosalie, you have not flattered her features."

"My father has done many flattering portraits of his mother. This is my meditation on death."

I studied the portrait more closely. Rosalie's shadowing intimated a skull beneath the skin. The transparent blue irises suggested ghoulish sockets or perhaps the faltering light of the soul. And the solid black of the dress and heavy pendant contrasted the fragility of the flesh. I had underestimated Rosalie.

"You have painted death and life simultaneously. Brilliant. Is it not, Edma?"

"I now see your intent. Yes, yes it is."

"Luckily her eyesight is poor," said Rosalie, deflecting the compliments. "Not for her sake, of course. Just mine."

As for my painting of Sidonie, Edma saw the thematic resemblance to *Le Déjeuner* immediately and gave me a look as though implying I had stolen or copied from her yet again. But in the next breath she said, "Your best yet, Berthe," and sounded only sincere.

Praise from Edma meant the world and I tried unsuccessfully to hide my pleasure. Rosalie was also complimentary and expressed astonishment that I was able to make Sidonie look like a beauty. I couldn't form a response because my throat had swelled.

"Your lovely preponderance of green, Berthe, brings to mind something I read recently," said Rosalie, "in Goethe's *Theory of Colour.*

He writes how colours diametrically opposed on the colour wheel will evoke each other in the eye. You have many shades of green, so—"

"Red," I blurted. If I was swollen with compliments, I was toppled by criticism. "It could use a stand of red flowers. Or a red-ribboned hat on the grass."

"I like the uniformity of tone," said Edma.

"Yes, red might be garish," I backtracked. Seeing the painting through others' eyes I realized that, unlike Édouard's daring, I had reverted to a traditional palette, a conventional horizon line and safe subject matter. Things that would please any Salon jury. How deluded I was.

"I was imagining something small only, a scarlet ribbon in Sidonie's hair. But you're quite right," said Rosalie, fearful that she had stepped on my cowardly toes. "Don't ruin the harmony."

Though I tried to put it out of my mind, I went to bed playing Rosalie's single note of criticism over and over in my head.

THE NEXT DAY, alone by the pond with my painting, my eye drifted aimlessly in its greenery, unsure where to look. With an angry spasm, I plucked the tube of scarlet #3, wiped some on my palette, grabbed a small brush and slashed a line of red across Sidonie's hair.

As though the objects in the painting had been afloat and roaming about, they now settled into place. I did another red stroke in the reflected image. The effect was striking. The red enthused the painting with the irresistible, however subtle. I later expressed my gratitude to Rosalie. She deferred all credit to Goethe and lent me the book.

I QUICKLY SETTLED on another landscape, one inspired by the exaggerated foreground perspective in his *Bullfight*. I would take advantage of his originality but improve on his perspective.

I painted a distant view of Marcello's cottage from the spot where I once spied on her, to record where our friendship first bloomed, a friendship I imagined as lifelong, such that in our aging years we might look back on this painting and reminisce. When it sat finished on its easel and was also dominant with greens, I took scarlet #3 and, though afraid of ruining the realism, made a swift stroke on a birch trunk. Again the painting shifted, its colours shocked and brought to clarity. I made a few more careful slashes.

Scarlet, I decided would be my secret signature. My hidden dare and quiet revolution. One had to start somewhere.

TO MY GREAT DISMAY, our last evening in Buezeval had come even earlier than expected—having learned we were summering on the Norman coast, Papa's ailing sister, taking no heed of the distance between Beuzeval and Lorient, insisted we visit—and the Reiseners had invited us for a farewell dinner. The table had been set in their garden and the wedding-band china shone like moonlight. Nicotiana and jasmine sweetened the air and the tree frogs were just beginning their chorus.

From his seat at the head of the table, Leo announced that Marcello had received a commission from the Emperor.

Marcello scoffed. "The sculpture is only for the garden at the upcoming Exposition. Nothing grand."

I was surprised she hadn't told me.

"Quite an honour," said Maman. "And the subject?"

"A bust of the goddess Hecate."

"Very good," said Leo.

I wasn't familiar with this goddess and knew Edma wasn't either.

I had recently confessed to Marcello my dream for Edma and me to have a studio separate from our parents' home. She was surprised this wasn't already the case.

"You must have an atmosphere unmuddied with the day-to-day. This is not a luxury, it's a necessity." She'd promised to "work on" my father at his next visit. Something I'd all but forgotten.

As the soup was being served, Papa brought up the recent uprising in Paris inside a steel factory. "Speedily quelled by the National Guard, its organizers are now behind bars."

"Banished to the *banlieux*," sighed Leo, "working under appalling conditions and for a pitiful wage, their children too. The workers will organize at first chance."

"You make it sound like Hugo's *Les Misérables*," said Maman.

"You may not witness such things in pretty Passy," said Marcello, "but that does not excuse their existence."

Leo's eyes gleamed in the candlelight. "When the revolution comes, we can all escape here."

"Organize to what end?" said Papa in disbelief. "Other than being jailed?"

Leo shrugged. "The Communard movement is a strong one. And one to which I can only be sympathetic."

"Come now, Leo. Do you really believe in a social commune where everything is shared?" Papa was launched. "Will you share your rooms in the city with the great unwashed? Someone must work the coal mines, yes? And some rule the country?" He nodded towards Marcello. "Does everyone possess the soul to produce art? Do you not think some men are quite satisfied by plowing a field or finishing a floor?"

Laure Reisener cleared her throat. "We come from a long line of cabinet makers who finished many a floor."

"Am I saying a floor finisher is lesser than a Prefect? Is it not that each man has his own talent and temperament? We cannot all be kings, can we?"

"Philosophical equality is hardly the issue," said Marcello. "The issue is that some men are paid far more for their labours."

"Because some labours can be done by many and others by few, no? Is it not a simple question of demand? Higher demand, higher worth, higher wages?" Papa seemed pleased and at his ease. I pictured him filling his workday with this kind of rhetoric.

Empowered by Marcello's friendship, I said, "When some go hungry and others live in lavish palaces, is that not too much inequality?" I recalled Eugène Manet's particular interest. "And how can there ever be equality if the working class is denied an education?"

Papa scrutinized his fork.

"Yes, yes, their lack of education is a grave disadvantage," said Leo.

"We should indeed be educating their children," said Marcello, "instead of having them make bricks or whatever."

"Some of my younger friends"—Leo smirked—"think we should not have servants at all. And each man should be responsible for cooking his own food, washing his own clothes, darning his own stockings. Where, I ask, would there be time for painting?"

"You are describing women's work, my dear," said Laure, "and that is how you have time for painting."

Leo laced her hand in his and brought it to his lips.

"Not that I could stop him, and nor would I want to." Laure looked around the table. "An unfulfilled man is an ill-tempered one. You, young ladies, if you want to be painters, must find husbands with no ambition of their own."

"But who," said Maman, "would desire such a limp-minded man?"

Papa's laugh was too loud and Marcello gave Maman's hand a commiserate pat.

Food arrived in proper order and we dined on rillettes, onion soup, celeriac salad, dorade and pigeon, each plate adorned with seasonal blossoms: purple chives, yellow and orange nasturtiums, white rose petals that tasted of strawberry. Maman complimented the food's presentation.

"Well, is it not true," said Laure, "that our eyes do the feasting first?"

Marcello winked at me then raised her glass. "I predict that all the painterly ladies present will have acceptances to next year's

Salon and hereby recommend we reconvene on Varnishing Day to toast our successes."

For three years now Papa had denied us Varnishing Day, and this outrage I'd shared with Marcello. "Splendid idea," he said now and Edma looked as surprised as me.

Then my clever friend, knowing Rosalie had her own studio both here and in Paris, praised our fathers for providing the necessary supplies and studios for their daughters' "voracious talents."

Papa hunched, miming fear, and repeated the word "voracious." But he'd taken the bait. "Edma and Berthe do their painting in their upstairs drawing room."

Marcello looked perplexed and turned to Maman.

"I can't bear the smells," said Maman. "Gives me headaches. Would it be too much to ask paint makers to add a little *eau de vie* to their tubes of colour or that awful linseed oil?"

"But where do you store the canvases?" said Marcello.

"In unsightly stacks against the wall."

Marcello rested her hand along Papa's arm, fully snaring his attention, and listed reasons why she herself found a studio essential. I didn't dare look at them. If Papa thought I was behind this, he'd dismiss the idea outright.

Leo offered to draw up some plans. "You'll want north-facing windows of precise height and placement."

Edma nudged my foot under the table and I nudged back, feeling closer to her in that moment than I had the entire stay.

AFTER ROAMING the Reiseners' vast property, in loose dress, with whole days given over to painting, it was torture to sit sweating in corsets and crinoline in our auntie's drawing room listening to her litany of ailments. Seeking our escape and inspired by the figure of our aunt's neighbour, the widow Mme. Pontillon, Edma asked Madame if we might paint her portrait. Mme. Pontillon was flattered and willing and Edma easily talked Papa into letting us spend our mornings working. Despite Mme. Pontillon's wonderful Roman nose and silver bouffant, I used the time to fuss over my Normandy paintings, still believing perfection possible.

Near the end of our stay, Mme. Pontillon invited us to dinner. Our aunt remained behind insisting we "have fun without her."

Joining us were what Madame referred to as "God's littlest angels." A dozen chirruping canaries fluttered freely overhead and perched on shoulders, chair backs and the potted ficus trees greening the corners of every room. The birds' ordure had bleached the trees' braided trunks a chalky white. On every wall hung paintings of the infant Jesus and the Virgin Mother or their sadder counterparts, Jesus impaled, his Mother crumpled at his feet. It was like dining in an aviary for Catholic birds.

The fowl course was being served when Mme. Pontillon's son, Adolphe, arrived unexpectedly. A tall, broad, thick-necked naval officer, he and his ship had returned early to port due to a torn sail. Amid much motherly commotion and introductions, the butler set another place, between Edma and me.

For a long moment after introductions, Adolphe stared speechless at Edma then stirred himself to compliment the blue of her gown. Edma barely noticed his fluster. With the exception of Édouard, she was long inured to the effect she had on men, her indifference only increasing her allure.

A red-speckled birthmark in the shape of a low-heeled boot marked Adolphe's left temple. Seated on his right, Edma couldn't see it, but she had a similar-sized red patch on her hip shaped like a foot. I looked forward to teasing her about finding the boot to fit her foot.

Papa asked to hear a military man's opinion of Prussia's Minister-President.

"My senior officer describes Bismarck as gluttonous, with gluttonous ambitions. Word is he has quietly annexed German-speaking fiefdoms and doubled the size of his army."

"So he was successful in Austria?"

"And Nassau and Hanover and Frankfurt. Many believe he'll renege on a promise to return land to France along the Rhine."

Adolphe Pontillon's voice filled out his chest, seasoned, perhaps, from calling out orders in the middle of an ocean. His erect posture and capable air made him appear more handsome than he was. As did his dark abundant hair which rolled in thick waves off his low brow.

"Adolphe has told me," said Mme. Pontillon, "that Bismarck refers to our Emperor as 'a sphinx without a secret.'" As if agreeing with her, a canary settled atop her great nest of hair. "I've no idea what that means."

"Has anyone read Dumas' new novel, *The Prussian Terror?*" asked Maman. "*Le Figaro* has been serializing it?"

The Pontillons only stared at her.

"The author says it's a warning to France of the Prussian war machine."

"A novelist is hardly a military strategist," said Papa, and our hosts looked relieved that novels were not going to be discussed.

"It's an interesting perspective," said Maman in her own defence.

"Are you in town long, Adolphe?" I asked.

"Just until the sail's repaired. Two or three days at most. To Mexico. We're to bring home the rest of our troops and hopefully Emperor Maximilian who stubbornly hangs on to a sinking ship."

"The papers say Maximilian will fight the Juaristas to the death," said Papa.

"I'm afraid death is exactly what he'll be facing if he stays."

"The conversation has become too dire," said our hostess. "A new subject, please."

Adolphe asked if we knew a Paris artist by the name of Manet?

Edma lowered her fork. "Édouard Manet?" She turned to Adolphe as if seeing him for the first time. He nodded dumbly.

"I remember that young man," said Mme. Pontillon. "Couldn't sit still and speak at the same time. As if moving his feet set the words in motion. It made me dizzy and I was forever asking him to settle."

"How do you know him?" demanded Edma. She searched Adolphe's face as if by some unholy chance he was Édouard in disguise. Visibly unnerved, he addressed the table at large.

"We met when we were sixteen, on board the *Havre and Gaudaloupe*. Six months sailing to Brazil and back. We had both failed our entrance exams to the naval academy, I'm embarrassed to say, and needed a certain number of months' sailing time to qualify. If you had to wash the deck with someone, no one made the time pass more quickly than Édouardo. That was what I started calling him after *mardi gras* in Rio."

Edma actually stuttered. "I, I... met him just this spring."

"We met him," I corrected. I wanted to kick her.

"I make a point of visiting him when I'm in Paris." He paused as if fishing for an invitation. "He's just as sure of himself now as he was then. He shows me his paintings which, frankly, I don't know what to make of."

Papa raised his glass. "That's putting it politely."

"His colours, though, remind me of Brazil. It was a flamboyant country. The clothes, the plumage of the birds."

Edma asked about the art of Brazil and their conversation soon became a private one that, to Maman's satisfaction, continued throughout dinner. Across from me, Adolphe's sister regaled me with arrangements concerning her forthcoming wedding and new home, then asked my "artistic opinion" regarding how she might arrange her hair.

"**YOU SOUNDED LIKE** a lovesick girl tonight," I told Edma as I climbed into our bed. "Someone mentions Édouard's name and you—"

"I don't demean you, Berthe. Please treat me the same." She turned away from me and blew out her candle.

"I was only teasing."

"Is that what it was?"

"I'm sorry, Edma." I put a hand on her shoulder. "Forgive me."

"It is forgotten." She briefly rested her hand on mine before it slid off again.

I lay awake long after Edma's breath grew deep and rhythmic, hating Édouard that much more.

We saw Adolphe once again, briefly, before his ship left port. Without consulting Edma or me, Maman arranged for him to join us for lunch.

"A fine gentleman," said Maman after he'd gone.

"Very fine," echoed Auntie, reclined on the *chaise longue* and vigorously fanning herself. "Not as handsome as his late father but still pleasing, still pleasing. He's a keen eye for you, Edma. In fact, I'd say that you, my dear, have unmoored that sailor. Set him adrift."

Maman gave Auntie an encouraging smile.

"You could do far worse, far worse," she went on. "You're how old now, dear?"

"I'm twenty-eight, Auntie."

"Hmm..."

"And have no intention of marrying anyone, as Maman well knows, as there would be no time for my work. It would be deceptive to let the fine Monsieur Pontillon assume otherwise." The defensive edge in her tone was new.

No longer smiling, Maman stood and left the room.

"Trust me, dear," said Auntie, unperturbed, "when you grow old and ill like me you will wish to have had children. It is my great regret. Well, I don't regret not having children"—she made a sour face—"but I do regret not having had grandchildren. Can you, Berthe, dear, please come remove my shoes. My feet have swelled terribly in the heat. Terribly."

WE ARRIVED IN Louveciennes to a continual flow of visitors. Our work, as I'd predicted, became not just secondary but nonexistent. The one person I had personally invited was Marcello, anticipating introducing her to our friends, and raising my status with Édouard. But despite her assurance that she would visit, she never did. And it would be months before I received her note of regret.

Édouard's first visit was of short duration. "I hate the countryside," is how he greeted us. "You can have your grass and fresh air, your watering holes, your slow-talking churchgoers and leave to me the stench and asphalt of the city."

Dressed in royal-blue gloves and vest, he brought along not his wife but a towering young painter named Frédéric Bazille. Meek and studious, Frédéric complemented Édouard the entertainer. Over the course of three days and nights, Édouard made us laugh with his stories, he teased and flirted, recited poetry and sang bawdy songs. He set up impossible croquet courses up and down steep inclines, using trees as obstacles. On the second day, he rented rowboats in which to drift downriver. Edma rode in his boat with Maman, and I in Frédéric's where our conversation never strayed from the subject of art, on which he was a veritable historian. When tired of being on the water, Édouard found a suitable place to come ashore, paid two young men to row the boats back and rented a couple of cabriolets.

The weather was idyllic and lovers seemed to be everywhere. In the water. Under the willows along the bank. Lying in each other's arms in rowboats. Holding hands across tables at La Fournaise or Grenouillère. As I'd come to expect, Édouard ignored me and lavished Edma with attention. My sensible sister, consistent master of her emotions, who never tried to impress any man, laughed too easily, smiled too much, agreed too readily. On the last evening of the visit, as we dined in the garden and the stirring melody of a riverbank violinist reached our ears, even Maman looked concerned for how Edma hung on Édouard's words, as if sated and senseless.

Perceiving my sister's weakness was like finding a soft spot in a stone. I could not help but feel sorry for her. For though he enjoyed winning her laughs and blushes, Édouard seemed no more invested in his victories than a cat who'd caught a mouse.

That last evening I found myself alone with Édouard, the others having momentarily dispersed on various errands. In the swing and shade of a weeping willow, we sat at a round oak table respectively at ten and six by the clock. We had never before been alone together. What to talk about to someone whose very presence I found an insult?

Since he dominated every conversation and initiated most, I sat confident he would open the door with another of his anecdotes or quips. Then I could tell him of my new works from Normandy, and because he thrived on flattery, how they were inspired by his themes and perspectives. But he who was never still or silent, sat still and silent, fingers turning the stem of his glass. Why was he not addressing me? Not even lifting his eyes to acknowledge me when it was just the two of us. Surely he couldn't be so blatantly self-absorbed?

He seemed to ponder the motion of the liquid in his glass and whether he might, some day, take another sip. Was I invisible to him? Or did he despise me as I despised him? If I weren't so well trained—one never left a guest alone—I'd have excused myself. No, I'd have left without a word.

A chickadee hopped along the terrace in search of crumbs. The humiliating silence persisted. What did I care for his attentions? Less than nothing. Our common gaze followed the slow swirl of Édouard's wine when I'd a sudden sense that Édouard was listening. Intently so. Not listening in general but listening to me. As if to hear my thoughts. No, not exactly my thoughts, but just hear me. Our eyes never leaving that glass, I listened to him listening to me. Sound loomed large. As though we were attempting to hear the notes of ourselves. Discern harmony or dissonance or something combined and new, it didn't matter. It was the listening itself that mattered, just like the process of seeing mattered in painting. I was in Normandy again, by Sidonie's pond, knowing exactly what to paint because some infinite awareness sustained it all. To speak was now unnecessary, for the wonder of the world was apparent. Everything appeared clear and bright and loving. Including his gross discourtesy and my anger.

"I was afraid of this," Édouard whispered. In the amplified air, the words felt like solid objects placed on the table in front of us.

Bazille stepped through the terrace doors waving the book to which he'd made reference. "Here's my proof."

"Let's see it then," scoffed Édouard. He lifted his glass to his lips and the spell was broken. The loss took my breath away. Like a drowning person breaking the water's surface, my lungs forced out air in a violent cough and Frédéric and Édouard both regarded me, expectant. I held up a hand to say I was fine, and reached for my wine. Édouard wondered where everyone had gone.

What had just happened? And why did he say he was afraid? Was our shared moment, for I was certain it was shared, so frightening? I wanted answers, though he now acted as though he'd said nothing and nothing at all had happened between us. Unable to ask my questions, I offered to refill his glass. He covered its mouth with his hand and didn't even look my way.

Edma returned, picked up the carafe and made the very same offer. He slid over his glass. "Please." She began to pour. "But wait," he said. "Are you, Mademoiselle, trying to get me drunk?"

A delighted Edma tipped the carafe too quickly and sloshed wine over the glass's rim and onto the table. I got up and left without explanation—as no one deigned ask for one.

After our strange intimacy, Édouard's flagrant disregard felt an even meaner humiliation. I was only glad when he left for Paris the next day.

ARRIVING SELF-SUFFICIENT with sketchpad and pencil box, a wheel of his favourite cheese and several bottles of claret, Degas sought out my company over Edma's. Despite being eight years my senior, he treated me like an equal and, unlike Édouard, made me feel respected, even clever.

A committed land animal, Degas loathed the water as well as games. Dressed in his summer-weight suit of the same cheerless brown as his winter ensemble, his tie tied and cuffs linked, Degas' idea of fun was reclining on a blanket in the shade—Maman on a blanket nearby—as he sketched and dipped bread into his wine, and made droll commentary on the figures and fashions of passersby. When we weren't disparaging strangers, we disparaged artists whose achievements we coveted. Ernest Meissonier, the most lauded and highest-paid artist in the Western world, was "a portentous elitist who painted in miniature in order to feel tall." His painterly son, "Charles' only real talent was being born." Gustave Courbet was "a red-faced solipsist who confused greatness with the size of his canvases."

Degas sharpened his pencil, blew on the tip and slipped it into its case. "Do you think that what men consider originality is merely a small adjustment of what we've already assimilated?" He plucked a buttercup, rubbed the yellow petals and studied the colour left on his thumb.

"A kind of enhanced theft?" I asked.

"Or maybe it's more like what this English fellow Darwin calls a random misstep or mistake. The artist surprises himself with an accidental line or colour mix and it develops from there." He had read the recently translated *Origin of Species.*

"And this mistake," I mused, "this slight mutation of the old, happens to catch people's attention?"

His eyelids lifted as though to let in more light. "Yes. For mistakes can't help but awaken the eye, in the same way a new combination of old herbs the tongue."

A ragged line of rowboats had positioned themselves on the river. On the shore, a man in breeches and cap pointed a pistol at the sky.

"So is there originality or not?"

Degas shrugged as the gun went off, the rowers cheered by a crowd on the patio of La Fournaise. "The tease and ache is that we can never know for sure."

My friend's morning routine was to skip breakfast and sketch in his room. Therefore I did the same, sketching outdoors before a spectacular peony bush in back of our cottage, ants hard at work on the partial blooms. I did two studies in charcoal, one in pastels and another in watercolour, though after Degas left and my auntie and cousins arrived, never found time to put it to oil.

The second time Édouard came to Louveciennes it was with his brother Eugène in tow. I couldn't tell if he was playing the matchmaker or simply hoping I'd take Eugène off his hands as he made sure we were seated next to each other at meals, shared the same picnic blanket and were paired in cards and croquet. Eugène's shy compliance irked me and I became contrarily bold. When Eugène couldn't answer whether he preferred the countryside to the city, I said with a conviction I didn't have, that it was entirely dependent upon one's stage of life. The country was good for young children who needed to unite with nature but not for the older child who needed to see all that man was capable of.

"Then the adult should have the country as respite from work and obligations," I insisted, "whereas the elderly need the comforts and distractions of society."

When he wavered as to whether or not he preferred to live in close proximity to his family, I said, "Family is crucial to one's emotional development."

He agreed.

"Living close to family stifles one's maturity as an individual," I contradicted myself but all I got was his gentle smile and admiring stare.

If we lost at cards or croquet, I picked at the faults of his game. Sometimes I ignored Eugène altogether.

"You're acting unjustifiably rude," Edma chided me after that second day. "Has he insulted you?"

"His passivity bothers me."

"He's shy."

"He has no backbone."

"He's a kind man who holds you in esteem."

"I'm not sure why it bothers me." And I was sorry, yet still unable to temper myself.

AFTER THE MANET BROTHERS returned to Paris, Edma became oddly quiet and introspective. We were walking along the Île de Chatou, tucked under our parasols, having left Maman and Auntie on the blanket finishing off the wine and madeleines.

"Something's bothering you."

She shook her head, one hard shake.

"I'm restless from the lack of work" – her eyes glanced off mine – "anxious to get back to it."

The admission made me gloat inside.

A flock of pigeons landed in our path before moving onto the grass. "I'll be twenty-nine soon. How time charges on without one even noticing."

The last few days with Eugène had seemed an eternity, so I couldn't agree.

"And how dreamlike the past," she added.

Sunlight fractured the river's dark surface into diamonds of silver and white. "Edma, look at –"

"It's just a game to him."

"A game? To whom?"

"Édouard. He revels in being admired and is only toying with me. He's married and so, of course, it's all he can do" – her voice caught—"but I have feelings for him, Berthe, difficult feelings"—she began to cry—"that I've tried to hide, mostly from myself."

"Oh, Edma." I grasped her hand. How had I not realized the extent of her suffering?

She sniffed back tears. "He's a married man! This is nonsensical!"

"He's not worthy of your feelings." How I despised him. "Not the smallest one."

She said nothing but her grief was palpable. It was almost too much for her to fish a handkerchief from her sleeve.

"If his hands weren't tied, I'm sure things would be very different," I said but could tell she didn't believe me. "But I'm glad he's married, because—"

"No, Berthe. It wouldn't matter. He has no comparable feelings toward me. It became clear this visit that I'm only making a fool of myself. Embarrassing myself and my family."

"Not at all!"

"You needn't be so kind. Maman told me my behaviour around Édouard had grown 'discernible.'" She closed her eyes as a group of children ran weaving toward us along the grass-bare path, swinging sticks to keep upright a wobbling hoop. I guided Edma aside.

"I used to think his flirtations were to make his wife jealous, but it's no different when she's not around." She smirked. "I've asked myself what might change if I offered to be his lover."

I stopped. "You really are in love with him."

Her laugh was feeble-hearted. "Not that I would go through with it, of course. Not as long as my father lives and breathes." She started walking again, eyes on the ground, unable to look at me. "But even such a perilous sacrifice wouldn't change things. His feelings are what they are. Friendly. I can no longer pretend otherwise. And since friends are all we can ever be, it's good he doesn't harbour the kind of yearning that I've allowed myself."

"He is utterly thoughtless and unkind to have led you on as he has."

"He's just being himself. It's my heart that's unkind." She took a measured breath, in, then out. "Real love must be mutual, the mixing of souls. Otherwise it's imagined. Nothing but a childish fantasy. I don't know how often real love happens but I do know that my own childish imaginings have gotten the best of me and proved a distraction from my work. So, really, Berthe, I'm grateful it's now over and I can put it behind me."

I pressed her arm. "Then so am I."

"Forgive me for taking you from Normandy. You were finally so inspired and—"

"It's fine. I'm fine. I'm only sorry you've suffered so."

We walked on in silence but, nearly out of sight of Maman and Auntie, we had to turn around.

She squeezed my hand. "What would I do without you?"

I squeezed back and kissed her cheek. Edma was mine again.

"THE LAST WINDOW was installed yesterday," said Papa. "I was determined it be finished upon your return."

As if simply grown up from the dirt in our absence, a miniature version of our home occupied the south end of the garden where a locust tree once stood—the same limestone walls and clay mansard roof, the same arched doorway and tin chimneypot. A new crushed stone path took us to the studio's door and, boots crunching, Papa led the way as pleased as if the whole thing had been his idea.

"North-facing windows so you receive consistent but indirect sunlight throughout the day." Inside, the north wall was a bank of glass whose attractive arch framed a delicate pink and gold sky. "We've used wood on the ceiling, see, to cut down on glare and reflection."

I shared a look of disbelief with Edma as he pointed out where best to plant our easels. "In this spot the light will bounce nicely off the plaster wall to give equal illumination to the room and your canvases." He ran his hand over the plaster wall to exclaim over its evenness, "which I oversaw myself." He pointed out the tongue and groove construction of the wall cabinets "supervised by Leo's man."

Suddenly overcome, I grasped his hands and kissed his cheeks. "Papa. Thank you. This means everything."

He smiled crookedly and looked to Maman, my rare show of affection awkward between us. It was not the fact of the studio that meant so much to me but what it represented—his blessing to pursue careers in painting. No matter any future change in his attitude, here sat a solid show of support that even he could not deny. Tears stained my vision as Edma hugged Papa and he lovingly kissed her head.

She said, "We don't deserve such a generous gift."

"But will accept it just the same," I laughed.

I wanted to move in our supplies that very afternoon but Edma claimed to be tired and wished to put it off till tomorrow.

THE STUDIO WAS barely thirty feet from the house yet proved a different world, the air ours alone to fill with our own thoughts and visions. It was permission to sit aimlessly and watch the changing light make mystery, make dust a choreography of scintillating dots, make shadow lend objects their dimension and gravitas.

When my work wasn't going well I kept away, not wanting to contaminate its atmosphere with self-doubt. The time away proved helpful and I would return with fresh perspective. In this way, the studio's threshold became a boundary that revealed to me my creative rhythms.

I HAD SEEN MARCELLO only once since Beuzeval—at the opera where she waved and blew a kiss from her box. She responded to each of my invitations—I had sent several—with warm notes of apology and a promise of lunch or a shopping trip. A promise that kept being deferred. Certainly she had many acquaintances and engagements but, after all we'd shared, I had anticipated being introduced to those friends at fashionable parties.

After the fourth note of regret from Marcello, I complained to Maman.

"You could not have expected her attentions would be the same here at home. Marcello walks in different circles where, believe me, you'd find the air far too thin."

I was mortified to think that being seen together around Paris might be inappropriate or cause Marcello embarrassment and immediately stopped all solicitation. And I could let go of Marcello, for I had Edma again. Just her and me, painting side by side by day, sleeping side by side at night, entertaining and being entertained by our artist friends. Maman, to her credit, stopped her talk of suitors and marriage. Edma appeared to have tamed her feelings toward Édouard. And, that winter, buoyed by yet another set of acceptances to the Paris Salon, we shared champagne fantasies of stunned critics and magnetized dealers.

1868

THE FOLLOWING SPRING the world descended on Paris for the Exposition Universalle. An estimated 50,000 exhibits swallowed the Left Bank, most of which I have more or less forgotten. There was that American invention—a chair on keels that rocked. Designed for seasickness? A primitive phonograph—music never sounded so terrible—and an amusing metal contraption with a claim to speed-writing when one would have to hunt down all those randomly placed letters. And a wooden contraption hung from metal cables big enough to lift my family into the air for a bird's-eye-view of the fair through its one narrow window. Heights unnerved me and I remained behind on the ground. Also on display were new weapons of war, as cold and ugly as their purpose, including a fifty-ton cannon from Prussia whose shells were said to weigh a thousand pounds apiece. I took one step inside that pavilion and turned back around, though if I could have predicted the future, I might have taken a morbid interest.

The single exhibit I recall in detail is the Pavilion of Japonaise Art. It was different from other pavilions in every respect, beginning with the limited numbers of visitors allowed in at a time and instructions to leave our boots in the ante-room. Two doors fragile as air slid sideways to reveal a silent white room with pale floor made of exquisitely woven grass mats that gave a little under our stockinged feet.

Sunk into the room's centre was a concrete pool curved like a woman's torso. Etched into the pool's white floor a scatter of grey outlines of singular leaves. Above which, nearly two feet from head to elegant tail, swam blood-orange fish like underwater fire. The fish were exotic and radiant but it was those ghostly leaves, fixed yet moving with the water and shifting light, that held my attention. I was in awe before I turned my attention to the art on the walls.

Unlike the walls of the Salon, smothered top to bottom with paintings large and small, these held canvases of uniform size hung in a single line at eye level. All that empty wall space worked to bestow the paintings with an insistent respect. Done in ink and watercolour, each was a landscape. Mountains and valleys. Rice paddies. Blossoming fruit trees. Rice paper houses. Like the walls that held them, these canvases too employed empty space, as though object and background were of equal value.

Standing in front of a painting of a stream running beside a leafless tree crooked with age, I found myself stricken, unable to move or breath. Or think. Thinking, or analysis, worked to ruin the effect, which seemed to rise out of the most extreme, yet gentlest simplicity. How was it possible to be so profoundly moved by these artists so far away? That day in the Pavilion Japonaise, perceiver and perceived arose as a single stroke and I understood that a painting was truly a living thing that could reach across time and space.

I turned to Edma to share my revelation when she whispered, "Close your eyes." She took my hand, led me a short ways and stopped. "Now open them."

We were now in front of the fourth and final wall in the pavilion. Unlike the other three this one was hung with hundreds of small pleated fans each bumped up against the next and each stained with watercolours. Close up as we were it appeared to be a random and meaningless wash of colour. Without a word Edma guided me back a step and then another and another until I saw the individual fans were arranged in the shape of one giant fan.

Three steps further and a picture magically emerged from the giant fan: a woman with long black hair, perfectly feminine in a flowing pink kimono decorated with... fans... her white painted face half-hidden behind... another fan!

I felt faint with wonder.

"A clever trick, no?" said Edma.

Clever? Trick? This dreamlike image of feminine allure hidden and revealed inside this most feminine of objects? "Edma, no, it's... it's breathtaking. It's genius."

She held aloft a program. "The colourful fish in the pool are called koi. Of the goldfish family."

How could she be so blasé? Or was I making too much of something merely foreign and new?

The next time I saw Degas, I felt vindicated as he too was astonished and inspired by the exhibit. He had even purchased a box of rice paper fans and was painting them as gifts for the women in his family. How satisfying, he said, to watch the image unfold piecemeal, pleat-by-pleat.

The pavilion devoted to the art of France was limited to former Grand Prix winners only. Édouard, in his arrogance and despite having acceptances in the concurrently running Paris Salon, borrowed a great sum of his inheritance—having convinced his mother he would earn it back in sales—and built his own pavilion directly across from the Exhibition grounds on the Right Bank, complete with flagpoles waving attention-getting yellow and purple pennants. "You have to invest in yourself," he berated the rest of us. "Where else will an artist get this kind of exposure?"

Edma, Maman and I were the only visitors to his pavilion one sunny afternoon, and we learned from Édouard's nephew, Léon, who manned the exhibit, the first visitors all week. Maman purchased one of the expensive pamphlets Léon was peddling. A photograph of Édouard graced the cover and inside was a list of the forty paintings on display plus a flattering article by Zola.

Not only would Édouard be left with hundreds of his own pamphlets, he wouldn't sell a single painting to recover his investment. Degas told me it was because of financial decisions like these that Édouard had been forced to live with his mother.

Weeks later, while hunting a misplaced bracelet, I discovered the pamphlet in the drawer of Edma's nightstand under some sketches of the view out our bedroom windows. Beneath the pamphlet were two postcards she had received from the naval officer Adolphe Pontillon. Postcards to which she told me she hadn't responded. So why keep them? It would be insensitive of me to tease her about the pamphlet but I did ask if she'd kept Adolphe's postcards.

She didn't hesitate. "No. Why would I?"

I knew my dear sister as sincere and honest. Had she forgotten having tucked them in that drawer? Or was she embarrassed to admit that cards from a distant suitor acted as talisman against any leftover feelings for Édouard? I kept such questions to myself though would have been better served had I not.

THANKS TO MARCELLO, Papa permitted us our first Varnishing Day. As she'd predicted, we all had acceptances to the Salon (Rosalie's first occasion) and though Papa kept his promise, Marcello did not. In Sienna, Italy, for a gallery opening, she sent an ebullient note of congratulations and her regrets. I was disappointed but hardly surprised.

It was exciting nonetheless. The rooms of the Salon swarmed with the Paris elite dressed to be seen and admired. Aristocrats were obvious from the cut of their clothes and size of their entourage, critics from the twitch and angle of their chins. Opera star Jeanne de Marcy was there, radiant in an off-shoulder blue silk, and the darkly handsome Jean-Baptiste Faure, whose apparent affability contrasted to the characters he played.

Lesser artists looked nervous being spoken to and sat alone on a folding stool beneath their work, or—like the three of us—in a stiff grouping with family or friends. Some more celebrated artists held private parties, with tables of champagne, bubbling fondue pots, and one with a huge cake in the shape of a swan. Another, a sculptor, displayed a replicate sculpture carved from chocolate. A painter brought a human tableau of Orpheo and Eurydice as they appeared on his canvas, only his Eurydice was wild-eyed as she struggled not to blink.

In Room C, Grand Prix winner Alexandre Cabanel slouched in a purple velvet armchair. Squeezed into his vest and coat, he looked like a dog resigned to unwanted petting as two young men, poised with notebooks and pencils, knelt at his either knee doing more talking than writing. Commissioned after the triumph of Cabanel's *Birth of Venus*, a life-sized portrait of Emperor Louis loomed behind M. Cabanel, its size and importance ridiculing any fantasies of my own small canvases garnering notice.

M. Cabanel had recently denounced Édouard in *Le Figaro* as "a disgrace to the profession of painting." Rather than be humbled, Édouard believed it would draw notice to his work.

Arriving in Room M, I located my paintings immediately—small and dark and very green, my daring scarlet marks imperceptible to all but me. After admiring the art of Japan at the Exposition, I thought them dense, the brush strokes crowded. Everything needed more light and air. Why was I so timid? Edma's cows, and portrait of Mme. Pontillon's dramatic profile with a bright yellow canary perched on her shoulder, were far more eye-catching. Still, people strolled by without a glance.

To our immediate left, one artist's work *was* being noticed.

"His best to date."

"Truly an artist of multiple visions."

"Extraordinary."

I moved around a gentleman's elbow to catch sight of the signature on the canvas. Manet. What? When did Édouard do this? Here was a seascape so clear and vigorous, it could only have been painted *en plein air.* Yet he mocked painting out-of-doors. The bluest breadth of a windswept sky, dancing angles of hulls and sails, I could practically feel my hat lifting. The work was so distinct from the paintings that had inspired mine I suddenly felt stuck in a past that Édouard had moved completely beyond. Since when was he capable of keeping secrets?

A large party edged our gathering sideways. I expected Papa or Leo to protest but they both just stared at the man at the group's centre as he answered a question from a reporter breathless from his sprint across the room. With wary dark eyes and an undeniably *air masculine*, his moustache waxed to needle-fine extensions, the man barely reached my shoulder. His hair cropped short, a dark river of beard poured down his throat to disappear under his collar.

One only had to look at the tiny canvases that hung behind to know it was M. Ernest Meissonier himself. Was it fortunate or unfortunate to share the initial M with the most revered painter in the world? His shrunken musketeers and brawling *bonhommes* were perfect likenesses. But to my eye that's all they were, likenesses, cleansed of body odors, of awkward passion, of human suffering. A critic once claimed, "Monsieur Meissonier is capable of painting the Sistine Chapel on the stone of a ring." Did that make it art?

On our way to see Rosalie's painting, we discovered a second Room M and there on the west wall, like ice water thrown in one's face, was the Manet I knew: big canvas, flat perspective, opposing colours and a shocking defilement of Cabanel's and Meissonier's Romanticism. Like the fly wheels starting up on a locomotive, his painting set the room in motion, with squeals of resistance and wonder belching into the future. But why had the Salon separated his works?

Here he'd painted a *fille de maison,* naked along her pillowed bed, her nakedness emphasized by heeled satin slippers, the thinnest of chokers, a gold bracelet and earrings and a single pink mum pinned over an ear. Her skin tone not classical ivory but yellowish and true. Hair grew free in her armpit and a thin furred path slid down from her navel. How did he dare? And was that fine hair on her arm? "A female gorilla," someone muttered. The veracity of her figure and the suggestion of her profession was monstrous. Again I was being invited to think and wonder on a world forbidden to me and couldn't look away.

Leo laughed. "He has really gone and done it this time."

The negress he'd mentioned to Edma had modeled as a maid presenting the prostitute with a bouquet of flowers from a client. Her marvellous skin tones were that of molasses. A black cat stood at the bed's end with its tail raised suggestively in the air. One could practically smell the aromas in that chamber. The painting's humour mocked the earnest intentions of every other painting in the Salon, including my own.

"However did this pass the jury?"

The jury needed to include his work, I wanted to say, as contrast, for what not to do and incentive to try the possible.

"Édouard," said Edma, "is truly the most honest person I know."

"What do you mean?"

"He paints exactly what he sees before him. Nothing more, nothing less."

Maman looked bewildered. "*Olympia?*" she read out the title.

"A common garden whore receiving a punter," scoffed Papa, sounding awfully conversant on the subject.

"The composition," said Rosalie. "Is it not Titian's *Venus of Urbino?*"

"Yes, yes," confirmed Leo. "Right down to the servant in the background. The placement of that hand."

"He told me it was an homage." Edma peered around the room. For Édouard?

"Instead of a sleepy dog, a rather lively cat," said Rosalie.

"What's she doing with that hand?" said a man beside us.

"Covering her *chatte*," snickered another, as if rudeness was now permissible.

"Judging by her bedding and those slippers, she looks rather well-off," said Maman, something hard in her voice.

"Let's move on," ordered Papa with a sharp gesture of his hand.

"None of the mawkishness of fashionable portraits, that's for certain," said Leo, staying put. "I wonder if—"

The silver handle of a gentleman's cane smacked the canvas, shocking us backward. He raised it again as a Salon warden rushed over. "*Ne touchez pas. Ne touchez pas.*"

"This vile thing must be taken down!" roared the man and others shouted their agreement. The guard looked panicked but put his body in front of *Olympia*. A stabbed finger tested him: he widened his stance and clasped his hands behind his back. It was time to leave.

"It will need more than one guard when the Salon opens tomorrow," said Papa as we filed out. And he would be right. *Olympia* would incite such violent reactions as to have to be cordoned off, with two guards stationed beside it at all times. Later we learned that Édouard hadn't attended Varnishing Day because he'd been warned by Salon officials to stay away. His honest eye aside, I couldn't decide if he was the bravest man I knew or the most in need of attention.

Marcello's bust had the honour of placement in the Sculpture Garden where we lunched. Serpent-haired *La Gorgone*'s mix of myth and modernity was far braver than my female Narcissus. Eating my egg with mayonnaise, I studied Marcello's stark collarbones. I'd told no one her secret about sculpting her own breasts but now imagined her telling random fieldworkers and maids, making them feel just as special as I had.

After lunch, I showed Edma and Rosalie Édouard's seascape. Astute Rosalie wasn't fooled for a minute by the similarity of signature. Who was this Monet?

AS PREDICTED, M. Cabanel's portrait of the Emperor was awarded the Grand Prix medal. Edma's and my meagre reviews resembled last year's and the year before and the year before that. *Lovely use of colour. Talented young ladies*—as though we were children. At least this time Edma's talent wasn't lorded over mine. I was content with small steps as long as they moved a forward course. Edma, though, appeared disheartened. "So much work," she said, "to what end?" For again there were no inquiries by dealers or gallery owners. No private offers of purchase. Yet the same could be said of most of our friends. Édouard's reviews had soared to a new level of scorn. I couldn't feel sorry for him—he should have expected as much—but I did for his model. In one of the kinder reviews she was compared to *a corpse in the Paris morgue, dead of yellow fever and already at an advanced level of decay.* Several critics called the painting morally contaminating and demanded the department of public health inspect the placement of her hand. One christened Édouard the *Apostle of Ugliness* while *La Presse* claimed Olympia *was art sunk so low the painter doesn't even deserve reproach.* Paul Mantz of *Le Gazette des Beaux-Arts,* and one of the most feared reviewers in France, refused to waste his ink on Édouard but instead heaped his praise on newcomer Claude Monet: *Do not for a minute mistake his name for Manet or you would do yourself and him a great disservice.* The Mouth of the Seine at Honfleur *is the most excellent seascape exhibited at the Salon in a decade. Manet or Monet? Monet! Though perhaps we have Manet to thank for the young artist's realist tastes.*

Like me, many critics had mistaken one painter for the other and later published retractions along with apologies to M. Monet. Édouard, though, received no such apologies. At his mother's on Thursday, he raged about the mix-up, believing Monet encouraged it, "in order to capitalize on my reputation."

"Reputation?" Degas whispered behind me and I laughed aloud. Édouard shot me a cold look in which I took great satisfaction.

No music played that night and the mood was subdued. Madame Manet was in bed with an unnamed ailment and her chair beside the fireplace sat empty. Suzanne had greeted us, gaze fixed on our chins as if the light of our eyes might give rise to a headache. Her manner was at once solicitous and remote. "I'm sorry to say that Eugènie is unwell and resting. She has asked that we enjoy ourselves but not too loudly." Without a piano protecting her, she seemed like an overexposed photograph, her boundaries blurred.

She moved with a slow self-conscious grace and took forever to guide us from hall to drawing room. If she was aware of any feelings Edma once harboured toward her husband she either hid it well or was inured to the idea.

She stood behind Édouard's chair as he held court, looking with consternation at the top of his head as though disturbed by a wayward curl or lick.

"Yesterday, an elderly gentleman," he complained, "if one can call him gentle, spat on my boot! In front of a café full of patrons! Over a painting! Then, today, I was challenged to a duel! Pistol or sword, I asked, before Degas, here, dragged me away."

Degas, an unlikely hero, smiled wryly.

Édouard spoke boastfully, yet it was clear by his manner that his confidence was finally shaken. I was glad to see it.

"People are afraid of change is all," said Edma in support.

"I was afraid of this," he said as his eyes pinned mine with a force that sent me backwards to bump into Eugène, who steadied me. I mumbled in apology.

"You might paint something more… mundane for next year," said Stevens and Édouard turned to him with raised eyebrows.

But what had just happened?

"An artist must never compromise himself." This from Zola.

"I am inspired by what I see before me," said Édouard. "I find reality beautiful and beyond defending. I've no intention to shock or offend."

Why had he repeated those words? Had there ever been such a confusing and frustrating man?

That evening the youngest Manet brother, the elusive Gustave, made a brief appearance. He was just dropping off some flyers but Maman made sure we were introduced. Dark-haired and taller than his brothers, dressed in an everyman's suit of inferior quality, he was formal and curt, in a hurry to be elsewhere. When Maman said we were painters, he replied, "A luxury few can afford."

He seemed to regard the gathering as a sinful indulgence though before he left I saw him discreetly fold a half dozen canapes into his handkerchief. I doubted they were destined for the poor.

MARCELLO'S RECENT SCULPTURE riled the critics almost as much as Édouard's *Olympia*, a review in *Le Figaro* particularly contemptuous. Had she rebuffed the critics's advances or in another way humiliated him? She received not a single positive review so I sent a note of condolence to which she responded promptly.

My dear, Berthe. Thank you for your sympathetic note. I've been told by a friend that as a female artist I should consider my poor reception a great accomplishment. Continued favourable reviews, he said, imply the reviewer feels no threat or challenge to his view of acceptable work by women. Only when we begin to provoke harsh critiques will we know we are being taken seriously. How's that for spinning gold out of straw?

I will travel to London from here where I will spend the month of May but upon my return to Paris I will look forward with delight at seeing you at your earliest convenience. Marcello

And upon her return I did receive an invitation, one I had every mind to spurn. Besides, I did not want Edma to feel left out, yet it was she who urged me to accept. "You never know when you might be in need of a friend. Especially one with influence."

Maman escorted me and waited outside in the carriage with her nose in a copy of Zola's "near pornographic" novel which she "could not put down."

Marcello greeted me with a warmth suggesting that not an hour had passed since Normandy. As we sipped her London tea, she regaled me with stories of her travels, asked after Edma, the new studio and my work, and how I was getting along with my father. Her forthright and unapologetic manner was as disarming as ever and to be at all concerned with what had not transpired between us felt childish. Knowing our next reunion could be months if not years away, I simply enjoyed our time together.

IN THE CARRIAGE RIDE to Mme. Manet's soirée, Maman nervously patted Edma's hand, turning it over and back until Edma gently removed it. I asked if there was something wrong.

"No, no, everything is wonderful," insisted Maman, though Edma's blank smile put me on guard.

As soon as we stepped into Mme. Manet's drawing room, Édouard, dispensing with greetings, placed a glass in Edma's hand and said he wanted to introduce her to someone. My presence, as usual, went unacknowledged though Eugène smiled at me from across the room. I pretended not to see him and followed Edma. The previous Thursday, Eugène had been constantly at my back, as if in wait, so that when I turned, I would accidentally knock into him and he would have a chance to heroically catch my elbow.

"It that Adolphe?" Edma said over her shoulder.

"Adolphe?"

"Do you know him?" Édouard clapped then rubbed his hands together. "Adolphe Pontillon is one of my oldest friends—and the very person I want you to meet."

Maman must have orchestrated this. How dare she? Her behaviour in the carriage now made sense.

Adolphe saw Edma and moved toward her like a beam of light. He wore his naval uniform—knee-length dark blue jacket, red Mandarin collar and pressed brass buttons—and seemed taller than

I remembered, his hair thicker, his nose and cheeks more sculpted. Now his hands took hers and kissed her cheeks.

Edma blushed, though whether with discomfort or delight I couldn't tell.

Adolphe inhaled as though to contain his pleasure. He nodded at me, distracted, and it was an obvious effort to let go of her hand and take up mine.

"How's your mother?" I asked.

"Here somewhere. She's been looking forward to meeting you and your family again." He returned to Edma. "She received your kind invitation and asked if I might accompany her on her visit."

Edma invited Mme. Pontillon? Without telling me?

"Maman thinks she's a celebrity now with her portrait on the walls of the Paris Salon. Édouard tells me it's exceptional."

"He's exaggerating." Edma avoided my glare.

Why had she not confided in me? I felt adrift and alone.

Édouard stepped in alongside his taller, broader friend. "I do exaggerate but not in this instance."

Edma looked from Édouard to Adolphe as though comparing fruits. As her eyes came to rest on Édouard, he threw up his hands, breaking whatever spell he still had on her and announcing that he must check up on his dear *wife*, drawing out the word.

"Maman will be pleased to see you again, too," Edma told Adolphe. "Oh, look, she's found your mother." Our two mothers had convened around Mme. Manet, whose finger stabbed the air as she spoke. Maman glanced over at us then quickly away.

Adolphe offered his arm. "Shall we join them?" As if making some kind of decision, Edma placed her hand with slow deliberation along his forearm. I watched them walk away, him say something beside her ear and Edma lift her face to his and smile a radiant smile. From now onward would I be watching her walk away from me? Had she chosen him over our life together? I had to tell someone or be sick. I located Degas in the far corner alone on the sofa and started over when Eugéne appeared and my skirts knocked into him.

"You're looking very well, Berthe." He steadied my elbow with a tentative hand.

"I am not well, thank you." I brushed his hand from my arm and continued. I denied Édouard's brother his many good qualities but could not deny his perseverance in the face of rejection.

Degas rose as I approached. "You look as though you could use a cup of punch." He signaled the butler.

"Do you see that tall man with Edma? The big-nosed one in naval costume?" I tried our common tone of cynicism, but couldn't maintain it. "He's going to steal her away."

Always sensitive when sensitivity was needed, Degas paused to allow my emotion its due. "Looks a proper thief. Handsome-ish, big shouldered, that wavy pelt on his head. I absolutely hate him."

"Edma invited his mother without even telling me. Behind my back."

"Deception always burdens the truth."

"When did I lose her confidence? When did she decide not to tell me she had written to Adophe's mother, knowing full well that Adolphe may accompany her?"

"Oh, dear Berthe. You poor women. Either you must marry and risk your lives bearing children or live with your aging parents, fluffing their pillows and putting up with their arrogance." He waved at Mme. Manet and her coterie. "A gold ring on the finger is always the more respectable in society's beady little eye, but I would call it a coin toss."

"If he's truly what she wants I can be happy for her, I can. But can I imagine life without her? If she gives up painting, I don't know if I..."

"Women can't steer a single course. It's your worst characteristic."

"We have more responsibilities than do men."

"Yes. It takes you longer to dress. And you have to oversee the *roux*, the dust, baskets to the poor." Sensing my offence, Degas backtracked. "If Edma has a choice in the matter, Berthe, then art is not her business. For there is love and there is art and we have only one heart."

A servant arrived bearing a crystal cup of wine punch. Degas rang his glass against mine.

"To dear Edma's happiness. May she produce many healthy bald cherubs for you to paint."

"To painting."

The corner of his lip lifted. The clink of our glasses felt like the sealing of a pact. If my painting life with Edma was at an end, I would need new supports.

"I blame Édouard," I said, watching him charm a small group to laughter.

"For?"

"For stirring up Edma's... needs."

"Needs are for the weak. Now tell me, dear Berthe, what it is that you're working on?"

I REMAINED SILENT on the carriage ride home. Not that it mattered since Maman talked in a continuous stream. "Adolphe's eyes followed you everywhere, Edma. His admiration for you hasn't waned since the summer. I'd say it's grown. Did you know the Pontillons have a country estate just north of Paris? In Maurecourt? Of seventy acres? And his mother told me Adolphe has bought a townhome in Lorient? Three storeys."

Edma tried to take my hand and I pulled it away.

Arriving home, Edma and Maman went into the drawing room to speak with Papa, who sat reading in his chair, a fire still flaming in the grate. Had he waited up for our return? Was he in on it too? Had all three conspired to keep me in the dark? For fear of my interference? My talking Edma out of it? I would never ever have kept such a secret from her.

My left eye had begun to water and sting as if stuck with an eyelash. I didn't want anyone to mistake it for weeping and retreated upstairs where I rang for Pauline.

Pauline unhooked the back of my bodice as I examined my eye in the glass. "Did Edma meet her young man tonight?"

"How did you know about that?" I demanded.

"I... I overheard Madame."

"You should keep your ears closed."

Pauline fell quiet and I felt all the more wretched.

I asked her to please brush out and braid my hair, something Edma normally did for me. Pauline's hands, rougher than Edma's, felt deserved.

When Edma came upstairs, I refused to acknowledge her and Pauline, busy keeping her ears closed, remained uncharacteristically silent. My braid complete, I climbed into bed with the Balzac Edma and I had been reading aloud to each other. Pauline helped Edma out of her clothes and into her nightdress before Edma dismissed her. She came and sat on my side of the bed, her hair still pinned and ribboned. Only now did I see how much care she had taken with it.

"I want love and I want my own family."

Hidden behind my book, my watery eye caused the words on the page to blur.

"I've had as much success with painting as I'll most likely ever have. Accepted to four consecutive Salons. Pleasant reviews. Not to deter you, Berthe. Truly I don't want to do that. I want you to keep on, I do. But it's not enough for me. Please know that my needs are no reflection on you." She stroked my arm, searing the skin. How were they not?

"Not that I desire accolades or money or great commissions... well, that would help"—she gave an ironic laugh—"but I do desire to be needed and loved. To have children before it's... too late."

"We made a vow, if I remember. At your instigation."

"People change, Berthe. Grow."

"Painting's now a childish pursuit?"

"I'm just not the same person as the one who—"

"I am." I lowered my book. "And half my love of painting is sharing it with you." My fears tumbled out. "If you, the more disciplined and talented, haven't the will to carry on, how can I?"

"Oh, Berthe. Please don't make it harder than it is."

"Harder for whom?" I slapped the book closed. "You will have love, little ones, a pretty house in… Lorient. I'll be left alone with Papa. Alone with my struggles in our studio and…" My eye burned as though sand had blown into it. "How could you deceive me, Edma? Why was everyone else in on it except me?"

"Let me explain."

"Even Édouard knew! Even Pauline!" My sore eye overflowed down my cheek.

"Édouard was not in on it. Oh, don't cry, Berthe, or I'll cry."

"I'm not crying. Something is wrong with my eye. This one."

"Let me see." She studied my eye then rang for Pauline to bring an eye bath.

"Yes, I invited Madame Pontillon." Edma pulled a thread from the lace of her cuff. "Was I hoping she would bring Adolphe along? Maybe. I wasn't sure she would. And if he did come I half-suspected I would feel nothing and that would be that. So I didn't tell you, Berthe, because I was afraid of hurting you. Needlessly."

I stared at her.

"Yes, I hoped to see him again in order to examine my feelings."

"Your feelings?"

"Yes."

"And after your… examination?"

She nodded. "I do like him. That much I discovered."

My heart withered. I had always only wanted Edma to be happy. If she wasn't happy in the life we had carved out for ourselves, what could I do or say? For I had nothing more to offer.

"Is he all I desire?" She moved quietly to the dressing table to take out her hair. "No, he's not."

"Because he's not Édouard," I said, unforgiving.

"He's not Édouard."

Pauline came with a cloth and bowl of *acide borique* in warm water. I thanked her, held the dampened cloth to my eye and pretended to read with the other.

When Edma climbed into bed beside me, we lay there not speaking, a cool wall between us. She rolled over and laid a hand on my shoulder.

"If I do marry, we'll still paint together, in summer as we always have. When you visit me." Her voice faltered. "You will visit me?"

Then I did tear up. And so did she.

"MONSIEUR PHILLIPE LÉVESQUE, this is my youngest daughter, Berthe."

Tuesday at Maman's soirée I was discussing photography with Degas, Rosalie and her father Leo—Edma and I had recently had our portraits done—when Maman sidled up with this pale and scrubbed-looking young man. Earlier I had noticed the man glance admiringly at himself in the glass over the console.

Maman laid a hand on my arm. "Monsieur is an accountant, dear, in your father's ministry."

Was I supposed to be impressed? Milky-skinned M. Lévesque bore the slimmest of moustaches, as if painted on with a 00 brush, and a pouf of dark hair sprouted from the dimple of his otherwise bald chin. His nails shone pink like the inside of a conch. I imagined him squeamish around pets and uncooked meat. All evening Maman had proudly introduced Adolphe as "Edma's beau from Lorient," so I knew what she was thinking; Edma's resistance had broken and therefore I, who always copied my sister, could not be far behind.

A confident sort, M. Lévesque was quick to join the conversation. "Isn't it only a matter of time before photography's truth renders painting obsolete?"

"Photography?" Leo sounded genuinely concerned for him. "A colourless picture of what the everyman perceives with his ordinary eye?"

Beside me, Degas sighed softly, "Truth? Whatever is that?" But M. Lévesque's clean ears heard nonetheless.

"This comfortable room"—he gestured—"these gas lights, this First Empire console and mirror. Me talking to you."

"Static forms." This from Édouard whose arrival had gone unnoticed. I stepped back to accommodate him in our small circle. His jacket smelled of his mother's potpourri. I did not have to like him though now felt dependent on his society. For if Edma were to leave Paris, his disinterest in me, the little sister, may well be shared by his company of friends.

"Look here," said Édouard as he guided M. Lévesque's attention to the white marble inlay of the console, then to the white blossoms on the settee, then to the white horse in the painting reflected in the mirror. "Now which colours in the room stand out to you?"

Monsieur said that all the room's colours seemed to have brightened.

"Good man. Now might this awareness of colour change how you inhabit this room? What if I move so that only half my face is lit?" Édouard stepped left. "Does this change your feeling about me?"

I was struck by Édouard's painterly eye but more so by the fact he had brought feeling into his description.

"Form," I said, determined to make myself interesting, "can never be static when seen with an eye toward feeling. This gives a picture meaning." Inciting murmurs of approval, I added, "Aristotle said the aim of the artist is to represent not the outward appearance of things but their inward significance."

Looking surprised I could speak in full sentences, Édouard turned and stared at me. Under the intensity of his gaze, I felt exposed, as though I had dropped my wrap so he could study my arms.

"The difference between painting and photography," said Degas drily, "is the difference between being hungry and being full."

On the defensive now, M. Lévesque sharply asked the question we were all thinking, "Your meaning, Monsieur?"

"A painting should never satisfy, but leave the viewer hungering for more of this truth you speak of. Otherwise one's truth is reduced to four walls and some nice furniture."

"A good painting," said Édouard, not to be outdone, "is like a sinus infection. It must flood the senses and create an exquisite pain in the head."

Leo laughed and clapped, three slow claps. M. Lévesque said he would think on these points, raised his half-full glass and went off to refill it.

"I read," said Rosalie, "that someone named Cros has recently invented a means of creating colour photography."

We all paused to digest the notion.

"Portraiture will pay the worst price," said Édouard.

"Photography may record reality, but it cannot interpret," I said. "Even colour won't change that."

Again Édouard stared as if seeing me for the first time. "Like water in a dammed river," he spouted, "artists will always find their way." We allowed him the last word on the subject knowing it would not have been dropped otherwise.

Leo asked what I was working on.

"Studies of a peony bush I'd like to put to oil but am struggling."

"Bushes," sniffed Degas. "What do they mean?"

"It's the particular light I found inspiring." If I didn't now question the whole endeavour, I might have talked about the black sheen of the ants against the wax-green casements, the powdery tones of those blooms already opened.

"You'll find a way to give your peonies meaning, Berthe," said Rosalie.

"Cut the flowers," said Édouard, "put them in a vase and bring them inside. Human intention equals meaning. Who cut them? Why? Where are they placed?"

It was good advice and I thanked him for it.

Stevens and his wife, Marie, had arrived and like filings to a magnet, several of Maman's guests were moving toward them.

Degas sighed. "There's something shameful about being known."

"Is that envy's green voice?" I said.

"Formulaic painting gives rise to banality," said Édouard, watching the Stevens. "Everyone's walls will look the same. Awash with pretty portraits of themselves. They will have to smash their mirrors though, if they want to avoid the truth."

As if on an impulse, he gripped my elbow causing me to start and asked if he might speak to me. Had he mistaken me for Edma? "I want your opinion on something, Berthe."

He'd remembered my name.

Rosalie gave me an inquiring expression but I was no less surprised than she. Édouard and I moved into a quiet corner. Across the room, only half-listening to whatever it was Adolphe was saying to Papa, Edma's eyes followed us. I leaned closer to Édouard to make her jealous and think twice of the society she'd sacrifice leaving Paris.

"You must give me your sincere opinion," he said. "What do you think are the greatest weaknesses about my work?"

The strange heat of his undivided attention made me feel as though under a spotlight. As if I were the last woman on earth. Was this his particular magic? Was this how Edma felt?

After his sordid reviews and failed pavilion, a medicinal dose of praise was in order. I told him how much his work had inspired mine over the years. He seemed pleased almost to the point of humility. I flattered myself though, that in seeking my opinion, he valued my painterly eye. Not wanting him to think me some adoring fan without opinions of my own, I offered that recurring bit of criticism I felt about his models. "But yes, your models' figures and faces could perhaps reflect more personality and feeling. To define their character as individuals."

Édouard started then took a step back, eyes narrowing as if to see better to whom he was speaking—definitely not Edma. Nostrils flaring as if hit by a putrid smell, he said, "Tell me now, would you have them smile? Shed a tear?"

I backtracked to try to explain myself but he stopped me. "A model's purpose is not to emote like an actor on a stage. I have no interest in their sad secrets. To me, they're no different from a bale of hay or one of your insipid peonies. It's my temperament they wear, nothing more."

He turned sharply on his heel and walked away before turning back, his tone clipped and pompous—"If you'd like, Mademoiselle, I could teach you how to paint a peony."

"Teach me?" The words just leapt out. "Perhaps, sir, I might teach you a few things, starting with civility."

His eyes widened, as surprised as I. Slowly, he came toward me, jaw set, hands clenched. My heart drummed in my ears. At the boundary of my skirt, he halted and I braced myself. His eyes roamed my face as though it hid some great mystery and he were looking to force a way in.

"Then let me paint you." His flat smile was insincere but I was determined to hold his gaze. "I promise to give your figure"—he paused—"great feeling."

"Lesson one. The intensity of your gaze is not civil. Lesson two. Arrogance is a failing, a precarious perch from which one inevitably falls."

He blinked. Had my arrow pierced his armour?

Bunching his lips, he framed my face with his hands. "I'll need lots of light to contrast your *obscurité*."

"Nor am I some sun-baked Moor." The delight in his laugh was confusing and I elbowed him aside and walked away, burning with hatred. How many bridges would I set fire to before I was left stranded and alone?

EDMA CLIMBED INTO BED, picked up her book but didn't open it. "I saw you flirting with Édouard tonight."

"Flirting? That is your talent, not mine. Being insulted is what you witnessed." I was at the vanity putting solution on my sore eye. I repeated our exchange and became angry all over again.

"He wants to paint you?"

"He wasn't serious."

"Of course not. Even if he was, Papa would never allow it."

Infuriating to think I needed my father's approval. I kicked out my foot and hit the wall. The pain satisfied but I would limp for days with a badly bruised toe.

By the time Adolphe and his mother boarded the train back to Lorient, his engagement to Edma was secured. The cleaving, that is, wedding, was set for mid-October. Only four months' time. Though short engagements were in fashion, the bride's advanced age had been taken into account.

THAT SUMMER WAS SPENT at the Pontillon country estate in Maurecourt so that the couple and two families could get to know one another and make wedding preparations. One such preparation was Edma's induction into the Catholic faith, something she called a formality yet felt like further estrangement. I had plenty of time to paint but couldn't, my recurring eye infection blurring the sight in my left eye.

The evening of the bridal dinner, while getting dressed, I broke down in Edma's arms. She held me and stroked my hair, such affection bringing more tears. She expressed regret in having hurt me, promised to write and to visit often, which only constricted my thoughts into a future without her. Something shook my body as if trying to wrench free.

"Think, Berthe," she insisted over my wailing. "We'll have two lives to share, so life will be twice as rich."

The false note in her voice was obvious even to her and she too broke down, something I'd wanted and was waiting for. Recovering a little, we laughed at our blotchy cheeks and reddened eyes before grasping each other again and holding on until Maman knocked on the door to admonish us that everyone was seated.

For their honeymoon, Edma travelled to Athens and the Greek Islands. She sent home a card from each destination. She sounded excited and happy, so I tried to be happy for her. My eye infection gradually cleared up, but too late to have anything to submit to the Salon.

1869

Jan. 18th, 1869

Dearest Edma, or must I now call you Madame Pontillon?

Maman wanted me to wait before writing you, insisting that after your honeymoon, you needed time to adjust to your new life. I'm sorry but I have waited as long as I can.

Rain again today, steady and dismal, the weather too lamenting your absence. You are missed by everyone. Papa keeps calling me Edma—wishful thinking on his part—and Maman feverishly jots notes throughout the day, afraid of forgetting what she wants to write and tell you. From the moment she opens my curtains to when she closes them, Pauline wonders aloud what it is you're doing, which is my constant thought too. She wistfully refers to your husband as the "pillow-chested Monsieur Pontillon." When I asked what she meant, she said, A chest on which a woman can comfortably lay her head.

Maman has lost whatever subtlety she may have once possessed and plagues me with platitudes such as: Women have an innate need for affection. Or: For a woman to try and make herself self-sufficient is to attempt the impossible.

She may be right, yet having no pillow-chested officer to liberate me from my father's house, I persist like the mule I am. I say that though I have yet to do any work, much less step inside our studio—I will always think of it as ours—for the mere idea only intensifies my loneliness. I prefer to sleep, pick out sad melodies on the piano, draw figures with my finger in the window fog and complain in my journal. I have lost all appetite and, so says Maman, am ruining my complexion. I indulge my melancholy—forgive me—and fear you'll dread my letters. Just know that you are profoundly missed and nothing is the same without you.

I want to hear all about your Lorient. I picture the bracing sea air and you with high colour in your cheeks, hat ribbons flying. A brand-new life in a brand-new place, how freeing that must be. Tell me: are you pleased with your home? Of being in charge of your own household? What sort of society does a naval officer's wife invite? Is marriage all that you'd hoped? You must write as soon as you're able. Don't spare any details. Please.

If our gossip here is still of interest to you, Édouard and Degas have had a falling out. Do you remember the painting Degas was doing of Édouard and his wife? The double portrait? It turned out to be of Suzanne playing the piano and Édouard listening on the davenport. Well, Degas sent Édouard the finished painting and Édouard considered the depiction of his wife "deliberately unflattering" and "a grave insult." So what did the madman do? He took a knife to it and cut out Suzanne's figure! Yes, without consulting Degas, he severed the portrait Degas had worked at long and hard. And then he returned it! In pieces! Who does such a thing? And I thought he reserved his antic boorishness for me. He is not a man in control of his emotions is all I can say.

When Degas saw the sabotage he immediately sent back Édouard's gift-in-kind, a painting called Plums, *and now refuses to be in the same room with the man. Maman and I saw the ruined painting. Though Degas does not flatter his subjects, he'd achieved an admirable likeness, right down to Suzanne's pink nostrils. I'm afraid Édouard, the realist, is not so realistic when it comes to his wife. Perhaps she was once pretty and his memory overrides the widened, reddened woman before him. Though clearly not effective in this instance, I imagine her passivity acts as an antidote to his volatility.*

They have recently returned from spending time in Holland with Suzanne's family so I have not seen nor spoken to him since our vile exchange last spring. You can imagine my shock when yesterday I received a note from him. But then he has no shame, not an ounce. I expected an overdue apology but no, he wrote that he'd a sudden inspiration and asked if I would consider sitting for him this Friday. I assumed it mockery and didn't answer, then received a second note the next day. This one was pleading—"Please say you are available." Is he sincere? And such short notice. Does he assume I've no social engagements? I don't, of course. And I will admit to my vanity overriding my pride because the idea of his daring hand painting my portrait thrills me. Barren of inspiration myself, I might as well be of painterly use to someone and I don't wish to lose his society. So I showed the note to Maman who, not so surprisingly, was intrigued by the idea of her daughter's portrait gracing the walls of the Salon, never mind the signature beneath.

But as you well appreciate, it isn't up to me or Maman to say yes or no to Édouard. It's up to my keeper. So at dinner last night I brought it up. Papa's reaction will also not surprise you.

Are you playing me for a fool? he said. It was not a question. He reminded me that he was as familiar with Édouard's paintings as the next person. Then thought himself very clever saying, What man would not want to paint your landscape?

Portrait, I corrected, pretending not to understand his innuendo.

Dear Maman reminded Papa of the friendly relations between the two families and that she, of course, would be there to chaperone.

I said that using colleagues as models was becoming more commonplace. But when does he ever listen to me?

Models are either dancers or prostitutes, he spouted, and if they're not, they're perceived to be. You must foremost consider, he said with an infuriating wag of his finger, your family's reputation.

Me? I said. What about your own consideration?

Oh, Edma, it just came out. I might have said worse but with a screech on the parquet, Maman pushed back her chair and excused herself. Papa was momentarily stricken, for which I was glad. In solidarity with Maman, I pushed back my chair but he growled at me to sit, more furious with himself, I believe, for mentioning a dancer and prostitute in the same breath. We ate the rest of the meal in silence.

I was certain I would not now nor ever be modeling for Édouard but later that evening Maman came to my bedroom and announced with a strained smile that she would be taking me to Édouard's studio on Friday. I said I was sorry to be the cause of argument between them and that it was not important, that Édouard could find another model. But I'm looking forward to it, Maman said. And that was that.

I will let you know how it goes with mine enemy. Édouard, that is, not Papa. We bring out the worst in each other, so it may all go overboard. From now until Friday, though, I will agonize over what to wear without you here to help me decide.

Tibby has twice brought home a young woman. Short, sweet of face and very buxom, she is the daughter of the proprietor of a printing press. A marked lisp makes her a bit difficult to understand. Maman despairs that he'll marry beneath him. I remind her of Tibby's fickle nature and that it's doubtful the relationship will last.

How it has relieved my heart to write. Oh, Edma, I've never known what solitude meant until now. I see just how dependent on you I've been all my life for I wake each day and don't know what to do with myself. Maybe you can write and tell me. Make up a schedule for me.

Also please tell me when it is appropriate to visit newlyweds without being a ridiculous third wheel.

Love, Berthe

Jan. 26th, 1869

Sweet, sweet, dear Berthe,
How strange to receive my first ever letter from you. I had hoped Adolphe wouldn't notice the emptiness I've felt without you and from which I believed I was beginning to recover. Then I received your letter. It made me smile to hear your voice again but by letter's end I began to cry and was unable to stop. Adolphe, full of solicitations, worried he was the cause. When I told him I was missing my sister, he insisted you visit sooner than later. He's never seen me so emotional. I'm afraid he believes he's ruptured some vital female bond and that my mind may be taken by fairies. To cheer me he suggested new paints and encouraged setting my easel in a corner of the drawing room. I cried harder. A corner of the drawing room? From where I can make pleasant conversation as I daub in a bouquet of poppies?

As for Adolphe, what can I say? Alone together, we are getting to know each other. Other than naval talk his conversation is a bit rudimentary. His is a regimented life and he assumes mine to be the same. He rises at dawn and the first thing he does is turn to me who's half-asleep and perform his morning's calisthenics, so to speak. As you know, I'm not a morning person. You may feel captive in your father's house but imagine feeling that your body is no longer entirely in your possession. Believe me when I say that if you, Berthe, were never to experience a man's physical love, you would not be the lesser for it. There is far greater transcendence in the act of painting than in that of lovemaking. At least for the woman. I am sorry if that dispels any romantic ideas you may harbour.

Don't mistake me, Adolphe is a gentle, considerate husband but, as I suspect it is with all men in such proximity with a barely clothed woman, the animal overtakes the senses. Judging by the look on his face, a blind violence over which it is clear he has little control seems necessary for him to reach his summit. Its duration is brief, thank God, and then he becomes a shy child in my arms. Oh, here I am, analyzing this most basic human act. But you know me.

And afterward, what is there to say? I pretend to sleep while he dresses then goes down for breakfast. I join him soon after and we eat and read the paper before he reports to work. He's home for dinner and if we have no guests or engagements we read to each other and play a few hands of Écarte.

He has made me promise to do a portrait of him while he still has his hair. I'll do it to please him though the only "art" I have time for now is arranging flowers and furnishings, overseeing the meals, the cleaning, our clothes. I could substitute the word duty for art but that would diminish my new life and I must believe that the role to which I've committed has import and meaning or I will despair.

Your life is still full of surprises and my letters will be tedious in comparison. Lorient life revolves around the navy and the commerce of the docks. The Emperor has made extravagant upgrades to the port since we visited Auntie, because it's to become the centre for the importation of France's coal—see how I'm learning things I never cared to know? All of France sends their goods to Lorient in hopes of fetching a higher price abroad. The train runs night as well as day and its warning bell often scares me from a dead sleep. Everyone here is a happy Bonapartist who still believes in his promise of being "all things to all men" though the cesspool farmers and chimney sweeps may have their doubts.

There is a market every second Saturday which has imported goods you won't find in Paris markets. Well, perhaps eventually, but they are seen here first. I have recently purchased African silk for a summer dress—you'd love the hot dusty colours—and exquisitely carved beads made from elephants' tusks for the embroidery. I found cotton lace collars from Portugal that are much heavier than Italian collars so they lie more evenly. There are fruits and vegetables and varieties of fish and fowl I've never seen and am not brave enough to serve. I will wait for you and we can be adventurous together.

I don't know if you recall the view of the bay from the bridge connecting the north and south sides of town but I thought you might consider painting it. At least I would if I'd the time.

As for my new house, I should have no cause for complaint. It's on a quiet enough street. There's a balcony off my sitting room from which the ocean is visible and I find myself coming here throughout the day to stare at the sea and daydream of home, our studio, Paris, you, Maman and Papa. I really must pull my head from the quicksand of memory and make more of my time.

The house is elegantly appointed despite a preponderance of blue and more blue. Adolphe's mother finds the colour "rational and calming." Cold is the word. There are two unfortunate rooms where the wallpaper and upholstery are of the same pattern. The worst is the drawing room where the maids are trained to line up the fat white and blue stripes of the settees and chairs with those of the wallpaper. The furniture melts into the wall with dizzying effect and I can't help feeling behind bars.

When we first arrived, Adolphe's family was here to greet our carriage. Before I was allowed to enter my new home, Mme. Pontillon handed me a duck's egg to crack open on the threshold—a family custom to ensure fertility. Or as my mother-in-law put it, "to aid you in your sacred obligation." Will I be sent packing if I can't produce an heir to the throne? Beheaded?

As for my scintillating social life. I pay regular visits to our elderly neighbours, and of course to Auntie who is always suffering some new pain and to Adolphe's sister who, having married last June, is now lying-in. And I host them in return though Auntie no longer ventures out-of-doors. I was recently introduced to the wives of a few of the naval officers who are Adolphe's friends. I plan to host them this weekend. Will report back to you.

I miss painting terribly and can't imagine anything replacing that sublime concentration that makes time a fast-flowing river that passes without obtrusion. Well, except maybe one thing—

my cook's bouillabaisse. Her name is Manon and she is an artist of the tongue's delights. I fear it's my destiny to grow stout as well as dull.

Please put aside all worthy novels and journals to bring when you come as the only books on my shelves are The King James Bible, books about mushrooms—the late M. Pontillon was an avid mushroom hunter—and military histories. I hope to introduce Adolphe to the novel as soon as I can get my hands on one.

Give my warmest regards to one and all and especially to you.

With all my heart, Edma

Feb. 4th, 1869

Dear Edma,

After I received your letter Maman found me crying with my nose pressed up against the wall. If we keep this up, we'll lose what's left of our health and beauty—not that it matters in my case but it does in yours. Thank dear Adolphe for the invitation. Maman forbids me to visit until spring but I will make it as soon as the day lilies bloom.

I cannot wait to see your blue home. How many servants do you have? And you will make a fine stout grande dame *by the sea. Never dull though. Oh, please be happy in your new life or I will be doubly miserable in mine.*

Speaking of country ladies, Yves is visiting with her "sacred obligation." Bichette is now running on plump little legs and has gained the happiest of dispositions. Last night, she even slept in my bed. How entirely reassuring to have a small warm body snuggled beside you in the dark. And what is that complex smell of a child's velveteen head? Something between freshly turned earth and currant bread.

Édouard and Degas have reconciled, though Degas says he won't be repeating the offer of a portrait. Ever. No one can stay angry at Édouard for long, says Stevens, because he's too forward looking and the past means nothing to him. I begged to differ after sitting for him but will get to that. First, speaking of portraits, Degas took a keen interest in Yves at Maman's soirée. Whenever Yves turned around, she found him unabashedly staring at her, his finger in the air sorting line and proportions. She calls him taciturn and strange, and would have refused his request to sit for him if it weren't for Maman who, since she rarely sees her eldest daughter, desires the portrait for herself. Degas told me Yves reminds him of an aunt of whom he was "overly fond." That man speaks in riddles half the time. He is maybe the most private person I know.

So yes, I had my first sitting with Édouard. Oh, Edma, I am still reeling!

We arrived at his studio in rue Gaudet at the appointed time. As he ushered us in, my skirts knocked over a forest of empty wine bottles beside the door. Reeking of soured wine and linseed, his studio is a true dandy's den: scarlet velvet pouffe and curtains, Persian rugs and brass candelabras. A singular woman's glove was laid over a book on the coatrack. Awaiting its owner? Consider yourself lucky to have escaped his adulterous net.

On the central easel beneath an enviable floor-to-ceiling window was a portrait of his Suzanne playing the piano. His touché to Degas? I didn't dare ask. Its shadows flattered Suzanne's plump figure and profile and she looked far younger than in person. He has recently painted Zola at his writing desk, now Suzanne at her talent, so I was glad to have brought my palette and brushes.

But rather than settling us in his studio, he was busy packing his painting things. We were going to his mother's appartement, he announced, where the other models were waiting.

Other models? Maman and I said in unison.

While in Holland he had seen two women seated on a balcony and was reminded of Goya's Majas on a Balcony. *He was planning an homage, he said, and Maman looked aghast. I did not want to concede that Papa had been right but we have all seen Édouard's homages and they're neither portraiture nor flattering.*

You are probably asking the question I asked. Majas? Édouard translated the word as "beautiful illusions," though when I later asked Tibby, he laughed and said it meant "women," nothing more. So off we went in his carriage, having sent Levin home with ours.

Arriving at Mme. Manet's, Édouard thrust on me a mass of white lace-choked fabric that I assumed were curtains, then pointed to a bedroom in which I could change. The curtains were actually a dress two sizes too big, with ruffles along every edge, enormous bell-sleeves and an ocean of skirt. To think I had fretted over what to wear and woke at dawn so Pauline could perfect my hair. Somehow I had forgotten his description of models as "hay bales who wore his temperament and nothing more."

I put on the white monstrosity—it must have been Suzanne's—and was too embarrassed to step from the bedroom. Maman found some pins to fit the bodice, though there was no hope for its drooping shoulders or dragging hem. But Edma, my frustrations were only beginning.

My black choker also wouldn't do. He replaced it with a green one that matched the balcony's shutters. The choker was hung with a fat bronze pendant—very ugly—and I was given earrings to match.

My fellow hay bales were Fanny Claus, the violinist friend of Suzanne, Antoine Guillemont and Édouard's nephew, Léon. Young Léon is now almost as tall as Édouard. He has Édouard's figure too and the same reedy pitch to his voice. I think there's more to Mme. Manet's story regarding him. I will prod Degas. Not that he'll give me a straight answer.

Édouard dressed Fanny in another white catastrophe, hers so short it revealed her boots! Antoine was in tails, a white starched collar and deep blue cravat. There was no sense to any of it.

My traipsing hem made for a perilous walk to the balcony and when I tripped and toppled a lamp, Édouard erupted in laughter. If the others weren't waiting and Maman enjoying tea and beignet *with Mme. Manet, I would have left right then.*

Once on the balcony, Édouard handed me a scarlet red fan—"Women love to remain cool"—and Fanny a blue parasol—"and they detest the sun." Antoine, he said, must have his hands free, ready for the unexpected. How ridiculous.

We three were to pose on the balcony for the passing world to gawk at while young Léon set tea just inside the apartment. Léon was almost completely in shadow so I didn't see the point of his even being there.

Édouard gave Fanny bright lemon gloves to wear. They were his own, brought back from Holland and absurdly large for her small hands. She laughed at them. I began to suspect this whole charade was some punishing joke for my remark regarding his painting.

Calling my hair arrangement too formal and without asking permission, Édouard began to restyle it. His thick fingers worked my pinned-up braid and I had to press on my scalp to keep it from pulling and hurting. Finally, the braid draped my shoulder like something killed. He undid it, teased curls on to my forehead then stepped back to assess the damage.

He attacked Fanny's head next and, to make her comedy complete, pinned a large silk chrysanthemum on the edge of her hairline so it sprung forward like a unicorn's horn. My sole comfort was that such silliness would never be accepted to the Salon so Papa would never see it.

He went around to the street below where he had gone to great trouble renting a cart loaded with, yes, bales of hay, on which to stand and thus level himself with Madame Manet's second floor balcony. The bales were covered with a makeshift wooden floor supporting an enormous canvas. He climbed the ladder to "his portable studio" and began to arrange our tableau.

Fanny and I were made to stand facing each other across a café table and Antoine to sit between us. No, we women were to sit and Antoine to stand. No, Antoine looks like a maitre'd, *he said, and changed us again.*

A horrid smell rose from the floor and I realized this was where Mme. Manet's pup relieved himself.

Édouard now spoke directly to me. Like Goya's Majas, this painting is about sisterly relations and the men that come between them. Fanny and Antoine both looked at me. I was too astonished to respond.

Now I was to stand, Antoine to sit. I actually believed we were in place. But then all three of us were to stand and look this way, no, that way, hold our objects open then closed, up, down, sideways.

In echo of our argument he said, Whatever you do, don't smile.

I barely contained myself.

Now we were to get rid of the table. Remove the chairs. No. He wanted one chair to remain. I'd had enough. Why, I asked, if this is a copy of Goya's painting, don't you just copy his tableau?

An homage is not a copy, he said, and the best ideas never static. Surely, he said, I had learned that from M. Corot while outdoors chasing his light.

You talk of fluid ideas, I shot back, yet are averse to changing light?

Steady light is a must for our trade, he said, and sheds no consequence on ideas.

I was fed up being a hay bale, fed up with his condescension. My corset was too tight and chafing under my arms, the lace of Suzanne's dress itchy. I hadn't eaten that morning. I snapped my fan closed, sat down on the chair, leaned on the railing and turned my face away from him.

And what did he do? Edma, you cannot guess. He said perfect. Nobody move.

Imagine my exasperation. The others breathed audible sighs of relief so I bit my tongue and held my pose. Maybe it's narcissistic, Edma, but I felt that everything he had done and said that morning was to provoke me.

As he sketched, he talked. Incessantly. About anything and everything: the conditions of the poor, the usefulness of windmills, an exhibition he had seen in Holland of a Dutch painter named Hals. He even recited Baudelaire's "Le Cygne." When Antoine tried to make the conversation two-way, Édouard asked him to please not move.

In the corner of my vision, I could see his pencil working as rapidly as his mouth. He could only have been making a mess on that canvas. After all our efforts, this made me the angriest. Was our time worth nothing to him?

But after a while I began to sense that one part of his mind was kept occupied by his endless monologue, or even distracted, so that the creative part might slip out while he wasn't watching. Similar to how Maman likes to be read to while doing her needlepoint, claiming she can hear better when her hands are busy.

When we were leaving, Édouard said that after seeing the paintings of Frans Hals, he had to admit I was right about his subjects lacking feeling. Then he thanked me for my insight and for inspiring him today. Can you believe that? On the carriage ride home, I felt so battered I fell asleep.

He has sent a note requesting more sittings. Once was more than enough for me but Maman says I cannot go back on my commitment now. How will I survive?

My love to you and to Adolphe, Berthe

Feb. 11th, 1869

Berthe,

I hope you received my package. What do you think of the shawl? It's from Spain. Fringed edges are popular there. Is it not lovely the way it flows in the wake of your movement?

How I look forward to your letters. I picture you writing at the desk in our sitting room, left elbow on the table, cheek and chin palmed, Pauline chatting and knocking about in the background. How delightful having our niece in bed with you, the dear thing. And modeling for Édouard! It's all enviable from where I stand no matter how trying it sounds. As for Édouard's erratic behaviour? He's a proud man, Berthe, and not as secure in his opinion of himself as you might think. Just like someone else I know. Yes, you.

Homage or not, I, for one, cannot wait to see what his hand has made of you.

Let me introduce you to my new society and you may look more kindly upon Édouard's. So... I hosted naval friends of Adolphe and their wives. I had planned to seat my guests according to Paris fashion but the women immediately sat themselves at my end of the table and the men at Adolphe's. Two separate conversations ensued. My attention kept drifting to the men's talk of the execution of Maximilian in Mexico and the grave possibility of France declaring war on Prussia. The wives, Pascale, Marthe and Cecilie, talked fashion and gardening and babies—Pascale and Cecilie each have one child and Marthe is expecting her first—all with casual indifference as if it would be distasteful to care too much about anything. Adolphe said later they only acted that way because they're intimidated that I'm from the city.

Cecilie brought up the subject of art and the one and only name she associates with it, Ernest Meissonier.

I asked if his tiny perfections moved her. She assured me they did.

Pascale professed to understand my decision to give up painting. You're at a terrible disadvantage, she said, not being allowed to attend art school and paint the foundation for figure painting.

It was obvious no one knew what she was talking about.

I said, quite innocently, Do you mean the nude figure?

Both ends of the table quieted and Marthe's husband raised his eyebrows boorishly.

Cecilie offered that it would be like a dressmaker trying to make a dress without measurements. Then the sweetly vacant Marthe said that to try and compete in a man's profession can unsex a woman.

Now do you appreciate Édouard's company?

Oh, and Pascale's husband asked in his weary tone if there were any paintings by women in the Louvre. When I answered no, he nodded sagely.

In a gallant though mortifying attempt to rescue me, Adolphe proudly marched everyone upstairs to view some of my work, including the portrait of young you. I had it hung across from my bedroom door so I can see you each morning. I admit to talking to it, to you, when I know no one can hear me. Anyway, when Cecilie saw my work, she became very excited and asked if I would paint baskets for the Church's spring fair. See, my talents will be put to good use after all.

Now that I am married, the more convinced I am that you wouldn't be satisfied with the arrangement. Do the utmost with your charm and wit to find a situation that suits you. Such as the support of a patron, but one who expects only art in return.

When you visit you may not recognize me. Lazy, insipid and, I fear, growing a little wider with each meal. What I wouldn't give to see what shocking thing Édouard has done with you and Fanny and Antoine. There are no shocks or surprises to be had in this house. Even the mourning doves wake me at the same hour each day. I now see great merit in resisting convention, not so much to change the world but for the sheer vitality of it. Forgive my whining and complaining, but you're the only one to whom I can freely express my doubts about the choice I've made. Oh, Berthe, I do doubt myself like never before. Only my cook's good humour keeps me from despair. I count the days until we are together again, Edma

Feb. 19th, 1869

Edma,

It is not like you to despair or doubt—that is my specialité*—and you have no cause to do so now. You have undergone tremendous change and it takes time to feel at home in a new place. I sound like Maman but cannot bear to think of you despondent.*

The shawl is perfect, your taste impeccable as always. Thank you. Edma, if you grow more voluptuous, you will simply grow more beautiful. Unlike me, apparently, for this is what dear thoughtless Tibby, back from his jaunt to England, said to me last night when we found ourselves alone. You're getting older, Berthe, and what with being so—he hesitated before coming up with slender but I know what he meant—you can't afford to be picky. He didn't stop there but lit up with sudden insight. You might do well to consider a rich older man in ill health who will die soon and leave you his property and money. That way you can have your own house and buy all the paint you could wish for. Then—what he really wanted to say—if in the future you end up alone and have spent all your inheritance, don't come looking to me.

I thanked him for his generosity of opinion.

Our spoiled brother has little direction. He drinks too much, spends his time gambling at cards and dice and is now studying up on the horse races. Maman says this is what young men do before settling down. Do they? The printer's daughter has come and gone and now Tibby's planning a trip to Portugal. Says he can't bear to be in one place for long. Another thing Maman cheerfully attributes to his youth.

She was cleaning out the studio today and sorted through my canvases to frame and take to Cadart's to see if he will display them. If my daughter, she said, wants to be a real painter, why should I not concern myself with her commercial progress? What do you think? Is this show of faith meant to inspire me back to work or mask her obsession to marry me off?

Cadart displayed four of Degas' paintings, which is where Maman got the idea, and at last night's soirée Degas quietly announced his first sale! I was so happy for him. Purchased by a man from Brussels, a minister to the King no less. This same minister has a friend who owns a small gallery in Brussels so now Degas is travelling there for a solo exhibition. Imagine that. He hopes this is the start of something. Édouard went silent at the news. He has painted longer than Degas and still sits on all his work. Though I do fantasize of my own first sale, my expectations are low. What collector brags of owning work by a woman?

Well… I survived several more sittings with Édouard. These, at least, have been civil. And because my flouncy white figure is central, so he tells us, two of those sittings were just he and I and Maman. Though on both occasions Eugène dropped by the studio to lean up against the doorjamb, neither in nor out, and watch in silence. With two sets of Manet eyes on me, I felt like a prize pig.

Édouard won't allow us to see the work-in-progress, insisting we wait until it's hanging in Room M at the Salon. As if it has any hope of acceptance. I can't say it without insulting him but what if, like his Olympia, *he's made me into a laughingstock? I've told him that I desired to see it before he showed anyone else. He said yes but now I'm unclear if that means yes, he is sure I do, or yes, he will show it to me first.*

Enough about my portrait and on to the one Degas is doing of Yves. Your sisters, I fear, have both become painters' models. Scandalous! Something to tell your new church friends.

Degas has finished three preparatory sketches of her and he starts painting tomorrow. I love watching him draw. His steady hand requires no ruler, his cross-hatch remarkably rapid, and his concentration so great that no one dares speak. Yves has trouble staying awake but he doesn't scold.

Speaking of scandals. I dared ask Degas about Édouard's nephew, Léon. He told me that Édouard and Suzanne shared quarters before they were married. Suzanne used to be Eugène's and Gustave's piano teacher, which is how they met. Mme. Manet knew about the affair but kept it secret from Édouard's father, who would never have approved. Then Suzanne disappeared from Paris for an entire year, back home to Holland, and returned with an infant in her arms claiming it to be her little brother.

So it's their child, I said. Degas told me that the boy's name is Leenoff, not Manet, then took his leave and left me hanging, as he likes to do. There are thirty and some years between Suzanne and her so-called brother. Wouldn't that make Suzanne's mother past child-bearing age. He looks the perfect cross between Édouard and Suzanne so I am convinced.

On Tuesday, Eugène mustered the courage to ask me a direct question. It was about you, actually, and whether you're now required to attend Catholic mass. Are you? It was apropos of the Vatican Council's announcement declaring the Pope "infallible." It was in all the papers so you must have seen it. What does Adolphe make of it?

I wanted to know who makes such a decision? The Pope himself? The Councilmen? Because logic follows that the judgement of those making the claim must also be infallible. How arrogant of men, I said, to believe themselves gods. Eugène agreed with me, of course, because he has no opinions of his own.

Do not despair, Edma. Things will improve and we will have great fun when I visit.

Love every day and always. Berthe

March 1st, 1869

Dear Berthe,
Your letter cheered me. Please never stop writing. But I have news. Unconfirmed news. The midwife has visited and tells me that I may already have an extra soul on board. Which, she says, could explain my sour mood and sour stomach, which no amount of wine sweetens. Homesickness, she concedes, could upset my menses, but she thinks it unlikely. Don't mention this to Maman or anyone else, please. The midwife also said that miscarriage is common the first time around. She called this nature's way of cleansing the nest. So repugnant. I'm queasy even thinking of it. I should not have broken that duck egg over the threshold. Some images will never leave.

It may be a slight against God to wish that this cleansing take place but I do. Though it would only be a matter of time before I found myself in the same state again. How ungrateful I sound. When I told Adolphe, he laughed and kissed me, calling it a blessing and a miracle. Every animal breeds, I said. He looked taken aback as though wondering who he'd married. I apologized, of course, said that I am not myself. But it's the truth—I feel common and base.

Manon, my cook, insists from the fullness of my face that not only am I indeed pregnant but carrying a girl. A boy, she says, sharpens one's features while a girl softens them. She now serves me sautéed pigweed at every meal, claiming it will help baby form strong bones. If she's any test to that, my baby's bones will be tree trunks.

If I am with child, Maman will want to be the first to know and first to announce. So for now, Berthe, let it be our secret.

I never expected to get pregnant so quickly, at my age. What sort of mother will I make? I'm exacting and critical and, in truth, scared of babies. I was afraid to hold Bichette when she was born. The way her eyes rolled around reminded me of Grand-mére on her deathbed. And her head, a cantaloupe on a weak stem.

Being pregnant would be inconvenient now that I have at last arranged a place to work in my sitting room. I did a pastel of wildflowers that truly cheered me. I even ordered a folding screen to hide my canvases and on which I had planned to paint a landscape. But worried about my age, the midwife says I must rest with my feet up as much as possible, at least until "it's taken." Like some horrid parasite. She recommended I take up crochet. To make itchy blankets and mushroom hats? My child will be wrapped in silk, thank you.

On top of my green stomach, I feel slow-witted and dreamy, something Marthe calls baby dust. And I just thought she was dim. Oh, I am a snob.

The midwife said the best thing I could do for the baby was to be happy. A happy mother, she said, makes a happy baby. So already I'm failing my child.

Adolphe believes a child will fulfill me because a child is what all women want. I should be happy. I should be. I knew this was what I was in for. I wanted it. I did.

Berthe, my life is changing so fast I'm afraid I soon won't recognize myself. That you too won't recognize me and I'll no longer be the sister you looked up to. Please forgive my self-pity and whining.

I must leave off, for the only thing that abates my nausea is eating. What sense does that make? And in particular eating Manon's foie gras *and buttered bread. So this* vache *must go graze. And then lie down. Though I want only to keep talking to you. I will finish tomorrow.*

March 2nd, 1869

Other than eating and dozing, I read the local paper. Most cows cannot read but this one can. Not art reviews or serialized novels or essays by philosopher poets. Lorient's paper is dedicated to predicting the weather, on land and at sea, knots per hour, the type of fish running and the most attractive bug or worm to catch them, under which moon it will be best to plant which variety of bean, when to expect the duck and geese migrations and how to clean your firearm. One columnist expounds on the exploits of the navy and another specializes in intrigue. This last is the one I seek out. A recent story involved two new mistresses of the Emperor. One is Baron von Haussmann's granddaughter, now pregnant with the Emperor's child though she's practically a child herself. The other is a former circus performer he has apparently installed somewhere in Passy. Maybe you've seen her? She has been spotted coming and going in a royal carriage and dressed in a man's coattails and top hat. Does the Emperor await her arrival at the Tuileries dressed in one of his wife's chinchilla-lined gowns? Such sordid tales don't faze Lorient's approval for their king. Within their Catholic notions, they admire his prowess. There seems a strange comfort in making earthly gods of men.

Speaking of which, the whole of Lorient, including Adolphe, is perfectly accepting, if not a little I-told-you-so smug, about the papal claim of infallibility. And yes, off I troop with my new family to Sunday mass each week, which is held in a beautiful fourteenth-century church with stained glass to rival Notre-Dame's. There's a moving sculpture of Mary and Child by an Italian sculptor whose name, sadly, no one recalls and a comforting elegance to be found in the rituals. Thankfully the local Bishop has some humour and wit.

Each Sunday, rich and poor leave their homes and jobs unattended and come to the service. "All are equal in God's eyes," the Bishop is fond of saying, though the church's patrons, like us, sit up front and the servants and tradesmen in behind.

It is pleasing to see one's liveryman, butcher and smithy dressed in their finest clothes and looking as dignified as their calloused hands and sunburnt faces allow. After mass the entire congregation gathers in the rectory for a meal of wine, bread, cheese and pickles. Because the meek shall inherit the earth and the Bishop wants all to have an equal chance at this inheritance, the property class serve their servants. You think I'm making it up. I'm not. It feels silly and contrived, but it's curious to see how the servants respond. Some are embarrassed and apologetic and can't raise their eyes, others rise haughty and proud, and a few are simply grateful and at their ease. Perhaps they're mirroring the behaviour of the ones they serve? Anyway, the whole exercise seems very telling, but of what I'm not sure.

This past Sunday, I ended up serving our cook, Manon. She had great fun with me. Asked for a cleaner serviette, pointed out a smudge on her glass, questioned the freshness of the bread. I'm afraid I am fussy about such things—Maman instructed me to be precise with servants in the beginning to set a tone—but how Manon made me laugh. I never feel so useful as I do at those Sunday meals. In the absence of you and Maman, Manon (a jolly woman, older than I am by seven years) is fast becoming my closest friend and confidante. Speaking of bosoms, she would be a favourite with Tibby. I do hope he at least finds a career that suits him, if not a wife.

As for Édouard and his nephew, I will reserve my opinion. Though by the sounds of the balcony tableau, perhaps placing his nephew in the shadows is symbolic. Mme. Manet is protective of her sons and seems perfectly capable of such a grand deceit. Perhaps his father would have disinherited him if the affair were revealed. For they married only after Monsieur's passing, no? So who knows what sort of arrangement was made between mother and son. Suzanne may feel indebted. But how tragic for Léon if he's unable to claim his father's name. Tragic for Édouard too.

But isn't it curious that after all this time he and Suzanne haven't had more children? Do you think it a loveless marriage? That he only married her because of the accident of the child? Which would justify that woman's glove in his studio. Like I've come to learn, intimate relations seems a physical need of men.

This letter is so long I must stop or will have trouble fitting it in its envelope. Besides, my parasite is demanding to be fed.

Yours, Edma

March 12th, 1869

My Petite Vache,

May this letter find your green stomach improved, though my own goes green at the thought of pigweed. But I am glad you're being looked after by someone who makes you laugh. Rosalie, who knows everything about everything as far as I can tell, says your cook is right. Greens are important during pregnancy. She says that the leaves should be picked at their early stages, as baby greens, while the baby is also at its early stages. She's been reading the ideas of a new German theorist, a Dr. Hahnemann. Something about "like affecting like."

Please stop worrying, Edma. You'll make a calm, practical and superior mother in all ways, and won't be fearful when it's your own baby. I will not speak a word about your possible condition to Maman but, personally, I'm excited for you. A girl, says your cook? I rather hope it's a boy, to whom life's doors are flung wide, the world a sumptuous feast laid before him.

Your church sounds more admirable than most and replete with the kind of societal leveling the Communards would hope to achieve here in Paris—minus the religion, of course. Will a heathen like myself be allowed to attend the service?

My news is that, without even telling me, Édouard submitted Le Balcon *to the Salon. And now has proudly informed me that it has been accepted! I couldn't hide my astonishment. I still haven't even laid eyes on it! I said. Apparently hay bales are not consulted on such matters. You will. You will, is all he said.*

I cannot believe it was accepted. Is its acceptance a ploy for ticket sales as the public clamours to see what new hilarity or blasphemy the madman has done now? He wants me to come to Varnishing Day. For moral support, or a side show, where people can laugh, then point to me, then back to the painting, then back to me? I said I would, because I'm determined to see it before all of France does and have it promptly removed if need be. I am dreading the day and have made Maman promise not to mention anything about its acceptance to Papa. It's all so inconvenient and may well force an end to Édouard's and my tentative rapport. He enjoys torturing me is what I think.

*He had also submitted a second painting—*The Execution of Maximilian. *This one was not only rejected but the government banned it from being shown anywhere in all of France. Even threatening to have it destroyed. Édouard considers this a great success! He says Emperor Louis is afraid it will expose the government's incompetence in Mexico and incite an uprising. I don't know about an uprising but I did see it—he had allowed me this— and its up-close, cool-handed killing is disturbing.*

Rosalie, I'm happy to say, had her Umbrella Stand *accepted and she credits you for your suggestion of the water droplets on the floor, which truly did put the nature in the* nature-morte. *With nothing to submit, I feel I've wasted my time this past year. My soul does feel in a knot. Though I believe I'm just lazy at heart and that it was your discipline not mine that spurred me to action. You may need to have a horsewhip ready for me when I visit.*

Degas had one acceptance which, as he says, is better than none. He finished his painting of Yves and I assure you she won't be pleased.

It's very modern with an emphasis on shapes and atmosphere. Yves' features are exaggerated just enough to distort them. Her long neck, for example, and fingers, the paleness of her eyebrows, the strong line of her jaw. Not flattering. He caught well that disembodied expression she gets when weaving her fantasies, but even her dress, that lovely one with the sheer sleeves and décolletage, was sorely undersold. Maman was hoping to purchase the painting but then she saw it. As you know, Maman does not hide her opinions. Poor Degas. He pretended not to care but I could tell he was shaken. Though how could he have thought otherwise? Maman used the dreaded "disappointing" and he immediately told us he had begun a second portrait in pastels with a different approach. We'll see.

I wonder why he feels the need to diminish his models' good looks. Do women wield some power over him against which he must rebel? This is not something I feel comfortable asking my willfully opaque friend. Beneath his snarling exterior, Degas is truly a sensitive soul, and it will take time before he reveals his underbelly.

Last Thursday at Mme. Manet's, Stevens brought along a neighbour, an aspiring young painter, Eva Gonzales. Her father is a novelist. Though I've never heard of him, Maman has read one of his books and was excited to meet him. His daughter Eva, only nineteen and humble to a fault, practically swooned when introduced to Édouard. Bumping her skirts right up against him, she showered him with flattery, mentioned his paintings by name and refuted his critics. He didn't stop her. Then she asked, right there in front of me, the Stevens, Antoine and Degas, if Édouard would consider taking her on as a pupil. As if he ran a studio!

He said he needed to see her work first and scarlet blotches bloomed up her throat like a sleeve collar. I felt sorry for her. She has all the green enthusiasm you and I had at that age but, really, we were never so obvious, were we?

You have probably heard from Maman that Papa is unusually tired of late. His feet are swollen by the time he arrives home and his boots take two servants to remove. The skin of his feet, Maman told me, is stretched tight and a shiny red. She tries to get him to take time off but you know how he is. The doctor says it's his heart therefore his blood is weak. So she's filling him with beef and chicken hearts. She's been reading the same articles by the same German theorist as Rosalie.

I must dress for dinner now because we are going to see the new Wagner opera tonight.

Love to you, Berthe

March 19th, 1869

Dear Berthe,

You and Maman should receive my letters with the same delivery announcing formally that yes, this cow is with calf. Let the nymphs and fauns dance and play their flutes. Nature rules us despite our higher intentions.

I do need beautiful things to look forward to, as little feels beautiful now that I am sick to my stomach several times each morning. According to the midwife this means the parasite has taken. The evil leaves me around noon and I spend the rest of the day warding it off with small plates of paté or duck rillettes *on toast. I should be able to float soon and stay warm in water.*

Even at night I wake to graze on the plate the maid leaves beside my bed. There is nothing less elegant than eating in bed in the dark and I have nightmarish visions of attracting rats—those I've seen at the docks are big as cats.

Please come soon and bring some excitement and vigour of the city. How was the Wagner? And congratulate everyone for me on their acceptances. I'm sorry your own work will not be on display. I feel responsible. Will you forgive me? Can I forgive myself? You must not give up. I may have been more disciplined but you, Berthe, have an original and inspired eye. Please use your fierceness and tenacity to believe in our dream and in yourself. Do it for me.

That your face and figure will hang on the Salon walls this year is exciting, no? Unless he has undressed you with his brush, you needn't worry about it being received like his Olympia. *And since his models bear little to no expression, you can feel safely undistinguished. Your personal pride is another matter but you knew you were sitting for a mad genius. So there is really no one to blame for the result except yourself. Well, maybe Maman who encouraged it.*

Adolphe's sister has had her baby. For having babies is all women do here. It a boy, Pierre, who sleeps during daylight hours and wails all night. One nursemaid has already quit. Perhaps he's a vampire. We'll see once his teeth come in. My mother-in-law is ecstatic at my news and says we are doubly blessed and God is looking kindly upon us. I don't consider retching a kindness. Sorry for the brevity of this letter. Housebound with my seasickness, I have little news and even writing tires me.

Love and kisses, Edma

March 28th, 1869

Dear Edma,

Official congratulations! Ever since your wedding Maman has worried your age might hinder you from having children. Now she brags to everyone how she was never in doubt you'd be with child by the new year. Already she is preparing for your lying-in. She secured the same midwife as Yves, the tall one with the Adam's apple, and the same chatty wet nurse with the eyebrows. When I visit, she hopes I can stay in Lorient long enough so we can return here together. That will be entirely up to you and Adolphe, of course.

I'm eager to see you in your new life and eager for a change of scene to spur some work. It's been nine months since I last did anything worthwhile. But Edma, I can't tell you how much your encouragement means to me. Please keep prodding me.

The reception of Wagner was a mixed one, some of the older patrons leaving at intermission. Granted, it was very long. His modern deviations wanted for melody and harmony—this alone fascinated—and there was an underlying musical force, driving in its precision, which I felt in my bones. Terribly exciting. Papa summarized the evening with one word: Germanic. He hated it.

So… Varnishing Day and Le Balcon. *Papa found out about its acceptance in* Le Figaro. *To reaffirm his disapproval, he did not accompany us. This eased my panic, but only a little.*

I insisted we go straight to Room M but we ran into M. Corot sitting and smoking his pipe beside his silver-flecked landscape Souvenir de Mortefontaine. *Edma, I wish you could see this painting. It is transporting. I was infused with wonder and, at the same instant, roused with nostalgia for that wonder. As though he had painted time itself! Truly Monsieur is at the peak of his talents. I cannot believe it didn't have a sold stamp beside it. If the day ever comes when I sell one of my paintings, I will turn around and purchase a Corot. Have it prominently hung so that each and every day I can be lifted out of my own banality. He asked all about you, Edma, and expressed his wish that you continue to find time for painting.*

When I'd asked Degas if he would be attending Varnishing Day he said he'd rather be on display in the morgue "where at least there's a plate of glass between you and the viewers." His acceptance is a portrait of a former ballerina. She's quite attractive in it so I must assume she is a true beauty in person.

She's arranged on a red divan and the sunset stains the wall in behind a deep blood-orange. Needless to say, the painting shines amid the Van Dyke browns covering the rest of the wall. It exudes passion and romance, which made me realize how little I know of my friend's inner life. I have yet to see him with a woman on his arm, nor has he ever shown interest in one. Édouard actually teased him about it last Thursday.

They don't scratch or bite, you know, said Édouard, except for the most excitable.

Degas had no retort. Those two couldn't be more different.

We found Édouard on the bench in Room L looking rooted to the spot. Perched on his either side were Antoine and Suzanne, who watched him like one might an unpredictable child. Despite his bright yellow gloves—the ones he'd had Fanny wear—and glaring vest, his usual optimism was muted. Antoine stood to greet us while Édouard stared at the floor. This did nothing to assuage my fears. Susanne, always solicitous, offered Maman her place on the bench which she declined.

I asked why he wasn't in with his work.

The truth? he said. I'm afraid Le Balcon *is absolutely terrible. Terrible.*

My stomach rolled over. Why? I stammered. What's wrong with it? I held back from reminding him that it may be his name on the painting, but it's my face and figure. And Antoine's and Fanny's.

He shrugged and contradicted himself saying that he knew in his heart it would be a great success. That I would bring him luck and fortune. Me? How? His erratic behaviour was not reassuring. I wanted to flee.

Maman said she would like to see it and took my arm. Antoine said he'd accompany us. Suzanne reached for Édouard's hand to comfort him and he snatched his away.

The smallish crowd in front of Le Balcon *meant that we were still clothed at least. And no one was laughing or yelling or spitting.*

We crossed the floor and I steeled myself. Maman whispered, We will sever all ties with the Manets if he has in any way diminished you.

Edma, the painting was as bizarre as it was incomprehensible—Fanny in those giant gloves, that chrysanthemum pinned to her head, boots showing, Antoine, all dressed up and doing who knew what, and me in that floppy dress and bulky jewelry refusing to look at him. But it is neither seditious nor sensational. That was a relief. If anything it is comical. I'm more strange than ugly in it. He has darkened my green eyes to near-black and darkened my hair and brows. He caught tension in my neck, my brooding, and my face and lips are pinched. Is that how he sees me? Dark and angry and pinched? But he had proved his initial intention. For I am not a hay bale, Edma. My face and figure are expressive and full of feeling.

Antoine insisted the eye trained directly on to me. It's clear, Berthe, that you have inspired Édouard.

You look menacing, said Maman.

In contrast to my figure, Antoine's and Fanny's expressions are flat and blank. As a message to himself? To me?

Maman asked why Mme. Manet's dog was under my chair with his toy ball. I hadn't noticed until she pointed it out. We need you here, Edma, to decipher things for us. What do Fanny's gloves represent and why is Antoine's hand stuck up in the air? Édouard never "explains" his work—but I don't think he himself knows the answers. He seems to paint from a different engine than logic, one free of analysis and parsing. Perhaps this unguarded way of working explains his vulnerability to criticism. I grant you, he is more complex a person than I've allowed.

Édouard appeared, announcing he had just been asked the price of Le Balcon. *He said I was bringing him luck. He disappeared into the crowd again without so much as a glance at his painting.*

"Who would even consider it?" said Maman. "Other than as an after-dinner amusement for his guests?" I had to agree.

I was hoping to see something more by Claude Monet this year, but Édouard cheerfully told me "the scoundrel's" paintings had been rejected.

Édouard and Monet had recently been introduced to one another at the Café Guerbois. Apparently Édouard described Monet as "young, short and dangerously confident." Monet was deferential, said Antoine, and referred to Édouard as "our way forward."

I will be sure to bring novels and newspapers as you have asked and you'll see that I didn't bring Édouard any more luck with the critics. Le Figaro *said Édouard lacks imagination.* Le Siecle *suggested he requires more training to improve his technique. These must have stung. But the worst insult of all, because he is—or was—a friend, is from Zola who wrote in* L'Evenement*: "This latest provocation was for the sake of controversy more than merit."*

They will have some making up to do.

Most infuriating, critics devoted more words to my painted figure than they ever have to my paintings. If you can believe it, several used the term femme fatale. *Me? Seductive and dangerous? Papa did not see the humour. Said I had compromised my dignity and embarrassed him. I informed him that modern art is a mirror of the viewer's own attitudes. You can guess how that went over. Without you here to keep the peace, Maman intervened, calling the painting a joke and both of us ludicrous for taking it seriously. He and I now avoid each other.*

Degas sent a note to tell me my figure was darkly feminine though he called the painting as a whole a meaningless circus. Eugène sent his compliments and described my figure as intriguing and mesmerizing. Having friends project their opinions and fantasies on to me feels vulgar. But don't tell Papa I said so.

Oh, my other news is that Édouard has accepted Eva Gonzales as his student. Not only that but he asked the fish-faced woman to model for him. Degas says she resembles "a turbot in a school of one." I know how unkind that sounds, and it is shameful of me to repeat it, especially about a fellow woman painter. See what's happening since you and your reason left? I'm not only compromised but cruel.

Edma, it just so happens that Uncle Octave has some business in Lorient. Auntie will accompany him and be my chaperone. So now I will arrive earlier, on April 22nd.

How I envy your ability to go about without a constant minder. I feel like some overgrown child. Degas, who has trouble sleeping, told me he takes long walks in the middle of the night. Alone. Just him and the feasting rats clearing the streets of horse manure. When I asked what that was like, he said it was like being Emperor of your own thoughts and the world your dreamlike creation. Oh, the fortunes of being a man.

So my packing has begun and I count the days until I am on the train to you. Papa, I suspect, is counting them too.

Love, Berthe

April 13th, 1869

Dearest Berthe,

I am sorry to hear that Édouard's work continues to go unappreciated. That Zola now counts among his critics must cut deeply. But he has not let censure defeat him before, and is too optimistic to let it defeat him now. I wouldn't have guessed anger in a woman could be interpreted as mystery. Perhaps femme fatale *is how Édouard imagined you. And the little dog beneath your skirts? Could it speak of his devotion to his family? There is a balcony railing keeping you apart from him, no? As well as your two chaperones Antoine and Fanny. I analyze from afar but maybe he harbours desires that are fraught with obstacles. Not desire for you, Berthe—I know the strained nature of your relationship—but for those* femme fatales *which you represent. Considering his curious relationship with his wife and popularity with women, he must contend with guilt. But honestly, no matter his intentions, if indeed he had any, I'm jealous that you inspired his hand as you did.*

Maman told me she invited Mme. Higgonet's nephew last Tuesday and that twice he tried to engage you in conversation and both times you pretended you had something pressing. If he looks anything like his aunt, I can't blame you. She has a mysterious Monsieur G still in her box of hopefuls so be forewarned. She believes painting brings you few rewards so won't rest until you're settled. Know that you always have my support. Being settled is just how it sounds. Especially now that I'm officially with child and Adolphe won't let me entertain in the evenings for fear of tiring me out. He's also afraid of touching me. I confess I'm content to be left alone, yet fear our time of intimacy was tragically short and that he may be disappointed, even frustrated, though he would never show it. Sex for a man seems as basic a need as water and food. Are we all animals in the end?

You won't like hearing it but I sometimes wish he had a mistress to go to. As long as it wasn't a serious union, it would satisfy my practical nature that one of my duties was being fulfilled. I really don't think I would be the least resentful. Love and sex, in my opinion, are not the same. Love is a meadow flush with wildflowers, crickets and field mice, while sex is a muddy underground creek running beneath a corner of that meadow. A small unsightly part necessary for watering that which grows above.

Lately my nausea has begun to abate. The midwife tells me that by the time you arrive, it will be safe for me to enjoy the garden and take walks along the harbour. As long as I can sit down on the job, I can be your model if you'd like. I would like to feel of benefit to someone.

See you so very soon. I count the hours, Edma

EDMA AND I EMBRACED and wept there in the train station, Auntie doing her best to shield us, Adolphe tipping his hat to onlookers, embarrassed.

"You look wonderful," I said through my sobs.

"You mean plump." She laughed, wiping at her eyes.

Though her pregnancy was not yet showing, her bosom was fuller, her movements more weighted. And what her cook said seemed true: Edma's features had softened to make her look exquisitely feminine.

I liked how Adolphe insisted she take his arm when walking, even from carriage to house, and fetched her pillows and footrest whenever she sat down. Their town house was clean and uncluttered, reflective of my sister's orderly nature. The cold blues and whites of the décor she had warmed with green plants and chocolate satin pillows for the davenports and sashes for the curtains.

To be reunited with Edma felt like coming home to myself. And because Adolphe forbade her from entertaining, I had her to myself, except on Sundays when she went to church and I opted to remain behind and work.

Her strapping and spirited cook, Manon, referred to me as Mlle. Little Sister. She insisted I was too thin and that "Women must have reserves to get through the trying times." She forced on me her buttery raisin cakes and dolloped *crème fraiche* into my coffee, tea and soup. Her cooking (there was duck fat in everything) was as delicious as Edma had claimed. I would gain eight pounds that summer, too many for my liking.

Away from my parents and united with Edma, I teemed with inspiration, the need to paint as essential as oxygen.

May 10th, 1869

My Dearest Daughters,
I am alight with envy that you are together once more in your secretive world of two. I trust that you, Berthe, will finally resolve to paint something. You shouldn't miss another Salon or your name will be forgotten. But do be careful not to exhaust your sister.

Edma, you must take exceptionally good care of yourself. La grossesse, *at your age, is difficult and* la premiere grossesse *the most trying of all. Keeping your feet raised will prevent them from swelling. Avoid all raw foods, very dangerous for the baby, and drink at least one full glass of wine each day. This will produce a nice calm child. I failed to do this with Berthe and Tibby and just look at them, one nervous and moody, the other a restless wanderer.*

Speaking of restless natures, I was returning some books borrowed from Eugènie Manet and Édouard was there with his protégé, Mlle. Eva Gonzales. I didn't realize she's not yet twenty. She cannot rival you, Berthe, in face, but appears to be a rival for you in talent. Édouard is unabashed in praising her way with a brush and how well she takes instruction.

So Berthe, you are out of Édouard's thoughts for the time being as he's now painting Eva at her easel with brush and palette. As he should have done of you if he had any sense. He said he believes Eva will be famous one day and the painting of great value. Talented female painters are a rarity, he spouted, right in front of me. But then he often says whatever comes in to his head without consideration. For he is a man with no self-censor.

I informed them that you, Edma, are expecting. You have their hearty congratulations. Édouard asked when you, Berthe, would be returning to Paris. I told him not until September. He launched into more praise for Mlle. Gonzales, insisting her debut at next year's Salon would bring a flurry of attention. I couldn't tell if he was lauding her or lauding himself as her instructor.

Eugène sends his regards to you both and especially to you, Berthe. The poor man is enamoured of you, that much is clear. I discovered his appartement *is in the rue de Monceau near the park. Very nice old homes in that area. If only he had a proper career or post of some kind. I cannot trust a man without a singular occupation. At present he is painting watercolours of his garden and helping to write Communard propaganda for Gustave. Such idealism can only lead to trouble, says your father. I'm glad Tibby has steered clear. One should never stir a pot that's not boiling, and yet Eugènie supports her sons' leanings unequivocally. Even when I told her what your father told me, that the police now have an eye on all the Manet brothers for subversive behaviour against the Empire. Do you know what she said? "Passion and youth are short-lived and must not be repressed. For all great things come of passion."*

Fine words until somebody gets arrested or killed. The whole family is a little off-centre if you ask me.

And then Suzanne came into the drawing room looking like a true song peddler, a rag over her shoulder, her moon face a shiny crimson. A tattered petticoat outlined her great stomach and dirty slippers her feet. She was doing the cleaning! She doted on Édouard as if he were a child, plucking at his jacket, arranging his hair. She was attentive to Eugènie's comforts, but really she had nothing of interest to offer the conversation. I suppose the piano is her singular talent. She is very accomplished; I will afford her that.

Tibby has returned from Portugal dark as a negro and suffering a poor stomach. But already he is planning a trip to America. I am trying to dissuade him out of it, at least until he is fully recovered. I'm at a loss as to the kind of woman that might sustain his affections though Eugènie mentioned a niece of hers who sounds promising.

Well, your father finally attended the Salon and saw Le Balcon *for himself. He thinks Fanny Claus looks Asian and decided that with her gardening gloves and "that cabbage" on her head she represents the Asian goddess Le Chou. Funny, no?*

He did not comment on your portrait, Berthe, other than to say he barely recognized you. Probably a good thing. I kept quiet.

Cadart, I'm afraid, has not sold any of your pieces, Berthe, and I am obliged to go collect them, which I will do this week. Perhaps seeing Edma's happiness will convince you, Berthe, to consider more serious commitments in your life.

Take care of each other until I see you again, your loving Maman

---

EDMA PROVED THE perfect model, her condition lending her an enviable serenity. Taking her suggestion of the view of the harbour, I painted her along its parapet, boats and their masts in behind, the town in the distance. After my painting drought, my brush surprised me with a startling discovery. One that had nothing to do with whether the object I was painting was cloud or hull, stone or reflection, large or small, dark or light, but everything to do with my feeling toward a particular object. My beloved sister in white dress and black hat weighted my brush with paint while the water of the harbour did not. I took comfort in the warm stone of the wall and saturated it with colour while the wood of the boats required less. And because I worried the people along the *quai* might disapprove of a woman painting in public, they too loaded my brush. Impressing my sentiments onto the canvas in this way magically relieved me. I can think of no other description of the alchemy I discovered there on the *quai*.

With a lighter hand I painted the morning sky, the townhomes along the far left shore, the water's storied reflections, its anchored boats. Patient Adolphe assisted me in rendering the details of the boats.

I did a second portrait of Edma, again dressed in white, seated in the upstairs sitting room of her new home. I discovered a thrilling secret about white: white did not merely reflect or offset other colours, white swallowed and absorbed colours. Like an overprotective mother, it held them dear inside its cloak of light.

After each painting was finished to my satisfaction I added my hidden accents of scarlet. Watching my newfound gratification, Edma questioned the point of a life deprived of artistic expression.

THAT SEPTEMBER Edma and I returned together to Paris a week before Edma's lying-in in order for Maman to host a gathering in her honour. Arriving home, Edma lamented with uncharacteristic sentimentality how much she missed Paris. She spent hours in our studio with her old canvases as if to resurrect her former self and former life.

I believed I'd accomplished something unique in Lorient and was eager to show my friends my paintings, especially Édouard. This business with Eva Gonzales poked at the beast of my competitive nature and I wanted to prove to him my artistic superiority. In anticipation of Maman's soirée, I took great pains to arrange the studio's candle lamps in order to present them in the best light.

Degas, as usual, was the first to arrive. As soon as he'd a glass of his favourite claret in hand, I invited him out to the studio. Incapable of pretense, he, I knew, would give his honest assessment.

He assumed the posture he does when appraising a painting: one arm across his ribs to support the elbow of the other, thumb hooking his chin, index finger running side to side along his hopeful moustache. If it had been appropriate for a woman to paint a man who was not her husband, I would have captured him in this pose.

He sniffed a few times in front of the harbour painting. "I like Edma's posture," he said finally. "The head's incline under her parasol. Bravo. A fiercely feminine presence. Without her the composition would be just another pretty landscape. And the stone parapet. The colours are textured. Accurate."

Stepping in front of the other, he sighed. "Oh, the sequestered passion of the bored." He moved in closer. "The red slipper and red fan are a superb touch. Gives an otherwise provincial scene a heart-beat."

It was not the reaction I had hoped for. I didn't yet know that this modest assessment was Degas' version of praise.

He asked me if they were finished.

"If you thought them finished," I said, "you wouldn't have asked the question. If you don't like them just say so." I had left swaths of space in each painting believing that, as in the paintings of Japan, such space is expressive in itself.

"Berthe, they're charming, they are. Have no doubt."

"Charming."

"It's not exactly the kind of scene that interests me."

In need of more effusive compliments, as soon as Rosalie had kissed and cooed over Edma, I dragged her out to the studio. She didn't disappoint. But then she couldn't help wondering aloud about the asymmetry of the harbour. "Perhaps a partial sail in the left foreground for balance?" And regarding the emptiness of Edma's sitting room she suggested a vase of flowers on the bureau, "to hide the wallpaper." To add to my misery she said, "Perhaps you're not finished with them."

I clung to and tried to convince myself of Marcello's words that truly original work will not be immediately pleasing to others. After all, this was something Édouard proved time and again.

Would he see that I had attempted the same turquoise-green for the window awnings in *The Artist's Sister at a Window* as he had used in *Le Balcon*? The same red tones for her fan as the one he'd had me hold and, just as he had dressed me in white, so I had dressed Edma. And that my whites possessed a depth his did not. Could he acknowledge that I might do some things better than he?

And certainly better than his Eva Gonzales?

He arrived to our soiree late, as always, and in high spirits, clapping men on the back and making love to the women. I had been away four months and just now realized how much I had missed his face and vigour, the way he cocked his chin to the side while telling a joke, the details paid to his dress—tonight a vest and cravat the deep blue of an evening sky, with silver and onyx cufflinks winking from his coat sleeves. He had kissed the cheeks of all the ladies in the room but mine. He doted on Edma to the point that I felt the familiar hollowness of the invisible.

As the evening wore on and he still had not acknowledged my existence, I insinuated myself into his conversation with Rosalie.

"Imagine what the walls of the Salon would look like if we ruled the jury," said Édouard.

"*Utterly* different," said Rosalie.

"It might be interesting," I slipped in, "to see the rooms arranged by style and technique rather than the surname."

I had felt lightly chilled all evening but under his sudden gaze I grew inexplicitly heated. I smiled. He didn't. Rather than a greeting or a welcoming me home, he said, "I wonder in which category you'd place my student, Eva. Now there's a young woman as dedicated to her craft as any man. You know she never misses a lesson and spends hours each day in her studio."

"I'm glad you're pleased with her," I lied.

"She's done a fifer, a tribute to mine. Even I have to admit it's superior. It's hard to believe she is—"

"Nineteen?"

"And how is your portrait of her coming?" I asked him, all innocence. Rosalie glanced at me. She had relayed a rumour of his struggles.

"No one sits as still. Remarkable. I'm having some difficulty getting her head right. But I'll get it."

"You should see the exceptional paintings Berthe produced in Lorient," said Rosalie, though I had no intention of showing him now, after being compared to his seamless student.

"They still require attention." My estimation of them had been deflated enough. If Édouard's opinion was less flattering, their ruin would be complete.

"So, Berthe"—Édouard now held my eye—"you were able to rise from your laziness and paint?"

With a mind all its own, my hand flew up to slap his face. He jerked back and I missed all but the hair of his bearded chin. Rosalie's small scream brought me to my senses. Édouard leaned in and watched me eagerly, as one might a wild animal in the zoo.

"What's behind this boorish remark, Édouard?" said Rosalie, graciously directing notice away from me to Édouard. "The painting not going well?"

I fled to my room. There I paced, swinging from fury to humiliation and back again. Wise Rosalie gave me time alone before she came knocking. I was concerned Edma or Maman had witnessed my behaviour and she assured me they had not. "He was deliberately provoking you, Berthe. Your reaction was understandable."

"It happened before I could think. I'm so embarrassed."

"It is Édouard whose behaviour warrants embarrassment."

I was grateful for her words but the evening left me feeling old and alone—yet, also, just piqued enough to excel in my work. During Edma's confinement I confined myself as well. I painted a double portrait of Maman reading to Edma and another of just Edma. For this one, and because it was Édouard's pride of colour to paint, I dressed her in black determined to outshine him. But this sum of all colour, full as a stuffed purse, sat flat and ugly on the canvas. Reflective of the light, it rejected every colour I used to try to give it dimension and life. Remembering Édouard's smugness and unapologetic face kept me from throwing down my brush. Maman protested that Edma's pregnant figure was not a suitable artistic subject and made me promise these two portraits would never leave the house. That I was breaking some unspoken taboo made me all the more tenacious. Alone in the studio, I painted into the night, studying the black beyond my lamps until my eyes ached and my head hurt.

IT WAS THE DISORIENTING dead of night when I woke to a candle lamp burning on my dresser and November's bite, the fire reduced to embers. Edma was in my room, by the window, holding open the curtains and looking out, her white housecoat a ghostly blue in the moonlight. Our attempt to share a bed had been cut short by her snoring and she had settled into Yves' former room. She dropped the curtains and hunched like a snared animal. A low groan climbed into a high-pitched whine.

"Edma?"

"It's started," she said at the top of her whine. "The baby's coming."

"Are you sure?" I fumbled to light my bedside lamp.

She came and sat beside me. "There's no looking back." And with that Edma began to weep as I had never seen her weep. As though darkness itself heaved up from the deepest part of her.

"I'll never paint," she sobbed. "I'll be chained... my life ordinary as any *housfrau*... my thoughts lost in fevers... and nannies and... and... and little clothes." The wail that cascaded up from her throat pushed me out of my quilts. I embraced her and her enormous belly which, pressed into my side, rose and hardened like a giant's fist. Her wailing gathered into an animal's growl.

"We must wake Maman. Send for the midwife."

"Wait," she hissed through clenched teeth. After a minute her pain eased, I'd climbed into a dressing gown, and the weeping continued. "I used to see the shimmer of light in and around objects, Berthe. Vision has gone. The world has turned from me."

I groped for a handkerchief in the bedside drawer and handed it to her.

"I gave up that gift for what? A man? Does he inspire me? Will—" Another low moan and she was on her feet, grabbing her stomach. My sister, who'd never shouted at anyone, shouted, "Take my arms." As I stood, her fingers dug into my outstretched arms at the shoulders. I grasped hers. Like the sumo wrestlers we'd seen at the Exposition, she pushed and I pushed back.

In the candle's flickering shadows her nostrils flared in quick breaths, her clamped jaw jutted forward and her eyes rolled back. My beautiful sister turned hideous. Now her face tilted to the ceiling, mouth unhinging with a descending cry as if falling into an abyss. Was this normal? Yves was the only other labouring woman I'd witnessed and there had been barely a noise from her—though during the worst of it, I had fled and hidden in the far end of the garden. Edma's grip slackened, her breath catching up to itself, and I was released.

"I'm calling Pauline." I slipped around her and found my slippers.

"My figure will be ruined," she wailed and paced inside the small circle of light. "My bosom will sag. My youth gone. My dreams. I never dared speak of them but I had dreams, Berthe"—she stopped and looked at me with swollen eyes—"enormous dreams. Medals. Paintings hung in the galleries of London, New—"

I moved for the door but she blocked my exit. "Again," she yelled and slapped at my arms. Arms locked, I pushed against her uncanny strength. A piercing keening began. Surely this would wake Maman, but it was Papa who hustled through the door on stiff discoloured legs, still tying his dressing down. We must have looked as though one of us were attacking the other.

"Send for the midwife," I said, struggling to stay upright. "Wake Maman and Pauline."

"Will she be all right? Edma dear!"

At the sound of her father's voice, Edma went quiet, dropped her arms and righted herself, casting me to one knee.

"I'll be fine, Papa," she said, chest heaving. Her face was blotched and puffy, her smile a grimace. She smoothed her hair. "Please go back to bed and don't concern yourself"—she sounded as if she'd not a care in the world—"and you'll meet your new grandchild in the morning."

The scene was grotesque and he left as quickly as he'd arrived. When the door closed behind him she wailed, "I cannot do this."

"You can, Edma." I was wholly unsure.

"I will give the child to Yves."

What was she saying? It was not a time to argue or plan futures.

"I will leave Adolphe." She stared hard at me, making sure I understood.

"Oh, Edma." To imagine her home again was my joy, yet no woman could ever survive such a fall. She crawled up on to the bed as though to escape from herself, folded over her knees and planted her weeping face in her hands.

The door swung open and Maman, hair draping her collarbone in two childlike braids, feet bare, took one look at her weeping daughter and became calm as still water. She spoke clearly and slowly, her tone offhand. "Your baby is finally ready to meet its wonderful mother. Will it be a boy or a girl? What do you think, Berthe? A handsome little Edme or beautiful little Jeanne?" These were the names Edma had chosen. Edme was Papa's second name.

"I don't know," I said, struggling to adopt Maman's pace and tone, "but I do look forward to finding out."

Maman had performed some ancient female magic, for Edma ceased crying, lifted her head and slowly sat up. I felt faint with relief.

Maman spoke to sleepy-eyed Pauline in the same slow, easy manner and Pauline left and returned with wine, which Edma dutifully drank. Crooning continually to Edma, Maman led the way back to Yves' room, I carried the lamp and Pauline ran ahead to set a fire. We stopped in the hall for Edma to press both palms to the wall and moan out her river of pain. I collected towels, silk blankets and extra quilts. Pauline was to boil water and bring soap.

The midwife arrived. Not the tall manly one who had attended Yves but one small and ancient. Under a dusty cape she wore a cheerless black smock and skirt. She had a vulture's hump and a face etched like tree bark. Ash-coloured hair, thick and greased, was knotted into a bun that rode the shelf of her back. As black as her clothing, her eyes were implacably aware.

Maman inquired after the nursemaid for whom she had long since made arrangements.

"I'm sorry, Madame," Pauline reported. "She's down with fever. An abscess in the breast."

"She tells us now? Stupid woman." Maman didn't take well to others frustrating her plans.

Edma whimpered, "What will we do?"

The midwife washed her knotty hands in a bowl of steaming water and dried them on her smock. "You're more than capable of doing the job yourself." There was disdain in her tone and Maman clucked her tongue.

"There's no shame," the midwife advised with cold clarity, "in providing for your own child." She rolled up one sleeve. "As women have done since first dawn." She was having none of our bourgeois ways. Dependent as we were upon her skills, Maman held her tongue.

At Yves' request neither Edma nor I had witnessed our niece's birth. So this would be a first for us both. I held one of Edma's hands and Maman the other. I wiped her brow with a cool cloth but could not keep my hand from shaking while Maman encouraged her in understated tones. Edma whimpered but no longer wailed. There was a stranger present.

During the final stages, the midwife turned Edma on her side to face me. As she pushed one body from another, Edma clenched my hands and stared directly, maniacally into my eyes. I didn't dare look away. Her emotions froze, she was all business now, engrossed in the bloody work of women. Her muted sounds that of the purest suffering. I synchronized my breathing with hers in an attempt to draw away and share her pain, an act that likely helped her less than it did me.

The sun had risen by the time the baby arrived, a tiny red-faced girl with a mat of dark hair, Adolphe's broad cheeks and, it seemed, Edma's even disposition. Unlike Yves' baby, whose post-birth howls reached the end of the garden, baby Jeanne barely mewled as she was placed wet and cheesy on Edma's pillow of a belly.

"A keeper," grunted the midwife, as if she'd hauled up a fish. She ordered us to remove Edma's nightdress.

Maman was perplexed. "Is that really necess—"

"Only if you want this child to survive."

Maman huffed but together we peeled Edma's moist nightdress over her head while Maman was quick to lay a silk blanket across Edma's bared breasts. Just as quickly the midwife snatched it away to cover the child where it lay face down on Edma, fists curled and bud-like. Stains bloomed on the white silk like black roses. Edma stared at her child, brow knit and frowning. I watched her carefully.

"You must wash the baby first," said Maman.

The midwife ignored her.

"And then wrap it tightly."

"Would you wash and bind a newborn puppy?"

"Did my daughter just give birth to a puppy?" Now that a baby was safely delivered, Maman's composure dissolved.

The midwife turned her back and addressed Edma. "Mother, look at me." Edma lifted her defenceless eyes. "Stroke her back, Mother, and talk to her. She'll know what to do."

Maman stiffened. "That's not—" She began to defiantly tuck the blanket under the baby's feet.

"Maman, leave them. Please!" If Edma did reject the baby, there was no wet nurse to take over. Maman threw up her hands and sat back down.

Edma, as instructed, stroked the stained silk and spoke to the rumpled face which responded by squinting up at her and licking its tiny lips. Then I saw it, the umbilicus running out from the bottom of the blanket. A bloodied and pulsing satin rope in dreamlike shades of blue, silver and white, living colours like glowing water. I was at once repulsed and scrambling for just what mix of shades could capture its life. Muttering about a nursemaid, Maman left us.

A peace settled in the room. The midwife clamped and cut the sinuous cord, its life having drained into the baby, then sat at the end of the bed, waiting silently for whatever bloody event might come next. I sat in a chair beside my sister, who watched her daughter with an intensity that reminded me of how she used to focus on painting. I stroked her hair and she stroked her baby's hair and all at once one of the baby's tiny hands bloomed fingers which it slowly pushed into the pursed circle of a mouth. Those dampened fingers made their graceless way to fumble Edma's nipple, which magically became erect, flushing a darker pink. The other nipple too.

"Another pain coming," said the midwife.

Edma barely winced at this last effort, which was placed in a pan on my side of the bed, a disturbing blackish organ smelling of butchered meat. I politely asked the midwife if it could be moved. She snorted but moved it to the other side of the bed.

Achingly slow and with heartbreaking intent, the baby wormed her way to Edma's exposed breast, her Sisyphean head bouncing on and off Edma's skin like a pecking bird before collapsing in exhaustion.

Edma's breasts were bloated and ripe, the white glowing skin streaked with fine bluish-green lines like underground tributaries. Before this morning, breasts had been swellings that gave shape to a dress or sculpture. Here they pulsed with near holy purpose. Looking uncertain, Edma continued to stroke and coo, guiding the baby's efforts lest she slip off and onto the bed. Adopting Maman's calm tones, I encouraged both baby and mother.

An hour must have passed since the baby arrived, yet she had still not fed. I approached the midwife as she sat in the corner whispering with Pauline and enjoying bread, cheese, apricots and wine, the birth as though forgotten. With deference I informed her that the baby was not yet feeding.

"You can't rush nature," said the midwife, filling her cup with more wine, "without ill effect."

"I fear the little thing's exhausted," I whispered. "Please, come and see."

She shook her chin at me, took a bite of bread and turned to Pauline. "The will to live is relentless." She proceeded to ignore me.

I returned to Edma and forced a smile. "You're doing everything just right."

New mewlings rose from the baby who now lifted her head and licked Edma's nipple. Then her head fell sideways with a deadened thump. I had never seen a creature work so hard. Edma seemed oblivious to time passing but as the minutes wore on, I judged the baby too weak to survive. Could we not force the nipple into the baby's mouth? Where was Maman?

With one last heroic effort and clutching the gleaming skin of Edma's breast in a fist, the baby raised her head, unhinged her small mouth wider than seemed possible and clamped her lips up and over Edma's nipple.

Edma gasped.

My breath let go.

"She's so strong," whispered Edma.

"The strongest are those that nurse on their own mother's tits," spat the midwife over her shoulder.

Edma looked at me with eyes I didn't recognize. "Manon says the very same."

"Does she?"

"Oh, look, Berthe, she's staring at me. Hello, Jeanne Marie Pontillon. Wherever did you come from? You truly are a miracle.

Just like your papa says."

That morning, I watched my sister fall as if from a great height into love. A choiceless plummet with no hand or footholds and a landing so strong and sure that nothing could upset it. This was not the sister I'd spent the summer with nor the one who wept and bemoaned her fate earlier in my room.

I stayed until she and baby Jeanne were asleep, Edma insisting, despite Maman's protests, that the baby sleep right there between her naked breasts and not in the new cradle Maman had had made and spent weeks outfitting.

IT TOOK FIVE DAYS before Maman secured a nursemaid but by then Edma was so fiercely attached to feeding her own child, she wouldn't even allow the woman to hold Jeanne.

"You will not be fit for your husband," warned Maman. "You will lose your strength and your baby will be spoilt and overly attached to her mother."

"I will nurse her until I am back home in Lorient. I will not discuss it further."

Maman was taken aback by Edma's tone but acquiesced that it was natural to be protective of one's child and left it at that. As for Edma's fevered threat of giving away her baby and leaving Adolphe—it was never mentioned again.

FRIENDS AND FAMILY sent notes and gifts to the house. Mme. Manet sent three jars of prune plums "to aid Edma's constitution," a special mix of herbs to "dry up her milk," and a bottle of wine to "help her sleep." Eugène's signature was on the card just under his mother's. An aluminum rattle tied with a pink ribbon arrived from Édouard and Suzanne. I read the note, wondering if he might have slipped in a belated apology but even his signature had been penned by Suzanne. I hoped Eva Gonzales' fishy face still eluded his brush.

When mother and baby returned to Lorient, I imagined Adolphe would not recognize his top-heavy wife who was as deliciously content as the child she nursed. Watching them go was like losing Edma all over again, only worse, for now our paths had permanently diverged. The house felt dreary and lifeless and Papa badgered me at every opportunity, to help Maman count the silver or sort laundry, or arrange flowers for company. He too was distraught at losing Edma.

I kept to my studio and fussed over what to send to the Salon. Despite tepid responses from friends and despite their "unfinished state," when the day came I let my two Lorient works be placed on the submission cart. It was my first time submitting without Edma and I couldn't help worry if previous juries had only accepted my paintings because of her superior ones. Perhaps Papa was right. I was useless.

1870

ALL THE TALK that spring concerned Prussia. I had no taste for the squabbles of kings who seemed to care nothing for the lives of ordinary people, but digested the name Bismark at every meal.

My Lorient paintings were accepted to the Salon and I wrote Edma to tell her what luck she had brought me. She promptly wrote back her congratulations but it was clear that any envy, longing or even interest in the world of art had been displaced by her infatuation with baby Jeanne. She even spoke of Adolphe with greater affection.

Turns out I am fiercely maternal. Jeanne is smiling now and I spend all my time trying to ignite that smile on her sweet face. I now know, without any doubt, what love is, unconditioned and unreserved.

Don't tell Maman, but I have not yet procured a wet nurse. Manon says all the wet nurses in Lorient have been feeding babies for so long — as many as seven at a time — that their blood is thin as water and so is their milk. I think it may be true since my sister-in-law's little boy has a constant cough and runny nose while Jeanne has had no illness to date. May we continue to be so blessed. The peasants really do know much more about these things than we. Manon also says nursing will ward off my menses and help prevent my becoming pregnant too soon. Though all I think of is having a second, and even a third, for I've not only an excess of milk but of love. As if the two go together.

Adolphe is, of course, privy to my decision to nurse Jeanne and doesn't seem to mind. In order to hide it from his mother and my friends, I hired a buxom nanny. Yes, I'm more housebound but for the time being am content in my own garden. You'll laugh, but in order to remain decent and provide Jeanne quick access to her milk, I sliced open four of my daywear bodices and even one evening dress vertically over each breast and added a curtain of pleated fabric from bust line to waist. A strange new fashion that doesn't look too bad. I tell everyone it's a design I admired in a Paris window display and they accept the vagaries of haute coutour without question. Maman would be horrified.

Edma's letter also contained a warning.

Adolphe's commander calls Prussia not so much a country with an army as an army with a country. He's expressed alarm over our Emperor's recent provocation regarding Prussia's liaison with Spain. I try and believe it's just an arm-wrestling match between the pompous and that nothing will come of it. How could anyone choose war when cherry trees are in blossom—it is as though a pink cloud has landed in the west corner. Jeanne is mesmerized by the sensation of those petals along her cheek and lips. Again, congratulations. I guess it is my turn to hang on the walls of the Salon and have my face and figure be judged.

Yours, Edma

THE PRIDE I FELT at my acceptances dimmed as I read in *Le Figaro* that the wondrous Eva Gonzales, submitting for her first time, had three paintings accepted. Three! Oh, how Édouard would gloat. I scanned down the list of acceptances. His portrait of her had also made the cut. I closed the paper and ripped it down the middle.

I did not ask to attend Varnishing Day nor Opening Day, certain that if seen together with Eva Gonzales critics would equate and compare us. We were, after all, of the same class, both admirers of Manet's work, and both had now modeled for him. Yet despite my effort, in each and every infuriating paper, the critics referred to me as a student of Manet—as if I too were a girl of nineteen—more than one wondering why my paintings were left unfinished. Eva's reviews, though, were numerous and stellar. As I complained aloud at breakfast, Maman regarded me with pity and Papa suggested I take up sewing.

I attended the Salon with Rosalie, chaperoned by her mother, Laure. Rosalie had not submitted work that year, her time spent caring for her grand-mère who had died at the end of February, and in receiving the attentions of Honoré Pousin, an architectural engineer fifteen years her senior. We had been introduced at the Reiseners'. A plain-looking man, fastidious in the way of architects, Honoré Pousin was economical in word and gesture, his humour limited to its lowest form—puns. The way Rosalie behaved with him suggested that, like Edma, she had given up on passion and was settling for decency. I asked Rosalie her feelings. From observing her parents, she told me, she had learned that love developed over time between loyal partners. "Passionate love exists only in novels. And even then it never ends well."

Approaching Room G for Gonzales and knowing how I felt about Eva, Rosalie suggested we skip it. But I had to see my competition. Édouard thought her superior to me in every way, the critics too, and I needed to know why. I liked to think I was woman enough to admit her superiority if it was deserved.

Though this was her Salon debut and not one of her paintings contained nudity, Eva's three works were centrally hung. Did her father have friends on the jury? Rosalie and I stood in front of her portrait of a uniformed boy playing a pipe, her homage to Édouard's *Le Fife*. She was well trained, that was obvious, her technique sound. I couldn't tell if she had an eye for colour, because her palette was a direct copy of Édouard's. But he had been right, her fifer was superior to his. There was an affecting seriousness in the work that even I couldn't deny.

"She's very good." I tried to sound magnanimous. "Exceptional for her age."

"She's copying, doing nothing new," scoffed Rosalie, and moved over to the next one.

"A woman at the opera," sighed Rosalie. "Vapid expression, lots of décolletage, a beaked soldier who has brought her a bouquet of violets with a single white rose. The rose represents the painter, no doubt, in all her virgin purity. An insipid personal fantasy."

Loyal Rosalie.

"And look at the face of this milliner," she said in front of the last. "Distorted as though reflected in a silver tea service."

I linked my arm through hers and together we strode off to Room H.

Édouard, Suzanne, Mme. Manet and Léon had spent the winter months in Holland; I had not laid eyes on Édouard since Edma's homecoming and was convinced I need never lay eyes on him again. He didn't deserve my attention and therefore, I told myself, neither did his portrait of Eva. Yet as soon as we entered Room M, my eye found his two paintings on the far wall. Brighter and louder than anything else in the room, they were like children clamouring for my attention. And like children, the more I refused them attention, the louder they became, following me like a second consciousness as we walked to where my Lorient paintings hung well below the centre line; one had to crouch to view them.

Rosalie pointed out all sorts of painterly abstractions I'd achieved. Laure kindly called them extraordinary. Like a beggar his heels of bread, I took any and all compliments.

I still believed I had done something original in *Harbour at Lorient* and clung to that thought as we moved ever closer to Édouard's paintings. Why was I anxious, fearful even, of seeing what he'd done with Mlle. Gonzales. It was nonsense. Yes, the portrait would reveal his feelings for her but I cared nothing for him so it didn't matter.

"This is curious," said Rosalie, having reached Édouard's paintings. I had let her drift ahead like a scout.

Why was my heart banging at my ribs, my eyes refusing to focus as I forced myself in front of his Eva?

"No one paints in a white dress," said Laure.

"No one paints in a white dress," I repeated and the painting came into focus. He had placed Eva primly on a chair in a fashionable white evening dress with short puffed sleeves.

One bare arm held her palette on its stick, whose end poked suggestively into the centre of her lap. I hiccupped a laugh. Her other hand extended her brush toward, but unable to reach, the painting on an easel. How difficult it must have been to hold up that arm. And then I saw that the painting on the easel was one of Édouard's. She was painting his painting. He was mocking her! Mocking her adoration, her copying his subject matter.

"It's very funny," said Rosalie.

Her face was even more fishy than I recalled and she had no true expression, none at all. She was as much a still life as the flower that lay on the floor by her feet.

"Yes. Very," I said but felt giddy at the thought: He feels nothing for her. Less than nothing.

Rosalie was saying that if she were Eva she would be mortified but my attention was fixed on the flower by her feet. A white peony. Perfectly executed. Had he not once offered to teach me how to paint a peony?

This portrait had been painted for my benefit. I was convinced of it. A tentative laugh escaped my throat, one I assume my companions took for scorn. The white peony not only professed the innocence of his relationship to Mlle. Gonzales but something more.

"Poor girl," said Rosalie. "Do you think she's seen it? Or has he kept it from her as he did to you with *Le Balcon*."

"Hmm…" Was the portrait a kind of test? As well as his blatant flattery of Eva in my presence? Exactly what kind of tests these might be, I didn't dare speculate for fear of the earth giving way under my feet.

But he had painted that peony for me. Of that I was certain.

ARRIVING HOME I rushed upstairs and wrote Édouard a note. Keeping in mind his treatment of me and in case I was completely mad, I kept it brief and simple.

Attended the Salon today. A perfectly executed peony, Berthe

I had the stable boy deliver it. The boy returned shortly thereafter with a note from Édouard.

Berthe, Praise for your Harbour at Lorient. *You have surpassed yourself. I am drawn in completely. My eye was led around the harbour, from one aspect to the next; all combined to create a single harmonious effect. It has a decidedly unfinished quality and yet that same quality feels like fresh sea air, cool water, hard rock.*

And the portrait of Edma at home. Her true expression. I'm not sure how you managed that. I do like the colour of your awnings. And the white of that dress has surpassed my knowledge of what white can do.

If you will, let me apologize for my unforgivable behaviour last fall. I was not myself. Édouard

Though I would refrain from sending it that night—such heated communication was hardly ladylike—I wrote a note immediately.

Apology accepted. And because I credit your daring for challenging me to try something new, I would like you to have Harbour at Lorient. *Berthe*

The gift was an impulsive gesture but felt right at the time. I sent off the note first thing the next morning and again the stable boy returned with a prompt response.

I would feel privileged to own a Morisot and twice privileged if you would sit for me again. A portrait of the woman. I have missed my favourite model. Édouard

I fanned myself with the card. If the peony was stating that he had no desire for Eva Gonzales, was he in the same breath stating a desire for me? But even if true… why take seriously a man who flirted with everyone and, worse, who toyed with my sister's feelings? Just yesterday I detested him.

I paced the room. What was the harm of another sitting? Of a little flirtation, as Edma once said. And this would be a portrait of me alone. The woman, he said. My skin shimmered at the thought. But why should I trust he whose moods were nothing but changeable?

I accepted his invitation with a caveat: *As long as you instruct me exactly how you'd like me to dress and do my hair.*

He wrote: *I'll leave these choices up to your good taste. No matter how great or few articles of clothing you wear, you will still be as lovely. I will be remaining in Paris for most of the summer season. When are you available? Missing you, Édouard*

Édouard Manet was making love to me. I folded the note and slipped it back into its envelope. I took it out and read it again.

I HAD PLANNED to spend the summer with Edma in Maurecourt but now told Maman that I wanted to attend the opening of Délibes' new ballet at the Imperial—Papa's poor health had ended his affair and Maman had magically regained a taste for the ballet—as well as witness the velocipedes race along the Seine. Then I slipped in, as a kind of second thought, that Édouard wanted to do my portrait.

"A proper one. Like Eva's?" Maman had admired what he'd done with Eva.

"I believe, yes."

She was concerned Edma would be disappointed but, in the end, we did spend a fortnight in Maurecourt early in June. Edma never looked so content and I never felt less needed by my sister. I did not share with her my correspondence with Édouard. I was not sure why except that the longer I kept it my secret the more delicious it grew. When Maman mentioned that I was to be sitting again for Édouard, Edma sat more erect in her chair.

"He may have been teasing," I downplayed. "You know how he is with me."

This was the beginning of my withholding from my sister. But withholding, I justified, just as Edma had done when she invited Mme. Pontillon to Paris, was not the same as lying.

I CHOOSE THE DRESS I personally would like to paint—my white day dress with the gold teardrops—curious how he would handle the subtle accents against the white. Catering to his favourite colour to paint, I added black highlights: hair bow, choker, waistband, slippers, a black-edged fan.

I practised how best to compose my face—dignified yet playful, relaxed yet lively. And arranged my hair so it hung partially loose.

On the carriage ride to Édouard's studio, everything felt disjointed. The ground under my feet seemed strangely far away. My thoughts raced ahead of my body or raced to catch up to it. To calm myself, I recounted, like a banker his notes, all the times he had slighted me. But I couldn't shake the notion that those exchanges were stepping stones, however slippery, leading up to this moment.

Édouard acted the gentleman and the professional. He doted on Maman, provided her a footstool and insisted she remove her shoes. On her side table, he set a plate of cheese, yellow plums, pecans "all the way from Mississippi," and a glass of her favourite claret.

Now that we were face to face, far more than deciphering if he harboured feelings toward me, was the problem of deciphering mine toward him. At ease in his studio, his sleeves rolled up and preparing his paints, he appeared preposterously handsome. Was the cut of his beard different? His hair more blond? His movements were as nimble as any animal's and the sight of the exposed muscles in his forearms ridiculously compelling. Some strange heat had ignited inside me, and I violently needed for him to find me attractive. To resent such feelings only intensified them.

I couldn't meet his eye, and allowed Maman to carry the conversation. I strolled the studio, pretending to study his paintings. When his canvas was prepared, he invited me to make myself comfortable on his davenport.

"Fine," I said. But how? Should I lie down like his *Olympia?* No, undignified. Sit? Yes, sit. And look natural. At one end? In the middle? Upright or leaning back? Ankles crossed or feet paired?

The davenport was surprisingly deep and as I sank into its soft cushions, my feet cleared the floor. Having forgotten to shift my crinolette to one side, I sat directly on it and snapped one of its bands. Had he noticed? Tucking one dangling leg under my skirt so I could turn enough to tug the cage sideways out from under me, I leaned back but the backrest was so distant I fell sideways, catching myself with my elbow to achieve an awkward slump.

"Berthe? Are you… comfortable?" said Édouard.

His tone made me contrary. "Yes." I flung out my arm holding the fan to drape it over the armrest. "Are you quite ready?"

"Yes. And you're all right like that?"

"Fine." Why had I said that? My neck was already growing tight. Twisted and slumped as I was, stays poked into my diaphragm, making a full breath difficult. But knowing Édouard, he would change my pose many times over.

"Very well. If you will, hold that pose."

Was he serious? I shifted a little to aid my breathing.

"Can you hold it, please?" He sounded so hopeful, I stopped moving.

I expected him, if not Maman, to keep up a conversation. But shoes off, she had settled into her novel and cheese and Édouard was quiet in his concentration. It seemed unfair to be looked upon in such awful silence but I could not bring myself to speak.

After a short period, he called for a break. Carefully I unwound myself within my skirt and climbed off the davenport, rubbing my back as I walked the room.

When we resumed, I feigned trouble recalling my pose in hopes Édouard would let me start over.

"Let me," he said.

Maman's chair now faced directly away from us. During our break he had turned it for the advantage of the window's light on her book.

His face came close to mine as I set my gaze on the far wall. Strong hands on my waist rotated my torso back to its awkward angle. His skin smelled like bread, like nourishment. He laid my hand holding the fan over the arm of the davenport then took my chin to tuck it down, his touch so painfully gentle I had the urge to push against it. He lengthened a ringlet along his fingers and laid it, too softly, across my shoulder. He lifted my slippered foot, one palm cupping my ankle, stopping as if unable to decide just how it had looked. Then a livelier pressure made me glance down. His eyes were closed and his lips pressed the top of my instep. A wind shook my spine. I stared blindly at the far window, using all my willpower to hold still.

Without a word he continued, placing each finger of my other hand upon the seat of davenport. He stood, plucked his handkerchief from his breast pocket, lifted it high and let it go. The white square briefly caught the air then landed on the cushion, a tiny flattish tent beside my hand. He returned to his easel.

He'd kissed my foot. Now his handkerchief lay there like a flag of surrender. Surrendering to what? The answer made me giddy—but why trust anything he said or did?

He approached again, knelt and spread out the hem of my skirt. I looked down just as he looked up. Betraying all I knew about propriety, I met his gaze. I needed to judge his intent. A smile played his lips but his eyes betrayed a sadness in which I recognized my own yearning. His hand shook out my hem. My eyes closed.

On the carriage ride home, Maman detailed the plot of the novel she'd been reading. My back was sore where stays had left their mark and my derrière numb from the heel of my shoe. Yet my body hummed and the passing world never looked so bright. The orderly lines of Haussmann's gleaming new *appartement* blocks, their flower boxes overflowing with colour, a dog scratching its scabrous coat, an old man hawking into his handkerchief, a skipping child with face raised to the sky.

What other apertures open along with the heart? And why was I not more afraid?

I would have two more sittings with Édouard, Maman mere feet away, our eyes saying what couldn't be spoken, my body's heat rising to his slightest touch. We walked a precipice of innocence, careful not to concede our feelings, and the necessity of denial made the tension ecstatic. Between encounters, I could focus on little else.

DEGAS ARRIVED EARLY and surprised Maman with a second portrait of Yves, this one in profile. Papa was not feeling well enough to escort Maman and me to the ballet, so Degas had offered to take us. He had acquired a keen interest in the "ballet rats," as he called them, and "the transformation of coarse girls into something unnaturally graceful."

This second portrait of Yves was a true likeness. He had achieved in pastel the definition and colouration of an oil, and I would spend the entire carriage ride trying to get him to reveal his technique. Having no impulse to impart knowledge, all he would say was, "I've already forgotten."

"Edgar," said Maman, "you've captured more than just Yves' features. You've captured my daughter's company! I look at this and believe she's in the room with me."

The corner of his lip lifted higher than usual. He insisted it was a gift.

"Ridiculous. You artists must take money for your work or what shall become of art?" She paid him more, I thought, than it was worth, considering it was a pastel. She had it hung on her bedroom wall with plans to present it as a gift to her son-in-law on his name day. But when that day approached, she decided to bequeath it to him in her will. "Théo, after all, sees her every day."

At the theatre my thoughts drifted on the music and I would later be unable to relay the story of the ballet other than that of a doll come to life. Marcello was there, in her box, looking exquisite in a black off-the-shoulder gown, hair swept up, a diamond necklace draping her collarbone. She noticed me below noticing her and waved her fan with just the right amount of enthusiasm. At intermission, she unexpectedly came downstairs and introduced her M. Carpeaux, a snob of a man who wouldn't even shake Degas' hand. Marcello, clearly embarrassed, kept our exchange brief. Before excusing herself, she kissed me warmly and whispered, "You look exceptionally well, Berthe. You're practically glowing." Her sideways glance implied I had a secret and her woman's nose could smell it.

ÉDOUARD INVITED MAMAN and me to join his family at the races at Longchamps. There, in the company of our mothers and his wife, Suzanne, and the ever-attentive Eugène – I was seated between the brothers when Édouard's foot pressed alongside mine under my skirt. I pressed back. Where our elbows shared an armrest I pushed against his in a game of resistance. When his elbow gave way, I jerked sideways, sparking Eugène's concern.

"It's nothing," I said, barely hiding my smile. "A cramp, already gone."

The horses were being paraded around the track.

"Who are you betting on?" I asked Édouard.

"I'm thinking of Infatuation."

"She's poorly favoured," said earnest Suzanne. "*Le Figaro* predicts Nonsense will take the prize."

"Nonsense," he said. "Poorly favoured means the odds will merit a good return. Besides, look at the legs on her. Long and lean."

"To outrun her pursuers," I said.

"She'll have to exert herself. That mare's legs, number five, look stronger."

"That's Windswept," said Suzanne, studying the probability sheets. "He's a favourite but I'm putting my money on Nonsense." For a moment I panicked thinking she'd seen through our innuendo. But no. The wager collector came around and, head down, she ticked off her betting sheet.

I could not resist. "Maybe Infatuation is not the best bet."

"I've faith that she will surprise me," said Édouard.

"I wouldn't make it too large a bet, dear," said Suzanne, handing him her pencil.

Such exchanges with Édouard felt like gold coins hidden in my hem. However shameful, fooling Suzanne was added jewelry. The fact that she was easily fooled diminished, in my eyes, true depth or intimacy to their marriage, thus relieving any guilt.

Eugène turned to me and shyly announced he had recently written an essay for Gustave's Communard newspaper to expose the hypocrisies of the Catholic church. "I'm hoping to make people question having priests and nuns in charge of the schools."

As I leaned my ear his way, I studied the lovely menace of Édouard's hands as they rested on his knees.

"Of priests preaching a superstitious fear of God in those too young to think for themselves, and thus engender submission."

I believed I could paint Édouard's hands because, as per his earliest advice, I could vividly imagine what they intended.

"Children's minds are easily influenced."

"Utterly," I said, hoping this an appropriate response.

I STUDIED MY OWN ANGLES, my eye jumping from mirror to sketchbook to mirror. My parents were away for the weekend, visiting friends in Pointoise, of which I made sure Édouard was well aware. I had talked them into allowing me to remain home by claiming inspiration. Which was true. I wanted to sketch my figure in camisole and bloomers, exposing my shoulders, arms and legs. Something I would not have done had my parents been home, or Pauline, who had Saturdays off. I sought to capture the hidden effervescence in my veins, of a woman breaking the rules without actually breaking them. Of being caught in a snare and finding the pain exquisite.

I sketched the womanly curve of my hip, my backside—were other women's backsides so flat? I poked at the flaccid muscle with the end of the brush when came a knock at the door. I jumped behind my dressing screen. "Who is it?"

Through the door, Thin Louis excused himself and said that M. Édouard Manet was here to see me. "Your parents aren't home. Shall I send him away?" His tone scraped.

"No. He's a friend of the family." Had my voice quavered? "I'll be right down."

As I received him in the drawing room his eyes ran down my figure and my legs grew watery. Like any good manservant, Thin Louis remained in the dining room behind us, making his presence known by reorganizing the cutlery. I gestured with my eyes and Édouard went and closed the doors between rooms.

"Now go put on your plainest dress and least fashionable hat," he said.

"Why?"

"There's a dance tonight in Montmartre. Outdoors, under the stars. The liveliest of music."

"Édouard. I can't expose myself like that."

He placed a hand over his heart and pledged to protect me and the Morisot name. His gloves and vest were of rough cotton and a drab shade of brown. "You will be... my cousin from Avignon."

"My father would—"

"Never have to know."

"Louis will know."

"I'll take care of Louis."

"Édouard." I couldn't help smile. "And if we run into someone I know or who knows my parents?"

"The threat will be neutralized for they'll have the same mud of Montmartre on their shoes. Now get dressed." He hooked my arm in his and walked me toward the doors. "You really must have such experiences, Mademoiselle. In the name of art if not of living."

Could I refuse such a taunt?

"There are women who are too loose and others who are too tight." The smell of wine lifted off his breath. "Through no fault of your own, you belong to the latter and I'm here to loosen your reins. Is that so bad of me?"

"Yes. But when have you ever been good?"

I chose a plain oxford-blue skirt and bodice with modest neckline and long straight sleeves. The needlework around the hem gave away its worth, but would hardly be detectable by moonlight. The carved ivory buttons also required a keen eye. My blue boots had been recently polished but would be dusty soon enough. I chose short gloves with pearl enclosures and a bonnet whose sides would hide my face. I would have to be careful not to be seen by neighbours.

Except for a distant lamplighter, the street was empty as Édouard helped me into his barouche and under the discretion of its canopy. We left a proper space between us but I could feel the warmth of him and imagined taking his hand in mine. Suddenly free of my chaperone, perhaps he was as unsure as I how we should act. In silence we passed Parc Monceau and continued out of town on the Boulevard de Clichy. Civilization soon came to an end and we bumped along on a rocky dirt road. Twilight bruised the edges of the sky. Squat homes and shops with dry thatch roofs now lined our track, the familiar smell of cesspools on the air. Shops were open and a surprising number of people, including women and children, were out.

"If you work all day," Édouard said, "you know how to make the best of a poor situation. I think of them as the freer class."

In a gap between shops, a woman in a torn skirt sang to the broken strains of an accordion, her voice so heartrending I asked if we might stop and listen. In front of the singer and musician, tall torches had been driven into the ground, defining the most primitive of ballrooms. Couples clung to one another, heads bowed, and swayed wearily in the dust, some kissing sweetly for all to see. Further on, a half-dozen miniature greyhounds resembling tiny bays bounded up milk crates to soar through hoops then stand on hind legs and turn in circles. Édouard clapped and tossed a few centimes on to the road. A foul-looking child scrambled after them on all fours.

As we climbed a hill, green rows of fruit trees filed out into the coming night and the air turned fresh. There was a surprising number of carriages on the road. The thought of Papa's cab travelling this route filled me with just enough defiance to dismiss any notion of consequences.

The sun had well set by the time we entered the village of Montmartre, where the streets resembled a Saturday afternoon on the Left Bank. Vendors hawked food, flowers, books, even paintings. Cafés spilled onto sidewalks. But here women leaned over balconies backed by gaudy red shutters and gestured lewdly to passing cabs.

"Thirsty?" a doll-faced woman called as she squeezed one rosy breast and a tiny fountain of mother's milk fell through the air.

"Cover your eyes," laughed Édouard.

"This reminds me of the old city," I said, to conceal my shock. Edma would never believe it. I hadn't dared to tell her of our flirtations, and the longer I kept it to myself the more anxious I was about revealing it. He pointed to a *café concert* whose gas-lit marquee illuminated worn gold letters—*Théatre Montmartre.* "We'll go there after we dance."

Under the lights, two women lit cigarettes between puckered lips then washed the air with their skirts while a man in a red top hat and tails beckoned people inside.

"And what could be worth the admission?"

Édouard sat face forward, as if picturing it and too excited to meet my gaze. "Twins. *Belgiques.* Two flaxen-haired oxen whose harmonies are… sublime, their timbres as identical as their sad figures. And there's a freckled fellow"—he laughed and tapped his knee—"who… no, I won't ruin it for you."

Up the winding hills of Montmartre, shadowed people in doorways and alleys stumbled, argued, embraced. A squealing mob of children ran across the narrow street in front of us and our driver yelled and snapped his whip at them. Through an open window came the gulping cries of an infant. I imagined it had been crying since birth, abandoned in a dresser drawer or apple crate. The smell of slop, of cooking meat and sour perfume rode the air alongside other scents I had no names for.

ÉDOUARD STEERED US around another man in top hat and tails who hummed softly as he relieved himself against a stone wall. Above him a wooden sign read *Debray's Mill.* Sadly moaning, the building's windmill turned in the breeze as the gayest of music rained down on us from above.

We passed a small graveyard whose picket fence was choked with red roses exuding their velvet perfume, then under a stone arch draped with more fragrant vines. Upon entering a walled courtyard we were greeted by a matronly hostess in an olive-green satin gown. A teeteringly tall, gold-painted Antoinette wig that smelled of rancid animal fat seemed to compress the woman's homely features and push her thick neck down between her shoulders. She flung her arms wide then seized Édouard's cheeks and planted a flurry of kisses around his face. Laughing, Édouard made an extravagant show of kissing her hand. He introduced me, his cousin, "Mademoiselle Bertrice Manet," and the matron's strong arm pulled me in and she kissed me roughly on the lips.

Laughing harder, Édouard said, "Cousin, meet Monsieur Debray."

Monsieur? "Very nice to meet you." With my silk handkerchief I discreetly wiped away the wetness and balled it in my fist until I could dispose of it. Édouard paid the man/woman, who still hadn't spoken but gestured us through.

"Debray," Edouard whispered at my shoulder, "lost his father and three brothers in the Cossack siege of '14. They nailed his father to that windmill for the villagers below to watch him die."

"Awful."

"Hasn't said a word since."

I glanced back at our host now putting a match to his cigarette.

"Let us get you, cousin, a drink."

Candled chandeliers hung from a wooden crossbeam overhead sent their light shimmering onto the leaves of two tall chestnut trees growing from the cobblestone patio. The effect was hypnotic, like being underwater. Benches, café chairs and small circular tables edged the dance floor where couples half-waltzed, half-jigged to a jaunty three-quarter-time piece. Women sat on their lovers' laps, kissing or being groped. In the floor's middle, seated on an old upright piano, two young men and one young woman shared a cigarette between them. Men wore straw boaters pushed back on their heads, while the women, gaudy with lace, wore no hats at all and no gloves. Despite my efforts I stood out like a cat among dogs. As soon as we found a table, I removed both bonnet and gloves.

On a raised platform, musicians played a curious mix of instruments—hand accordion, viola, violin, cello, a gypsy's tambourine, cans and salt boxes filled with dried beans. Édouard handed me a squat glass of something pink. Like some heavenly summons, a bright ringing now wove through the melody, delicate crystalline notes that raised the hairs of my neck. The ringing ascended to a crowning note, making me squint, and then began to scale back down.

"That sound?" I said, dazzled, and he pointed up.

Ascending and descending in size, brass bells were strung overhead from wall to tree and tree to wall across the courtyard. The rim of one bell struck the next and the next in an endless loop. Finally one of the musicians reached up to still the line and the sound faded into the distance, taking my soul with it.

Édouard touched his glass to mine. "To making the most of it all." The champagne was sweet as candy.

As I watched the merriment, I wondered what Paris would look like under this working-class government Édouard championed. Might all women be free to be out in the dark, unchaperoned? Might I be at ease sitting on Édouard's lap in a public place? Being kissed, or worse? Did I want such a thing?

"Eddie," called an approaching young man whose creeping beard concealed all but two pale half moons beneath his eyes.

"Is that Eddie?" said his companion, her cheeks rouged like a puppet's.

Édouard knew everyone. He introduced me, Cousin Bertrice. Albert kissed my cheeks as if we were intimates. Nanette asked for my dressmaker.

"Handed down from a cousin," I said, avoiding Édouard's eye.

"How many cousins do you have, Eddie?" said the woman.

"A fish bucket full!"

The couple laughed and wandered toward the dance floor.

"I'm not sure I should be here," I whispered.

"Let's dance." Before I could reply he grabbed my hand and waist and waltzed us into the whirl of dancers.

Beneath the chiming trees, we danced, some tempos so vigorous I had to sit out the next in order to keep sweat from staining the underarms of my dress. I loved the slow waltz best, my eyes on his and his guiding hand pressed to my back. He was a smooth, confident dancer. My instinct to lead rather than follow made me less so. But in moments of surrender we moved gracefully together.

A bowl of black cherries was passed around the dancers, plump and ripe enough to stain hands and lips. Édouard scooped a fistful at speed but, imagining all the hands that had touched them, I passed.

I noticed a man tucked under a tree, his face hidden by his cap as he scribbled in a sketchbook by the light of a chandelier. I asked Édouard if he knew "the artist among us."

Immediately he danced us over and introduced "Monsieur Auguste Renoir from Limoges."

M. Renoir had the manners to remove his hat, which made his wariness apparent.

"But I was born in Limoges," I said, to put him at ease. By now I was feeling the effects of the pink champagne. "I lived there until I was seven. Until the revolution." I was about to say my father was the Prefect but thought better of it.

When M. Renoir asked which years, we discovered we were the very same age and had lived within a half-mile of each other.

"For all purposes, you would have lived in different cities," Édouard corrected us. "Renoir is the son of a tailor."

Even so, we shared memories of the limestone Virgin Mother in her sky-blue cloak, paraded through the streets at religious festivals. And the harvest fair with Bertrand, the singing pig. The pig had been trained to grunt along to his master's fiddle playing. We children threw him kernels of corn after each song, which he caught in his mouth like a dog.

"Renoir," said Édouard, "is a comrade of that devil Monet."

"Really? Is that true? I greatly admire his work."

"Though Renoir here claims to be a painter of *la vie moderne*, he's a helpless romantic. I don't think one can have it both ways but wish him the best of luck."

"I didn't catch your name," said M. Renoir.

"Berthe Morisot," said Édouard. Having long since taken off my bonnet, I now felt completely exposed. "And she is a painter as good as any man." The compliment eclipsed my worry.

Édouard laid a heavy hand on the artist's shoulder. "If only you knew, Berthe, what Renoir here says about women painters, you wouldn't be so friendly. I think 'ludicrous' is the word? Or is it 'ridiculous'?"

Flustered, Renoir said, "I meant only that art is a tyrant. You have to give yourself over entirely and to live such a life would be to sacrifice a woman's natural inclinations."

I could see his words were kindly meant. I asked to see what he was drawing, unable to imagine good work coming from this chaos of models who didn't stand still. He passed me his sketchbook. He had caught the dancers' moondrunk expressions and half-lidded eyes, their curving arms and necks, the impossible closeness of bodies. His faces were cherubic and yes, far more idyllic than reality, but the gay atmosphere was absolutely true. I was moved and told him so. His tight-lipped smiled revealed his pleasure.

After meeting M. Renoir, I confessed that my feet were getting sore—I had never danced this much—and Édouard announced it time for other entertainments. I felt light-headed as we made our way back to his cab, my hand in his as if we were lovers. Husband and wife. I imagined describing the evening to Edma in my next letter. What would she say?

Once inside the golden doors of Théatre Montmartre, the heat was crushing, the floorboards sticky underfoot and the air a mix of beer and cigarettes. A candlelit hall led to a short flight of stairs and then into a bowl of a room whose floor sloped drunkenly toward a raked stage. A bluish haze floated under the ceiling. Tables were set with lone candles and mottled tablecloths that had once been white. The gas lamps along the stage's lip threw grotesque shadows of the performers onto the scrim behind.

We wove between tables seeking one for ourselves, people muttering they couldn't see the magician doing something with an audience member's top hat and a pitcher of beer. I wished I'd my bonnet to hide myself, but after removing it and my gloves at the dance, they had promptly disappeared.

Our table had uneven legs and tipped wildly. As Édouard ordered champagne, I studied the room for anyone I might know. Many respectably dressed men but none were familiar, at least not in the dim light. Then, from down near the stage, a woman's tripping laugh. I knew that laugh. It had to be her. Marcello. One arm draping the neck of the man beside her—M. Carpeaux?—she held a cigarette to his pursed lips, then to her own. Her hair was pinned up, her neck ringed with a gold necklace. She had not dressed down but could have come from the Opera House. Yet here in this underground hovel, she appeared at home, as free and unconcerned as any man.

I positioned my chair out of her sightline. My narrow sense of propriety embarrassed me and yet was so ingrained I didn't dare let myself be seen. I pointed her out to Édouard.

"I've seen her down here many times. She knows how to enjoy herself." He tipped his hand side to side. "Not too tight, not too loose."

The champagne arrived, my glass cloudy and finger-marked.

The next performer was dangerously thin, with bulging eyes and a rude Adam's apple, his face a pox of freckles. Cymbals were strapped to the insides of his knees, tin horns wedged in both nostrils and a larger horn in his mouth. The largest horn, though, stuck out through a hole in the back of his pants. It was the lowest thing I had ever seen. But when out from his orifices came a tuneful, spritely rendition of Offenbach's "Infernal Gallop," I laughed until I cried. Marcello's unrestrained laughter carried an octave higher than the men's, so once more we were together sharing an unguarded moment.

Wearing matching skirts of candy-red satin, the next act walked side by side on to the stage, shoulders touching and feet moving in unison. They swung around to face us and I gasped along with half the audience. The young women shared a single ropelike braid of pale-blonde hair which draped their conjoined shoulders and hung past the three arms between them. People went quiet, either out of horror or respect, as the twins hooked the fingers of their outer hands together in the pose of an opera singer, their third hand dangling below. The master of ceremonies instructed us to close our eyes. Perched forward on his chair, Édouard had already closed his. Without musical accompaniment, the young women began to trade soft notes back and forth in a slow harmonious build of melody and song until the dingy theatre disappeared. Muscular and rapturous braids of sound like currents in a river. Édouard swayed in his seat unaware of doing so. I was brought to tears, partly from knowing their unfortunate shape would confine their genius to performing for a pittance and cold soup in theatres such as this.

PEOPLE STREAMED FROM the theatre and into the streets. Young, often coarse-looking women were escorted on the arms of wealthy grey-haired men who could have been my father. Headed where? To do what?

Stinking of smoke, and champagne that the uneven table caused me to spill on us both, I was escorted back into the carriage. Édouard asked if I desired to be delivered "back to my pretty cage."

"Not when you put it that way."

"Very well then. There's one more thing I would like to show you." He ordered his driver to "take us to the top."

Édouard had played the gentleman all evening, treating me like the cousin I pretended to be. There were no kisses, no confessions of love, no passionate embraces. Not even here in the privacy of his barouche. I was disappointed but also suspicious. Were his flirtations mere sport performed near the safety of chaperones and wife? Did he relish teasing women, seducing their affections as he had with Edma, and attach to this no deeper meaning? Was he all show and bluff? Even faithful to his wife? Was I truly like a cousin to him?

The driver could proceed only so far up the steep slope. It was mad to be out in the dark villainous countryside walking a narrow goat path, in a champagne haze. I trudged dumbly content on my sore feet, holding up my skirts with one hand, my other fast in his. The stars were close, their light tremulous. It seemed that, with the right effort, one would be able to hear them.

We reached the peak of Montmartre. Stacks of hay squatted in the dark like unlit cottages, dung soured the air, and a nearby cow groaned in warning. Further on was an actual cottage, a single buttery yellow window. Outside the fence, Edouard squeezed my wrist and said, "Stay here."

I heard a mongrel growl and Édouard's louder rebuke. The door opened to a man whose candle illuminated his broad face and the tam that lay on his head flat as a crêpe. I couldn't make out the whispered conversation.

Édouard returned, said his friend would be right out. I complained again of my sore feet.

"You can put your feet up for the rest of your days," he said.

"You have no sympathy."

"Only for your sheltered life."

He guided me to a kind of stage in the middle of nowhere. And through a little gate to a bench inside a small enclosure whose nature I couldn't discern in the dark until it was too late. He directed me to sit, which I happily did, my head spinning not unpleasantly in the warm air. He sat beside me, put his arm around me and kissed me, soft but forceful. He stopped short to see my reaction. I reached for his face and kissed him again.

"Why, cousin," he exhaled and we kissed more fervently.

I would have laughed but my mouth was overcome with the feel and taste and heat of his lips, his tongue. I half-heard him ask me to keep my eyes closed. "Will you, Berthe? Until I tell you to open them."

"Why? What is it you mean to do?" I joked. My lips landed on his smooth hard teeth as he spoke.

"Just promise."

"I promise."

I closed my eyes as he kissed the palms of my bare hands. I felt pliable as water as he nosed under my hair, kissed along my nape igniting sparks behind my eyelids. I kept my promise despite a sudden flare of light and the whooshing sound of a fireblower. Was his friend to perform for us? I found his lips again. If Edma could see her younger sister, kissing the man she once so desired. Would she be horrified or happy for me? Another bright whoosh followed by the galloping sound of horses and the floor beneath our feet began to tip and rock. What? All promises off, I opened my eyes and tried to stand only to fall hard to my seat and see the cottage below magically shrinking. My stomach lurched. I grabbed the bench for all my life.

"We're flying," said Édouard.

"I can't, I don't—" I shut my eyes again. "Go back down. Please, Édouard. Stop it. Stop it now."

He pulled my back against his chest and bound his arms around my waist. I seized fistfuls of his jacket. "It's perfectly safe, trust me," he said.

"I'm frightened by heights."

"Too tight." He kissed my neck, nipped at my earlobe. "I've got you." A hard tug jerked the basket's corners and we stopped. My stomach lurched with nausea.

"See, I've stopped it as you asked. Now can you open your eyes?"

"No."

He laughed. "It's really worth it. Just don't look down." He kissed my ear.

I took a deep breath. Pride made me open my eyes. I stared straight ahead to a distant city. Paris had melted into nervous points of light. The Seine was a dark, winding absence, a black snake which swallowed those lights into its transparent stomach. Radiant stars above, radiant stars below.

"Imagine painting such a miracle," he said.

"It's a wonder but I would like to go down. Please. Now. Unless you'd like me to be sick on your boots."

It wasn't until we disembarked that I realized we'd been tethered to earth with a stout rope, and that Édouard's friend had been in the basket with us the whole time, managing the gas flame.

I DON'T KNOW what time Édouard delivered me to my door but Thin Louis was there to greet me, his eyes cast down. Too tired and famished to care if he would indeed keep my secret, I asked for a plate of cheese, greengages and buttered bread. I made my way upstairs and Pauline soon arrived with the food and to help me undress.

"Did you enjoy your evening, Mademoiselle Berthe?" Her voice was hoarse with sleep.

"Fine," I downplayed.

"Does Monsieur Manet dance well?"

How could she know? Did the working class commiserate? Pass information like spies?

"I did not hear you." When she began to repeat her question, I said, slower and more clipped, "I did not hear you."

She stopped her questions and I asked her to wash my feet and rub them with hypernicum oil.

The foot rub and food sent me into a stupor of exhaustion. I lay in bed weightless and floating, recalling his hand in mine, the feel of his beard, lips, the surprise of his tongue and imagined a freer society. Where girls and women attended Beaux-Arts and painted the nude. Walked anywhere, without one's mother or aunt in tow. Rode the top of the omnibus, ankles glaring. I didn't fall asleep until after the morning light stained the curtains.

ÉDOUARD WHIPPED AWAY the sheet and flung it to the floor. He had invited Maman and me to his studio for the unveiling of my portrait.

Maman was silent, then politely flattering, a dead giveaway of her low opinion. He had caught it all—my twisted slump, my crinolette to one side like an ant's abdomen, my fixed stare, my pretense of nonchalance, my palms on the davenport as if steeling myself against an attack. To top it off, my shoe and white-stockinged ankle stuck out from beneath my skirt.

I burst out laughing. Maman stared at me and cleared her throat. I assured Édouard that I was not laughing at his work but at myself.

"I was so ill at ease."

"I took that as a compliment."

Maman appeared confused but I understood.

"I believe I would be more comfortable now."

"I'm glad to hear that. I hope to witness your evolution as a model model."

I laughed even louder, embarrassing Maman further. I was standing on the edge of an abyss, dizzy with secrets and dreams of a different future. Ignorant of any danger. Maman asked him a question I didn't hear. I couldn't. I now understood the wisdom behind unmarried women having a chaperone. Not just to protect against those creatures called men but to protect women from our own animal natures.

I was in love with Édouard Manet? Apparently I dressed for him and arranged my life around seeing him. I was in love with Édouard Manet. We wrote to each other of our engagements so as to be in the same place at the same time. I was in love with Édouard Manet. I woke in the morning thinking of him, I painted in the afternoon thinking of him, I went to bed thinking of him and in my dreams did things with him that woke me in the night to heave away my quilts.

I ached to write and tell Edma that I too knew what it meant to fall in love. And that she had been right in saying that real love had to be mutual. I would not lord it over her, but I believed he loved me as I loved him, body and mind and spirit. Why else would he risk himself as he did? My entire being rang with this conviction and I, fervent member of the realist movement, gave myself up to the ideals of romanticism.

I didn't write and tell Edma. I kept telling myself that revealing such a thing in a letter lacked propriety. I would tell her in person next time we were together. For how could I keep such a secret from my beloved sister?

Whatever the germ that makes a country hunger for war, that summer Paris caught it. As Adolphe predicted, Prussia reneged on their promise to return Rhineland to France. And now the Spanish crown was being offered to a Prussian prince. Such a union would surround France with Prussian-friendly territory and our Emperor demanded the offer be removed. To Papa's surprise and relief, this demand was honoured. But then Emperor Louis demanded the promise extend into the future *ad infinitum* and hate propaganda escalated on both sides.

Our Minister of War made the official announcement in front of the Hôtel de Ville. He reminded France how our Emperor's famous uncle had trounced Prussia "in a matter of weeks," and roused *esprit* with the promise that our soldiers would be equipped with the newest in artillery as seen at the Exposition—the chassepot rifle, and France's "secret weapon, *la mitrailleuse,* whose rotary barrels fire 150 rounds per minute."

"This campaign against the Prussian Terror," boasted the Minister, "will be an artless stroll in the park, walking stick in hand."

The city erupted in patriotic fever. Flags were strung like laundry across rue de Haussmann and flung over the railings of every bridge. Beating pots with wooden spoons, marchers filled the boulevards each evening chanting "*Vive la guerre!*" Whenever the bells on the butcher's door announced a customer, the shop parrot shrieked, "To Berlin. To Berlin." Each morning, Mme. Sasse, a soprano with the opera, who resided at the end of our street, announced the sun like a rooster by belting out "Le Marseillaise" from her upper balcony. Though I heard but never saw the singer, Mme. Higgonet told us she wore a Pompidou wig and the white, red and blue costume of Mother France complete with her "heart's breast on display."

Making Maman gush with pride, Tibby was among the first to enlist. Though glad to see my brother apply himself to something resembling work, I wondered about his suitability. Pampered and spoiled, changing his surroundings whenever it suited him, he had proved loyal to nothing but his own comforts.

It had been a fortnight after that glorious evening in Montmartre when my bliss came to a confusing end. There were no more coincidental meetings in the Bois or Louvre, at concerts in the Tuileries. No more invitations to the races. Édouard didn't come to Maman's reinstated soirées—Papa having regained his humour—nor attend those in his own home. I gazed hard at our intimacies, our helpless kisses. What had changed? Had his wife found us out? His mother? Yet his family's attitude toward me appeared unchanged.

Could his interest have already waned? Been usurped by another? I wrote to him and he didn't respond. I wrote again.

Silence. A devastating and infuriating silence. The only thing that kept me from despising him was the nagging, or perhaps desperate belief, that he kept his distance out of love, out of trying to protect me. We had not done more than flirt and kiss but it was only a matter of time and opportunity before things became more compromising. For me, that is. A possible pregnancy would reveal all. I would be shunned from society. Our two families would become sworn enemies. My family's reputation would be forever stained, though Mme. Manet, I was sure, would manage to salvage theirs.

Such complications seemed unreasonable and unfair when love itself was so simple and immediate, as natural as reaching for a glass of cold milk when hot and thirsty. Like the sun or the seasons, my love for Édouard was not something I had manufactured or created, and therefore was also likely why, even in anger or despair, I felt powerless to undo it.

"IF THIS IS a war of fashion," said Mme. Stevens, stroking invisible dust from Frédéric's uniform, "we will certainly be victorious."

It was Thursday evening at Mme. Manet's and Frédéric Bazille had arrived in a gorgeous ensemble of bearskin shako, gold braids, cutaway tunic and red-tasseled turban. From a military family, he had been called to serve as an officer of the Army of the Loire. I could not picture this gentle scholarly painter leading men into battle.

"Disarm them with beauty," said Degas. "Mount masterpieces on every shield."

Stevens laughed. "Shield. It's not the Middle Ages, Degas."

It was the height of summer and no one took the pending war seriously. The weather was sublime, the outdoor cafés boisterous, the parks alive with the squeal of children.

"Mount them on poles, or barricades," Degas continued. "Plant white marble statues on the hills of the battlefields."

"Flatter the lumpy Prussians with compliments," said Stevens. "Tell them how fine they look upon a horse."

"Choose art and love, not politics and war," said Mme. Stevens and we all raised our glasses.

I was desperate to see Édouard, to know if it was regard or regret that kept him away. Across the room, Eugène was looking at me with the same absent absorption as one might gaze at falling snow. I excused myself and walked over. As if I was an apparition, disbelief lit his face. He gave a quick glance behind him then adjusted his jacket.

"Édouard's not joining us?" I tried for nonchalance. "Not ill, I hope?"

"No. No. Preoccupied with work. Insists that inspiration can't be deferred."

I leaned in, uncharacteristically eager to hear what Eugène had to say. "But… in truth, I don't know why he's unsocial of late. It's not like him." Peering at me as if I might know something he didn't, he reached out a hand before gently retracting it. "Are you all right?"

No one, not even Degas, had detected my unhappiness. My cheerful front was effortful and Eugène's concern threatened to reduce me to tears.

"I'm well, thank you," I mumbled and excused myself.

THE WAR GAVE my father a new *raison d'être.* All the frustrations harboured against his ailing body he now directed against this other, less formidable enemy. Or so he believed. Among those opposed to this war was Deputy Minister Thiers, who predicted a ruinous outcome. His lack of support earned him the moniker "the unpatriotic trumpet of tragedy."

Assigned to the headquarters of the Army of the Rhine, Tibby, eager and bright with thoughts of adventure and the promise of free whiskey, left Paris on the fifth of August on a cloudless day.

"This is the way real men behave in the face of peril," spouted Maman. "Cowards talk, heroes act."

I didn't know if such maxims were for her sake or for Tibby's. Nor did I recognize my own mother.

Edma, still in Maurecourt, wrote that Adolphe's ship was to take part in a blockade along the Prussian coastline. *And to support any military landings on the mainland. He fears the French government doesn't know what it's up against. I am anxious for his safety. Though I would prefer to return to Lorient to be near him, he insists I take Jeanne to join Yves in Mirande. Maurecourt is too close to Paris, he says, and Paris is not just a target but the aim. I trust you, Maman and Papa will join us if, heaven forbid, the time comes.*

Papa dismissed her concerns. Then things happened faster than his ministry and the government could keep up with or remedy. In the thousands, volunteers arrived in Paris from the countryside to enlist in the Grande Armée. While waiting to be posted they made camp in the Champ de Mars and Bois de Boulogne. Papa reported that though the funds had been allocated, there was not just a shortage of tents to house the men but of sugar, kettles, coffee and rations to feed them. Not to mention the wonderful chassepot rifles. The amazing *mitrailleuse*, of which all the papers had printed detailed drawings, apparently existed on paper only. Somehow, though, despite these crucial shortages, there was plenty of the free whiskey Tibby had bragged about. Daily Papa lamented that someone in the Ministry of War was misdirecting money but could never pinpoint who or how.

During Sunday's stroll in the Bois, Maman, Auntie and I came upon soldiers, clearly drunk, bathing naked in the upper pond, while others urinated openly in the lower. When a gunshot flushed birds from trees, we crouched and grabbed for each other. A volley of shots ensued and crackings and fluttering from the trees. They were shooting off tree limbs for cooking fires, and at pigeons and squirrels to roast over them. A ringing in my ears persisted for the rest of the day and it would be our last walk in the Bois for a very long time.

Reports that the Armée was underprepared, that too many unskilled men had joined up just for the rations, went unheeded. And on a sanguine summer's day early in August, our Minister of War ordered our troops stationed in the north, many lacking a weapon or proper boots, to cross the border onto Prussian soil and take Forbach by surprise. His military strategy? Whichever army took the initiative would win the fight.

Mere hours after the battle began, word arrived of France's defeat. Two days later, another defeat at Wissembourg. By mid-August, Prussians were on French soil. Thank goodness Adolphe had the prescience to keep Edma from returning to Lorient. Now the war was all anyone could talk about and Maman began to fret about Tibby. Papa assured her that his company, at France's headquarters in Metz, was far from trouble.

Residents fled the besieged cities and poured into Paris. They set up shelters under trees along Haussmann's new boulevards, in alleyways and parks, including the park beyond our garden wall. If there was no wind, the air grew fetid. From the comfort of my sitting room I watched women tend cooking fires, children run wild and old people lie on blankets on the ground. What would they do when it rained?

As if truly a machine of war, the Prussians took Chalons-sûr-Marne, a week later Gravelotte-Saint-Privat, and then Vionville. Vionville was a mere three and half miles from Metz. From Tibby. Joining Maman in her worry took my mind off the elusive Édouard. My heart, so recently awakened, had grown numb and heavy. Unable to paint, I sketched from memory his hands, his face. Surely the next time we met things would right themselves like an overturned glass, which could then be refilled with feelings shared. Until then, life was stripped of its dazzle and this losing war seemed not out of place.

In early September, Maman, doing her best to carry on, asked me to accompany her to the Bon Marché to see the Fall fashions. The day was warm and sunny, the canopy removed from the carriage. We reached Boulevard Haussmann yet the street sign on the corner building had been covered over with a placard painted with bold black letters: *Boulevard Victor Hugo*. It made no sense. After his denunciation of the Emperor's treatment of the working class, the writer had been in exile in England for five years now. We turned onto the boulevard. Criss-crossed overhead down its length, fluttered red crêpe paper strung from lamppost to lamppost.

Maman clucked her tongue. "The Communards are getting bold. You can bet Gustave Manet is involved. His brothers too. Eugènie should have insisted they sign up for service." I could not picture Édouard stringing crêpe in the night, let alone shooting a rifle at a Prussian.

We drove right into a chanting mob which choked our way forward. A celebration was taking place. Flags waved and pots banged and glasses of champagne were passed hand over hand above the cheers. For what cause? I scanned the crowd for Édouard and saw him in every face under copper-coloured hair. A shot rang out and a cheer heaved up. Our horses whinnied and one lurched back, pulling the other with it and the carriage weaved and tipped up on two wheels. I slammed against the carriage edge, Maman banging against me. She yelled at Levan to get the animals under control, the horses already settling. As the chanting soared, Maman and I looked at each other. Had France managed to win the war after all? Then we heard it, "*Vive la République*! *Vive la République!*"

"What's the meaning of this?" Maman asked Levan.

"The Emperor has been captured at Sedan, Madame. The Empire has fallen. A new republic was declared this morning at the Hôtel de Ville."

"How do you know this?"

When he gnawed at his lip and said nothing, she asked, "Under whose rule?"

"The opposition, Madame. Monsieur Gambetta."

"Gambetta? Turn us around. We're going home."

The government had fallen? Was this Édouard's new republic?

As Levan tried to turn the horses, at my elbow a young man in labourer's clothes gave me a sneering smile. Before I could look away, he hurled himself up to rip my parasol from my hand and dropped back down laughing.

"Scoundrel." Maman closed her parasol to brandish like a sword. The carriage lurched forward, my heart thudding as I watched the man run through the crowd, my fringed yellow parasol twirling away from me.

"Take le Pont Neuf," ordered Maman.

Le Pont Neuf, we soon discovered, was also blocked.

"L'Iena then."

Levan just sat there.

"Levan."

Then we saw it. From the garden of the Tuileries, hoisted on ropes and a cradle of beams, the statue of Emperor Louis swung precariously above the cheering men. Easily twenty feet tall, the limestone image floated toward the bridge rail. We stared in wonder. With one great lurch and cry the men sent the statue toppling headfirst over the railing and into the Seine. Like a skilled diver, it broke the black water with only the smallest of splashes and disappeared from sight. Cheers, corks popped and champagne bubbled over onto the street. It was really happening. Édouard's and his brothers' dream. Was it my dream as well? What did a kingless and classless society really look like?

That evening a special edition of *Le Figaro* reported Emperor Louis' capture along with half the Grande Armée. The exodus out of Paris began. That very night the Empress stole across the English Channel with the royal dentist, a man rumoured to be her lover.

The wealthy and the titled retreated to their country homes. The government ordered their own Ministries of War and Interior closed and all personnel to vacate the city. Papa's Ministry remained open, though there was much confusion over who was in charge as its Minister had fled. Believing affluent Passy would be a prime target for looters or worse, friends and neighbours loaded carts with their most precious of belongings and left, the Great Terror not forgotten.

Papa was undaunted. "Everyone is being hysterical. Gambetta is a moderate and will protect the bourgeoisie," he claimed. "And as long as Issy and Vanves are in French hands, Paris is protected from the Prussians."

No matter, several of our servants left with or without Papa's consent. Whether they feared a Prussian invasion or joined the Communard cause, we'd never know. The local butcher closed his doors, followed by the *pharmacie* and bakery. Despite dwindling clientele, Passy's market continued for the time being.

Papa's faith lay in M. Thiers who, despite no longer being a Minister, left on a mission to garner support from other European countries. Thiers had lost the vote to Gambetta for interim leader and refused to take part in "this hastily formed, pretend government."

"I have a job to go to," Papa announced at dinner. "And though I don't believe Paris is in any imminent danger, someone must oversee the remaining servants. Therefore I will stay behind." He then insisted Maman and I take the train south to join Yves and Edma in Mirande. "As precaution against the unforeseeable."

Maman looked offended. "Of course I'm staying, Tiburce. You're not well." She turned to me. "Though events are never as morbid as people's imaginations, go and be with your sisters. It will make Edma happy. You can paint. Help with the children."

"What if something happens to you?"

"We will leave well before then," said Maman.

I made them promise. I was loathe to go anywhere before

seeing Édouard and putting an end to this tortuous guessing game but regretfully began to pack. I sent him a note telling him I was leaving Paris and absolutely must see him, that his silence was a slow death. Again no response.

The day before I was to leave, a letter did arrive, from Mme. Manet. Maman read it aloud at breakfast.

Sept. 16th, 1870

Dear Cornélie, Édouard says that between the Prussians and the civil unrest, Paris is no longer safe. He has found a place for me to stay with friends of his in the Basses-Pyrénées. Suzanne and Léon will accompany me. Édouard, Eugène and Gustave will remain behind to assist the new government and do what they can to stop the Prussian Terror. I trust you and Berthe will be joining your other dear daughters and wish you a safe journey. I am told the trains are running at capacity and regretfully we may have to sleep in the station. A small sacrifice compared to our valiant young men. May Gambetta prove to be what this country needs. My most fervent wishes for your son's safe return.

Eugènie Manet

Papa grumbled about "the new government," as if to blame Mme. Manet and her sons for its existence. But all I heard was that Édouard was to be alone in Paris. Without his mother or his wife. Had he encouraged such a letter? Was this his backhanded response to mine? If I were to stay and he truly cared for me… he would worry… he would come and talk me out of it. There would still be time to leave. I knew I would have no peace until I spoke to him and told my parents that I could not live with myself if anything happened to them and refused to leave without them. When Papa objected, I worried he might decide to leave after all, so cut him off. "I'm staying here with you and there's no point in trying to talk me out of it."

"It is not up to you," he said to my retreating back but did not pursue it further.

I wrote and told Edma that I would be staying to help Maman care for Papa. To be lying to her about my real reason for staying made an uncertain situation feel all the more isolating and lonely.

Berthe, To stay in Paris is pure foolishness. Do you not realize the danger? Papa hardly wants Maman's much less your ministrations. I am upset enough at Papa's recklessness and now you! Please listen to me and leave before it's too late. I have written and pleaded with Papa to no avail. It's hard enough to bear the thought of harm coming to Tibby. If you don't come to Mirande, I will worry myself sick. Yves has plenty of room. We will be together again. And Jeanne wants to know her auntie. I will model for you. There are some lovely landscapes here, meadowlands sugared with wildflowers, wide cumulous skies. Please heed this letter. Edma

Dear Edma, Please don't be anxious. Perhaps we're being foolish, thinking we're romantic heroes and heroines defending the homeland but Papa is well-informed and would never put us in undue danger. We will leave together when the time comes. So forgive me for not heeding your warning but I have my reasons. We will, I'm sure, be together soon for I too want to know my niece better and love you deeply. Berthe

Was that how I saw myself? A romantic heroine willing to put her life at risk? And for what? For a man who refused to communicate?

TO MAINTAIN EVERYONE'S SPIRITS Maman continued her regular Tuesday soirée no matter how few might come. The first night, Leo arrived alone, Rosalie and the rest of the family having gone south to safety. He looked thin, tired about the eyes, and was less talkative than normal. Ten minutes later, Degas and Eugène stepped into the drawing room. I rose to greet my friends but my heart sank.

Édouard had not accompanied them. Now I felt truly abandoned. And foolish. Like Edma once said, it was all a game to him. Perhaps love itself was a game to him. I had chosen Édouard over Edma and I had chosen wrongly. I would leave tomorrow, on the earliest train.

Suddenly exhausted, I wanted only to go to bed and sleep. Then I heard it, the pitched tone of his voice in the hall saying something to Thin Louis about gloves. He was here. He had come. My hand shook as Eugène lifted it to his lips. "You are cold?" he said and began to rub my hand between his. I gently pulled my hand away.

When Édouard stepped into the drawing room, the air brightened and everything came into focus. Biting back happiness, I had to resist going to him. He greeted my parents in turn. He was dressed down, similar to our night in Montmartre, and my thoughts soared back to that time. As he reached me, he made a diversion to the tray of pickled white asparagus. I wanted to grab his face, force his eyes to mine.

He took a random chair. A Communard rally had taken place that afternoon at the Folies Bergére and Édouard spoke passionately of this and nothing else. He sat with feet planted and his body pitched forward into the conversation. His eyes addressed everyone but me while I looked at no one but him.

Not since the Second Empire seized power could such an event openly take place. He, Degas and Eugène had all been there to toast the Emperor's capture. I willed him to keep talking so I could rest my eyes on him without giving myself away.

The height of his chair set Papa slightly above everyone else. He spread his elbows on the armrests and sat not forward but back. "How is that different than raising a glass to the Prussians? Are you prepared, Édouard, to start learning German?"

"We celebrate France's liberation from royal excess, censorship and the oppression of the working man," said Édouard. "Now, with any luck, a true Communard will replace Gambetta, and we'll finally have a fair and modest society."

Eugène had posted himself beside the fireplace, which placed me in his direct line of vision.

Neither of us disposed to argument, Degas and I sat outside the fraying circle. I was overdressed and embarrassed for it in my grand-mère's gold earrings and necklace and a new silk gown cut in the latest of fashions: enormous puffed sleeves and scooped neckline. I had spent an entire hour deciding which pair of slippers to wear in case he came. Now I felt a prime example of the decadence he denounced.

"So you'll be handing over your properties to the collective?" Papa said. "Giving away your paintings to the smithy so he can hang them around his work shed?"

Édouard went still. It was like watching a firework's fuse being lit. "If those with palaces and mansions do some sharing, we might all live as well as you and I, Monsieur Morisot."

Papa slapped the air with the back of his hand. "There will always be success and failure, rich and poor. These are natural antagonists and one does not forgive the other."

Leo played the diplomat. "Gambetta's not my pick, but I say we're lucky he's a moderate. No one's more eloquent than Gambetta and—"

"Eloquence is a pacifier," said Édouard. "Gambetta's enough of the old guard to support the status quo."

Degas leaned in to me and whispered, "Do you think Gambetta spit polishes his glass eye?"

Gambetta had a glass eye?

"He did nothing to stop today's rally," said Leo.

"Because he feared being shot or hanged?" offered Édouard. His arguments were usually lightened with humour but not tonight. The broadness of his anger made me believe some of it included me.

"Or is it a show of tact on his part?" Leo said, nodding, agreeing with himself. "Gambetta could well be the bridge between the old and new, the monarchists and the Commu—"

"Idiot radicals," said Papa.

Positioned behind Papa's chair, Maman placed a hand on his shoulder and then nodded to Thin Louis to refill glasses though they were only half-empty.

Édouard laughed meanly. "The Commune has its share of doctors, lawyers, and bureaucrats like yourself, even a few aristocrats. Idiots? I call them altruists who recognize that a ten-hour work day is a reasonable desire."

"What do you know of the working class?" Papa's face was a blank canvas.

"I support a reasonable work day," said Leo, "though worry a democracy may in the end promote more factions. A democracy requires every opinion be accounted for, and there are as many opinions as there are men."

"Of course it will," said Papa. "When no single man holds power, challengers will vie to fill that hole. There'll be coercion, bribery and threats."

"Already plenty of that," said Édouard.

Degas whispered. "I wonder where the Emperor's gold crown is now? Being paraded around on the head of a kitchen maid? Nested in by mice?"

Papa was not finished. "Nothing leads to more hunger for power than a democracy. Royal blood, thankfully, limits the contenders to the throne."

Édouard scratched his head. "What about actual hunger that comes from not having enough to eat?"

Papa gripped the arms of his chair. "Let's just picture this ideal government of yours. First, you can say farewell to beauty."

Maman gestured for me to go to the piano. I shook my head. I was not going to give Édouard the opportunity to miss his wife's far superior playing.

"Your new government may well plant root vegetables in the parks instead of flowers, to fill those hungry bellies you speak of.

Graze pigs in the street. The wood framing your masterpieces? That should heat some homes, no?"

"Did you know," Degas whispered, "that owls swallow their prey whole?"

I stared at him.

"And after digesting the meat, regurgitate a furball filled with bones and teeth?" He held up thumb and forefinger to demonstrate just how small those teeth would be.

"Under a truly liberal republic"—Édouard's voice rose—"artists will stop having their spirits gagged. There will dawn a new age for art and—"

"Such grand words, Édouard." Papa clapped and Édouard reddened. I was terrified he might leave. "So what you really mean is that quality be damned?"

"True art will always be recognized." Édouard spoke to his hands.

Please don't go.

"By whom? A democratic jury populated by bakers and lamplighters? Maybe women, why not? Children too, if everyone's equal."

"Is not the Prussian army making its way towards Paris?" said Maman. "Are we not all French and on the same side? If the answer is no, we might as well surrender right now."

This led to a momentary truce. Leo reminded us of Gambetta's call-to-arms that had been posted on every lamppost. A civilian militia was being organized to bolster the weakened army.

"Paris may be blessed with too many artists and not enough soldiers," said Papa with a snort.

"I can assure you, Monsieur Morisot, we artists will do our duty," said Édouard.

"Oh, now I'll be able to sleep at night."

Beside me, Degas raised two pistol-shaped hands and shot them off with whispery explosions.

As I'd feared, Édouard rose, thanked Maman for the wine, and moved toward the foyer. My heart lunged after him but I rose slowly, excused myself and followed.

"You're leaving?" I said. Thin Louis held out his hat and scarlet gloves.

"I cannot believe your father is allowing you to remain in Paris." He tore his hat from Thin Louis' hand. I nodded to Thin Louis, dismissing him. "Does he not realize what could happen?" He yanked on his gloves. "Does he want to see you mangled? Your legs blown off?"

Finally he looked at me, eyes furious yet frightened, his brow an agonized question.

"It was my own decision to stay."

"You're being irrational."

"Is this about rationality?"

"Berthe, go to your sister's. I implore you to leave on the first train." He needn't have said what he said next, as I could read it in his eyes, but he said it anyway. "Not for you. For me."

I'd made the right choice. I took his hands and brought them to my lips. "I'm not afraid."

"Do not romanticize war."

Seeing movement out the corner of my eye, I dropped his hands and wished him good night. I'm not entirely sure how much Eugène had seen or heard.

AT BREAKFAST, two days hence, Papa read out a dictate received from the Ministry of War. My studio would need to house members of the National Guard. It was no great sacrifice by any standard but the loss of my refuge and what meagre autonomy I'd been allotted made these hard-won battles feel inconsequential.

The day's papers announced President Gambetta's latest declaration, a kind of ecstasy of hopelessness: "Paris will die on her feet. We will defend her till our last breath." While Edma's latest letter, which Papa shared aloud, was filled with warnings gleaned from Adolphe: *The French military attaché in Berlin says that Paris's resistance is ill-advised. The Prussian army outnumbers the French army by half and they are in possession of the most menacing of displays from the Exposition—fifty-ton long-range cannons. Adolphe urges you, and now I beg you, Papa, to leave Paris immediately and join us here in Mirande.*

"Bismarck will not risk ruining the city he covets." Papa folded the letter and slipped it in its envelope as if to make it disappear. "He'll starve us first, to keep our treasures intact."

"Is that supposed to be a comfort?" I said.

He scowled. "No one is keeping you here."

In that he was wrong. And just as I'd hoped and imagined it would happen, Édouard and Eugène spontaneously stopped by just before the dinner hour with a bottle of good claret. Bereft of so many friends and neighbours, Maman was happy to set out a couple more plates. Even Papa, despite his difference with the brothers, seemed to welcome their company and debate. Seated in the drawing room, Édouard announced with a defiant tip of his chin that he and Degas had signed up as artillerymen for the National Guard and Eugène the *Garde Mobile*—an unskilled fighting force backing up the front lines. To picture my artistic friends wielding anything but a paintbrush or pen was difficult but it was impossible to imagine Eugène in an aggressive pose.

Stevens, Édouard told us, was a staunch pacifist and would not enlist. Now he spoke to me. "That rogue Claude Monet is marrying his mistress." My heart sang. I kept my face neutral but my eyes danced for him. "By the time the Prussians arrive, he will be conveniently across the channel on his honeymoon."

"Cowardly timing," said Papa.

Maman tsked.

"Unless he had little choice," said Papa.

The choicelessness of love, I thought, surprised at my father's romanticism. Then his raised eyebrow told me he spoke of a more scandalous, practical matter.

"You'll never guess who's to be Degas' commander," laughed Édouard. "Ernest Meissonier himself."

"Excellent." It was the first time in weeks I had seen Papa smile.

"I'm sure his orders will be short and precise," I said.

"His men's uniforms spotless," said Édouard. "The medals for heroism he pins to our breast tiny."

Maman mentioned the guard would be making use of my studio and Édouard told us he had sent a number of his paintings to a friend's well-vaulted basement for safekeeping. "The rest I'll cover with blankets and store in my studio cellar with my fingers crossed." Did this include my gift of *The Harbour of Lorient?*

I had forgotten Eugène was there when he spoke up and urged me to do the same.

"They're not worth the trouble." I waited for Édouard's refutation but Papa had his ear.

Eugène, whom I was beginning to see was stubborn in the way of a boulder in one's path, wouldn't hear of it. "Each painting is an historical document," he said. "Not just of the times but of your progress as an artist. Someday they will be important."

Such optimism. My own worst critic, I felt no compunction to protect my work, but that night Eugène convinced Maman of their significance and the following week would personally oversee the business of wrapping them and storing them in the cellar. The seventy-some canvases Edma had left behind remained locked in the studio cabinet.

When Édouard and he were leaving, Eugène said to me with no hint of self-pity, "I don't expect to survive this invasion. But I'll think of you and your family, and know my death had meaning."

"Eugène, you're being dramatic," I said, a seed of fear taking root. If harm could come to Eugène, it could come to Édouard.

"Édouard," I blurted, "before you go, I need some advice on a painting I'm struggling with."

"It's my brow and hair," Maman said, believing she knew the painting in question. "She can't get it quite right." My painting of her reading to Edma during her lying-in was the only portrait I had ever done of my mother and she was overly concerned that she turned out well.

As Édouard followed me outside, I saw Pauline spying from the third-floor window but she moved from sight. The sun had begun to set, the air still warm and heavy. The pears in the trees hung like gold pendants. Pink gladiolas bloomed a flower fence around the pigeon pens and the birds cooed, luring in the night. The gardener walked shaking ashes from a pail and a loose hen strutted over to see if he carried food. The scene was idyllic, a stage set for lovers, and it was hard to conceive of preparations for war taking place just outside these walls.

The evening light dissected the studio with long white blades, the air tart with the vinegar water used to keep the windows clear. As soon as Édouard closed the door behind us I was flooded with so great a happiness a part of me hated that such feelings relied on him.

"Berthe, leave Paris while—"

I took his face in my hands. "Tell me how much you've missed me."

He tried to shake his head free but I held it firm. "Tell me you're sorry for not answering my notes, for making me suffer."

"I am sorry, Berthe. I've missed you but cannot risk wanting you."

"You? The risk is all mine and so it is mine to take."

He closed his eyes as if I didn't understand, and I struck him in the chest. His eyes sprang open. He grabbed my beating fists and I tried to keep my voice down. "Don't ever reject me again. And if you do tell me why and tell it to my face."

Fitfully, he pressed me to him. Our anguished kisses soon turned slow and savoured.

"It is not my intention to reject you. Only..."—again he hesitated—"to protect you."

"I can protect myself."

An ache of a moan parted his lips.

"Promise me."

"I promise you."

Despite our clothes and flesh, I felt not an inch of separation between us.

WITHOUT WARNING, the next day the city's borders were closed and the trains stopped running. Our chance to escape south to Edma had passed. There were reports of Prussian brutality—a convent desecrated, young novices raped, villages burned and its citizens systematically shot. Papa called it propaganda but I began to have trouble sleeping.

The landscape of Paris changed again. Brick and mortar barricades were erected at the ends of boulevards, ugly black trenches dug in behind. Wooden storehouses appeared on street corners to house gunpowder, oil or food. For fear of supplies being cut off, cows, goats and sheep were brought in from the countryside to graze in the parks. Thousands of oxen roamed the Bois de Boulogne and shat amidst the tents of the National Guardsmen. Crates of chickens were dumped in the streets to provide the army with eggs. The birds roamed free, and those whose necks weren't wrung by hungry peasants or crushed beneath carriage wheels, laid eggs in all corners of the city. Gare du Nord was turned into a makeshift mill and bakery.

Less concerned about invading Prussians and more about "thieving Communards thinking they're owed something," Papa ordered the remaining servants to crate up all of our First Empire pieces to be stored in a repository in the Elysée.

With half our furnishings removed, the rooms of our home looked barren and unlived in, our voices suddenly too loud and lonely; it was as though furniture possessed an ability to listen. Only now did I see how these pieces I had known all my life—sideboard, drawing room console, the desk filling the bay window, my dresser,

Papa's chair—animated the rooms of our home. How memories could come to reside in a chest of drawers.

A group of four bushy peasants arrived from Toulon with their meagre sacks of belongings and crowded into my beautiful studio. They had been issued cots and food rations and we lent them bedding and cooking pots. They would mark the floor with cigarette burns and boot skid, scratch the walls with games of x's and o's, and manage to create a meandering crack in the highest and most essential window. I cried upon seeing that crack. The garden corner where the hostas grew tall was turned into a latrine and the flowers withered overnight. Our orchard became a butchery of carcasses strung between the fruit trees, each preserved in a mayonnaise coat and flies. Only when the mayonnaise grew green and the meat odorous, claimed the soldier with a rash that darkened one temple and cheek, was it ready to roast. Which they did, in the pit they dug behind my studio. Many evenings, after dinner, the men drank and sang to a sourly tuned accordion. Papa considered these sacrifices our contribution to the war effort and refused to listen to Maman's complaints.

M. Thiers' mission failed to garner foreign support and each day more sobering defeats headlined the papers. *Orleans Falls. Rouen Captured by the Enemy. Bourges Surrenders. The Army of the Loire Defeated.* The Army of the Loire was what Paris counted on as its chief defence. *The Emperor's palace of Versailles has been taken, without a single shot fired.* The war had indeed been "a stroll in the park," but not for France.

Edma wrote: *You must now face the facts and prepare yourselves. It is only a matter of time until the Prussian Army is knocking down Paris's door. To say I told you so brings me no relief so I send you my prayers and my strength, Berthe, to endure.*

But I see Edouard almost every second day, I wanted to tell her. We steal kisses in the foyer and under the stairs and once again share coded looks and words.

Then on the front page of *Le Figaro*—now a third its normal size—came the headline we had been dreading. *Marshal Bazaine capitulates at Metz. In a single day,* read the article, *fifty-two generals and 174,000 French soldiers relinquished their weapons and surrendered to the Prussian enemy. Is this performance one of cowardice or acumen?*

Somewhere in that stumbling stream of prisoners was Tibby. Maman could not be consoled. She ordered Thin Louis to have her trunk packed and a carriage readied.

"I am going to find my son and make sure that he is being properly treated." Thin Louis advised it was not safe to travel and she screamed at him to do as he was told before gusting upstairs to pack on her own. Neither Papa nor I could persuade her otherwise and Dr. Rafinesque was called. I was more worried for Maman, believing rightly or wrongly that Tibby's self-concern would somehow carry him through.

Degas and Édouard came the following night to offer support. Édouard kissed my cheeks and squeezed my hand with intent. "My love," he whispered beside my ear and I was foolishly content. As he let me go, a desperation to keep him close clenched my jaw.

They wore their required uniforms: navy-blue pants with thick red stripes down the outside seam. Jackets with a double row of brass buttons, red-trimmed collars and matching caps. Seeing them in uniform made it feel as though we were all characters in a play. Édouard looked achingly handsome in his costume, his brass buttons glinting in the light. Degas' costume was smudged with dirt and worn at the knees. Degas was thinner too, though he appeared stronger, more defined, as if he had just now taken up residence in his body. Dark crescent moons set under his eyes, eyes that had always belonged to an older man but now looked ancient.

Édouard reassured us that "resourceful and clever" Tibby would come through just fine. Dosed on laudanum, eyes glazed, Maman hung on his words and didn't stop nodding. "No need to worry about that young man, Madame Morisot."

That very day, he and Degas had hiked up the hills of Montmartre to purview the surrounding countryside.

"Hundreds of fires ring the outskirts of the city," said Édouard.

"Prussian ants in their hideous grey uniforms," said Degas, "are burning hayracks to deny our livestock their feed and trees to deny us our heat."

"So the siege has begun," said Papa.

"Is't time, dear? Shou' we pack 'n' leave?"

"It is too late for leaving, my darling." Papa took Maman's limp hand.

"Our mettle will be put to the test," said Édouard brightly.

Degas stared at the floor. "France has already failed that test. Now we see how far we bend before we break."

My role in this play felt of another genre. The young woman in love, carefully appointed, foolishly content in the presence of her optimistic soldier with the shiny buttons. She wanted only to be held and kissed, hear words of love whispered in her ear, imagine a future together, a new order where men could leave their slow-witted wives and marry anew.

That evening, like a scorched fog, pungent smoke rolled in over Paris and stayed. Behind this paste of smoke, the sun turned an eerie copper pink and all around the neighbourhood confused roosters repeated their morning calls.

WITH THE EXCEPTION of military correspondence via the balloon corps, mail in and out of Paris came to a halt. I wrote Edma anyway, out of need, saying what I dared not say, then tossing it in the fire.

Oh, Edma, the war and its horrors has only now become real to me. Dear sweet talented Frédéric Bazille is gone. I'm tearing up, unable to believe it. He has been killed in battle. A bullet to the head, Édouard said, his height, you see. His poor family. Édouard wept when he told me the news and I held him in my arms and cried with him. To be held by the man I love is what I live for these dark days. I've been too frightened to tell you, Edma, but he and I are lovers. Not in the biblical sense—not yet—but in every other. I promise to tell you everything when we are next together. We will be together again. I must believe that. Oh, Edma, it was mad to stay here but Édouard is like the sun to me. Or the earth to my sun. I now understand the power he had over you because love is simply vaster and stronger than we are.

Papa stops Maman from speculating about Tibby, though as soon as he is out of earshot she conjures dire scenarios. I am glad you're not here to be shocked by our mother on her knees wailing and beating at the floor. It is unbearable. Laudanum is the one thing that calms her.

My stomach's in a permanent clench from the blast of cannons which daily shake the earth and rattle our windows. It's not so dire as it sounds. Not yet, anyway, for these Prussian cannons are not aimed at Paris but at those on the perimeter trying to save Paris. As Papa predicted, Bismarck appears to want to preserve the city and starve us into surrendering.

For now we have enough food but it's being carefully rationed. Hardly matters to me for I've no appetite, though lately in my dreams I am eating Manon's creamy soups. Did she accompany you to Mirande? Our cook says the markets are half-full at best, and a bushel of potatoes sells for triple the normal price. Yesterday a bidding war for the last cabbage at M. Remy's stall fetched fifteen francs! The gardener patrols the grounds at night for fear of starving citizens slipping over the walls. But still pears and apples disappear from the trees, there are holes where beets and carrots should be and rabbits are going missing. Papa thought one of the servants was stealing for his family and tried to force a confession. Then one of the guardsmen owned up to helping himself to our rabbits after stupidly killing not one but two pregnant females. Though I had the feeling he was covering for someone else. I have trouble feeling these men are our protectors. One took a bath within sight of my sitting room window and as if proof of M. Darwin's theory he was covered in black whorls of hair. If he were a more handsome specimen and I had any humour left, I might have taken advantage of having a nude model to draw. But I find no inspiration, beauty, or dignity in our situation. How, I ask, can men killing men be a solution to anything? Death is only a cure for life.

M. Gambetta pleads for Parisians to stand united in our national will. He has pledged "to die before surrendering." Sounds heroic, yes, and I understand the importance of keeping up morale, but if the Army of the Loire saw no point in fighting, how can the mismatched, underfed soldiers of Paris have any chance? How can the likes of Eugène Manet make a difference at the front? How do brick and sandbag walls stop a cannon? Gambetta's pronouncements are hollow and perilous. My opinions infuriate Papa but I would gladly take learning German over a cold grave. Besides, French bluster is what got us into this war in the first place.

My candle is running short, for they too are being rationed. I pray with all my heart that you and Yves and my beautiful nieces are safe and well fed. Berthe

---

Dearest Edma, The Champ de Mars has become a field hospital after two chemical plants inexplicably caught fire and exploded. The air is acrid and the injured moans and screams carry across the river. I sleep with my pillow wrapped around my ears if I'm to sleep at all. Vagrant children wander Passy's streets, thin as sticks and lacking proper clothes. The gardener shoos them away when they come to the gate. How awful to regard children as threats. In my guilt I rummaged up old but still decent woolens and fabric ends to send to the poorhouse.

Édouard and Degas visit when they can, Maman drilling them for news of Metz and Tibby. They have heard nothing but, at Papa's behest, make up news of a positive nature. Degas is a terrible liar and Édouard an overly enthusiastic one. Maman is catching on to the deception. Their visits are my joy and solace. Degas arrives hungry and dust covered, having done an honest day's work. M. Meisonnier weights their rifles with sandbags which they must press fifty times overhead morning and evening. After target practice they load burlaps with sand and build walls, or carry buckets of water from the Seine for washing, or transport gunpowder supplies where needed. I sometimes wonder if Édouard, whose uniform remains pristine, reports for duty at all. It looks as though his day's work is no more than trimming his nails and beard. I tease him but am pleased he looks out for himself. If I lost him, Edma, I don't know what I'd do.

Degas said he doesn't think he'd have the courage to shoot another man no matter the circumstance. Édouard mocked him for it but could Édouard? What man has such tremendous arrogance that to silence another's life he'd not suffer from it for the rest of his. Surely it tears the very fabric of one's humanity.

I'm weary all the time and accomplish nothing. I mostly daydream of my lover, read, make flaccid sketches of this and that and, to please Papa, sometimes fiddle on the piano, my fingers stiff with cold. We must use our limited coal and wood for cooking only and walk about the half-empty house in our capes and gloves. It's all so strange. My handwriting is ragged because I can't get warm no matter how much tea I drink or how many warm bricks support my feet. I never thought I'd envy the cook and scullery maid who now sleep in the kitchen beside the stove.

Thin Louis went to the candlestick shop only to find its windows boarded. One stroke of luck still to be had, he ran into Leo and the dear man came by the next day with a gift of ten dozen candles and a gallon of cooking oil. I asked after Marcello. He told me she has escaped to Italy.

I wonder: do these so-called leaders of men not bleed like we do? Is their pride so all-consuming that they are indifferent to suffering? Are they like bored children seeking excitement, however deadly? There is word going around that our Emperor was inspired to war by the agonizing itch of his piles! Before his capture he was seen parading on his white horse back and forth in front of his army as if in bravery but perhaps the saddle eased the itch. Or was he hoping to get shot and end his agony once and for all?

To picture you and my sweet nieces as healthy and happy keeps me from despair.

Berthe

Edma, my beloved sister, The sun still rises, oblivious to what it illuminates. Yesterday Maman and I ventured the block to check on Mme. Higgonet, who also remained behind. Two children were asleep in the doorway of the boarded-up patisserie, one curled sweetly around the other. A passing guardsmen ordered them to move and when they did not, he poked at them with his rifle then rolled their unresisting bodies with his boot. Their faces, pale as chalk, were tinged a haunting blue. Edma, they were dead. Children. The youngest, a girl, couldn't have been more than seven. When I close my eyes, I keep seeing those frozen faces. Children are dying, I want to scream. Stop this madness!

The city's gas has been cut off and our candle supply, Leo's too, has run dry. Dinner is eaten at 4:00 so that there is still daylight enough for the servants to clean up. We are consumed by darkness at half-past five and our even darker thoughts. If there's a moon, we play another round of cards but otherwise make our way early to bed in hopes of sleep. It is the dull routine of animals.

I've lost the weight I gained in Lorient, maybe more. I suffer dizzy spells—Dr. Rafinesque thinks I might be anemic—and must cling to the railing to climb the stairs. A dry persistent cough and a burning in my stomach wakes me in the night. The cold takes its toll. I had such chills last night so Maman called in Dr. Rafinesque. Siege fever was his diagnosis. Do doctors invent these names? Is naming an illness supposed to be a comfort?

To conserve heat, he has ordered me to bed. So here I lie, of no use to anyone, in anticipation of the thudding blast of the next cannon jarring my organs.

The summer with its glorious entertainments and gaiety seems an impossible folly. I want only to sleep and dream of those times. I cannot wait to tell you about Montmartre. Such memories sustain me, not the unrecognizable twisted roots and withered greens on my dinner plate. The grey meat. I don't dare ask how many horses are left in our stable. A butcher in the 5th is selling paté made from rat.

My love, my Édouard, hasn't visited for ten days now. Degas tells me he suffers a bad stomach from eating rotten meat. I am desperate and asked for Dr. Rafinesque to be sent to tend him. I am waiting to hear. I imagine him sharing my sick bed. That such closeness would heal us both. I imagine being as man and woman. No matter what you say, I want to know carnal love. A life would hardly be complete without knowing such love. My body longs for his, aches to touch and taste and know every inch. And to be touched by him. His hands. I love his hands. Oh, if I could only share such thoughts with you in person. If we get through this war, I will. I hate keeping secrets from you and know you will be happy for me.

Degas remains strangely steady. He appears unsurprised by our circumstance as if expecting as much from his fellow man. Pessimists are better suited to handle such as war. He calls this siege "reality intensified" and sounds more curious than afraid.

Le Figaro *reports that the city's poor, both starving and freezing, are filling the hospitals and the morgue. Can we bourgeoisie be far behind? Is it not just a matter of time? My stomach feels as though on fire yet I have chills that shake my pen. This letter may be legible only to me.*

President Gambetta has shown courage, in my opinion, by flying off in one of Nadar's balloons—one bullet to those silk balloons would surely be the end of it—to organize remaining troops outside the capital and bring an end to this siege. Though why he might succeed where others have failed is beyond me. Papa considers the balloon trip different. Sees Gambetta as a coward trying to save himself. That's the opinion of all those hoping M. Thiers will be invited to step into this new void of governance.

Maman writes daily to Tibby, sometimes twice. It was my idea. Only instead of burning her letters like me she addresses them to the military headquarters at Metz and gives them to Thin Louis who pretends to post them. It seems to have helped for she only needs laudanum at night to sleep. Papa does not allow her the newspaper until he has read it and removed any upsetting articles. He remains strangely strong, never complaining of his own ills, though sometimes he needs not one cane but two. My hand is too tired to continue.

Please be safe. B

Oh Edma, a sickening revelation in Le Figaro. *The zoo has been emptied. Where have those beautiful and innocent animals gone? I can hardly write the words: the rich have been dining on steaks of kangaroo, antelope, zebra, elephant and more.*

Better, says Papa, for these animals to feed the French than the Prussians. I couldn't listen. Such decadence makes me want to don a red scarf and join the Communards. Have I partaken and been kept in the dark? My stomach heaves at the thought.

Édouard's stomach also cannot take food. It makes me feel closer to him despite our distance. Degas said Dr. Rafinesque gave him something to drink which made him retch but then he felt a little better. I was so happy to hear it. If I felt stronger I would find a way to go to him.

My infirmities give Maman renewed purpose and she is finally off her laudanum. So I am of use after all. Or maybe she simply ran out of it, for Dr. Rafinesque has fled Paris. Either that or gone underground. Has he caught my 'siege fever'? Maman feverishly hunted down a new doctor for me. This one has bootblack hair and a buttery complexion the colour of café au lait. *His breath smells of the licorice root we used to clean our teeth with as he handles me like the finest of china—feathers the hair from my forehead, gently eases up my eyelid as if something other than an eye might lie beneath. His stethoscope horn on my back was so delicately placed it made me shiver and then cough uncontrollably.*

He pronounced my lungs clear and diagnosed the coughing as a constriction of the larynx. Said my stomach ailments were related.

We couldn't make sense of anything he was saying.

He told us his grandfather, also a physician, hailed from East India—that explained the complexion—and according to an eastern model each of our organs are related to an emotion. Stomach disorders are caused by anger, he said, and strings of anger from my stomach have risen up to constrict my throat. He searched my eyes and asked, "Are you feeling angry, Mademoiselle Morisot?"

"Am I angry?" I shouted but my throat reduced my words to a whisper. A stupid question. A needless war is causing great anguish to everyone and everything I care for. The people of Paris are dying. Children are dying. My brother is missing. The man I love is ill. Yes, I'm angry, I wanted to say, aren't you?

He recommended more bed rest and the puerile advice of thinking of happier times. "What do you think I've been doing?" I said but he didn't hear.

Our Emperor, wherever he is, should be tried for the murder of the people of France. What gave him the right to gamble with our lives? He is no god. And in whatever dank prison he is being held, I wish him suffering in equal measure to that of his subjects. May his piles increase tenfold, may they cover his face. And, I hope that, like us, he is learning what it is like to be poor. The deprivations of war have finally made all Parisians equals. Communards rejoice! The only difference is that some of us have larger prisons in which to freeze and starve.

This letter is composed of nothing but anger. Apparently it's my illness. I would like to believe I am sick with emotion and nothing more. Such a thought instills in me some sense of agency at least, far preferable to helplessness.

I miss Édouard and I miss you, Edma. I need you both here beside me. My burning heart would keep us warm. B

1871

Jan. 3rd, 1871

My dear daughters,
The balloon corp has promised to begin taking civilian mail so I wanted to wish you a bonne année. *I hope that you were able to celebrate in some authentic style. I've grown fashionably thin these past months and swim within the layers of clothing I don for warmth, the weight of which is making me strong as a circus pony. Your father is surprisingly robust despite the hardships. His work gives him purpose though he must now do what he can at home for it is no longer safe to travel to the ministries.*

Your sister's health has not been good. I believe that an ulcer is the cause of her stomach pain and anemia the reason she's unable to warm herself. To stop her shivering, I must get into bed with her and wrap myself around her. As for her cough, I am not ruling out consumption.

We had been following the advice of Dr. Rafinesque as well as another doctor and her condition only worsened. I feared we had tried everything.

But then Édouard and Eugène came to wish us a bonne année. *All of us were covered in a film of dirt and grime that only heated water would wash away. Our clothes no better. As for our bodily odours, thank heaven for potpourri. I put several sachets in and around Berthe's bed. I had nothing to offer our guests but watered wine and some canned cherries. Édouard was thin and his skin resembled parchment, his fiery ebullience extinguished. He was so despondent that, if you can believe it, Eugène did the talking.*

He has matured away from his mother's skirts and speaks his mind with a slow deliberate effort, even holds my eye satisfactorily for once. Édouard's sunken cheeks make him look gaunt and aged, but on Eugène the same is an improvement. I had not thought him handsome before now.

They were appalled to see the state Berthe was in and sat on either side of her bed, holding her hand as if to split her down the middle. She only had eyes for Édouard—whatever do you girls see in him?—who mumbled and fumed that we hadn't left Paris when we could. He questioned why she'd not been seen by a doctor and I assured him she had been seen by two. Eugène insisted that she be seen by a third, a physician friend of his, "young and abreast of medical advances."

Dr. Dally arrived that very night. A tall willowy figure with striking blue eyes, a trim moustache and clean-shaven chin. I wanted to ask him where he finds the soap for shaving as your papa's unshaven face makes him look old and common. Dr. Dally wore a very fashionable long black wool coat, which I know Berthe would have admired. After a lengthy examination, he told us he did not believe Berthe's condition is in any way permanent and that he had every faith that after this war had ended she would recover. Some souls are more sensitive, he said, with what I thought was true appreciation. I think you'd agree that being so finely strung, Berthe would do well to have a doctor for a husband.

I was vexed that he recommended the exact opposite treatment to that of the other doctors. He wants her out of bed and moving around as much as possible. Said this would bring warmth, improve her circulation, stimulate her appetite and help clear her congestion. So now we're trusting this doctor's advice and putting it to the test.

Berthe complains she's too tired and her legs too weak, but Pauline and I each take an arm over our shoulders and force her to walk up and down the hall, telling stories to distract her. We are fast approaching Berthe's thirtieth name day and, as incentive, I promised a gathering of sorts. Already I think a little colour has returned to her face.

I had asked Leo if he could track down a particular painting of Camille Corot's that was at this past Salon. He managed to find it at Cadart's, despite the gallery being boarded up. He is resourceful, that man. I wrapped the painting in a sheet—all parcel paper long burned—to present to Berthe on her name day but decided to give it to her today. Watching light fill her face and tears stain her eyes, I wished I had thought of it sooner. We've hung it over the fireplace where she can admire it from her bed.

She sends her love, as does Papa. You are both thought of day and night. Adolphe and Théo too. We send our hearts to Bibi and Jeanne. How we long to hear news from you.

Never stop wishing for your brother's safe return and please be well.

With deep affection, your Maman

Jan. 16th, 1871

My darling daughters,

Please read this letter strong in spirit. It has finally come, the Prussian bombardment. They have turned their cannons around to face our fair city. Today you can no longer hear Paris breathe. Homes and shops sit hollow-eyed. The streets are vacant and death is everywhere. Bodies shattered, starved or frozen amongst the rubble. Is it not enough to deprive and starve us? And now this?

Though aimed at the city's core, cannon fire fell so near Passy that every last window shattered on our fourth and fifth floors. Luckily no one was hurt—of course our servants are now few—but nonetheless all the furnishings had to be moved downstairs, the windows boarded.

The Pantheon and Grenelle quarters bear the worst of it. Auteuil has been hit and the Pont du Jour. Leo was wounded in his leg by a shell falling in rue Bayard but it's not too serious. The gratitude he expressed at his right arm being unscathed seemed extreme. He said he would sacrifice both his legs for his right arm. He is a true artist, I suppose.

Oh, the bluster of General Trochu. He's even worse than Gambetta, proclaiming Paris will never surrender, not at any cost. I say, we've endured enough. I've come over to Berthe's side and don't give a damn about such humiliation. Our present stink and filth, of eating soup made from the bones of swallows, is what's humiliating. I'm ready for this war to end, and us all to be together again. Fly the white flag! France has been shamed since the day this war began and it is mere bravado that pretends otherwise.

My only good news is that Berthe has regained a little strength and is able to stand and walk on her own. Now if we can only get her stomach to accept more food, I believe she may recover. Though I wouldn't call it food exactly. Dr. Dally checks up on her every few days and I think his reasons are more personal than professional.

Your father's health seems stable. I would swear he is sustained more by famine than feast. Though I know, by how little he speaks of it, that he worries terribly for your safety and for Tibby's, from whom we also have not heard. I write letter after letter to the military headquarters in Metz but have received nothing back. I believe in my heart that your brother is alive and when the war has ended will return to us.

We wait with breath bated for word from you, Maman

Kisses to my grand babies.

"I LOOK AS THOUGH aged ten years."

"Your lack of colour gives your dark eyes and hair a certain mystique." Maman had sent Pauline to help in the kitchen and taken over doing my hair. The house still standing and with word of France's imminent surrender, Maman planned a gathering in honour of my name day. Mme. Higgonet and Leo were invited, as were Dr. Dally, Degas, Eugène and Édouard.

"My hair is dark with dirt and grease."

"Dr. Dally thinks so too."

I sighed.

"He saved your life, Berthe. That's no small thing."

It was because Édouard still lived and breathed that I was alive, I wanted to say.

"And, I haven't told you, but the doctor has offered to take a painting of yours in lieu of payment."

"As in take it off my hands?"

"It was not like that." She held up a dark blue and a cream-coloured ribbon to weave through my braid.

"The rust one, please."

"But these match your dress."

"Exactly."

"It's no different than selling a painting."

"It feels lesser."

"He comes from a good family in Bordeaux."

When I didn't respond, she said, "Be reasonable, Berthe. A future alone is just how it sounds."

The cook had somehow procured four pigeons to roast and, at my request, had saved a jar of pickled asparagus for the occasion—Édouard's favourite. Dr. Dally came with dried figs, "a gift from a patient." Eugène arrived with a wheel of hard cheese he bought off a man whose shop had been hit. Eugène apologized again and again for the moldy bits, though no one cared. Leo arrived with two splendid bottles of Spanish wine.

"Where in this god-forsaken city did you find them?" asked Mme. Higgonet.

Leo went quiet and Madame looked confused, then flustered. No one asked after that. Many of the homes in his neighbourhood were flattened.

Degas brought a box of stale crackers. Édouard came late and empty-handed. As he greeted me, he whispered, "My lips contain your gift when we find a private corner."

I flushed with warmth. "You're so thin," I said, saddened by his sunken eyes.

"That's the kettle calling… whatever that expression is. Soon we'll all be transparent and light enough to float. We can convene in the rafters for a new perspective."

"No balloon required. Wonderful."

To laugh was so unfamiliar, my lungs ached. Our small party sat in a circle around the coffee table, Maman careful to divide the food evenly onto our plates. Everyone did their best to make things last and not act the hungry savage. I imagined mayonnaise for the asparagus, and a baguette under the cheese, though we made do with the dry crackers. For the first time in a long time my stomach stopped whining.

Beside me on the divan, Édouard excused himself and Dr. Dally came and took his place. He smelled of soap and bootblack. Did he hoard crates of soap in his cellar? Perhaps I should trade a painting for a crate?

"How's the patient?"

Édouard had stopped in the drawing room doorway and watched our exchange.

"Warmed by this gathering," I said and, misunderstanding me, he pressed the back of his palm to my forehead.

"Perfectly normal."

Like you, I wanted to say. Because he was. Perfectly normal. Handsome enough with his summer-blue eyes and high cheeks.

But normal.

Édouard walked back to us.

"I'd say Mademoiselle is out of danger," Dr. Dally directed his diagnosis to Maman.

"Of one kind," Édouard muttered behind me.

"Mademoiselle Berthe," said Dr. Dally, "would you be so kind as to show me your paintings someday?"

"Are you a collector?" said Édouard.

"No, but I have suggested to Madame that—"

"A connoisseur?"

"I am not, but am fond of landscapes—"

"Mademoiselle Morisot is more than a landscapist. She is a painter of truth and the human soul. Do not demean her."

"Édouard." I was embarrassed.

"It was not my intention to offend," he said calmly. "Please, if I have—"

"It's all right, Dr. Dally," I offered, when Édouard didn't.

Dr. Dally trained his blue eyes on me. "Call me François."

"François. Maman mentioned your offer. I will think on it."

"Very good," he said, standing. "Now I believe I have taken your seat, Édouard."

"I have paintings you might be interested in," said Édouard. Across the table, Degas gave a little me-too wave. Dr. Dally, François, nodded at Édouard and excused himself.

Alone in Papa's study under the pretense of retrieving a book, I received the first of my gifts from Édouard.

"Don't you dare give him a painting," he said.

"It would be payment for services."

"Even more degrading."

"I know."

"Don't."

"I'd no plans to."

He kissed me again then cupped my face to study it. "Thirty?"

"Thirty."

"Old for a woman."

I slapped his arm. "Perhaps I need a doctor."

"No, love is the best medicine."

This man was not normal. Not at all.

FINALLY, two weeks later, on January 28th, Paris stopped its heroic pretentions and surrendered. When Pauline opened my curtains and relayed the news, I crossed the line between master and servant to hug her and kissed her long cheeks. In return, she patted me on the back.

"It's over." Tears of exhausted joy swelling in my eyes making the room swim. I wondered if I could possibly paint this.

"Until the next thing," said Pauline, turning to the wardrobe. "What shall you be wearing, today, Mademoiselle?"

"THE ARMISTICE is to be signed in the Hall of Mirrors at the Palace of Versailles," Maman said and looked up from the paper.

We were at breakfast: one stewed prune each, a tiny strong-smelling egg with a greenish-blue shell, and a stone of bread made from roasted acorns.

"Fitting that the vanity of this war," I said, "be reflected back to our ministers a hundred-fold."

"We should have held out a little longer," said Papa. "Shown more muscle in the end."

"What? We're filthy and starving. Others have lost their lives, their homes." I barely refrained from mentioning Tibby who for all we knew was dead, threw up my hands and left the table. And we still hadn't a single word from Edma and Yves.

OVER THE FOLLOWING WEEKS life returned to something resembling normal. The hollow rooms of our home were filled with those old friends, our missing furniture. The guardsmen disappeared one by one from my studio. New glass was ordered for the missing upstairs windows, including one for my studio. The gardener began the long process of filling in ground holes and firepit, burning the soiled clothes, hay beds, and magazines left behind. He would have to wait until spring to replenish the damaged gardens. Some of the stores along our street reopened. A small market was set up in the square selling jars of pickled things, cheese curds and fresh-caught eel. My stomach was able to accept only small amounts at one time or else seize with cramps.

Shortly after the last guardsman was gone, Pauline gave notice. She packed her few belongings and left without so much as a tear. Maman couldn't understand it. Pauline had been with us since she was fifteen, nearly eighteen years, and Maman considered her part of the family. Pauline and I hugged warmly. I thanked her for all her care over the years, especially during the siege, and wished her every good thing to come.

"It is my turn," said Pauline, defiant.

"Yes, it is," I agreed though she didn't elaborate.

To have love? A home and family of her own? She also didn't say where she was going but I assumed from her timing that she would not be going there alone. Her waist, I only then noticed, was slightly broader. It couldn't have been from overeating. Had the guardsman who'd stolen the rabbits, and probably the fruit and vegetables too, been stealing them for her?

I missed Pauline more than I had imagined. I missed her frankness and air of mischief, the comfort of knowing she was near. And I often found myself wondering what she was doing at any given moment. I was a little jealous that she had lost her maidenhood when I had not.

Each morning I sat with Maman while Papa walked the short two blocks to the post office to check the casualty postings. At the sound of the gate upon his return, she clutched my hand, both of us dreading to read the expression on his face.

Coal once more burned in the grates, its warmth akin to food for our bones. The city's gas was turned back on and again we had the miracle of evening light. Papa bought new carriage horses. The market expanded, though many basic items such as flour and butter were not to be found. Nevertheless, the scent of real food floated on the air to whet the *appétit* and when Édouard and his brother stopped by we had palatable meat to serve.

The government was a skeletal one as we awaited public elections, yet the trains began running again and a rudimentary mail system was put in place. One snowy morning, Thin Louis brought in the mail tray holding a packet of letters eight inches thick. We just stared at it. Papa's hands shook as he untied the string. He shoved the tray at me and the letters tumbled onto the table. "Read"—his jaw was rigid—"the most recent first."

Quickly I checked the postmarks and found one a mere week past. The address was in Edma's neat handwriting. No bad news, please. My fingers fumbled the letter knife and Maman gently took it and the letter from my hand. Opening it she read to herself first, then aloud: *We are ecstatic at the news of the armistice. We have been praying for this day. I trust this letter, at least, will get through to assure you that we are all fine.*

I wiped away tears of relief.

Though we have not heard from you, we understand that Passy was spared. We have received word from Adolphe. He is unscathed, the navy having little role in the conflict after all. The babies have grown fat—

Papa's gulping belch startled us. Maman stopped reading. His head fell to his hands and he wept in hoarse sobs and without control. I hadn't believed my father capable of such feeling. Maman continued, louder over his weeping, though the effort to keep her voice steady was obvious—*fat and full of life. Jeanne is fascinated by her cousin's every move and alert to the sound of her voice. I run on, forgive me, for I have far more important news. Adolphe made it his mission to track down Tibby. And though it took these long weeks, he finally located him*—Maman gasped, one hand clawing the air for Papa's hand—*in Perigueux in the Dordogne.*

One hand pressing her chest, Maman passed the letter to me to read.

Our little brother is quite heroic in my eyes now. You will hear the details from Tibby himself but, in short, after he and his fellow soldiers were captured at Metz they were taken to Mainz and the largest of the prisoner camps. Over 25,000 men some say. Imagine the conditions. As you know, our Tibby does not take well to being inconvenienced and managed to escape by digging under a fence then slipping onto a collier in the middle of the night where he hid in the hold. The collier was headed to Hamburg! So he sailed right into enemy territory where he jumped ship and swam to shore and somehow managed not to lose any toes to the cold. Then he forged his way on foot all the way back to Bordeaux where he promptly reported for duty! Oh, and he was promoted to lieutenant for his bravery.

Maman laughed and wept at the same time. Papa, now recovered, slapped the table. "Clever boy. Yes. Resourceful boy, our Tibby."

That night Maman got drunk at dinner, but no one scolded or blamed her. After that most happy of days, my appetite improved and slowly my body grew stronger. But after six months of holding strong for our sakes, Papa's health began a slow and gradual decline.

MY RENEWED HEALTH brought with it renewed desire. I sent a note inquiring after Édouard, whom I had not seen for nearly a week's time, urging him to visit. I anticipated his prompt response but received nothing back. Two days later, Eugène showed up at our door, alone. The day's cold whipped about by wind, a red silk scarf was wound around his neck and his chapped ears and nose were of the same cheery red. He pinned a hen under one arm and held a basket containing an angry rooster in the other hand. Sprouting from his coat pocket was a bottle of Maman's favourite claret. She clapped when she saw him. As she kissed his cheeks, his gaze sought mine for any sign of pleasure at seeing him. And I was glad to see him and thankful for such practical and generous gifts, but my worry for Édouard took centre stage.

"Is Édouard well? He's not with you?"

He kissed my hand. Behind his attempted smile lay a sadness, a resignation. It was then I realized that not only did he know the depth of my longing for his brother, but he understood it. Because he loved his brother too and he also longed for his attentions. Our love for Édouard was something we shared and in that moment I experienced a kinship with Eugène I had not felt before.

"His spirits are good," Eugène told me. "Maman wrote and insisted he come to her. He has journeyed south or would be here himself, I'm sure of it." He looked at me askance, not comfortable lying, and added, "He had to hurry to catch the last train." His failure to mention Suzanne and Léon made it even worse, more glaring. They had seemed so far away these past months, I had all but forgotten their existence.

Édouard was going to see his family. I was not his family.

"His Maman and family are well?" I managed.

"Yes. We're all very relieved. Yours too are safe." The hen clucked then stabbed its beak at Eugène's gloved hand.

"Yes, even Tibby," said Maman gaily. "He's come through unscathed." She ushered us along to the drawing room. "Come now, let's raise a glass to the end of war and worry. Where's Louis? He'll take the fowl."

Settled in the drawing room, Maman and me on the flowered settee and Eugène at his post at the mantelpiece, we were joined by Papa. Papa and Eugène spoke of upcoming elections and who might lead the nation.

What had I been thinking? That Suzanne and Léon would remain forever in the south? Or worse, that they'd been killed? Of course, duty to family came first and I wouldn't respect him if he hadn't reunited with them in haste. Yet, why not inform me? How long does it take to pen a note?

FEBRUARY'S ELECTION swung conservative. Though most Parisians had rallied behind M. Gambetta, country dwellers preferred tradition. In place of a monarchy, the new National Assembly, sitting for the time in Bordeaux, was dominated by grey-haired men advocating caution and restraint. When M. Thiers won the vote to lead the country, Papa felt vindicated. All I could think was that Édouard's and his brothers' rising hopes for a new *republique*, which included hopes of my own, had been stamped out. I wanted to reassure him and myself in the process and paint him a picture of a future beyond this election, a future that included us. But though Eugène had passed along his mother's address, I had my pride. It was he who must write me first.

Edma wrote with fresh concern: *These men do not feel like men of the hour. Adolphe fears these election results may incite the reactionaries.*

Having joined hands to fight a common enemy, I did not believe the people of France could turn against another.

The peace terms laid out by the Prussians were harsher than anyone expected. A war indemnity of five million francs was to be paid. Alsace as well as Lorraine ceded. To top things off, until ratification, the Prussian army would encamp in Paris.

TIBBY RETURNED HOME. Maman could not stop touching him, stroking his head, his shoulder, his hand, and exclaiming over how thin he was. Except for a full beard and hair long enough to drape his shoulders, he appeared the Tibby of old. Confident, boyish, restless, spoiled. He bragged that his *appartement* in the 5th had not a stick broken. That even his larder was still stocked. When he kissed my cheeks I smelled wine on his breath though it was barely afternoon.

Maman laid a feast in his honour and Tibby, flushed with his own bravado, regaled us with his hardships. Like a waterwheel, my thoughts turned again and again to Édouard's thoughtlessness. Papa announced that he had written to President Thiers of Tibby's "unheralded heroism" and had received a letter back offering Tibby a position in an exclusive section of the National Guard. Tibby drank the remains of his glass then shook it high in the air for Thin Louis to refill.

"And Louis, bring my skinny son more pork," sang Maman.

"This very elite division," said Papa, now doing the boasting, "is to be called *The Friends of Order.*"

Friends together with Order sounded incompatible, but we all raised our glasses.

"To life returning to normal," said Papa.

Normal? Was that what we had suffered for?

AS WINTER SHED the cruelest of the cold, a Communard demonstration of an estimated one million people took place in the Place de la Bastille, marking the anniversary of the revolution of '48. Eugène told us that demonstrators had built a huge barricade in the Champs-Elysées. "To prevent the Prussian victors from marching its length. Then others set it on fire." I had smelled the smoke from my balcony.

"When a gendarme tried to intervene, he was killed," said Eugène, offering no details. In *Le Figaro* the next day, the murderers —"ruffians from Belleville and members of the Guard"—had burned the man to the point of begging for his own death and then promptly drowned him in the nearest fountain.

With Pauline gone, my bedroom curtains had not been drawn, and outside, as if unwilling to conceal the day's events, a full moon illuminated the night. I ran my hand around my breasts, assessing their fullness. Curls of smoke from chimney stacks were shredded by wind. Mongrel flakes of snow flew sideways. Across the river, small fires dotted the landscape. These fires, I knew, belonged to battalions of the Guard kept on to clean up rubble and debris. But how many of these men were Communard hopefuls disillusioned with the outcome of this war and pent up with fight they never had the opportunity to unleash?

THE DAY the Prussian army marched through the deserted streets of Paris, the cloudless sky was a gleaming lavender blue. Ever since I could only think of it as Prussian blue.

Behind our bolted doors and shuttered windows we listened to the approach of a thousand boots hitting the cobbles in percussive unison. I pictured the greenish-grey lines of unsmiling pickel-haubes, their chins tipped and turned a neat thirty degrees, the rifles on their backs polished and loaded. Surely they felt the hatred radiating from inside each sealed-up building. I couldn't hate them. As Maman had said, they were simply following orders. It was the heads of our governments I despised. Papa expressed his fantasy that the cannons which, since France's surrender, had gone missing from artillery storehouses would emerge from alleyways on either side of rue d'Iena and in one coordinated effort obliterate the lot of them.

Eugène dropped by to say a quick hello, his battalion having been installed nearby to ensure the march went off smoothly. I couldn't stop from asking if he'd heard from his brother.

"My brother has not much use for the pen," he said, reading my mind. "Maman writes that they are staying put until"—he hesitated—"everything is worked out."

"Worked out?"

He lowered his voice. "I cannot say more as I don't know any more. But Édouard hopes to return to Paris very soon."

Whatever the glint in his eye was supposed to mean, I felt suddenly hopeful. As if something was afoot and everything would magically work itself out.

PAPA PRESSED EDMA against his chest as if he would never let her go and to which she gracefully surrendered. She then took my hands, tears budding. "Look at how thin you are, Berthe. You should have come. You should have come."

"I know. You were right all along."

The tremble in her embrace made me truly sorry to have burdened her so.

Traveling north to rejoin Adolphe, she had stopped first in Paris. Poor tired baby Jeanne received so many fervent kisses it set her wailing. Edma brought gifts: two dozen bottles of wine and a dozen wheels of cheese. One entire trunk was filled with jars of *rillettes*, goose paté and dried apricots, coveted sacks of flour and wooden tubs of butter.

"I'll soon fit my clothes again," sang Maman, and Papa, giddy with happiness, groped for her *derrière.*

To have Edma home was the single cure for my loneliness. I dearly wanted her counsel so decided to tell her the real reason I'd stayed in Paris. For who better to understand my feelings?

We were cloistered in Yves' old bedroom away from the eyes of Maman, who still believed Edma's buxom maid doubled as a wet nurse. Edma lay nursing one-year-old Jeanne, and I perched on the chaise beside her.

"Edma, I need to…"

She looked up and I stopped.

"I'm so happy you're home." Why was I hesitant?

"It's a relief to be here. Yves and I, well, she's particular about everyone doing as she does. Was horrified I was nursing Jeanne. I had to make her promise not to tell Maman though I can't trust she'll keep that promise."

She removed Jeanne's hand from reaching into her mouth. "Maman looks exhausted but how I admire her resilience. And you too, Berthe, but you need to eat. Lots."

"Édouard has gone to the Pyrenees to collect his mother." There, I said his name.

"And his health?"

"He looks like the rest of us."

She feathered Jeanne's hair off her forehead.

"But is as handsome as ever."

"So now you find him handsome? Thine enemy?"

"No. Well, yes. He has become a friend."

"I'm glad. He's the type who is a loyal friend in the end. Just maybe not in the beginning. Or middle." She laughed.

"I confess I... oh, Edma." I moved to sit beside her on the bed. "I've been dying to tell you something."

"What something?"

"It's... well, it started with Édouard's portrait of Eva Gonzales. You remember her?"

"Of course."

"Well, I have made a complete reversal"—I was speaking too fast—"and now believe Édouard that, well, that his hostility toward me, as you witnessed, was the result of his repressed feelings. For me. Remember how we came to blows not once but twice?" My nervousness made me titter.

"Yes." Edma looked confused but didn't interrupt me.

I wanted to tell her everything from the beginning. I described the peony he'd painted, our letter exchange, my posing alone for him. I detailed my discomfort and his touch, the kiss on my ankle, the silent exchange of our eyes. Growing giddy, I told her of our coded communications at the racetrack. She shifted the baby to take her other breast, turning on her right side so I couldn't fully see her face. I might have exaggerated our night in Montmartre, the *guinguette*, the heavenly bells, of seeing Marcello at the *café concert*, his kiss inside the basket of the gas balloon, and all the stolen kisses since.

"Edma, I wanted to tell you sooner, I did, but was... afraid for some reason. But never have I dreamed there could be such feelings for a man." I paused for a reaction. She was silent.

"So, you see, I was not entirely honest with you about why I decided to stay in Paris."

"Oh?" she said without turning her head.

"He'd stopped speaking to me. Was trying to protect me, or himself, or us both, but I didn't know that and had to see him before I could leave. By then it was too late. Well, perhaps there was time but I'd have him to myself. His family having gone south."

Her silence was making me nervous and I kept talking. "I know it was mad to stay but my heart needed to be near him. I wanted to be near you too, of course. And then the trains stopped running and it wasn't possible. But now I don't know what to think. He's gone to bring Suzanne home—which, of course, he must—but he didn't tell me he was leaving. And it's been a month and I haven't heard word."

She turned, breath rising as if about to speak but then her gaze returned to Jeanne, whose eyes had closed.

"Let me assure you, Edma, we have been very discreet and Maman and Papa suspect nothing. And Suzanne and Madame Manet also remain perfectly ignorant."

"Oh, Suzanne is used to his straying eye." Her dismissive tone was jarring. "Like most wives, she knows her husband's penchants." She buttoned her nightdress and lifted the sleeping baby into the cot. She gave a light flippant laugh that couldn't have contrasted more with how it felt to have just exposed my heart. "I have to say, I expected more... originality of you, Berthe."

"Pardon?"

She buttoned her bodice closed. "Here you are following in my wake again. So shall I assume you'll be getting married soon? Not to Édouard. One can't marry fire. But a naval friend of his, perhaps?"

"Edma, this is far more than... what you and he had. I felt a profound kinship from that first day we saw his work at the Salon des Refusés. As if I had—"

"As did I."

"As Tibby once suggested"—I wanted to shock her into silence—"a lavender marriage might suit me, yes, someone old and rich. But only so that I can be Édouard's mistress."

"Let's see... where have I heard the mistress idea before?" It was not like Edma to be cynical. "Wait." She stopped and stared. "You haven't been intimate, have you?"

"No, no."

"Of course not." Only now did she give me what felt like her full attention. "If you are having such drastic thoughts, Berthe"—she laid a hand on her heart—"as you know, I once did, it's high time to find a marriageable man. Not a lavender one but a real marriage. I'm not encouraging you to stop painting. I would never do that. But if this distraction with Édouard continues, your painting will wither. Have you considered this Dr. Dally Maman mentioned?"

I rose and went to the window. "Me. A doctor's wife."

"Why not?"

Below, the gardener was pruning the stringers off a cherry tree. Edma rang for her maid, telling me how thirsty she found herself after feedings.

"Because I'm not you," I proclaimed as much to myself as to my sister.

"I've angered you. I'm sorry, Berthe. It is a delicious fantasy, two rebellious artists in love. I know it well and feel for you, I do. And because I care for you, I can't allow you to delude yourself as I did. He's a passionate man who elicits a passionate response from women. Have you ever wondered how many others have felt as we have?"

Now it was the sincerity behind her words which rattled.

"Besides, Édouard is a gentleman and, as you say, a friend. He'd never allow you to compromise yourself. And who could admire such a man if he did? Have you actually forgotten, Berthe, how you once felt about our father's infidelities? Do you want to be that woman?"

I couldn't think straight.

"Enjoy the flirtation, but don't let it steal your sense. Really, Berthe. Have you learned nothing from my suffering? And now, you say, he's left without a word to be with his wife? And not written since?"

I couldn't respond.

"Sounds like the impetuous, changeable friend we both know and love."

The maid knocked and entered with a jug of water. Edma poured herself a glass. "What I'm doing is trying to broaden your perspective. Perspective is always narrowed by infatuation. If not erased." She took a long draught of water and sighed a fat contented sigh. "Berthe, I know right now you must hate me but I'm only saying this because I love you."

"I could never hate you." I turned from the window. "I just feel confused. And embarrassed."

"As was I. So don't be. What you've been through is completely understandable." She drank more, then tucked a blanket around the baby's feet. "You'll come down to earth like I did. Because what other choice is there? And take your work more seriously as you should be doing."

She was right about my work. War and sickness aside, it had been the last thing on my mind.

"Or should I ask Maman to invite this doctor fellow for dinner? I'd like to meet him."

"Dr. Dally. François."

"Maman tells me his eyes are the blue of cornflowers and he's a marvellous sense of fashion."

Was normalcy more desirable than this heartache? I risked my life to be near him and now where was he?

"You didn't answer my question about inviting François for dinner."

THE DINNER WAS perfectly lovely. François was charming and engaging, attentive to me without being oppressively eager. I couldn't predict everything he was about to say, nor see his limitations. He listened patiently to Papa's complaints and recommended foot rubs and a tonic. He held and bounced baby Jeanne, who was normally shy with strangers. He even told a couple stories that made us laugh.

He was normal and decent and good. Perhaps more handsome than Édouard. And he possessed a chest on which a woman could comfortably lay her head. Edma called him "appealing in all aspects."

Maman invited him the following week too. This time when he requested to see my paintings, I showed him. He praised them but was not effusive so I believed him sincere, and he expressed awe at such a refined skill as painting. Then he asked if he could purchase—Maman having already paid our bill—*Study, At the Water's Edge*, my painting of Sidonie as a female Narcissus.

It was not painted with you in mind, was my first thought. None of my paintings had anything to do with you.

"Let me think on it, please," I said and he took my hand to press to his lips, not too hard and not too soft.

THE DAY BEFORE Edma was to return to Lorient, a letter arrived for me. Maman, Edma and I were at breakfast, Papa having taken his upstairs, the excitement of having Edma and a baby in the house wearing on him. There was no name on the envelope and no return address. But I knew Édouard's handwriting. Edma saw the change in my expression and as I slipped the paper from its sheath she stared at me in warning.

In answer to Maman's curiosity, I said it was from Eugène. "He has joined his mother in the Pyrenees."

"Thoughtful of him to write." She flared her eyes at Edma. "I don't believe he's a true radical like his younger brother. I really don't. Though I do consider it a moral failing not to have a profession of some kind, he does manage his accounts with acumen. Now Dr. Dally has both a profession and an inheritance."

I could not leave the table without giving myself away. Édouard had a magician's timing.

Feb. 26th, 1871

Berthe, May this letter find you regaining your vitality. Eugène tells me you are looking more like your beautiful self. Please forgive my sudden departure and for not writing sooner. Maman is a tyrant and I am not much of a letter writer, though if you could know my thoughts your name and face are foremost in my heart and as constant as the birdsong outside my window.

I wish you could have come with me. It is so good to be away from Paris and the sights and sounds and memories of the war. I urge you to leave for the countryside. It will speed your recovery.

I now tell you something in secret and with hope ablaze in my heart. I trust you won't speak of it and will make sure no other eyes read this letter. There are plans underway on the Communard front to overtake the present government. I hope to return to a Paris on the brink of real change and lend my support to this noblest of causes. France will never be at peace until all men are seen as equal—not just in the eyes of God but in the eyes of their fellow men—and treated accordingly. I am optimistic regarding France's future and for the future of painting. And of our future too. I miss you. I miss painting you. I miss kissing you. As soon as you are strong enough, you must sit for me again. No one gives me such inspiration. Édouard

Keeping a neutral expression while my heart rocked and rang like a church bell, I tucked the letter back into the envelope and slipped it under the side of my plate. Edma's eyes darted to it as if she might snatch it.

THE NEXT MORNING, knowing my habit of waking at eight and lying in bed pondering all and nothing until half-past, Edma came knocking. I invited her in and she lay on the bed beside me, picked up my hand and studied it.

"I've wanted to say, Berthe, that I can believe that Édouard is in love with you. Your personalities strike a certain balance, he so outgoing and you so pensive. You are both attractive and bright. You both share a passion for painting."

I squeezed her hand. I'd known all along she'd understand.

"But I've held back from saying this because"—she turned on her side to face me—"you know as well as I this relationship can only end in grief."

I let her hand go.

"I know you have too much integrity to be someone's mistress and ruin your marriageability so I needn't say anything. Not to mention denigrate the Morisot name." This was a new and sharper angle.

"It's curious," I said, "how a married man taking a mistress does nothing to harm his reputation. In fact, it elevates him in the eyes of men and even most women."

"That may be true, Berthe, but it does nothing for your situation."

"What is it you want to say, Edma?"

"I think marriage was invented to help men focus. A kind of homing device for when they lose their priorities. Men simply have too much freedom, too much choice, which inevitably brings the burden of complication."

"You think we women are more fortunate then?"

"In that our lives are simpler."

"You mean limited."

"Appreciating what we have is called satisfaction. Wanting what we can't have brings no end to dissatisfaction. I want you to find satisfaction. Happiness."

"Do you?" My anger forced me to sit up. "Because the very things you have given up—painting and loving Édouard—are the very things that bring me happiness. And neither is in the least bit simple!"

She lurched from the bed and strode to the door.

"Are you happy, Edma?"

Hand on the door's knob, she stopped. In her hesitation I felt the familiar tenderness for her that nothing could scrape away. "Edma—"

"Happiness isn't given to you by another, Berthe. Happiness is a choice." She pulled open the door and closed it soberly behind her.

PRESIDENT THIERS ARRIVED in Paris from Bordeaux to recover the now-estimated 226 cannons—along with crates of ammunitions—that had gone missing from the Guard. How something so obvious as a cannon could go missing, much less 226 of them, was a riddle if not a joke. Unless, as Édouard had hinted in his letter, the deed had been long in the planning. But I said nothing about it to anyone.

Before the elections, Papa's position in the finance ministry had been "reallocated." Complaining at every turn of being "confined to the home like a woman" and sensing an opportunity for reinstatement, he sent President Thiers an invitation to dinner. Thiers accepted and plans were begun for the guest list and menu. That dinner, however, was never to take place.

A generous reward had been posted for any information concerning the missing cannons and a claim came forward: the cannons were hidden in the hills of Montmartre, in hayrack barns. In the early morning hours of Papa's dinner date with Thiers, before the sun and the people of Montmartre rose from slumber, the cannon recovery operation was underway. The regiment in charge was the Friends of Order, and Tibby was among them.

"We rode out to Montmartre armed only with the threat of arrest," Tibby relayed when he arrived home late that afternoon, his pants and shirt caked with dust, hair plastered against sunburned skin, his feet blistered and bloody. He drank wine like water and would sleep in his old room that night, too drunk to see his way back to his *appartement*.

"We located the barns and hacked open the doors with axes." We were in the drawing room, Tibby's feet soaking in warm salt water and leaves of witch hazel. He blinked excessively as he spoke. Maman asked if he'd gotten dirt in his eyes. "There were sixty of us," he said, ignoring the question, "and all we had were a few stupid axes." His laugh was mirthless.

"By the time the barn doors were opened, the sun was dawning and the local farmers well aware of our presence. So there we stood, staring down the black mouths of row upon row of cannons as the generals clapped each other on the back."

Thin Louis arrived with a plate of toasted rounds, paté and pickled onions. Tibby drank, and even as his Adam's apple rose and fell he eyed the near-empty wine bottle with concern.

"Perron, whose every thought shoots out of the cannon of his mouth, said 'It's a pretty sight, but I don't know how we're going to move them.'" Tibby snorted. "In the event of actually finding the cache they hadn't arranged horse teams to drag them away."

"Stunning incompetence," said Papa, as if he would have known better.

"You must eat, Tibby darling." Maman nudged the plate toward him. He waved away the idea of food. Of mothers.

"The locals arrived in numbers. With rifles. They untied our horses, our only means of escape. It was obvious they would outnumber us soon." Tibby fingered the cross-hatch of bloody scrapes darkening the side of his neck. "I slipped out."

"I'm glad you're safe," said Maman, reaching for Tibby's hand as he pulled his away.

"Me too," I said, for what it was worth.

Papa gazed out the window. "There's no purpose served in anyone else hearing this."

I realized why Tibby was so filthy—he'd walked all the way from Montmartre. Or run. Kept out of sight in the weeds and thickets, losing his jacket and cap, snubbing the pain in his feet.

This was all we knew about what happened until the morning papers filled in the rest.

Fighting erupted between the Friends of Order and local Communards. The unarmed Order was quickly subdued and the two commanding officers, General Claude Martin Lecomte and former chief of the National Guard Jacques Clément-Thomas, were captured. Their hands and feet bound, they were carted to the rue de Rosiers. There in the square they were summarily executed by firing squad. Ironically General Clément-Thomas was himself a devoted Communard.

News of the mishandled operation and the murders have emboldened the Reds. They recognize the weakness of President Thiers and he and his army have retreated to Versailles, leaving the city undefended. There is jubilation in the streets among those who want a new république.

So Thiers never arrived for dinner, nor the mayor of Paris, Jules Ferry, whose municipal offices were housed at the Hôtel de Ville, and was seen lowering himself out a back window before fleeing. The Tricolour was removed from the Hôtel de Ville and replaced with the red flag of the République. Another red flag was unfurled down the length of the belfry of the Town Hall, while the tocsin of Notre-Dame, which had not been rung since the revolution of '48, rang every hour on the hour. Papa dismissed it as a terror tactic but I knew this was the plan at which Édouard had hinted. He would now be on his way to Paris. I would soon see and touch my love. And in this freer new world, we could rewrite the social rules.

As Communard leaders settled into their headquarters, a dozen of the missing cannons were positioned around the grounds of the Hôtel de Ville. The *quai* and main streets leading to the hotel were blocked with sandbags and wooden barriers. Any time Maman and I dared venture out, someone somewhere was chanting "*Vive la République.*" There were disturbing rumours that men were being rounded up and tried for nothing other than the fine cut of their coats or quality of their boots.

I tried to excuse the brutality as an unfortunate yet necessary means to a fairer and freer society. Of course sacrifices would have to be made but Édouard and his brothers would, in the end, be on the right and moral side of history.

"THIERS MAY HAVE fled," announced Tibby, "but the bourgeoisie must show we're not afraid and that we support a peaceful solution to our differences." He and friends were organizing a peace march at the Place Vendôme. Perhaps he was only trying to win back Papa's respect but I was proud of this measured call to action, certain such a dialogue would have Édouard's support too. Could any reasonable man want more fighting? More death?

The first outing attracted upwards of 200 marchers. Luck or something smarter prevailed on both sides and tempers were restrained. Tibby boasted of its success and the plan to repeat the march "every day until the leaders of the Reds put down their guns and are ready to talk." Papa apologized to Tibby for not "having the legs" to participate.

The following day drew more than twice the numbers. It was sheer chance that Tibby ran into the son of Dr. Rafinesque, who he had not seen since their school days, and fell out of step with his fellow organizers up front and into the belly of the crowd.

When the marchers reached the square, a Communard leader ordered them to disperse. Tibby paid little attention to the shouted voice over the megaphone until one impatient Communard fired his rifle, whether into the air or into the unarmed crowd no one could agree. A confusion of shots ensued. The crowd reared backwards, people toppling into and over one another. Nine marchers, six of them Tibby's fellow organizers, were dead, and a dozen wounded. Because of his inability to resist a new set of ears to tell his stories, Tibby lived to tell us this one.

The papers called it the *Massacre in the rue de la Paix*. Reporters asked the question we were all asking: *Who were these men killing their fellow countrymen?*

Papa was quick to lay blame. "Liberal intellectuals for stirring up the working class! The likes of Gambetta, Hugo, Baudelaire and your Manets. Probably condone killing as necessary."

"No one condones killing," I said in Édouard's defence, though I had wondered the very same thing.

Secretly wanting to punish Edma for making me feel foolish, I had not written to her since she left Paris. Being the more mature, she wrote first. Her letter made me feel loved and chastised in the same breath.

Please, Berthe, let's not let men come between us. I appreciate your being honest with me. It was not easy to do so and my response was not what you'd hoped. Know that I am here for you—though I trust your good judgment.

As for this Communard takeover, and the killings of unarmed men in broad daylight, Adolphe predicted this kind of unrest. Is Tibby staying clear? Have you heard from Édouard? Is he still supporting his brother in this? By all reports there are violent factions involved and I fear that Paris may no longer be safe for those of our class. And we thought the war was over. I know Papa's wait-and-see attitude but promise me, this time, if the situation takes a turn, you will leave. Know, Berthe, that Édouard is a grown man and can take care of himself.

Shortly after her letter an influx of men from the ghettos of La Villette and Ménilmontant were to descend on Paris. Now Papa did feel terrorized. Again our neighbours stored valued possessions and fled, only this time we were the first among them. How ironic it was to fear our own citizens more than a foreign invader.

Thin Louis again crated and stored our First Empire furniture. My paintings remained in the basement. We packed as much as we could carry. Believing President Thiers would soon put things right, Papa did not feel the need to venture any further than the nearby village of Saint-Germain. Tibby was called to Versailles to rejoin the government forces.

Levin drove us to the station—the horses carefully without ribbon or feather. We passed young men crowbarring up cobblestones to heave them through the window of the *pharmacie* and apartment above. Two women sat on the back of a nearby cart swinging their exposed ankles and eyeing us with malice.

"Bourgeoisie pigs," yelled the blonde one, and Levin swung the whip and the horses stuttered then clattered faster as a cobblestone crashed somewhere behind us.

Turning into the rue d'Iena, a well-dressed man sat slumped against a storefront, chin to chest, legs stretched before him. The shadow in which he sat was his own blood. A rat nosed his bared ankle. His hands splayed along his legs. I looked away then back again, realizing his gloves were crimson red. I knew of only one man who wore—

"Stop the carriage." I stood and the hard dip of a wheel sent me back to my seat. "Stop! Stop it!"

Levin slowed and Papa shouted at him to carry on.

"Don't look, Berthe." Maman grasped my hand.

I covered my mouth as three ragged children ran up to Édouard, the rat scurrying off, to rummage his pockets. The smallest knocked his hand palm up and pale on the dark cobbles.

"It's just blood." I breathed.

Maman put her arm around my shoulders and pulled me in. "We don't know him," she cooed. "It's all right."

I pitched forward and vomited. Papa groaned and shifted in his seat.

WE SETTLED INTO a cramped four-room *appartement* in sleepy Saint-Germain-en-Laye to await what came next. A second election was held by the reigning Communards and in Paris only. With the moderate and conservative voters all but gone, the results were a clear victory for what was now being called the *Commune de Paris.* The painter Gustave Courbet was elected to represent the 6th. An artist in the government? I believed this a good sign. A first step. Courbet's first order of business was the toppling of the Vendôme Column, his second to abolish the Académie des Beaux-Arts. I was thrilled. He announced the academy's closing in a published letter in *Le Figaro. The artists of France are avenged. Now true genius will soar!*

Édouard's vision was coming true.

As Papa read the letter aloud in our small dining room he kept glancing at me, daring me to show my true feelings. When Papa read with disgust that my former teacher dear M. Corot was also a member, I knew in my heart that only good could come of it. I pictured Édouard and Degas inside the Hôtel de Ville alongside Eugène and Gustave toasting their triumph and wished I was there. Though no one could know what this new order would look like, the lack of predictability alone was exciting.

I ignored my parents' lament that we would now lose everything—our home and belongings, our servants and status. But strictures around art could be liberated, I wanted to say, women allowed in drawing studios, allowed to walk about free as any man. Married couples allowed to annul a loveless marriage. I kept quiet though, amid reports of mobs looting the homes of the rich before setting fire to them.

A note arrived from Tibby. *Having learned from our mistakes, President Thiers has changed his strategy. The now very well-armed Friends of Order are preparing to take back Paris. President Thiers has ordered that every means be used and says resistance will not be tolerated. I am confident of our success and certain that you will be able to return to your rightful home before too long.*

What did he mean that resistance would not be tolerated? Was Édouard aware of Thiers' plan? That evening's meal sat leaden in my stomach. We woke the next morning to the sound of cannon fire and smoke smearing the distant sky. Like some terrible *déjà vu*, another war was being waged. A so-called civil one. Where was Édouard? My cough returned and I retched whatever food I managed to ingest. Maman insisted I leave immediately for Edma's and would not hear my protests.

Though I could not know if the letters would reach them, before leaving I sent warnings to both Édouard and Degas urging them to leave Paris.

EDMA WELCOMED ME into her home with sisterly affection and concern for my health. She asked after Tibby, Maman and Papa, and then, unable to stop herself, asked if I'd heard from Édouard.

"No, but assume from Eugéne's letter that together they returned to Paris. I worry for their safety." I shared the scene of the dead man and what I took to be his red gloves—"I thought it was him, Edma"—and suddenly overwhelmed, I began to weep, just as Adolphe stepped into the hall with Jeanne in his arms. Abruptly he turned and left. Edma embraced me, one firm hand pressing my head against her collarbone as if I were a child. As soon as I caught my breath I apologized and assured her this would not be indicative of our visit. She kissed my forehead and did not bring up his name again.

Lorient had been untouched by war and looked just how I remembered it. But we could not escape the newspaper reports or the flow of letters from Maman, now in close correspondence with Tibby. *The Trocadero has become the artillery site for Thiers' army, and our street, rue Franklin, their headquarters. Tibby and his fellow soldiers occupy our house and sleep in our beds. It makes me happy to think of Tibby in his childhood bed.*

"At least our house will be safe from looters," I said to Edma.

"But now Passy is a prime target." Her logic, as usual, outpaced mine.

Outnumbered, the Communards built barricades using anything and everything—stones pried from Haussmann's boulevards, overturned carriages and omnibuses, sandbags, wooden signs, fine furniture, even sculptures and paintings. As government forces surrounded the city's core, those inside began a reprisal of symbolic destruction. The Tuileries, first stripped of its royal riches, was burnt to the ground. The finance building where Papa had worked for the last twenty-four years was destroyed, along with the Cour des Comptes. Half the buildings in the rue Royale disappeared while a wing of the Louvre was lost to fire, and more than 100,000 rare books. The Hôtel de Ville was blown open from one end to the other and set ablaze, its murals by Delacroix, Ingres and Cabanel gone forever. The elderly Archbishop of Paris, imprisoned since the Emperor's capture, was executed along with ten of his monks.

"Who is it issuing such orders?" demanded Edma.

"I'm sure this was not part of the plan."

"Whose plan?"

Édouard's, I didn't say. Mine.

Adolphe was of the understanding that the Commune's moderate leadership had crumbled and vindictive groups now ruled the day.

Worry burned my stomach as though something scraped it raw. Edma's cook, Manon, made it her mission to keep me from losing more weight. I developed a tremor in my painting hand. Already the furthest thing from my mind, painting was now an impossibility.

Maman wrote: *Tibby tells us that President Thiers is resolute and will be pitiless until the expiation of the Communards is complete, down to the very last. I say Paris must be delivered back to citizens who have respect for their culture and for others' property! Thiers' own mansion in the Place Saint-Georges, which, if you recall, was a veritable treasure house of books and artworks, was desecrated by miscreants in ways too vile for my pen to record. The Friends of Order has grown to 130,000 strong and counting. Papa and I are very optimistic.*

I forward a note from Eugène to Berthe though I've every mind to burn it. If he and his brothers are foolish enough to be involved in madness, they deserve whatever befalls them. They must bear some responsibility for the way things have gone.

May we be together again soon, Maman

April 27th, 1871

Dear Berthe,

I am writing from La Rochelle on the coast, where I am with Maman, Édouard, Suzanne and Léon. The seaside town is a balm for the nerves, its ocean vistas restful to the eye. I think you would find many perspectives worthy of your brush.

After Thiers retreated from Paris, Édouard and I returned with great hope for a new chapter in France's history. I'm sorry to report that we were profoundly disappointed. Militant radicals—not true Communards—had taken charge. Paris was a dangerous place for men of our dress and manner, and we left immediately with brother Gustave in tow. Poor Gustave feels he has failed in his life's mission. I tell him that the working class has unleashed decades of anger upon Paris, an anger which will have to be spent before calmer heads prevail. Édouard too is in despair. He sleeps a lot these days and, if you can imagine it, has nothing to say. He is unable to paint and spends long hours staring at the sea as if lost in a dream.

Though things are not as any of us had envisioned, I tell both my brothers, and now you, I believe it is a beginning still. However misguided. Rome, as they say, was not built in a day and neither will be a free and equal France.

I was very relieved to hear that you and your family have left Paris. I think of your well-being often. Until we meet again, affectionately, Eugène

I couldn't have felt more grateful to Eugène for allaying my fears. I freely shared this letter with Edma.

"An entire family of dreamers," she said after reading it, adopting Papa's clipped tone.

THE FRIENDS OF ORDER marched on Paris. Defeating stronghold after stronghold of Communard defences, they took men, women and children prisoner and left the rest dead in the streets. Three weeks later to the day, the final barricade fell in Belleville. The defeated men put down their arms and put up their hands. For that they were taken to the cemetery of Père Lachaise, penned into a corner and gunned down with a *mitrailleuse*. The heralded weapon was not ready in time for the war with Prussia yet was ready to use against our own. This execution was but a prelude to Thiers' grand campaign "to end all future rebellions."

Beside the charred rubble of the Tuileries, every last Communard rebel, in the fashion of an assembly line, was led to the banks of the Seine. There they were gunned down, their bodies tossed without ceremony into the river. Women and children included, as if they might carry germs of dissent in their blood. Dear straight-spoken Pauline, we would learn, was among the slaughtered—estimated at 25,000. Did a child in her womb sink with her below the waters of the Seine? Did she recognize Tibby among the executioners? Did Tibby recognize her?

Le Figaro reported that the blood of corpses turned the river oily and black. They gave the slaughter a name: *La Semaine Sanglante*. I stopped reading Maman's letters of praise for Tibby's courage and the heroic President Thiers as *the man who saved Paris*. Edma explained away the horror as "a tragic yet necessary evil. Violence begets violence," she said, "and now that it's over we can only pray for the souls of the departed and for the souls of those who pulled the trigger." She had become religious whilst I wasn't watching. A believer. But where was this newfound God of hers when Pauline and the dead bodies of children were being tossed into the river by her own brother?

"Animals have more humanity," I said. "The French have lost theirs."

"Terrible choices had to be made, Berthe."

Nothing made sense, not even my sensible sister. I couldn't erase the images of slaughter. Sleep my only escape, I began retiring early and sleeping well past breakfast. During my waking hours I sought out Manon in the kitchen, where I begged to shell peas, scrub potatoes, perform any helpful but mindless task. I sought out Jeanne and her nurse in the nursery to help stack blocks and read storybooks, pour invisible tea for dolls with stony faces. Anything not to think. Not to feel.

Though the Friends of Order were consigned to help in the cleanup and restoration of the city, Tibby abandoned his post and left Paris without so much as a goodbye to his mother. It would be more than a year before I next saw our brother. Eyes dulled, his nose reddened from drinking, any youthful élan he once possessed was completely extinguished.

We heard that Fanny Claus, my fellow hay bale in *Le Balcon*, had given birth to a son during the Prussian siege but two months later she was dead from malnutrition. Two former schoolmates of Tibby's had been shot in the street for the sin of wearing blue scarves. Mme. Higgonet died of heart failure after her house was bombed during Thiers' campaign and her butler, who'd stayed behind, burned to death trying to save her valuable china.

The ground under my feet less and less solid, I watched where I stepped in case it gave way, or my ankles crumbled. How could I continue to believe in the social contract to which I belonged? Or in the men who designed and upheld that contract? The patriarchy had proved depraved and immoral, so was it not absurd to take seriously its rules? The signposts that had guided my life for thirty years seemed little more than vanity and chintz.

Days passed. I felt an innocent child again. Wide eyed, empty-headed, I couldn't see what was so important about eating. About putting on clothes and moving about. Talking. What good were words? But no one could answer these simple questions, which, of course, were not simple questions. Not my parents, who inhabited a different reality altogether. Not Edma, with her ready logics. Whose happiness was built upon what I believed was a denial of her own free will. Every morning, every night and before every meal, my sister uttered Catholic prayers with a closed-eyed resolve and pursed-lipped smile. Where she was once my sun and moon, she had become a dark pond reflecting the light of others: her God, husband and child. And not Édouard, who was so very far away. Who'd run to his wife. Not once but twice. It had begun to seem that I'd dreamed him into existence. Certainly I'd dreamed myself into believing I might be the jewel in his sky.

My parents reprieved south to stay with Yves. I was to spend the summer in Lorient. Edma prodded me from bed each day, cajoled me to dress, eat and bathe. She read to me, made one-sided conversation. With my hand in hers, she led me outside to walk in the garden, or down to the harbour to watch the boats, or to the market to finger the silks and cottons. Everywhere seemed painted with the same loveless brush, the same distant perspective. How terribly impersonal that life continued on, without one's consent, like an empty boat along a river.

I HAD BEEN IN Lorient for ten weeks when a letter arrived addressed to me. It was a year since the war with Prussia began and the world I knew smashed like a vase on a stone floor. When I saw my name written in his hand, my pre-war self emerged as from behind a curtain and I could see her. That young woman was in love, passionate about her art, her appearance and her pretty things. This woman, fingering her cold toast, looked forward to an afternoon nap, a game of cards, an early bedtime. The exhilarating need I'd felt for him seemed exaggerated. The excitement when he entered a room and our eyes met an indulgent fantasy.

His name had not been mentioned since the day I arrived and now Edma downplayed the letter. She wondered aloud if Édouard was back in Paris. If his studio was still intact. His mother's *appartement.*

"Édouard is like a cat," said Adolphe, "and will land on his feet no matter how far the fall." He glanced to Edma to see if it was all right to have spoken of him and received her twitch of a smile not meant for me.

Letter in hand I excused myself, though I knew Edma would be upset by this, worried its contents could push me into an even deeper abyss. Or to a heaven of my imagination's own making. But I was past caring what people thought. Even her. Though her worry was warranted. If the optimistic, defiant spirit that I knew as Édouard Manet was extinguished, my despair would be complete.

Dearest Berthe,
I have returned to Paris for the time being. I have missed you and think of you every day. I trust you have regained your health and that your strength of spirit has survived the disgrace and sorrow France has brought upon herself. Here neighbours are blaming each other for their actions or lack thereof, but the truth is we are all at fault and must all bear the blame for what has happened. It will be a scourge on France's soul forever, one whose lessons we must learn well or risk repeating.

I wander the streets in gloom and confusion at how things could have got so out of hand. Anger and denial colour the air. To be here is to breathe it in and be addled by it.

I cannot paint. My days are spent riding the train with M. Gambetta each morning to Versailles (he sits in the National Assembly now) to listen to our so-called leaders discuss our future. The events of the past year have moderated Gambetta's views, as they have mine, and he continues to call for measures to enhance social equality. His is the one sane voice as far as I can tell and I regret having once thought less of him. He describes France's bankers, aristocrats and Bonapartists as a class of "dictators and ruffians." He expresses equal dismay over the "unforeseen explosion of the working class, who obeyed their blind fury." He is the voice of the middle road while Thiers sits looking down his imperialistic nose at him, at everyone, as if he's some god instead of the inhuman beast he has proved himself to be.

Gambetta has proven himself wise, a great man even. I have offered more than once to do his portrait but he politely declines. I try not to take it as an insult. It may be a case of self-consciousness about his disfigurement and glass eye. Even when I suggested a profile, he refused.

My studio was badly hit, but I've found another, next door to Maman's appartement *which, miraculously, or I'd hear no end of it, survived the fighting intact. I want to do a picture depicting Thiers' firing squads but my hands are unsteady, nor does my imagination spark. Still, I feel it my own and every artist's duty to record these events before the blood dries and memory scars over.*

Degas was here in Paris though for only a short time. He is not painting, but drawing caricatures of the battles' dramatis personae, *and likenesses of his former fellow soldiers. Some of the caricatures are very funny but in the extreme way of also being horrific. We all find our ways of coping.*

You'll have heard the heartrending news about Fanny. Suzanne was distraught and upset to have missed the funeral service. The child is being raised by Fanny's eldest sister. I ran into my friend Camille Pissarro who, like Monet, had also taken a honeymoon in England at the start of this mess. The poor man returned to his home in Louveciennes only to find that the Prussians had turned his studio into a butcher shop and used his canvases to catch the animals' blood and wipe their hands. Only forty of his nearly 1500 paintings have survived. He was fatalistic about it but I wanted to weep for him.

And then there's Meissonier. Gambetta told me Meissonier didn't bother to hide away his work but believed his reputation so great that any man who occupied his studio wouldn't touch them. Including Prussians. And he was right! Apparently they placed his canvases in neat stacks along the walls and covered them with clean sheets. For that much I'm grateful. Though they did slaughter his cows and horses.

Eugène is in Bordeaux visiting our cousins. He told me you were much stronger the last he saw you, which gave me heart. It pained me greatly to think of you ill and suffering.

My doctor says I'm suffering what he calls nervous depression. Who isn't, was my response. Nonetheless he recommended time away from Paris at the seaside where I will spend the months of August and September with my family. I believe it will do me good and I will try and paint happier things. Picnics on the beach, Léon playing at croquet.

When we are both healed in body and spirit, we will meet again and pick up where we left off. If that is not possible then we will pick up where we are. That is my fervent hope. Yours, Édouard

I CRUMPLED THE PAGES in my fists, squeezed them to find some blood of the man I once knew. Nervous depression. Shaky hands. He would try to paint happy picnics on the beach? Games of croquet? Anger reared up like a starved animal smelling food on the air. I screamed at the pages in my hand, whipped them down and stomped on them. I threw myself onto the bed to pound my pillow and muffle my screams lest I scare the baby.

Edma wisely left me alone. I would not have unlocked my door in any case. I ignored the gentle knocks of the maid announcing dinner left outside my door. I don't recall falling asleep but woke the next morning to Edma's voice through the door. "I've brought breakfast."

I had not changed out of yesterday's dress and my ribcage ached as I made my way out of bed to let her in. The floor felt extra hard against my stockinged feet, my lightheadedness a floating curiosity. Edma tenderly kissed my head, poured cream into my coffee, rearranged the chaos of bedclothes and propped pillows for me to breakfast in bed. She placed the tray over my lap and urged me to eat in the same voice she used for Jeanne. "Things will work out," she soothed, "for everyone. In time. Trust me. Don't let this further wound you."

How was it that she knew what I was thinking and feeling?

"I know it seems hard now"—she glanced off the crumpled pages on the floor—"but you'll see, Berthe, that it's for the best."

What was for the best? I studied the rather pleased look on her face. Did she think Édouard had written to put an end to our intimacy? To rescind his proclamation of love? That, like her, I had been rejected by him in the end and she quietly revelled in the idea?

Her misunderstanding made me sit up. I suddenly saw just how intact was Édouard's and my intimacy. Nervous depression was the perfect diagnosis for me too. His hand shook like mine. He couldn't paint. Nor could I. He wasn't the person he used to be. Nor was I. We could not pick up where we left off but we could pick up where we were. For the first time in months, I didn't feel alone. I drank the proffered coffee. The bitterness felt right in my mouth as did the burn in my stomach. Even apart, he and I experienced the same leaden vision, tasted the same sorrows and wished for each other's company.

"It a beautiful day out," said Edma, swinging open the shutters. A stream of white light caused the floor under her feet to disappear. For the first time I noticed the wallpaper, pale blue patterned with fleur-de-lis.

"Yes, it is."

Her pursed smile could mean many things.

"Is there notepaper and ink in my desk?" I said.

There was the slightest of hesitations. "Yes, I believe so." She went and pulled out a drawer. "Are you sure, Berthe, that it's wise to respond?"

"Wise?" How I was feeling and what she was saying were like putting a hat on upside down.

"Please, Berthe, don't subject yourself to more anguish."

Was the concern in her voice even genuine?

"I'm sorry, Edma, for last night and for being such dour company these many weeks. I'm feeling stronger this morning."

"That's good, that's good."

"You and Adolphe have been so… selfless," I said, only now waking to the fact and marvelling at it. "So patient with me."

Edma batted away the thought. "You're my sister."

"I don't know how I can ever repay you."

"You never need to repay family."

"No, but I will try."

I regarded my plate of lightly browned toast, shiny with apricot jam, the triangle of soft cheese the colour of parchment. It looked delicious.

The empty boat on the river sat lower in the water, inhabited. The current beneath surprisingly strong.

"MADEMOISELLE BERTHE," said the maid through my bedroom door, "a parcel has come for you."

I asked her to come in. Young and bright, her hair the same shade of ginger as Édouard's, she looked hopeful we might open it together. I thanked and dismissed her.

It had no return address and no note. Nested inside were dozens of folded paper fans, tassels dangling from their bases. There must have been 200, if not more. I took one out and spread open its blank white folds. I knew at an instant who the fans were from and the meaning of the gesture. I stretched the folds until they were nearly flat then further still, harder until it tore the corner.

We had not been in touch since I left Paris, but I knew that this was Degas' quiet yet pointed nudge back to painting. I also knew that if I set fire to them all, that would be fine with him.

I left the box on my dresser. When Edma learned they were from Degas, she understood too. "He's a good friend" – she said this as though in contrast to Édouard – "a caring man."

With each day that passed, the box of fans demanded more of my attention. Occasionally I'd finger them, sometimes lift one out and examine its blankness, fan myself with one or two, snap them closed and toss them back. Then, one day, I set a chair by a window. On a table, I placed a bowl of clean water. A fresh rag. Edma lent me her paint box and palette, whose wood was no longer visible for the hard smears of paint. Choosing the four smallest brushes, I arranged them by size and in a vertical row. Then rearranged them in no order. I stood and paced the room waiting for the urge to sit again. It didn't come.

The following morning I stared at these objects and, like an amnesiac, tried to make meaning of them. The handle of the brush against my knuckle made me realize the soft spot there was once calloused, protected. With my index finger I stroked the tip of the smallest brush, drew the stiff hairs across my lips and chin. The tremor in my hand made the brush tip tickle.

The next day I opened a jar of watercolour and tipped out a tiny hill of chalky pink powder. I dipped the brush in the water bowl, dropped a wobbling bead at the edge of the powder and watched it creep in, creating a pool of deepest scarlet. The change, the creation of colour, made me feel godlike. With the same deliberation that little Jeanne tackled a new skill, such as holding a crayon, I touched paint to a fold of my tiny pleated canvas and watched how the paper absorbed colour. I continued the line onto the next fold. My unsteady hand made it jagged. So what? The line reminded me of an image from the Japanese exhibit – a plum branch. After dashing off several blossoms, I laid the fan aside.

On the next fan, I painted the bold line of a bald mountain and daubed in tiny green triangles for fir trees. The folds bent and shifted the track of my brush. The thin paint sprouted halos around my objects and bled one colour into the next. Fine. They were paper fans. On the next I tried a koi. Then a lily pad and an ill-defined lotus flower. Singular images from the remove of memory and a culture not my own. But the memory of a brush in hand, intending marks on paper, acted like an inquiring voice. Shall we try this? Try that? Leave it blank? What about this colour? I painted eight before my hand tired.

The next day, when I took up my brush, my eye was drawn by the things living in my room. The paper chain of dolls I had cut out for Jeanne. The vase of daisies past their point. The paisley of a scarf. That day I painted fifteen fans. My lines a little more true.

The following day, just when I had seated myself at my small table, the maid came with an invitation to join Edma and Jeanne in the garden. I asked her to please bring my painting things, along with extra brushes in case my sister wanted to join me.

Edma laughed at the idea. "It has been so long," she said, but joined me anyway. The two of us painted side by side again, each with a wondering brush in hand. But before long Jeanne wanted for Edma's attention. Together they sought butterflies "for your auntie's fans."

I painted the ribbons fluttering on Jeanne's hat, a bird splashing in the birdbath, the missed butterfly. Images that changed moment to moment, second to second, and demanded a looser hand, even a trembling one, and that my eye too, remain fluid.

I tried to paint a leaf as it spiraled to the ground. The very instant I believed I could capture the action, I lost the quality I chased. But my brush made swift stabs and feathery dashes, and brief aerated composites bloomed on the fan. More intimations than objects. Temporaneous living things. When Edma and Jeanne brought me their captured monarch, I painted its escape.

To attempt to fix an image killed it dead. Movement was life. If I thought too much about what I painted, my hand shook in hindering ways, my arm became heavy, my eye no longer seeing. The purpose of a fan was to flutter, to move the air. A fan was not so much a thing but an action. Life too was an action, perception a fleeting moment of engagement. And then another, and another. And to keep this engagement fresh, it required letting go of it, every second of every moment of every day.

Painting those fans was my first sense of freedom in a long time.

I sent Degas not a note of thanks but a fan painted with a ruby-throated hummingbird hovering above an orange nasturtium. I imagined him unfolding the fan and the corner of his lip lifting ever so slightly.

When the last fan was finished, despite Edma's protests I gave them all away to Edma's grateful church group to sell at the next bazaar. My hands now as steady as they ever were, I began to paint in earnest.

I did two larger watercolours of Edma and Jeanne in the park. Teetering on the edge of sloppiness, of carelessness, I painted the fragile, transient moments before me, their furious, hopeful colours and shadows full of grief.

When Edma saw the paintings, I could tell she thought them terrible. Being good was not the point. Painting was the point. I did one of her and Jeanne indoors on the divan, which she said she liked and asked if she might keep. Of course. What was I going to do with it?

On our trip to Cherbourg, ready to weight my brush and my hand and commit, I switched to oil. The oils slowed my brush but not by much. Edma was relieved to see me engaged again though sometimes a look passed over her face, as though it was hard to watch me paint while she had a child to see to. We did not speak of it nor did we speak of Édouard. I let her believe him a thing of the past and a subject that would pain me. While I believed him a thing of the future and a subject that would pain her. We shared much that summer but we could not, did not, share Édouard.

I had planned to return to Paris early in September but then we received a letter from Maman. All but one of the windows of our home had been blown out, the main chimney crumbled and our front gate gone missing. Edma grew teary but my memories of the house were so tainted I imagined that ornate iron gate to be the pride of some poor farmer's wife and could have heaved a chimney brick at the remaining window and completed the job.

I was sad to learn that the studio had been hit by a shell and burned to the ground. *Gone forever,* wrote Maman, *the paintings and studies you, Edma, had left behind.* This information sobered Edma and she asked if my work had been lost. "Eugéne insisted mine were stored in the cellar. He came to oversee their wrapping."

"That was good of him."

"I had no intention of saving them, Edma."

"Or of saving mine?"

"No one expected this. I'm sorry, Edma. I thought you'd taken the ones you wanted. But if for a second we had known—"

She told me not to worry. That it was a case of nostalgia on her part and she would get over it. Her eyes were less forgiving. I felt selfish and not without guilt.

Like me, Maman decided the war had *soured our memories of the house and grown too big for our dwindling family.* She'd let a small three-storey a few blocks east in rue Guichard.

Starting fresh made flawless sense to me, though I'd one worry: living with my parents in even smaller quarters. I wrote to Maman with my concern and she assured me that I would have my own floor, "a separate *appartement,*" and all the privacy I wanted. She requested my preferences in wallpaper and curtains, wanting to have everything ready for my arrival.

So I stayed in Lorient until early October. I had more than overstayed my welcome, but Adolphe and Edma were skilled in not letting it show. I was anxious to get back to Paris. To Édouard.

I OPENED THE CAGE DOOR and the greener of the two parakeets squawked, hopped onto the door frame and rotated its head to regard me with one suspicious black and yellow eye. The other bird on its perch stabbed its preening beak under a wing.

Here in Paris, people were putting their lives back together as if nailing them into place. Routines and decorum of French life were clung to vigorously along with an unspoken insistence on conformity. Any deviation from the expected, whether in fashion, cuts of meat or choice of music, caused a mild panic. I understood the instinct perfectly because it was my own. External order mitigated the internal confusion caused by recent events.

Mama indulged my request for white curtains, white slipcovers, white bedding and wallpaper in a pale grey and white striped moiré. I had new distaste for clutter and excess and demanded no extraneous furniture or adornments of any kind. My bedroom was for sleeping and dressing. My sitting room for painting and receiving visitors. The small room off the sitting room would house canvases and supplies. I could not bear knick-knacks or art objects. I wanted to know every item I owned and be able to register its place of belonging. The only painting on my wall was my treasured landscape by Corot above the fireplace. To the women's asylum I gave away any clothes that were neither black nor white. Bright colours seemed frivolous now, attention-getting. I gave away slippers, hats, hair ornaments, stockings, jewelry and fans. I hung my few remaining hats on hooks on the back of my front door.

A parakeet fluttered to the floor, tucked its head down and began to pace. Maman had bought the two lemony-green creatures as a homecoming gift, "to keep you company." They were excessively bourgeois and I hated to imagine from what jungle they'd been torn. Pitying their caged lives, today I had decided to leave the cage door open. Though I took evening meals with my parents, ostensibly I now lived alone and the parakeets' skittering claws, songs and squawks did prove company of sorts.

I set one of my Cherbourg paintings on my easel and the bolder of the two birds launched into the air to flutter beside my ear. I flinched as it clutched my shoulder.

"What are you going to do to me?"

Several minutes passed and neither of us moved. The small weight of him was not unpleasant. "Fine then, so what do you think about this one? Good enough for the Salon?"

STRUGGLING TO MAKE SENSE of the Communard uprising, everyone looked for something or someone to blame. My aunt and uncle decided absinthe was the cause, claiming the smoky-green drink produced a temporary madness. They gave up alcohol altogether and started a temperance society. Whenever we were invited to dinner, Maman enjoyed a glass or two en route in the carriage to avoid their sour looks.

Like Papa, the newly appointed Director of Fine Arts, Charles Blanc, blamed left-leaning bohemian intellectuals and took upon himself the "sacred responsibility" of re-educating the next generation of artists. Thus he devoted an entire wing of the Palais de l'Industrie to a new museum housing "the ideal of the beautiful"—full-scale replicas of Michelangelo's frescos in the Sistine Chapel, Ghiberti's *Doors of Paradise* and more. The Museum of Copies, he claimed, would "restore our standing in the world and provide guidance for the young painters of the future." In other words, painters were encouraged to regurgitate what had already been done.

Back from a trip south, Degas stopped in for tea. How happy I was to see his somber face and brown wool suit, his sad honest eyes. We didn't speak of the horrors of the past year but of his trip, of Edma's life and of Blanc's new museum.

"He's employing Meissonier and Cabanel for the job," I told him.

"Reducing France's best to copyists. How ingenious."

"Where is the *Musée Moderne?*"

"Whoever thought one could long for the days of Emperor Louis?"

We wondered what might sway this year's staunchly conservative Salon jury.

He never once mentioned the fans so neither did I, the omission like a shared childhood secret.

Marcello also surprised me with a visit. Said she needed to see firsthand how I'd "come through the trials."

"You are a different woman," was her quick appraisal as we took tea in my sitting room.

"More faded and jaded?" I had noticed a number of white hairs of late.

"No. I would say you seem more… yourself."

Marcello was as she always was. Graceful and forthright. Not too tight. Not too loose. "Poor France will never be quite the same."

I poured tea. "And yet our government seems to be looking to the past as a way forward."

"Government is a horse's ass moving backwards as the horse steps in its own dung. So I plan to submit to the Salon under a new pseudonym."

"Oh?" I raised my eyebrows.

"Léonardo da Vinci."

Because the sun was shining, after our tea we took a stroll around the lake in the Bois. Having been bombed, its trees felled for firewood, livestock eating all its grasses and shrubs, the *parc,* like the rest of us, was hard at work renewing itself. The manure the livestock left behind sprouted new green growth and tucked among the grasses was the ivory glint of day lilies hanging their angelic heads.

I KEPT MY EASELS out at all times, ready to paint every female relative requesting to see me. I coerced Yves and Bibi into posing on the Trocadero—using the same perspective Édouard once painted of the Exhibition—and then again on my balcony, with Bibi peering out between the black iron railings. Though unable to forget Paris under its pall of smoke, its flaming buildings and makeshift hospitals, I painted what I now saw before me. The past was past, the future unknowable, this present moment forever dissolving before my eyes.

I painted my sister and niece in watercolour to expedite the process—Yves had no patience for modeling—and transposed the paintings to oils indoors. Why hard-and-fast rules about anything, painting included? Inside or *en plein air*, I didn't care. My work was to capture change: reflections, ambiance, the expression of a hip or tip of a chin.

Hunting truth with my paintbrush had now become my route to meaning. As for what gave Edma's life meaning, a few weeks after my arrival home we received news that she was again with child.

IT WASN'T UNTIL autumn's end that Édouard returned to Paris. I had responded to his letter to say I understood exactly how he was feeling, and that there was no need to belabour in words our present, temporary anxieties. I told him our country's tragedy of errors was over. That our souls were united now and always. I told him: *We must reserve our sensitivity for our work. Through which we can hope to heal ourselves and others through the beauty of truth. To show me you understand, do not respond to this letter.* That put an end to further correspondence. Perhaps I wanted to punish him for having left Paris without telling me. Though I might always be second to his family, I refused to be made to feel so.

Mme. Manet reinstated her Thursday evening soirées, and her first was a shrunken affair, with no Fanny Claus on the violin, no Frédéric Bazille's studious face gazing off above the rest. Degas had left for America to visit his brother in New Orleans. Rosalie had married her architect and was travelling in Italy. And as it was not a good time to appear allied with radical elements, others feared that association with the Manets would prove bad for business and stayed away.

I had to persuade Maman to go, begging just a little and playing up my loneliness. Still searching to lay blame on who had sent her son running from his country, she held mixed feelings towards the Manets. It had been nine months since Tibby disappeared and we had not received a single letter or note.

When Maman and I arrived, I thought it was Eugène there in the hall to greet us. His shoulders rounded, his arms slack by his sides as if having forgotten their purpose, his hair disheveled, his grey suit and black vest ill-fitted, he looked as though he had been standing there for hours, if not days, and I didn't recognize the man I loved. Maman realized she was missing her fan, and the butler escorted her back outside. So it was just him and me.

Édouard approached shyly, his smile mere surface tension. His hands were cold in mine and he kissed my cheeks with a meek reverence. His playfulness had vanished along with any hints of our former innuendo. He stared as if we were strangers, his eyes removed from the act of seeing. The effects of laudanum?

I could not bear that, after all our time apart, this was his greeting. The war might have tamed Édouard's volatility but it had made me more contrary. A consequence of giving up hope, after all, is losing one's fear as well.

"We need to repeat that greeting," I said. I let go of his hands and flicked mine as if wet. Cleared my throat. "Now." I held out my hands.

His confusion held a hint of curiosity, of life. As he took my hands, I squeezed his as hard as I could. He went to kiss my cheeks and I stiffened my arms, forcing him to pull me in. This time his lips on my cheeks had some blood in them. We stood facing each other. Though things now felt more awkward, it was preferable to feeling nothing.

Maman arrived, waving the forgotten fan, and we joined the party.

Mme. Manet's *appartement* looked the same except a little greyer, as if coated in a fine and permanent layer of dust. Quiet formal conversations floated between the notes of Suzanne's impressive études, performed with, I felt, new depth. Or perhaps my ears were new. Every ten minutes, as we made our separate rounds through the room, Édouard and I lifted our heads from our conversations to locate each other's whereabouts, our former flirtations replaced with melancholic glances. The fire that once crackled noisily now a single burning ember, condensed and waiting.

Suzanne kept a close watch on her husband. She'd had him to herself these past months, nursing him back to some distant semblance of himself. Her newfound possessiveness was understandable.

Having done one circuit of the room, Édouard and I found ourselves alone again in the front hall. I asked if he had begun to paint.

"I'm nearing my fortieth name day, Berthe, and am no longer young. I have to admit that my best work is now behind me." He leaned against the wall and snorted. "And I took such pains to protect my paintings from the war. Paintings of which I've sold none."

Who was this piteous man?

"Since when do you judge your work by such mundane standards?" Flushed, I sought my fan. "Have you forgotten what you're up against? What we're all up against?"

"Oh, Berthe." The stroke of his finger along my cheek felt patronizing. "I have wasted my inheritance and must live with my mother. My studio is a poor man's garret from which I take no inspiration. I question if I have any originality left."

"You're still alive. Still in possession of your arms and legs. What is it, Édouard, that suddenly frightens you so?"

Suzanne appeared, hovering at the end of the hall.

"Berthe, you're looking well," she said, sweetly.

"And your playing is even more sublime."

She blushed a high pink and took Édouard's arm. "Your mother is looking for you. Excuse us." And like some docile child, he let her lead him away.

I found Maman and requested we leave. Immediately. She said she'd be right along and while I waited in the front hall for the butler to bring our capes, Eugène arrived, late to the party. His happiness at seeing me was evident and he kissed my hand with assurance. Did his newfound confidence come from seeing both his brothers knocked from their pedestals?

There was an honesty between Eugène and me now and therefore an ease. He had seen me at my lowest point. He knew my feelings for his brother and we both knew of his feelings for me. Though we were too well bred to speak of our imbalanced situation, there were no secrets between us. In other words, we had a healthy foundation for friendship.

Sounding pleased, he told me of the progress he had made on his novel. He had just met with an interested publisher, which was why he was late.

"And the name of your protagonist?"

"I've decided to name him Eugène," he said without irony.

"Really?"

"A different surname, of course."

"You don't think that's self-aggrandizing?"

"It's just the name that suits him."

"Hmm..."

"Would you like to know the name of my heroine?"

When I hesitated, he laughed. "It's Jeanne."

"Good."

"She has an independent mind that resists generally accepted ideas."

I looked at him.

"You may have inspired her."

"Should I be flattered?"

"You either are or you aren't."

In truth, I didn't know which way I felt.

1872

THE CALL WENT OUT in the papers for Salon submissions, accompanied by this plea from the Minister of Arts, M. Blanc, who apparently fancied himself a poet: *I call on the divine genius of France's artists to raise up the past ideals of the beautiful behind the flickering shadows of the fallen world.*

His language was meant to inspire, but the message was clear. Depictions of the tragedies of the recent past would not be accepted, and the Realists, the painters of *la vie moderne,* not tolerated. Word got around that Meissonier himself had painted two "patriotic" paintings of the destruction of Paris, but now would not be submitting them.

When Degas heard that the rejection of Courbet's submissions was based solely on his role in the uprising, he boycotted the Salon altogether.

Édouard remained not so much distant from me as lost. He had not managed a return to painting but I insisted he submit two of his older works. America was seeking reparation costs from England for the sinking of their naval ship *The Alabama,* and details of the battle were in all the papers. So I suggested his painting of the battle, and a second, *The Kearsarge at Boulogne.* Convinced of rejection, he saw little point, but I made Suzanne promise they would make it onto the collection cart.

I submitted two seascapes I had done in Cherbourg. Knowing how fragile Édouard's confidence, I was more concerned with his paintings than my own.

TO TRY AND CHEER her melancholic son, Mme. Manet held a celebration in honour of Édouard's fortieth name day. He entered the drawing room to polite applause from the dwindled group of friends. In contrast to the last time I saw him, he'd colour in his cheeks. A new suit tailored to his thinned figure made him look taller. Or was it his carriage? He shooed the dog from his mother's footstool and stepped upon it, smiling. Turning forty was nothing to smile about. What had happened? He extended his arms.

"Name for me, my friends," he said, "an artist who can't flog a thousand francs' worth of paintings in the course of a year."

A resounding, "You!" from the painters present.

And me, I thought, and Degas and Antoine.

He hung his head then peered up at me with a glint of mischief. I instinctively moved closer.

He roared, "How wrong you all are!" Then he laughed a true laugh. How I'd missed hearing that laugh. Like a tide lifting the boats of a harbour, every spirit in the room rose as he boasted of a dealer and gallery owner who'd come to his studio, a M. Durand-Ruel. Only one boat seemed to sink in the wake of Édouard's buoyancy. Eugène, who with a kiltered smile scratched the back of his head.

"The dealer had hardly stepped foot inside my studio before he offered to buy two of my paintings at 800 francs apiece!" He shook his head. "I was so dumbfounded, I let them go without a counter-offer. He came again the next day and offered to buy twenty-four more!"

Mme. Manet clutched the arms of her chair. "Is it true?"

"Yes, Maman, you heard me, twenty-four more for a grand sum of 35,000 francs! This time I bartered. A little."

I swooned at the very idea.

"I didn't dare ask the gentleman questions for fear it was a dream," he said. "But he returned again the next day and took away a third cartload and a promissory note of another princely sum." He flung up his arms. "Now I need a drink! To toast myself!"

The details came out over the course of the evening. M. Durand-Ruel had recently returned to Paris to reopen his little-known gallery in rue Laffitte. During the war he had fled to England with his collection of Corots, Courbets, Rousseaus, Millets and Daubignys, took a risk and opened a gallery on Bond Street. Though French landscape artists sold poorly here, their work charmed the English. So, while in London on their honeymoons, Claude Monet and Camille Pissarro visited the gallery and shamelessly introduced themselves as "the future of French landscapists." They bought the dealer a drink and sweet-talked him into hosting a show of their work—M. Monet had a gift for persuasion—which the London critics likened to their own beloved Mr. Turner.

It was Monet who gave Édouard's name and address to Durand-Ruel, in hopes of paying back some of the debt owed to him. Degas told me that Édouard had twice bailed his nemesis out of financial troubles. He added, "He secretly envies Monet's way with a brush."

I left that night with the dealer's address. I suddenly didn't care about the upcoming Salon. I wanted to sell paintings. Since I wasn't to marry, I needed to ensure my future independence and security. I had become a pragmatist, my feet not only on the earth but of the earth. Would not Edma be proud?

TO MY IMMENSE HAPPINESS, both of Édouard's works were accepted to the Salon. The acceptances, it turned out, meant a great deal to him and he thanked me over and over for pressing him to submit. Unfortunately, Suzanne and my mother were present. If we were alone, I wondered if his thanks would have been more personal. I missed the feel of his lips, his hands on my waist.

My two paintings also made it past the conservative jury. And though my reviews would be of the same familiar and benign nature—the term *feminine* in every mention—Édouard's reviews, were, for the first time, exceptional. Amidst walls filled with the expected and the bland—for which Director Blanc was roundly chastised—it had become clear to everyone how Édouard's pieces invigorated the eye and spirit. Even the feared critic Albert Wolff, who'd once ridiculed Édouard as *amusing, with the eye of an artist but not the soul of the one*, bestowed his seal of approval. *Manet,* he wrote, *has become a man of the world. Rest assured: it is now safe to hang a Manet on your walls.*

To cap his sudden and unexpected success, Édouard was commissioned by a collector, a wealthy racehorse owner, to paint the view from the man's box at the Hippodrome—for three thousand francs! His success and happiness felt curiously like my own, but I had needs as well, and was no longer afraid to admit this, neither to myself nor to him. I waited, patience growing thin.

THAT SPRING, Edma came home for her second lying-in. In contrast to the first, a peaceful birth brought forth a boisterous baby girl full of personality and noisy demands. Baby Blanche had the heart-shaped face and round woodland-green eyes of her grand-mère Morisot, who did not protest this time when Edma refused to use the nursemaid.

"It saddens me, Berthe," said Edma at dinner one evening, "to see you living so cloistered."

Papa was eager to elaborate. "Dressing in white or black, ignoring her social commitments, painting at all hours, parakeets her only company."

"Tiburce," scolded Maman half-heartedly.

"It's embarrassing," he muttered and even Edma did not contradict him.

I had become an eccentric old maid even by Edma's measure.

"I must work," was my only defence, "and it takes all my time."

The day before she was to leave, the two of us alone in my *appartement,* Edma said that I fussed over my canvases "as if they were my children." It was not said meanly. Then she pointedly asked after Édouard. I knew what she was asking and could honestly say the childish flirtations between us had ended. "Though the roots—"

On the floor below, the baby woke with a scream that made Edma grimace.

"I'm relieved to hear that, Berthe. Very, very relieved." She squeezed my hand. "There are other men, you know, and you're not too old for real children. Not yet." She stood, unthinkingly weighed the fullness of her breasts to gauge which to feed from, then kissed me goodnight.

I couldn't bring myself to disturb her peace and finish what I was going to say, that the roots of my former feelings for Édouard now reached deeper, more mature sources of water and nourishment. And that I hoped it only a matter of time before new shoots broke through the earth and clamoured toward the sun.

SHORTLY AFTER Edma and baby Blanche returned to Lorient, Édouard came by the house. It was sheer luck that Papa, keeper of the castle, was sleeping. Maman brought Édouard to my rooms where she remained, gazing at a book whose page never turned. It was so absurd, the three of us there. I was thirty-one years old.

He stalked around my easels, commended me on my works from Cherbourg.

"I haven't seen anyone treat oils the way you're doing."

"Without respect, you mean?" I came and stood beside him.

"With such abandon."

"Abandon is the very thing I'm after."

"And with such passion."

My heart beat faster. He was flirting with me. He studied my balcony painting of Yves, commented on the child's point of view behind bars. "I feel much like that child."

"As do I." Had Maman heard the waver in my voice?

"I have rented a fancy new studio, I have my first commission, but the truth is I don't know where or how to begin." He touched my painting to run his finger down the length of Yves' back. My spine ached with it. "I've this gnawing doubt I'm no longer capable of painting. Anything at all."

"A temporary inhibition." I made it a statement. "It is impossible to paint from the same place as before the war. We're different people, our hands new hands that have to learn all over again."

As if forgetting Maman was present, he took my hand and brought it to his lips. "So might these hands start by painting you?"

"They may."

He kissed both my cheeks, slow and lingering.

To her credit, dear Maman said nothing afterward. I was well beyond her influence and she knew it. Despite her heroic efforts, it was obvious, even to her, that Édouard inspired feelings in me like no other man. And though she could not say it, I think she was secretly happy for me to know and experience such feelings, even if they could not be fully gratified.

"A SCULPTURE OF Venus?" I traced my finger down her hard cheek.

"I must try to make potential clientele comfortable," said Édouard as an excuse.

His new studio was as elegant and grand as I imagined Meissonier's might be. High ceilings, oak walls, Venus in the foyer, an imposing fireplace carved with Corinthian plasters, a dark blue velvet *chaise longue* in the corner, candelabras.

"With some exceptions." I pointed over the fireplace to my old friend *Le Déjeuner sur l'herbe* and to *Olympia* on the main wall, two paintings for which even M. Durand-Ruel knew he could never find a buyer.

I had been chaperoned to Édouard's new studio by dear Rosalie, now a respectable married woman. Like Edma, she too had given up painting, insisting she no longer had "the necessary focus." At my request, Rosalie had walked me to the studio door and then left on errands.

"After all these years Édouard's like my brother," I told her. "A brother who needs a willing model and some encouragement. I couldn't bear wasting half your day." If Rosalie, in her goodness, believed she was compromising my reputation in any way, she would never have agreed. Then again, I always did underestimate her.

Édouard had ushered me inside then stuck his head back out into the hallway.

"I'm too old for a nanny," I said. "Rosalie will be picking me up in four hours' time." I held his gaze. "Please don't give me away."

He shut the door and I began to remove my gloves. I had anticipated a vigorous response to our finally being alone. I had taken care to lighten the dark moons under my eyes, fussed with my hair, even rubbed my décolletage and ankles with dried rose petals. But it was clear that he was preoccupied.

Instead of hanging my coat on a proper hook, he tossed it over the shoulder of Venus. "I'm unsure how I might arrange you. Maybe you've some ideas?"

He was asking me?

I removed my black-ribboned hat.

"Shall we have you standing or sitting?"

I put my hat back on, only sideways. "I think you should paint me in my hat."

He stared at me.

"And maybe in my coat." I pulled my coat back on. "And scarf." This I pulled from my pocket and wound around my neck. "And then I will sit down inside, all dressed to go outside."

He laughed a little, one nervous screw loosening. "Fine, then. Shall we move a chair into the light?"

"It's your chair, your light and I'm your model."

He set the chair at an angle in front of enormous windows hung with white sheers. "The black's pleasing," he muttered, another screw unwinding.

"Maybe I should put on my gloves?"

"No. No gloves."

Finally, he was using his eyes. Now his posture gained height and breadth, and I could tell he was seeing not just my person but a painting.

"A touch more colour. For contrast," he said and took the stairs two at a time. He returned with a bouquet of violets. Water dripped from the stems. "Hold these."

When a woman accepted violets, the flowers of love, from a man, she was accepting him as her lover. I smelled them, my eyes asking the question.

"Higher." He saw only composition and light. I lifted the violets between my breasts. "Yes." He took and reduced them into a small bunch "to pin at your corsage."

"At my corsage," I flirted. The screws were being tightened again and he couldn't play. Behind his canvas, he lifted his pencil and stopped. His shoulders flagged.

"What if it's no good?" He stared at me accusingly.

"Then I will never speak to you again."

He huffed a laugh despite himself.

"Please let it be terrible. Then we can buy more paint." How ironic to be saying such a thing to the man once referred to as a pariah of the art world, whose paintings provoked and shocked. But it was clearly the right thing to say, for his focus returned and his hand began to move deftly and quickly.

He must have drawn only a vague sketch, for already he was mixing paints as if afraid of his inspiration fading. Or maybe, I flattered myself, he was influenced by my newfound approach to oils.

He paused to fetch us both some wine.

"Is it terrible thus far?"

He let out a big breath. "Brilliantly bad."

NEARLY EVERY DAY for the next two weeks and against my father's wishes, dear Rosalie escorted me to Édouard's studio and then left us alone. He painted one portrait after another. Each more "terrible" than the next. I brought along a veil, a fan, my velvet housecoat and slippers. I puckered my lips, batted my eyelids. I hid behind my fan, showed off my ankles, posed with my hair up and with it loose.

We were like children play-acting, I the eccentric model, he the serious painter. But I was no one's hay bale. He inspired me and I inspired him. Some canvases were, in fact, terrible, and he whitewashed them and began again. I enjoyed myself, and came to understand that expression in a whole new way. I liked who I was, was not afraid of who I was. I was not the perfect daughter, perfect sister, perfect citizen, perfect painter. Nor had I ever been these things. Yet I wasn't sure who I was, for such a notion was as fleeting as anything else.

Édouard and I didn't even kiss. Not once. To cross that boundary would have threatened our ease. One morning, Suzanne showed up bearing dried figs and currant buns for her husband. I could tell, despite her bucolic face, that she was surprised to find the door unlocked and Édouard calling to whomever it was to enter. And after entering on whispery feet, to find me sitting there dressed in my coat and hat, my face veiled. She apologized for interrupting, eyes blinking around the room.

"Your mother, is she... upstairs?"

"Oh, Rosalie escorted me. She's just stepped out and will be right back." I peered over my shoulder out the window.

Édouard did not invite her to stay and thankfully Suzanne didn't wait for Rosalie to appear.

"Suzanne," I ventured after she'd gone, "was your brothers' piano teacher, I understand. So that's how you met?"

His paintbrush stopped moving, his figure gone rigid.

"I apologize," I said. "It has nothing to do with me." After another heartbeat, his shoulders let down and his brush continued.

ON WHAT WAS to be our last day before he began work on his commission, I brought along one of my recent Salon paintings which, of course, had not sold: *The Harbour at Cherbourg.* I asked straight out if he would show it to his dealer, M. Durand-Ruel, and recommend me. I could never have been so bold before the war but still my cheeks grew warm.

When he hesitated, the hollowing of my stomach leapt in anger. He needed time to consider it?

"You are aware"—he took the painting from my hands and placed it on a nearby easel—"that Monsieur Durand-Ruel is a staunch monarchist and devout Catholic. His tastes in art are conventional and—"

"But he's representing modern—"

"Only because there's a profit in it. Like most businessmen he's more than willing to compromise his principles."

"Are you saying work by a woman—"

"Might be a challenge for him. So I was thinking"—he tapped a finger against his lips—"how to appeal to him as a businessman. Hmm... I could tell him that if he's committed to representing the *avant-garde,* here is his opportunity to be the first to represent its leading female painter."

I stepped up to him, took his face in my hands and kissed the place that had spoken those words. His lips responded, his mouth, his hands, his arms, his hips, all responded and my body seemed to open at invisible seams to join to his. Hand on my lower back, he pressed his length against me and I pressed back. Just then the bells of Rosalie's carriage announced her arrival on the street below.

"Why did we waste all our time together painting?" he said, breathless.

"It was more than painting." I kissed him again. To have to leave him at that moment was like leaving behind my skin.

"I WOULD LIKE YOU to open it," said Papa, sliding over the mail tray as the soup was being served.

A parcel had arrived for me that morning but since Papa inspected each and every correspondence entering his domain, he had prevented Thin Louis from delivering it to my rooms.

I took the package, a perfect square, wrapped unevenly in brown paper and too much string, and placed it beside my plate. "I will open it when I'm alone, thank you, Papa."

"You will open it here at dinner, for I want to know who's sending you a package."

"I understand your desire, but my mail is not your business, it's mine." I pictured Édouard's hands clumsily doing the wrapping, a job normally reserved for his wife.

"As long as you are under my roof, you are my business."

Papa's words held such cold rage that the servant, in the middle of filling my bowl, stiffened and soup dripped loudly off the bottom of his ladle. He was young and new to the household.

Maman kept her eyes on the actions of the server.

"I am your grown daughter who deserves to have her privacy, like any oth—"

A strange growl issued from my father and something flew across the room to pierce the far wallpaper before it fell with a thunk to the floor. His fork.

Maman gasped. The servant stumbled back. I struck the table with my fist.

"I am nobody's... business."

Papa looked stunned, then shame dropped his eyes to the table. I was not proud of provoking my father in this way, old and ill as he was, but scraped back my chair, took my package and left. I had to pause on the stair landing to calm my heart.

I locked my door and leaned against it, hugged the package to my chest to brace for whatever came next, seizing the outrageous thought of just how liberating it would be when my father was no longer alive.

Minutes passed and no one arrived to demand my return to dinner. I went to my desk for my letter knife, clipped the tangle of string then tore back the paper. I stared at the small canvas in a carved mahogany frame, one which Papa must never, ever see, and was overwhelmed by the most joyfully complicated emotion. Clear proof of his re-found abilities, here was a brilliantly rendered still life of my corsage of violets. Tied with ribbon, it was laid on a table alongside the red fan from *Le Balcon*. Beside these, a painted note was folded to reveal only the words at the note's beginning and at its end: *To Mlle. Berthe… Manet.* What might have been said in the middle had been left for me to imagine. If I were not imprisoned by Papa, and social mores, I would have run to him.

"AS AN UNMARRIED WOMAN"—I directed my words to Maman only—"I will someday be in need of an income. And therefore an occupation. And my chosen occupation, as you know and for which I am wholly indebted to you, my generous parents, entails purchasing paints and canvas."

"We are not dead yet." Maman glanced across the dinner table at Papa. Such levity told me she understood I was up to something and was trying to help.

Thanks to Édouard, I had received the much-anticipated note from M. Durand-Ruel. He had requested to visit me in my studio and view my work. I wrote back immediately and suggested a day and time. Unfortunately, my studio was in the home of my parents, to which Papa held the keys. I'd no assurance that he would allow a strange man into my rooms, much less commerce to take place under his roof. Since the fork incident, I'd been careful not to provoke him. But having already committed to the dealer and having left it to the last hour, I had no choice but to bring it up. I timed my speech for after Papa finished one glass of wine and two courses.

"There's an art dealer, a Monsieur Durand-Ruel—"

"The man who purchased Édouard's paintings?" said Maman and turned to Papa. "He paid 800 francs per painting."

"The very man. He owns a gallery over in rue Laffitte."

"And one in London," added Maman, drawing out the city's name.

"Well, Monsieur would like to see my work."

"Here?" Maman looked from me to Papa and back again.

"My studio is my sitting room so, yes, here. Tomorrow, in fact. In the afternoon. At 2:30." I held my breath. I'd revealed that I'd made the appointment. Without his consent.

Papa took a deliberated sip of wine, then slowly set it down.

I folded my hands in my lap.

He cleared his throat, an ugly-sounding process that required a handkerchief. Then, "I will agree to the dealer's visit on one condition."

He paused, but I was not going to ask the question.

"The condition is that I, as former senior officer in the Ministry of Finance, do the negotiating."

I met his eye and he nodded just slightly. He was asking, not telling.

I struggled to sound calm. "Thank you, Papa. I would appreciate that. I know nothing of such transactions."

He asked Thin Louis for more cream sauce for his dorade. "So at what time did you say I should expect the gentleman?"

"2:30."

"Fine. He can use the merchant's entrance."

I looked hard at Maman.

"He may come from a good family for all we know," she said. "Besides, shouldn't we try to flatter him a little? For Berthe's sake?"

PAPA WAS THE ONE who greeted the dealer—in the foyer—and escorted him upstairs. I was in my drawing room as instructed, pacing and praying Papa wouldn't insult him. Wouldn't ruin this singular opportunity, perhaps my only opportunity, to maybe, someday, make a living off my work.

Younger than I expected, Paul Durand-Ruel had a friendly face and an easy composure. If Papa dropped his officious armor, he might have liked him. Due to a needlessly crisp agenda, introductions were curt. I sat drinking tea, ladylike, trying not to spill it while Papa followed the dealer around the room, peered over his shoulder and ordered Thin Louis to place this one or that one as requested on the easel for inspection. Every painting suddenly looked unfinished to me. Amateurish. I wanted to explain my choices, my inspirations, point out this or that abstraction but Papa was to do the talking and I act as though such business was beneath me.

With great authority Papa commented on where this one was painted, during which summer, at the home of which of his daughters. His accuracy surprised me. He even got most of my titles right. I didn't correct him on the others.

M. Durand-Ruel stood with his arms hanging in front of him, one hand gripping the wrist of the other. He nodded at Papa's commentary, made quiet hmms or sighs out of his nose. Now he took several paces back from my portrait of Edma in Lorient, then moved in close. When he pulled a monocle from his pocket, I nearly spit my tea. I knew how messy and shambolic my strokes were up close.

After he had studied the last picture upon the easel, Monsieur turned and nodded once to me. I had no control over my face, my smile as likely an idiot's grimace. He turned to Papa. "I would like to offer twelve hundred for four pictures."

Four! I wanted to scream. Jump out of my chair. I bit the inside of my lip to focus on the pain.

He pointed to two oils, including the original harbour picture

Édouard had passed on, and two watercolours. Watercolours? Really? It was all too wonderful.

I rose to walk over and offer my hand.

"Fifteen hundred and they're yours," said Papa, his voice strangely deep.

I sat again, hard enough to jar my bones. Maman had revealed at dinner how much Édouard had received for his work. Yes, this was less than half but his were bigger canvases. And two of mine were watercolours!

"She's a true and original talent," Papa said, to my horror, "and just think, she's young and not yet at the height of her abilities."

Please. Stop. Now came a silence so oppressive I felt faint. It was only the cinch of my corset that held me upright. I needed the window opened to freshen the dying air. Outside a rusty blue barge floated downriver carrying open crates heaped with red apples polished in sunlight. In pure madness, I began to paint the scene in my mind's eye.

"Fourteen," said M. Durand-Ruel.

I coughed, reaching for my tea. Say yes. Why are you not speaking? If you don't speak, I will be forced to.

"Fourteen it is."

Fearing my legs wouldn't hold, I remained seated so M. Durand-Ruel came to me, which my father would consider only proper. We shook hands like men, which felt strange but fitting. He complimented my work in the practiced way of someone who doesn't actually believe his compliments. I didn't care. My work had sold, and for a respectable sum. I couldn't wait to tell Edma.

All evening Papa joked that he might have a new career ahead of him and asked what sort of commission I was planning to pay him. He had not been so jolly for some time and tonight the redness of face seemed a healthy thing.

I wrote Edma with my news. She promptly wrote back, the letter's tone as though intent on dampening my excitement.

Congratulations on your first sales! Officially a professional painter! You have achieved something of our dream, Berthe, and even if your career fails to progress you can be proud of having accomplished this much. I can't say I'm not a little envious, but one cannot have everything one wishes for. I am happy to hear that Papa supported you in this venture. He sounds as excited about the transaction as you. I know how he worries for your future. Perhaps he can worry a little less now for the time being.

I am well yet somewhat distraught. Unlike Jeanne, Blanche is fussy at the breast and cries inconsolably most afternoons for hours at a time. The doctor says she'll outgrow it, as does Manon, but right now it is hard to bear the little thing's suffering. I should not complain for both children are healthy and my life is blessed with goodness.

Love, Edma

"SO THIS IS WHAT making money does to a woman's appearance?" Rosalie peered at me in her curious yet knowing way until the carriage swerved to avoid hitting something in the street.

"In that such a transaction makes one want to wash, yes."

She laughed. "You are modeling a great deal for Édouard. You might start charging him for your services."

Uncomfortable where this might lead, I changed subjects.

I had written to Édouard with my news and to thank him for his recommendation. He wrote back. *Selling is a grand feeling, no? When can I see you alone again?* I had turned around and wrote Rosalie for my answer. Though the day was warm, I wore a cloak to conceal a new black gown—a V-cut neckline with frothy lace—and a black velvet choker. Hardly appropriate day wear, but an outfit I hoped would inspire my lover beyond his brush.

When I stepped into Édouard's studio, I locked the door behind me with a properly loud click, so he would hear. As I pulled off my gloves, he spoke of having been to the racetrack and finding an inspiring angle and perspective. "Finally," he said, "I have begun my commission."

I slipped off my cloak and he stopped talking, his eyes dipping into my décolletage. Without hesitation, I stepped in to kiss him, wrapping my arms around his neck—but he ducked and scooped me into his arms like a groom his new bride.

"Oh?" I startled, my laugh an uneasy hiccup.

He carried me to the *chaise longue* and laid me along it as if he knew exactly what he was going to do next and next and next.

"I've barely said hello." Embarrassed by my inexperience, my confidence dissolved as he knelt on the floor beside me. "Is this mad of us?"

Édouard no longer appeared able to hear or speak. He kissed my lips closed while dragging my sleeves off my shoulders. Edma once described Adolphe's carnal needs arrogating his senses. Was deaf-muteness how it began?

Sobering concerns competed for my attention. I could end up pregnant. My name ruined. Moist kisses across my ear, shivers cascading over my bared shoulders. Papa would disown me.

"Should I stop?" he whispered, then licked where his words had entered. My head swung left for his lips to travel the length of my neck. I could arrange a quick marriage of convenience as cover. Small bites of his teeth along the narrow ridge of my clavicle caused my toes to point. Or I could move to the country. He feathered kisses down to the very bottom of the V of my décolletage. Paint under a pseudonym. So light was his touch, my back arched of its own volition, seeking more pressure. Feign my own death. His strong hands cupped my breasts and pushed them upward. Someone moaned as he kissed the hills of flesh and teased my nipples with his teeth, the skin so sensitive it felt like a tearing. I pressed my fists against the chaise.

His kisses travelled the centreline of my bodice and continued down the front of my skirt. The surface of my skin felt hot and swollen as his too-slow hands lifted the layers of fabric and crinoline and removed my underclothes. He kissed the inside of one knee open. The other. Anticipation reduced me to a single point of where his mouth touched next, my breath a racing train as his head dipped from view. I cried out when the sensations threatened to blind me, and then couldn't make any sound at all when they did. Afterward, I was afraid to open my eyes, certain to find nothing but white light. Edma had never mentioned this... ecstasy.

All this pleasure had been his to give, for he had not removed a stitch of his own clothing. In my post-bliss happiness, I pulled him onto me. "Lie with me," I begged, and kissed his chin and cheeks, eyes and lips.

"Ahh... *la petite mort.*" I had not heard the expression but had no trouble understanding its meaning. He kissed my hand and released himself. "Your expression at this moment... unrivaled."

"I am a woman in love."

"You are a woman indeed." His eyes searched the room. "And I... need to paint that woman."

"You're mocking me." I rolled on my side, my limbs loose and warm, to watch in disbelief as he dragged over three easels. Lined them even with a floorboard.

"Three?"

"I want to capture every inch of you."

He disappeared upstairs and returned with a canvas as tall as him, staggering and struggling to place it horizontally across the supports.

"I'm not helping you"—I laughed—"because you are being foolish."

"I see truth before me and will not let it be lost."

I understood then how a woman could give up her personal ambitions for a man. Could succumb to marriage and bearing a child, the tangible proofs of love. But my lover was already married. Not intent in confining me to his house to oversee his meals and the refinement of his children, my lover was intent on putting me on a canvas for all the world to see. If, that is, they had such eyes as his. And the painter in me understood this was, perhaps, a more elevated union.

I lay languishing in my contented fog, still dressed, only my undergarments and slippers missing. He poured us both wine. Semi-upright on one elbow so I could drink, for the next three hours I watched him paint. Watched his gaze slide around my cheeks, embrace an ear, trace my lips, reach again and again into the exposed V of my chest. As his eyes caressed my breasts, I could not say which I enjoyed more, which made me feel more cherished – his lips upon me or the genius of his gaze. I told him I wanted all of him. That I was his. He pleaded with me not to speak. We drank, toasting our impossible predicament.

He said he wanted to capture me from head to slipper, so that he could gaze upon his painting as if upon me.

"There's not time," I said, but he didn't stop. We had more wine. He spent so long on my face and bust that when his gaze moved to my hips, we were both a little drunk. As he painted my skirts, I lifted them, slowly, taunted him with the sight of where my garter met my stocking. He groaned, brush clattering to the floor. And though still he would not unite with me, our urgent hands sought to give each other pleasure. To hear his rising pleasure in my ear was unbearable and my bliss grew even higher and wider than my first go, something I didn't believe possible.

We lay shoulder to shoulder under his high white ceiling, huffing to catch up our breath. Spent and tipsy, I began to laugh, not me exactly, but my body. My body began to laugh, without control, and would not stop. My back arched and contracted and arched again. I felt like that young girl in the old city that I once saw heaved skyward from a dusty blanket, newly released from gravity's rules.

"What is skin and bones," I said when I could speak again, "but a tiny and temporary home for a universe of love?"

"Such a romantic, Mademoiselle Morisot."

I kissed along the outer shell of his ear. "No. I'm a Realist."

"Hmm…"

"Do you remember that afternoon in Louveciennes," I said, "when we were alone in the garden?"

"Of course I do."

I propped myself to see his face. "But you denied it."

"I did not."

"Then you did not acknowledge it."

"How could I? It was impossible to speak of." He brought my palm to his lips.

"I thought I was mad."

"We were mad and we are still. Look at us. But I have left off on your hand, this hand, and must finish what I've begun." He kissed my palm again and sat up to re-button his pants. Then fitted my slippers back on my feet.

My body felt heavy as though filled with sand and my eyes drifted shut.

At first I dreamed of Rosalie's carriage bells in the street below, of Rosalie surrounded by packages wrapped and twined. Then I heard them again. Closer and more insistent, like a warning. I started awake, scrambled up from the chaise. Édouard threw up his hands.

"Ruinous! What shall I do with you?"

I slipped into the toilette to settle my hair as best I could, brushed out my skirts. Frantically threw on my cloak.

"Wait, wait, slow down. She's only just arrived. Come."

He pulled me in front of his canvas, wrapped his arms around me and tucked his chin along my neck. "Here you are. What do you think?"

"Édouard—" I struggled to get free but he held me tighter. "Where are my underclothes?"

"First things first."

I looked across at the painted figure still wet and glistening and stopped my struggles. Was that me? Her lips, pinched in his other portraits, were smooth and plump. Her brow, her cheeks, even her nose appeared to have softened, become fleshier. The skin of her chest too. Soaked with light. She wore a smile that wasn't quite. Her gaze, as if she'd never had a care. I didn't even mind the exposed fan of my ear and lazy swing of my tired eye, for who but Édouard Manet could capture an honest portrait of a woman sated in love?

The carriage bells rang again.

"The legs," I said. The bottom half of the painting was foreshortened and all out of proportion.

"I know."

"And my hand." The right hand was stiff-fingered and strangely large.

"The wine."

"But the rest."

"I know."

"I love it as I love you." I leaned back against him. "It's a shame to have to hide it away."

"Why would I?" He sounded offended.

I pushed out of his arms. "Because, Édouard, people will guess."

"You give people too much credit."

"Anyone who knows me"—I was certain—"would see that I had been ravished."

"People have poor imaginations."

Was he so drunk or did he truly not understand? Or worse, not care? "Where are my underclothes?" I got down on my knees to peer beneath the chaise.

"Leave them for me. A souvenir." He clapped his hands. "Let's invite Rosalie up and see."

"No, we absolutely cannot." I scanned the room.

"Where is that woman I just painted? Carefree and in love."

"She is right here and cannot risk being exposed."

He was indifferent. "I promise you, Rosalie will see what she wants to see and nothing more."

"No. Stop your teasing. This is not a game."

He strode to the windows and, to my disbelief, threw them open. "Rosalie, come up. I have a new painting."

"Édouard! Rosalie is the most astute woman I know. Do you *want* to expose me?"

"Berthe. Trust me."

"You're drunk." How quickly happiness could sour. "I'm going downstairs." I located my hat and glanced around again for my bloomers.

"Berthe, wait. I only want to reassure you."

"You are doing exactly the opposite."

I opened the door and there stood Rosalie, her hand poised to knock. "Rosalie."

Édouard stepped up behind me.

"I'm so sorry to keep you," I said. "Let's be going."

He gently urged me aside to kiss Rosalie's cheeks. "Now come, see what I have accomplished today in so short a time."

"I... Maman is expecting me." With my eyes I dared him to disregard my warnings. Trust me, his eyes said back.

"This will only take a minute." Édouard guided Rosalie by the elbow and positioned her squarely in front of the painting.

Then I saw them, my white bloomers at the base of the white sheer curtains. In clear view. My heart pounded in fury and fear as I positioned myself between Rosalie and that corner of the window and asked if she'd found the book she was after? If there was anything new at the Bon Marché? She answered my questions but didn't take her eyes off the painting.

How would I explain myself to her? I would confess everything, beg her forgiveness. Beg her not to tell Maman. And to please, never say a word to Edma. Edma would... I didn't know what Edma would do.

"Berthe looks..." said Rosalie, and I couldn't breathe, "like she's just woken from a wonderful dream."

"I didn't sleep well last night," I said quickly.

"You see, Berthe," said Édouard, too loudly, "I knew she would guess it."

"You've captured her at her most peaceful and most beautiful," continued Rosalie.

"Thank you." Édouard stared hard at me. "I agree."

"But the legs," said Rosalie.

"Not enough time, you see."

"And the right hand."

"She had awoken then and wouldn't keep still." He smiled sheepishly, seeking forgiveness yet believing himself vindicated.

Men have affairs without consequence, I thought, unsmiling. I left without saying goodbye and without my bloomers.

Rosalie did not bring up the painting on the carriage ride home and I didn't dare. Because she avoided the subject, I feared she guessed what had gone on, though Rosalie was too smart to presume to know what was best for another. Or perhaps she did presume, and had come to the conclusion that whatever he and I were engaged in should not be interfered with.

"I've not yet told Edma of my recent modeling for Édouard," I said, "to encourage him back to painting." I knew she and Edma corresponded and hoped she understood my meaning.

"Do you think she still harbours feelings for him?" She opened her fan, lazily beginning to fan herself.

"Do you?"

"She asks for news of him in her letters."

"Oh? Funny, but she never mentions him in her letters to me."

Was she using Rosalie to spy on us?

WHEN I NEXT SAW the painting, Édouard had cut away the lower half, there being no cure for it. As for everyone else who saw it, Édouard turned out to be right. They saw what they wanted to see and no one was the wiser. Not even Suzanne. Or the shrewd Madame Manet. Or Eugène, who said I looked "sixteen and in the full bloom of youth." Maman, when she saw it, said I should have paid more attention to my hair and that she thought it rude of Édouard to paint my eye adrift. "He should have traded his Realism for kindness. But otherwise you look young and admirably feminine in this one."

The next time we were alone in his studio, he apologized profusely for upsetting me. "How can I make it up to you?"

I paused. "Undress yourself."

"You want me to—"

"Undress yourself. Now."

Smiling, he tore off his cravat, dropped his suspenders. Unbuttoned his sleeves followed by those of his shirt and removed it. He worked open the buttons of his pants. I watched his pale skin's gradual revealing. Arms, chest, torso, genitals, legs, feet. I had not seen a man's genitalia except in painting and sculpture. The dark profusion of hair still a surprise, the un-erect member more humble and lowly than it had felt under my hand. I tried not to laugh when, as if a separate striving creature, it rose up like a compass arrow to point at me.

"Now you must remove my clothes."

At this command, he took his time until I couldn't bear the pace and helped him along.

Exploring hollows and furrows, curves, the thickness of bones beneath, the textures of hair, skin, its colouration and heat and fragrant odours, I understood there was more to painting a nude than what the eye registered. Again he refused to make me a woman—"too dangerous"—but then again with his mouth satisfied me to the point where I could not imagine better.

1873

"WELL, THE KING is dead." Maman had brought my breakfast tray herself, along with *Le Figaro*.

"Who is dead?"

"Emperor Louis." She tsked as she pushed the front page toward me. "Apparently lived quite high since his capture."

After a brief capture by the Prussians, the Emperor had been released and then hopped on a boat to England. There, reunited with the Empress, he enjoyed a comfortable exile in Chislehurst, tended by five dozen servants and playing host to British royalty.

"Do the aristocratic class stick together no matter what their sins?" posed Maman. I pictured Marcello in that dirty marvel of a theatre and how, the next time I saw her, she was surrounded by government ministers in the great hall of the Opera House. Recalled our meeting in her garden house—painting herself naked. She could expose herself in ways I never could. Were I in her place, I thought, I would be spending evenings with Édouard dancing at the Moulin de la Galette or travelling together in foreign lands, not sitting alone with a paintbrush and two green birds for company.

Maman shook out the fold of one of my curtains. "President Theirs has proposed a new law that all children of France, no matter their class, be educated—albeit in secular institutions. He's not a religious man, as you know. Wasn't that Eugène's cause? Oh, and he's proposing all factory owners be forced to pay workers a fair wage."

"Do you think that these proposed laws are reparations for his soul, or a bid for one?"

"Now, Berthe."

IN RESPONSE TO THEIR monarch's death, a loyalist faction within the government began a quiet insurrection. Contending that the newly proposed laws would give control to the "very barbarians who nearly destroyed our moral fabric," these men managed to spread enough alarm among parliament that, following a non-confidence vote, President Thiers was forced to resign.

The new president-elect, former general M. Marshal MacMahon, set about "restoring moral order." His first mission: to design a Catholic basilica for Paris's most rebellious neighbourhood on the butte of Montmartre where two of his fellow generals had been executed. Conceived in white stone, to "expiate the sins of the Commune," the future Basilica of Sacre-Coeur would stand as "witness of repentance for deeds past and a beacon for the moral future afore us." It would be built high enough to be seen from all corners of the city, lest anyone forget what had taken place there. He seemed of the belief that two senseless murders overshadowed 25,000 others.

The esthetically paralyzed Charles Blanc was dismissed as Minister of Arts for his sin of "liberality" and replaced with the Marquis de Chennevières, a man famous for his editorials against the evils of atheism. The Marquis wasted no time destroying the pantheist murals of the Pantheon and replacing them with religious allegories. Next he rooted out atheists on the Salon jury to ensure that "nothing frivolous, scandalous, or decadent sully France's reputation."

The Salon jury was so rigid in scope that a cry went up for a second Salon des Refusés, a cry once again loud enough to concern officials. And, for a second time, an alternate Salon was announced. In ten years' time the art world had come full circle, ending where we had begun.

Thursday at Mme. Manet's, speaking uncharacteristically loudly over the music, Degas called this secondary Salon an "insulting consolation prize." He snorted. "This jury wants to exhume the dead, so let them. If painters striving for originality are rejected on that principle alone, then I reject them."

He told us that Claude Monet and Camille Pissarro were also boycotting the Salon. I imagined that, having gained respect in England, it must feel all the more insulting to be rejected in their own country.

After last year's stellar reviews, Édouard was undaunted.

"If this year's jury is of a Romantic bent, give them something Romantic. We can play their game better than they, no? Besides, what's our choice? The Salon is the only game in town."

"For now," said Degas, enigmatically.

"For now?" said Édouard. "Where else will you find the same exposure? What else carries the same cachet? Not the Kensington in London, not whatever it's called in Brussels and certainly nothing in your America."

No one could argue with him. As encouraging as it was to have my works now at Durand-Ruel's galleries here and in London, they had attracted neither critical attention nor buyers. Like Édouard, I would again submit work to the Paris Salon.

ON A RECENT TRIP to Holland, Édouard attended a retrospective of Frans Hals. With the Salon jury in mind, he went to work on a romantic tribute to Hals' *The Merry Drinker*. His model, a stout friend and engraver by the name of Bellot, was getting ready to leave his studio when I arrived mid-afternoon for no other reason than needing to touch and be touched by my lover. Rosalie had become my accomplice, though she was far too sophisticated for me to know whether this was wittingly or unwittingly.

"Pretty young women do not visit engravers," M. Bellot announced in his pleasing baritone. "I'm in the wrong business." The smell of beer was strong on the man's breath, his cheeks a crimson red, his eyes smiling.

Édouard clapped his friend on the back. "Your being too fat is the reason."

M. Bellot wagged his finger. "I didn't even charge him for my time and he insults me."

"You're now immortalized in paint! You should be paying me."

M. Bellot moved into the hall. "Now, to salt my wound, I must use the merchant entrance."

"And you drank all my beer!" laughed Édouard.

When the engraver had gone, Édouard showed me "my period piece with beer. *Le Bon Bock*."

It was a warm study in conventional mud-browns and rusts, complete with a bitumen undercoat and scumble glaze. In it, M. Bellot filled out his chair, his knees spread to allow the glory of his belly. He wore an otter-skin cap and smoked a long white-stemmed pipe while his plump hand gripped a half-empty glass of golden beer crowned with white foam.

"You, my love"—the endearment like a new flavour on my tongue—"have immortalized a round man's *joie de vivre*."

"If you, with your relentless critical eye, say so, then it must be true." He wrapped his arms around my waist.

"It's a portrait of contentment. A *bonhomme* that Meissonier himself might have painted."

"Who happens to be on the jury." Édouard tapped his temple.

"This glass of beer equals—no, surpasses—Meissonier's accuracy. The beer alone is admission to the Salon." There was nothing that incited my lover's affections more than flattery. Today was no exception.

Time and again, at the height of my desire when all thoughts of consequence vanished, he still refused to take his prize. Afterwards I could only be grateful for his restraint and love him all the more. A child would be ruinous. Or perhaps he believed I might still marry.

Édouard announced he would submit two paintings to the Salon, *Le Bon Bock* and, to my dismay, the ironically named

Repose—the self-conscious portrait of my first solo sitting before the war. I protested but he insisted it was the perfect foil to *Le Bon Bock.*

"You must be strategic with a jury like this one. Look here." He dragged over a second easel and placed *Repose* upon it.

"Your portrait is bright, see, where Bellot's is dark. Your figure is distinctly feminine, Bellot's distinctly masculine. One speaks of innocence, the other decadence. Here a young woman is perched gracelessly in her slender body"—I swatted him—"while here a fat old merchant is long since settled into his."

"You should have changed my pose and put me out of my discomfort."

"I would never. It was too expressive."

"So how exactly are you being strategic?"

"The jurors will not be able to separate their appreciation of one for the other. That way, they'll take both."

The contrast he failed to mention was that *Repose* was the weaker of the two works, which made *Le Bon Bock* stand out all the more. I knew it and he knew I knew it.

He encouraged me to also think strategically. "Send in a proper piece for a woman. A pastel. Of something sweet. Thus appeased, they will overlook your insolence and consider your oils."

That March, I confidently submitted two oils and one water-colour and yes, a last-minute pastel in case Édouard's theory was true. The pastel was a small thing, a portrait of a neighbour's pretty daughter. It had taken me all of twenty minutes.

In the middle of April, each of my works was returned stamped on the back with a big red R. All of them, that is, except that insipid little pastel. After nearly a decade of being accepted to the Salon, I felt chastised by the Académie for the sin of being born female. I was furious at myself for submitting because what buyer was going to want a painting with that damn R on the back screaming out that it was not up to French standards. The jury might as well have taken a knife to them.

My foul mood lasted weeks, though I was cheered to hear that Eva Gonzales had been rejected outright. In comparison to previous years, acceptances by women had been more than halved. Marcello also hadn't made the grade. Perhaps because of her brazenness of taking on a masculine name?

Fueled by rejection, I painted feverishly that spring. Thankfully, my parents now left me alone. Papa even recruited family and neighbours to pose as my models. I painted my cousin Mme. Boursier and her daughter, which my dealer purchased and shortly thereafter sold to my dear friends, the Stevens, for 800 francs.

That sale gave me the confidence to put my portrait of Yves and Bibi—*View of Paris from the Trocadero*—on consignment in M. Durand-Ruel's gallery. It sold the following week to a department store owner, a M. Ernest Hoschedé, for a respectable 750 francs. It was my first sale to someone unknown to me. Maman was astonished. Never in her lifetime, she told me, had a female family member earned a single franc. I couldn't tell if she was proud or if it diminished me in her eyes. I don't think she knew herself.

Papa, of course, handled the transactions. He was fond of money no matter its source, and my sales seemed the one thing that cheered him.

Shortly thereafter, Papa was in the middle of rising from his chair and found himself unable to straighten. As if time had stopped, he remained pitched forward, facing the floor, back locked into place. The doctor could do nothing but suggest the use of a push-chair and of moving his bedroom onto the main floor. In constant grimace and pain, he slowly retreated from the world, never leaving the house and spending most of his day in bed. Resigned to my having to fend for myself once my inheritance was spent, he made a point of instructing me in basic economics of rent, servants and the stable.

My insipid pastel did not warrant a single mention in the papers, nor should it have. My figure in *Repose,* meanwhile, warranted any number of them. For Édouard had read the judges correctly and both his paintings had made it past the jury. The *Revue des Deux Mondes* called *Repose* "a puzzlement defying all explanation." Another critic dubbed it *Seasickness,* which summed up my emotions at the time. Another *The Woman Who Squints.* A critic for *Le Figaro* simply called it "a horror."

The reviews that truly bothered me were the ones that described me as one of "Manet's promising students." I would rather have been called his lover. At least that would have implied some equality.

Édouard was hardly discouraged by the poor reviews of *Repose,* because in continuing his theme of contrast, *Le Bon Bock* was the talk of the Salon. The portrait of the good-natured engraver wooed even the harshest of critics and proved so popular that Édouard achieved an unaccustomed celebrity.

In our uneasy times, wrote the critic Mantz, who had once called Manet's visions monstrous, *this even-tempered drinker represents eternal serenity. His blushing cheeks and portly figure tell us he knows no sadness. This former fiend, Manet, who came forth from the abyss to frighten ladies and children, has proved himself a noteworthy painter and a genteel and distinguished man.*

THE STEVENS HELD a party in celebration of Édouard's success. In their elegant new *appartement* overlooking the Luxembourg, my painting of Mme. Boursier was prominently on display over the sideboard in the dining room and nicely complemented by the dark damask wallpaper. Seeing it there, I was struck that a painting was a kind of ghost, or chalice for the spirit, and I marvelled that a part of my soul now inhabited another's home, perhaps even carrying its own influence. As I stared and wondered, two hands landed on my shoulders.

"Not bad, for a student of mine."

"You should write in and correct them."

"But you are a student of mine," he whispered.

If we had been alone, I would have bitten his lips closed.

He was all smiles that night, cocky and confident and attractive. His mother didn't even try to downplay her pride. "I knew it was only a matter of time before Édouard's genius was recognized. And there is greatness still to come. Still to come."

Suzanne, for a change, had also accompanied him. Sitting alone on the divan observing the fluttering leaves out the window, she savoured her cheese and rounds as if a private pleasure, dabbing the corner of her lips with her serviette. I'd always believed she was made shy by his friends, intimidated by their class and wit. But suddenly I saw her as a female version of Édouard's engraver in *Le Bon Bock*. Serene and sensual, without regret or ambition, she appeared content on her own and happily ignorant of whatever it was her husband might share with another woman. Or was this my guilt speaking?

Just as Édouard's portraits of me and of Bellot contrasted one another, so did Suzanne and I. I was thin and she was plump. I was fiery and she sedate. I was ambitious, she retiring. Did our differences serve him in the same way as his two paintings? Did it take one to appreciate the other? Could his clandestine love for me depend on his dull marriage to her? Did he love her more than I'd allowed myself to consider?

Eugène arrived late, loitering at the edge of whatever conversation I was engaged in, waiting to catch me alone. I was content to let him wait. Édouard described how the new Arts Minister, the Marquis, had personally congratulated him. "Perhaps men of religion have limited narratives, but he called me the prodigal son."

"Much like the critic," said Stevens, "who claimed a more sober Manet has put water in his beer."

"That's a lie. It was pure Haarlem beer!"

"They think they've reformed you," said Degas.

"So you'll have to paint something wicked for next year," said an excited Antoine.

"Perhaps a portrait of the prodigal son?" Édouard looked at me. "In the nude."

"Perhaps the Marquis will pose for you?" I said.

"In the nude!" roared Antoine.

The conversation turned to talk of a society Camille Pissarro had initiated. Degas confessed that he had already joined and was part of a planning committee searching for members. "We are putting on an independent exhibit of modern work and have recruited Monet, Renoir and Paul Cézanne thus far. I've been encouraged to ask, Édouard, if you might—"

"Sorry, my friend"—Édouard made a frightful face—"I'm not brave enough to throw my hat in with Cézanne."

"I'm surprised he's still painting," I said. "Not one acceptance to the Salon in all these years, he must be the most resilient painter alive. Or the most arrogant."

"Much like someone else we know?" teased Mme. Stevens. "Whose paintings have required armed guards to keep them from being destroyed?"

"Oh, Cézanne is far more arrogant than I," said Édouard. "But can we not admit I show more promise?"

Degas shrugged and tipped his hand side to side.

"Pah," said Édouard. "Even you, Degas, have to admit his paintings are the visions of nightmares. Let me qualify—I like the man well enough. Yes, he's morbid, has no personality and needs a bath, but he's not a bad person." Stevens choked on a laugh. "But really, Degas, you should not encourage him."

"Cézanne is completely sincere," said Degas. "Now his most recent work... in landscapes, employs angular shapes and—"

"Landscapes?" Édouard lifted his face skyward, hands in angélie. "Heaven help him and us."

Degas ignored him. "The group is called the Société Anonyme Cooperative. Designed after the union of bakers. Sixty francs buys you the right to exhibit with the group and a share of the profits."

"This bread will never rise," laughed Édouard.

Having been shut out of the Salon, I was curious.

"Pissarro," Degas explained, "wants to give Paris an entire exhibit to contrast with what people see at the Salon. To see modern work in large numbers, he believes, would function as an antidote for the fatigued Romantic eye. And I agree."

When Édouard had no witty remark, he pressed on.

"The exhibit is planned for the spring. There'll be no jury, no honours and no limit to the number of paintings one can exhibit. Within reason, of course."

"Can you submit to the Paris Salon as well?" asked Antoine.

"No. That will be the one requirement. We want to deprive the Salon viewers of *art modern*. Make them hungry for it."

I pictured my tiny pastel crowded into an obscure corner of Room M. "How does one become a member?"

Édouard stared at me, incredulous.

"By invitation. We plan to recruit only painters of substance," added Degas.

"Like Cézanne?" sneered Édouard.

"Like Berthe. Like Stevens. Antoine."

"So it's a juried show after all?" said Antoine.

Édouard twirled a pickled asparagus on its toothpick. "Everyone's a judge in the end. But come now, to join this group would be to give up on any serious career. Besides, am I not proof enough of the rewards of working within the system?"

"No one can argue—" Degas began but Édouard wasn't finished.

"To change people's appreciation of what constitutes art is a slow process."

"Too slow for me," said Degas.

"For you? The slowest painter I know," said Édouard, but his levity fell flat.

The topic closed, Eugène made his approach. "I was sorry to hear of your Salon rejections, Berthe."

"No sorrier than myself."

"Very unfair in my opinion."

"I couldn't agree more."

"I think the idea of a modern exhibition a good one. I think people are ready for it, even if they don't yet know it."

"Or... in this conformist milieu, people will view it an exercise in self-aggrandizement."

"Or as a business venture. One that incorporates Republican ideals of cooperation with conservative views of commerce."

"I have come to like both those aspects." Then I added, more to myself, "I would very much like to meet Monsieur Monet."

"If the membership dues are an obstacle for you, Berthe, I'd like to help."

"I would say thank you, Eugène, if I didn't find your offer so insulting." I left him mumbling apologies.

EDMA HAD COME DOWN with fever and I was summoned to Maurecourt to help with the children. The cause turned out to be a breast infection which, once diagnosed, was soon remedied by herbal potions from Manon and manual expression of excess milk. One morning while wandering the upstairs hall with my morning café, I came across a glass bowl of whitish blue milk, forgotten outside Edma's door, a disturbing skim of yellow fat on top. I almost regurgitated my café.

Edouard had accepted an invitation to Argenteuil and the home he had helped procure for Claude Monet. Though the ache of separation possessed its own sweetness and we corresponded frequently, what I would have given to accompany him. Not proud of my deceit, I hid these letters from Edma by bribing my assigned maid to sort them from the rest of the mail and to keep mum about it.

Monet's invitation to Édouard had contained a challenge my love couldn't resist—*Will you, M. Manet, finally abandon the false shadows of the studio in order to capture the true light of the outdoors?* Therefore Édouard's letters were full of the frustrations I well knew: *The fickleness of clouds. Damn bugs in the paint. Wind in the eyes.*

The weather has a mind of its own, one that doesn't care for your cares. But he soon wrote of the positive things I'd hoped for him. *The world is a living, breathing creature. Its processes not unlike painting itself. It is forever being reborn, changing shape with the wind, changing colour with the sun and changing texture depending on the moisture in the air. To paint outdoors is to attempt to capture life itself, the very nature of which defies capture. Just like art.*

He described the day he painted the Monets with their son Jean in the garden. *Claude tended his flower beds while his wife and son rested on a blanket and I asked to paint the contented domestic scene. After a while Claude set up an easel in order to paint me painting him. No sooner had he began painting than Renoir dropped over. Seeing what we were up to, Renoir insisted on borrowing a canvas and paint in order to do his own portrait of Camille and Jean. How amusing to be working at once, under the sun in the open air. Though nothing new for those two, for me the camaraderie was enchanting. We jibed over who would finish first, whose would be best, and fetch the highest price. No one paints faster than Claude. It's remarkable really. As for whose painting is the best, well, our styles are stark in their distinctions and you can be the judge. But only if you pick mine will you be richly recompensed. My greens tend toward blue while Renoir's toward yellow and Monet's to true green. Wherein, my love, lies the truth?*

I fantasized of Édouard and me painting in the country air together, exposed to the elements and each other, complaining of the gnats, pointing out this abstraction or curious detail, and when the best of the light had gone, making love in the tall grass.

Edma remained my willing model. I painted her in a marvellous striped day dress sitting alongside Blanche asleep in her new cradle. The light in the nursery was extraordinary and the cradle, with its sheer white canopy and pink border, a goad to my brush. When she saw the finished painting, Edma moaned that she looked tired and matronly.

I apologized.

"No. That is the reality of a mother of two and you have caught it brilliantly."

Praise from Edma still made me feel rotten with promise. An ancient power older sisters wield over younger.

My favourite work from this visit was a figure landscape of Edma with little Jeanne, in their church clothes playing *Cache-Cache* in the garden, though Edma asked if I might defy Realism a little and flatter her waist, "to give me something to live up to." I was happy to comply.

Knowing Édouard would appreciate the juxtaposition of nature and Paris fashion à la *Le Déjeuner sur l'herbe,* I decided to present *Cache-Cache* to him as a gift when we were next together.

WHEN I RETURNED HOME in late August, Maman appeared worn and aged. I scolded myself to have left her to tend Papa alone though it was he who'd insisted I go and not return "until your sister is well and you have several new paintings. Good ones."

Maman and I spent the next several months nursing him. I read him his daily papers, asked his "professional" opinion on the monetary value of my paintings and played piano for him. On occasion I rubbed his blistered feet and legs, a necessity that made us both shy and uncomfortable. But Maman needed the respite, which he reluctantly understood. As the weeks wore on, his pride waned along with his strength. One day, after I'd finished reading an article in *Le Figaro* and paused for him to digest it before commencing another, I found him staring at me with wonder in his eyes, eyes that now protruded as though the sockets were in retreat. His voice was a hoarse whisper. "I didn't think you cared for me. Thank you, Berthe."

I lifted his cold bony hand to my lips. It is hard to hold a grudge against the dying.

AS SOON AS ROSALIE was available I arranged to meet Édouard and deliver my gift. When I arrived at his studio he was not alone but with an older couple, wealthy too, judging from her fur stole and the gold handle of his cane. After the success of *Le Bon Bock* these visits had become commonplace, buyers seeking another such cheery *bonhomme*, though Édouard had painted nothing like it since.

After introductions, I sat and waited for the tour to finish. Édouard had a slight limp in his walk. I imagined he'd turned an ankle during his time in the country and vowed to kiss it better. The couple shared a private look of incredulity as Édouard showed them *The Railway*, the painting inspired by mine of Yves and Bibi behind the rails of my balcony. Once again, he had used his Olympia, Victorine Meurant, as his model. She of the "splendid" gaze. It was obvious to me how much she'd inspired him and I tried to not wonder if this lowly bar singer inspired him in other ways. And in this very room.

"I don't see the railroad or the train," said the man.

"But the girl can," said Édouard.

"Hmm..."

"Can you not smell the heated metal of tracks through the smoke?" Édouard stirred the air in front of his nose, performing for me.

"What's that in the mother's arms?"

"That is a baby seal."

The couple's eyes widened before they took a closer look. I disguised my laugh with a cough.

They left soon after, empty-handed, but Édouard was nevertheless in high spirits. He seemed heartier, his cheeks full of colour, which he blamed on the smoothness of the Bordeaux wine. Working outdoors had bleached white the hair on his forearms, which were tanned to a dark gold. As he unwrapped my gift, he boasted that he had finished twenty-seven canvases since the beginning of the year and that between his two galleries Durand-Ruel had managed to sell a total of thirteen. "At a pretty price, too."

"Bragging suits you."

He cleared an easel and set my painting upon it. I noticed his limp again and asked about it.

"It's nothing," he said irritably.

"Are you sure?"

"*La haute couture* finds itself hiding in nature." He guessed my intent as I knew he would. "You've left out the naked men. Wise of you."

I smiled wisely, but he did not look.

"Motherhood has ripened Edma's beauty," he said.

Surprised to feel old jealousy, I almost revealed her waist as fakery. "She would have ten if she could. And Yves is expecting again."

"Your sisters are doing your duty for you."

As if the breeze through the open window carried an unborn soul seeking to seed itself, the thought of never bearing a child suddenly weakened me with loss. I looked at Édouard. What would our child look like? Sound like? Feel like in my arms? Having misinterpreted my staring, Édouard stepped behind me and pulled me to him. Teasing my ear with his tongue, he wedged a hand down the front of my bodice. For a short moment, I felt common and cheap.

PAPA SLEPT through most of the day and night now. We could do little more than sit with him, administer occasional sips of water, most of which ran over his chin to wet the collar of his nightshirt. Sometimes I sketched his profile or hand, the outline of his long flattened figure barely raising the quilt. These sketches I burned before Maman saw them.

A year after his disappearance, and as if sensing his own usefulness, without warning Tibby arrived home from wherever he'd run. Only recently had Maman given up writing him, newsy letters that filled two baskets on the floor beside her desk, awaiting a destination. When Thin Louis escorted Tibby into the sickroom, Maman didn't recognize her own son. His trim Italian suit and full beard couldn't hide the bloat of his face and discoloured nose. He looked a decade older, yet he was alive and home, and this was a timely gift. Maman, too weary to rise, waited for him to come to her, take her hand and kiss her cheek. She then pressed her cheek against his hand and silently cried. It was a heartbreaking sight and I wanted to yell at him for his thoughtlessness for having made her suffer. But it was clear he'd suffered too, in different but perhaps equal measure.

He took his turns at Papa's bedside but these would be few. As if relieved of a final concern, Papa died two days after his son's return, in the late afternoon, the sky a dray-white as if emptied of all feeling.

Though I'd anticipated a grand exhale of relief and freedom, it was not to be. Every time I passed the drawing room, my eye wandered to his tall chair, seeking his suspicious looks or greeting. His empty seat at the head of the table was haunting. The man who had dictated the parameters of my life was not on a business trip, not with his mistress, at the office or drinking in a café. He was not at the dining table reading his papers with Maman or standing on the balcony smoking a pipe with Uncle as the sun set over Paris. He was not suffering in his bed, staring at the ceiling, legs swollen, back burning. Not even an echo of himself, he was literally nowhere. Such impressive finality was impossible to comprehend, and to try was to fall into an abyss of my own making.

Maman was even more bewildered. She had lost him for good this time and when she took to her bed, she stayed there and rose only on the day of the funeral. We had hoped for Tibby to make the arrangements but since Papa's passing we rarely saw him, and when we did, he had drink on his breath and an excuse on his lips. When Eugène offered to help, Maman and I accepted. Having been the one to organize his own father's funeral, Eugène knew what procedures to follow and how to ensure Maman wasn't fleeced by the grave tender or stone mason.

Mme. Manet sent meat pies, a currant cake, a bottle of bitters and a note from one widow to another. *We live for our children now. And you, Cornélie, for your many grandchildren. Don't despair. There is still joy to be found.*

I sought refuge in Édouard's arms. He listened to my recounted memories of Papa, of battles and resentments and reconciliation. He insisted he paint me in my black mourning hat and veil.

"Looking old and ugly with death," I said.

"Beautiful with reality," he said.

I was putting on my cloak to leave and casually mentioned that I was considering joining Degas and Pissarro's new Cooperative.

"What?" His shift in mood was shocking in its swiftness. "You'd put your name alongside Monet's, a grocer's son? Renoir's father, if you recall, is a tailor. And no matter his peaceful paintings, Pissarro is a Jewish Creole who extols the virtue of anarchy. And if you think Cézanne's pictures are ridiculous"—he was now irate—"you should see how he dresses!"

His hypocrisy was not to be believed. "Are you," I asked him, "the same Édouard Manet who supported the efforts of the Commune? Who extolled equality among men?"

He grabbed up his brushes for cleaning. I followed on his heels.

"Are you the same man who drinks most evenings with those you slander? Who spent the summer eating the food served to you by Monsieur and Madame Monet?"

He roughed a rag over his brush tips.

"Does art not transcend the boundaries of class and money?"

"The venture might prove fruitful to some." He had calmed down, but only a little. "Maybe even to you. But you realize you risk never being considered by the Académie again."

"The Salon is not celebrating *me*, so I risk nothing. And how ironic, Édouard, that after all the vitriol you've directed at the Académie, you now clamour for their good opinion."

He stopped his cleaning. "A decade of mockery and I have finally earned their respect. I may sound shallow, but I'm enjoying not being spat on."

"And what does that have to do with this Cooperative?"

"Come, Berthe, even if I don't endorse the Cooperative, I will be pegged its unofficial leader."

"A leader of a Cooperative you refuse to join?"

"People will have to blame the audacity on someone. Who better but me?"

"I certainly blame you. Is that so very terrible?"

"I'm unsure." He looked at the brushes in his hand as if he'd forgotten what they might be called and what he was to do with them.

1874

BOTH YVES AND EDMA along with their families returned to Paris for the funeral. Upon her arrival Edma rushed into my arms and, as if they'd awaited a container, her sobs came. A scolding Blanche gripped and pulled on her skirts, crying even louder.

The house was overrun, its atmosphere almost festive with sorrow highlighting its missing piece and patriarch. I kept waiting for his old self, upright and commanding, to come round a corner, muttering about the chaos, directing us or subduing misbehaviour with a few curt words. Tibby joined us for the day of the funeral only, alcohol burning his breath at two in the afternoon. Before dinner, and to Bibi's and Jeanne's shrieks of delight, Tibby acted the clown and performed coin and cards tricks then danced them around in turn, their small feet planted on the tops of his boots. By the time dinner was over, his conversation was incoherent and I ordered Levin to deliver him home and make sure he made it into his own bed and with jacket and boots removed.

The funeral procession from church to cemetery was a staid, glum affair, but boasted a respectable number of carriages. M. Thiers' impressive black four-in-hand trimmed in gold leaf, which I could only view as sinister, was among the empty ones. Maman would send him a note of gratitude for the honour. There were neighbours' carriages and carriages of those Papa worked alongside. Leo and Laure Reisener rode in their coupé while Rosalie and her husband arrived in their cabriolet. Mme. Manet, along with Suzanne and Léon, came in her handsome though worn four-in-hand, Édouard and Eugène riding well-dressed horses on either flank, Édouard less at ease on the animal. Edma sat slumped on my shoulder and took no special notice of Édouard though Adolphe rode beside him at one point and they seemed pleased to see each other. Degas, who considered horses "resentful behemoths waiting for the opportunity to bite or fling you," rode in a hired cab. The sun came out briefly, as if to take one finite look at a man's life.

As the casket was lowered into the dark, we children were invited, one by one, to toss in a yellow rose. Adolphe held Edma, unsteady with weeping, as she leaned over the grave. I'd brought a symbolic paintbrush to tuck alongside my flower's stem. When the wooden stick made a skittering against the coffin's lid, the priest frowned and peered discreetly into the hole.

A week after the funeral, I accompanied Adolphe and Edma back to Lorient. Maman had requested time alone, insisting that I be around life and not death at this time. It felt entirely wrong to leave her, I argued, but she remained adamant. It would be years before I understood the instinct to guard one's child, no matter what age, from seeing her mother fall to pieces.

I didn't want to leave Édouard but it felt good to be in motion. I loved a train's gentle rocking, the industrious rattle of wheels against track, the shifting landscapes feeding the eye. We had a nicely appointed cabin—seats of stiff brown leather, green velvet curtains swept sideways with gold braid and a table that unfolded from the mahogany paneled walls on which Edma and I played cards. I told her of the Société Anonyme Cooperative and its gathering of artists who shared a modern eye, and that Degas was still looking for enough respectable names so the critics would be unable to ignore the exhibition.

"He failed to entice Stevens, Édouard or Antoine to join but asked if we might consider submitting some of our work."

"Me?" Edma was taken aback but clearly flattered. "Can you imagine what Adolphe would say? A wife and mother?" She looked into her lap. "And, what, I have maybe ten canvases left which I deem of any value."

"And if I joined?"

"Are there any other women being considered?"

"You and I are the only ones."

Edma shook her head, as if to clear it. "This is not the Salon, Berthe. This is a rebellion. By men. Of who knows what sort."

"Our status, Degas believes, both socially and within the painting world, may entice others."

"Oh." She folded her fan of cards. "So… let me understand. Degas, as one of our class, has been enlisted to recruit artists of the *haute bourgeoisie* in hopes our social stature will lend this rebellion legitimacy."

"It's more than—"

"Berthe, surely you see that these men are trying to take advantage of us."

"That doesn't mean they don't hold our work in regard."

"What man respects a woman's work?" Her tone was bitter. "What does Édouard say?"

Now that his name had been spoken, she watched me carefully.

"He is shocked I would even consider it. Says I risk future acceptance to the Salon, and that, yes, I may be ruined socially and professionally. But, Edma, I don't know if I care."

"If you value his opinion"—her eyes searched mine—"then there's no question."

"I do value his opinion but not to the exclusion of my own. He is not my father." Nor my husband. But had Rosalie mentioned our meetings? Was Edma fishing for the nature of our relationship? "And if I'm rejected from the Salon again this year…"

"You'll try again the next. The jury will evolve, eventually."

"But imagine a gallery filled with only modern paintings… reflecting the world we live in, the feelings we live with… what we see and *how* we see it."

"Do you even know whose work will hang on those walls?"

The door opened as Adolphe and the maid returned with the girls. In the maid's arms, Blanche whined at an irritating pitch and thrust her arms out for her mother. They'd come from the observation room and, over the whining Jeanne, announced that they had counted fifteen cows and twenty-six sheep. With a wince, Edma settled Blanche at the breast.

"So have you submitted to the Salon?" she asked me.

"The cart comes next week. I picked out three paintings for Maman to submit in my absence."

"I'm glad." She sounded satisfied. "I'm sure you'll have better luck this… Ai! No biting." The baby screamed, and Jeanne buried her face in her father's coat.

SPRING CAME EARLY to Lorient and I filled the hours with painting Edma and my nieces in a series of figure landscapes. When the best of the light had faded, I played with the children, drawing, making tiny marzipan cakes for their dolls, reading to them. Blanche had little patience for books and would tear at the pages. I'd have to ask the maid to remove her, which inevitably set her to wailing. Not long into my visit, shy, sweet-tempered Jeanne requested to sleep in my bed. This Edma not only allowed but encouraged, perhaps hoping to incite my maternal urges. That first night, before my little niece clambered into my godless bed, she knelt, bent her head over hands folded at her chest and began mumbling to herself in a tiny, sincere voice.

"Are you not praying?" she asked.

"Of course." I was not about to argue God with a three-year-old. I knelt beside her and wondered if this wasn't another second-hand lesson from Edma.

I COULD NOT PREDICT when Edma might spontaneously weep or be short with the children. Edma had loved Papa without reserve. Yves and I had been surprised, and a little piqued, to hear that since she had married and left for Lorient, Edma and Papa had corresponded twice monthly. Yves had had no such correspondence nor, she admitted, would she have known what to write. It seemed familial love was as much a two-way street as any.

Edma and I were in the garden one unseasonably warm evening, the sun blinking, pink and gold, through gaps in the trees. On the terrace table, candles flickered, the saw of crickets livening the dark. The children were asleep, Jeanne in my bed, and the servants retired. Adolphe had left that day for a naval exercise so it was just the two of us sipping Manon's cherry wine as we recounted memories of Papa at his best and worst, teetering between laughter and tears and feeling as close and intimate as we'd ever been.

"Forgive me," said Edma without warning, refilling her glass and mine, "but I must bring it up." She took a tiny sip of wine, took my hand and smiled a sidelong smile.

I grew nervous, convinced that she was going to ask about Édouard. That she not only knew of my solo visits to his studio but that I had underestimated the devotion of Edma's servants, and the maid during my last visit had revealed our correspondence.

"Don't you think, Berthe, my sweet, talented sister, that it's time to seriously consider marriage? Before… well, before it's too late?"

I wagged my finger but was relieved. "Maman has put you up to this."

"The truth?" Her eyes grew wet. "It was Papa's final request of me before he died. He worried so much for your future. Mentioned it in every letter."

I was both touched and annoyed to hear it. "And here I thought he had begun counting on my talents to maintain the family fortune."

She kissed my hand. "Having your own child is a joy and satisfaction like nothing else in life." Even Blanche? I thought. "You're still within childbearing years."

"No child of mine could be as dear to me as your Jeanne is already."

Edma huffed a smile. "And she adores her auntie but you're changing the subject. I'm not suggesting you give up painting. I think if any woman can do both, it would be you. In fact, I'm sure of it."

"I would have said the same of you."

"No, no, no. My soul was not wedded to painting like yours. My process was more… external." She pointed a tipsy finger at me. "You have changed the subject."

I sipped my wine as she tightened her grip on my other hand as if to keep me from running. "Now don't tell me, Berthe"—she leaned forward and peered up at me—"that, our beguiling Édouard aside…"—she tittered like a schoolgirl and placed two impish fingers to her lips—"yes, yes, I still find him beguiling."

What to make of her wine-fueled confession?

"But that is neither here nor there." She waved the notion away. "This is about you. You cannot tell me that there is not one man in all of Paris up to your standards. That captivates you even a little?"

I hated keeping my secret from her.

"No one's perfect, you know," Edma said eagerly, misunderstanding my tilted smile. "Every relationship, Berthe, is a compromise of sorts. That's just its nature."

Édouard is perfect, I wanted to say. My life is perfect. I have a career in painting. The most beguiling of men is in love with me and I with him. A man who shares my ambitions and understands me as a painter. The fact of living apart frees us from dreary domestic concerns and the clandestine necessity of our rendezvous fans the flames. Yet even the most clandestine of affairs longs for a witness, as confirmation.

"Love deepens over time." Edma gave my hand a little shake. "I can say that firsthand. And in ways that are most surprising. You might think of it like painting. How with practice and dedication you not only get better at it but it works its way under your skin and into your heart."

"Love and painting," I said.

"My dearest sister." She inched her chair closer. "Are you keeping something from me? Someone? You know you can trust me with your confidence."

I took a long draught of cherry wine. Of course I could trust her. Why ever did I believe otherwise? "Yes, I've kept something from you. And it has made me feel distant from you, which I don't like and don't want."

"You *have* met someone." She clapped her free hand down over our joined hands. "And kept it secret." She smiled. "It's someone… Maman would not approve of?"

"Well—"

"Is it Degas? You two seem—"

"Degas is a dear friend and that is all he can ever be." I did not want this to turn into a guessing game. Under her earnest gaze, I spoke to our entwined hands. "I'm afraid that the someone is… well, our beguiling friend."

Edma's eyebrows pinched together.

I bit my lip but then out it came. "Édouard. I helped him return to painting and then, our relationship, it became… intimate." My happiness betrayed me and I smiled shyly yet proudly at Edma.

She wrenched her hand from mine and stood. "I cannot believe—" she looked down from an imperious height—"I refuse to believe it. Tell me, Berthe, it's not true." She stamped her foot. "Tell me you're teasing me. You're lying." She tugged fiercely at her shawl though it wasn't cold. "Or were you lying when you told me the flirtations had ended between you?" Her upper lip peeled back and her teeth gleamed in the candlelight.

"I... I have not lost my virtue, Edma," I stammered, "only my innocence."

"What in God's name are you talking about?" she practically screamed and then walked in a tight angry circle. A servant moved on the other side of the terrace doors.

I scrambled to make the notion agreeable. "It means... that he and I are equals in our love, and there's nothing frivolous or untoward about it. Our intimacies are a natural expression of our—"

"If Papa could hear you." She spat the words. "You disgrace his name. Our entire family." She strode to the terrace doors.

I stood to defend my ground, my chair toppling over with a bang. "How are we so different from any married couple—"

She whirled around. "Don't you dare compare your adulterous acts to my marriage."

"Edma! Why not? Love is not made greater or less because of laws and rules."

Disgust crept across her face. As if she couldn't stomach my existence.

"Why do you want to deny me love?" I begged. "I'm thirty-two. Edma..."

She didn't bother closing the terrace door behind her. I stood there, unable to think or move, my breath loud in the sudden quiet. Shadows swam overhead, bats hunting their dinner. The candles' flames burned as steady witness to our exchange. My welling tears caused their light to bend and stretch.

Why had I confessed now? It was late and Edma was tired and grief-stricken, the wine making her emotional. Should I go after her? No, she needed a good night's sleep, as did I. Everything, I tried to assure myself, would look better in the morning. I pushed my chair to the table, and then Edma's as well, as if this would restore our former order. I blew out all the candles save one to guide me.

I wended my way through the dark house, stepping as lightly as I could on the stairs, feeling sullied and unwelcome. As if my presence might defile the children, spoil the milk. When I got to my room, little Jeanne was no longer warming my bed.

I undressed and lay there, unable to sleep. Was Edma jealous that I had succeeded where she had failed? That, on top of Papa's death. To have revealed my affair at this time was insensitive. Tomorrow I would apologize. And if I must, plead for her forgiveness.

RAPID KNOCKING on my door woke me. Morning light through the sheers was thin and pale, the hour ungodly.

"Mademoiselle, Mademoiselle," came the guileless voice of my maid, the one I'd paid to keep secret my correspondence with Édouard, "Madame's neighbours, the Vaniers, are on their way to Paris, and have agreed to chaperone. Your train, Mademoiselle, leaves at 8:10 sharp."

I stumbled from bed and swung open the door. She promptly dragged a trunk in over the threshold, leaving faint white scrapes in the oak floor. "Your painting things and pictures are already packed." She sounded efficiently proud. "I will assist you with the rest." Slowly her words were sinking in.

"Little Jeanne will be disappointed that you've decided to shorten your visit. She's so very fond of you." She shot me a sideways glance, looking not so innocent after all. Her insolence shocked me awake and propelled me out the door to Edma's room. I knocked softly on her door, leaned my forehead against it to keep my voice low.

"Please, Edma, we cannot, must not end like this." There was no answer. I knocked a little harder. "Edma, I'm so sorry if I hurt you. I should have told you sooner."

I waited, listened for movement inside, then hit at the door with the butt of a fist. "Speak to me."

My maid came around the corner. "Madame is out visiting," she said, her tone almost gleeful.

"At this hour?" I pounded harder, raised my voice. "Edma! Open this door! Please! I beg you!"

The butler and two other manservants appeared at the top of the stairs to stare. I had failed to put on my dressing gown or slippers. My hair was loose. The three men spread themselves out as though prepared to drag me to the train if necessary.

"How dare you look at me," I said, and two sets of eyes fell to the floor. The third man, a youth with long black hair and a flat broken nose, kept on staring as if assessing the one rotten tomato in a basket. I strode back to my room, threw on my dressing gown and went to the nursery. It was empty. I went to the dining room, the drawing room. Empty. In the kitchen Manon stood stirring something on the stove, her wide aproned back to me. I could tell she knew I was there. Whatever she was making smelled wonderful and I already missed her cooking.

"Good morning, Manon, do you know where Edma may have gone?"

"No, Mademoiselle Little Sister, I do not."

I waited, sensing she had more to say. She usually did.

"I do know that she loves you very much and could never bear to see you ruin your life."

She had shared my private confidence to a servant? "What did she tell you?"

"She did not tell me anything. This much I know."

I steadied my voice. "When do you expect her and the children to return?"

"I expect not until you are gone. She is very decisive, that sister of yours."

"Yes. Yes, she is."

When I returned to my room the maid had nearly finished the packing. A dress of her own choosing was laid on the bed.

"How dare you?" I pulled the dress to the floor, went to my desk and began a letter of apology to Edma. Halfway through, I set it aside. It was she, not I, who need apologize. I crumpled the page and threw it in the still-open trunk. "The grey striped," I said calmly to the maid.

THIN LOUIS TOOK my cloak and hat. My three Salon submissions sat stacked against the wall. Had Maman forgotten to submit them? I tipped them forward. Each was stamped on the back with a fat red R. I breathed deep and even. Papa's death, thrown from my sister's home, now this. I laid my head against the wall when Maman appeared in the doorway.

"You're home?"

"Maman." I kissed her warm cheeks. "I'm home early because I missed you and worried about you being on your own. A happy coincidence"—I smiled—"Edma's neighbours were travelling to Paris and agreed to be my chaperones. This way I could save Adolphe the trip later. I hope you don't mind."

"No. Of course not."

I asked how she was feeling. She gazed into the middle distance. "The sun still rises."

I kissed her again, wanting to be held by her, have my hair stroked. My eyes grew wet.

"Oh, don't be too disappointed." She gestured to my paintings. "What do those old men know?"

I smiled and wiped my eyes. "Thank you, Maman."

She told me she had received a note from Degas. "He's pleading with me to urge you to be part of some exhibition. I don't know what to make of it."

"Degas?"

After overseeing the unpacking, I sat with Maman at the dining table and she read me his note.

Dear Madame Morisot,
I am writing to implore you to allow Mademoiselle Morisot to become a member of a newly formed Cooperative of modern artists and take part in our inaugural exhibition. I understand she has been rejected from this year's Salon, but believe me when I say that her work is too good to go unseen. M. Nadar has generously

donated his former studio to be used for the exciting exhibition. It is a very fine second-floor appartement *in the tourist district of Boulevard des Capucines. The programs are in the process of being finalized and I am sincerely hoping we can count on Mademoiselle Morisot to add her name. She would be welcome to submit up to ten paintings of her choice and we have reserved a wall with exceptional light on which to hang them. The exhibit will open in mid-March, two weeks before the Salon.*

To have your daughter's works in our exhibition would be an honour. The organizing committee is in hearty agreement that her originality and talent really must be on display.

Sincerely, Edgar Degas

EVEN IF, as Edma believed, the committee sought my social standing more than my work, the note lifted my spirits. Degas was practically begging, and he was not one to do so.

"He sounds very intent." Maman regarded me, a weariness about her eyes. "I try to imagine what your father would say. If he would allow it."

"He would say that no one is going to buy my paintings if they're not on display. And the Salon is not displaying them."

"I trust you won't be the only woman."

"I believe I will."

She sighed. "What kind of men's club seeks to include a woman in their business? I trust these are respectable men?"

I knew she meant of our class. "I believe so," I lied.

She took her hands off the table, and folded them into her lap. "I'm at a loss over what to do with you, Berthe. But you are a grown woman and it is time for me to say that this decision and its consequences are yours alone."

I wrote to Degas immediately, thanked him for his letter to Maman, told him I was fed up with Salon juries and included a list of the nine paintings I would like to submit to the exhibit. Four oils, three watercolours and two pastels. *Though I am not bold enough to attend the opening,* I added, *I would like a chance to meet my fellow exhibitors.*

Dearest Berthe,
I was delighted to receive your note. Thank you for supporting this venture, lending your talent and your elegance. In order to drum up some press to attract the public, there is to be a private viewing for critics the day before the opening. I am suggesting a celebratory gathering at noon for Society members, a Varnishing Day if you'd like, before the critics arrive at 2:00. Artists can mingle, put any finishing touches on their work and complain about their placement on the wall. I will bring champagne. I hope you and your mother do us the honour of attending.
E. Degas

I WAS IN MY sitting room touching up one of my submissions when Thin Louis knocked and announced that M. Manet was downstairs. Only yesterday I had sent him a note informing him I was home. I was thrilled that he was so eager to see me.

"Send him up, please."

"Madame Morisot is not—"

"She will be home soon. Please send him up."

I hung my smock on the back of my chair, pinched colour into my cheeks and checked my hair in the glass. Then the man I loved was framed in my doorway. Dressed impeccably in a burgundy vest and gloves, his hair more auburn as it tended to in winter, his beard flecked with the light of tiny white hairs, regarding me with those warm copper eyes. I made to move into his embrace but he took me by the shoulders and delivered two sharp, formal kisses to my cheeks. I dropped my arms, smiling at how well I knew him now. His impersonal greeting was not about me, he simply had something on his mind.

I pouted. "That's all I get? When I've missed you as the earth misses the sun in winter?" I reached for him again, but he stepped around me to the painting I was working on—the double portrait of Maman and Edma. He picked up my brush and palette and dabbed ivory highlights into the skirt of Maman's dress.

"Édouard!"

"So, you're joining Degas' carnival?" He put down the brush.

I touched his shoulder and he crossed over to the window. Still that small limp in his gait.

"Your leg, it has not im—"

"Does he know you submitted?"

"He knows I was rejected from the Salon, so, yes."

"That's against the rules, is it not?"

"It doesn't seem to matter to anyone, except you." My humour was faltering. "What's wrong, Édouard?"

Something on the street below held his eye.

"Are you truly upset with me over this? The Salon offered me no recourse."

He didn't respond and my hand went to my heart.

"Édouard, you weren't rejected too?"

He shrugged one shoulder. "Two rejections but two acceptances."

"I'm so glad. *The Railway*?"

"And a watercolour of *Polichinelle*."

"A watercolour?"

"Yes."

"Since when are you doing watercolours? Is that Monet's influence?"

He returned to the door of my room, which Thin Louis had left slightly ajar, and pushed it closed with a click.

My joints softened and I couldn't help my smile. "This is not the time or place, my love."

He leaned against the door and fixed his eyes on some absent object. "You must marry my brother."

I waited for the absurd sentence to continue, and laughed.

He looked up. “You must marry Eugène.”

“You shouldn’t tease me like this. I’ve had a terrible week.”

“I am in earnest.”

I shook my head to begin again.

“Berthe. Listen to me, you must—”

“Why do you keep saying that? Who are you to tell me what I must do?” I grabbed fistfuls of my skirt to have something to tear.

He bit his lip. “I mean to say that you should, Berthe. You should marry him.”

“Why would you suggest such a thing, when the only man I have ever loved is standing here in front of me?” His expression was unyielding and my voice shrank to a whisper. “Are you here, Édouard? Are you still here?”

When he didn’t respond, I sought my chair.

“Please, listen to—”

“I’ve just lost my father. My sister has thrown me out because I confessed to our intimacy. My work has been deemed worthless by the Salon. And now I am being rejected by the man that I believed loved me as I love him?”

He remained by the door. In case of a quick escape?

I dug the heels of my palms into my eyes to stay tears and heard his boots cross the room. A chair pulled up beside mine. When I felt the warmth of his hand on my neck, I collapsed over my lap, my tears turning to sobs that caught as if on hooks in my throat.

He stroked my back. “You misunderstand what I’m trying to tell you,” he said over my ugly weeping. I wanted him to stop touching me and also never to stop. “Our love is true, Berthe. I will always love you as you love me.”

I clung to the ache in his voice.

“But I can’t sit by and watch you grow old on your own, forced to live with a sister. Having to be chaperoned whenever you venture outside. I can’t be the cause of your having no child to love and renew your spirit.”

Slowly I sat up. He offered me his handkerchief and gently removed the hair from my eyes. "If I have you and art, I have no need for renewal. You could give me a child, Édouard. I wouldn't care what people thought. I would disappear to the country or I could marry your brother as a guise and—"

He stood as if to leave and I seized his hand. "Don't leave me."

"Have you never wondered why Suzanne and I had no more children after Léon?" He eased his hand away and walked to the window. "I would have loved a houseful. Maman continues to lament over this dearth of grandchildren. Because, for all her pride"—his tone turned grim—"she refuses to acknowledge Léon as her blood. I can't even give the poor boy my name."

A pigeon fluttered onto the railing of the balcony. Why tell me this now?

"Suzanne has had more miscarriages than I can count. And whose fault is it?" He faced me and flung his arms wide. "Mine. It's mine." His arms fell to his sides. "I'm ashamed to say it… but I… have infected my long-suffering wife with syphilis. I did that. Me. She suffers headaches that keep her bound to the house." He began to pace. "Her hearing has begun to fade. The day may come when she will be unable to hear her own music."

It was my turn to look away. Syphilis? The notion was repulsive. But Édouard looked fine. He looked perfect.

He pushed his hand through his beard as if to find his flesh behind. "My doctor says I have three years before… before my health becomes… untenable. And before I die, I need to know that you'll be taken care of."

My feet and hands had gone cold.

"If you marry Eugène, who is a good, kind man and who has been in love with you since he first laid eyes on you, you will be a Manet, a member of my family, and I'll know you'll be cared for. We'll be able to see each other freely and often." He came and took my face in his hands and held it till I looked at him. "It's out of love,

Berthe, that I urge you to marry my brother. Love." He dropped into the chair beside me. "There. I've said it all."

The cold invaded my chest. From whom did he catch it? His Olympia whore? From one of those women of Montmartre who called him Eddie? From a respectable woman who caught it from her own faithless husband? Was he no different from my father? Having his privileged fun? If he loved me, how could he conceive of me in the arms of his brother? He was practically prostituting me to keep me near. To be tortured by his proximity and that of his ill wife. I understood now that we would never consummate our love. That there would be no child with him. Had a child been my secret hope? Edma's scolding face reared up. Did she know that this is how married affairs end? In anguish? Was she only trying to protect me? My hands, still gripping my skirt, began to ache as the blood returned.

"When did you fall in love with me?" I demanded. Could he pinpoint the moment? Was it distinct from the other women he had made love to? Or was it a blur of mindless desire? Were we all just a blur?

"My love for you built up in me like a head of steam, until I had no choice in the matter. I did my utmost to push you away because I knew this day would come."

"You should have told me of your illness then."

"I could not yet admit it to myself."

I brushed out my skirts, dried my eyes and handed back his handkerchief. "Well, then, we have three more years," I said, as if speaking of kitchen accounts, of market prices. "And what do doctors know? Doctors are fools."

"No, my love. Eugène has waited for you. He can't wait any longer."

He leaned in to kiss my cheek, but I jerked away. "You cannot call me that now."

He rose slowly from his chair as if his back were stiff, as if everything hurt. I stood too and shoved him so hard he stumbled back and came down heavily on his sore leg, wincing. His syphilitic leg? He glanced at me, wary, and went over to retrieve his hat from the table beside the door.

"Go."

"I hear you have an opening next week. Though fingers will wag your way, and my way too, I'll talk you up to my rich acquaintances."

"How can you joke when you've thrust a knife into my heart?"

He raised his palms. "And Eugène. On a platter!"

"I don't love him," I screamed. "I love you!" I covered my face and yelled it again into my hands. There came the creak of the front gate. Maman.

"I am so sorry, Ber..."

Maman, in the courtyard below, asked Thin Louis whose horse was tied to the lamppost.

Édouard cleared his throat. "And I love you. But my brother will care for you, Berthe... in ways that I..." His voice broke. "Will be unable."

In the sunlight, motes of dust floated lazily, with an indifference almost human. He wiped his eyes with the handkerchief already moist with my tears. "Eugène is a good man who has invested his inheritance well. I am not a good man. I am a scoundrel and a fool. And today I am paying the price. With love."

"If you are not a good man," I said, "what does that make me?" I felt numb. Nonexistent. I lifted my smock from the back of the chair, slipped my arms through its sleeves and stepped before my portrait of Edma and Maman. Édouard's skillful dabs had brought Maman's skirt forward into the light. Brilliant.

"Where was I?" I picked up my brush and palette.

He opened the door.

"Oh, yes," I said, "I was putting in my secret signature." The colours of the painting began to move in a slow swirl, like water in an eddy.

"My love?"

"Hiding heartbeats of scarlet #3 in my paintings to invigorate them." I wanted to add that they represented my desire for him before I even knew I loved him. But that's not what came out of my mouth. "Slashes in the skin." I painted over his highlights.

He closed the door behind him, and my palette whipped across the room. It would leave permanent paint stains on the door and I would have to invent yet another lie for Maman.

NOT A WEEK LATER, Maman suggested that, this summer, we vacation with the Manets.

"In Normandy. It's a favourite place of yours, no? To paint? Eugènie has a friend with a house on the beach where we can all stay. We could visit the Reiseners. Maybe Marcello will be there? Édouard and Suzanne plan to join us. Eugène too. It will be good to get away, no? Think of happier times?"

The wheels had begun to turn.

I had hoped to give the show the name The Nasturtium, wrote Degas, *after the name of the boulevard and location of the studio, but was outvoted. The title is a case of the avant-garde trying to sound conventional. I had to pick my battles.*

Had I been one of his battles? Degas had sent me a mock-up of the program. Squeezed on to the cover was the onerous *La Société Anonyme Coopérative à Capital Variable.* Thirty-one artists in total, and, between paintings, pastels and engravings, 162 works. I was the only woman. Despite what Degas said, I could guess that not all the men were in agreement about my participation. Indeed he had warned me that my joining was *very brave but, in the eyes of many, for a woman, indecent. The press will be sure to pounce on you.*

Let them pounce. I had no one to answer to now but myself.

The following morning at breakfast, Maman read aloud from a letter she had just received from Edma.

Berthe's involvement in this modern exhibit is an affront to the Morisot name and a grotesque show of disrespect for our father, so recently deceased. I am shocked she doesn't know better. And that you, Maman, have allowed such a self-important display.

I heard the words as code for what she couldn't say. Yet Edma's wish that Édouard and I end our intimacy seemed to have been granted and I wondered if her daily prayers were more magical curse. Now was she praying to end my career too?

Maman's hand dropped onto the table. "I don't know what to do, Berthe. Is your sister correct? Should I stop this right now?"

I panicked that Edma had revealed my affair.

"The exhibition?"

"Are you not listening?"

"Edma is missing Papa," I said, "and her anguish is misplaced. Papa would see it for the business venture that it is. And that's how I see it. An investment in my art. Also, my name is in the program. To back out now would be disruptive and unjust."

She shook her head.

"Most importantly, Maman, I want to do it. This exhibition is all I have."

SOMEHOW MARCELLO GOT WIND of my scandalous involvement in the Cooperative and sent along a note postmarked Amsterdam. *I'm thrilled to see you're breaking free of the confines of the Salon, and narrow minds. May your reviews be scathing and your conviction true. Wishing you every success. Your friend, Marcello*

I wrote back asking when she would next be in Paris. *I need to share my heart with someone and feel that you alone will understand.*

She did contact me upon her return and we went for a long walk on the *quai*. I confessed my liaison with Édouard, including seeing her in Montmartre but being afraid to expose myself.

She seemed delighted by Montmartre especially. "So you have seen the classical horn player! Laughing like that feels vital, like expelling old air to make room for new. Not unlike Monsieur Tremblay!"

I told her of Édouard's proposal that I marry his brother. And though it wasn't mine to tell, I also told her of Édouard's illness. When I'd finished, she kissed my hand. "How fortunate to have found the person to unlock your heart."

My sorrow spilled over and she held me, people staring as they passed, boatmen pausing in their work to watch the female spectacle. Some man whistled. She didn't care and I hadn't the strength to.

"You're drowning," she said beside my ear, "but with time, good woman, you learn to breathe underwater."

The fat pink petals of tulip trees whirled at our feet. She lifted my chin with her gloved hand and I saw the Seine through my tears, now all spark and flash.

"And if you are anything like me, you will love the world more equally. All of it. Including your dear future husband. Why? Because it will take many people to fill the vastness where your heart once beat."

She drew a handkerchief from her décolletage and dabbed my eyes. The river changed. "The one salve I've found for the pain of living is the making of art. But then you, my friend, already know that." She leaned in, conspiratorial. "We artists. We are the lucky ones."

"Yes. We are."

She kissed my hand and linked it through her arm. "Shall we continue on?"

"WE SHALL NOT STAY LONG," said Maman as the horses came to a stop, speaking both to our driver and also to me. The chestnut trees were in bloom and the Boulevard des Capucines crowded with carriages, vendors and those with money to spend. Maman repeated, again, Uncle Octave's belief that Papa would never have allowed such a "reckless disregard for propriety."

Stepping from the carriage, she gazed about for who might recognize us. No one paid us any attention except an urchin eyeing our clothes and the weight of our reticules. I had decided that if my fellow Cooperative members expected me, as a member of the upper class, to bring a bourgeois legitimacy to the group, I would dress the part. Putting aside my black and white wardrobe—to Maman's relief—I had ordered a new dress in two shades of mauve silk with a brocade train, its cuffs and neckline trimmed with white ermine. The bodice was embroidered with two rows of pearls, silver-blue satin bows in between. I finished off with silver-blue gloves and a matching hat whose extravagant white ostrich feather draped over one side. Whenever I moved my head, the feather swayed in the air like a lazy afterthought.

Degas was there to greet us, somberly elegant in a new pale grey suit and not his brown standard. Like the connoisseur he was, he paused to admire my outfit.

"And…? Do you approve of my armour?"

"Mademoiselle Morisot, you are a work of art."

"Are you going to ask me the significance of my feather?"

"In Egypt, ostrich feathers represent Ma'at, goddess of order and truth. Of realism."

"You made that up."

"But now your bows…"

"Are just bows."

"We cannot stay long," Maman announced.

Before escorting us upstairs he handed me a program, a pleasing white booklet of quality bond, the ponderous group name in a bold black font—"fresh from the printers."

The balloonist's studio-turned-gallery appeared to be made of light. The main room ran the length of the building and floor-to-ceiling Roman pillars drew the senses upward to its soaring ceiling and skylights. A procession of windows opened the north wall, while colourful paintings animated the other walls with the modern subject. Voices could be heard down the hall from what Degas called "the work room." Judging by the noise, the celebration was in full chorus.

All nine of my paintings hung in the middle of the principal wall, sunlight illuminating every inch and corner. Never had my works been so prominently and respectfully displayed. They were mounted in carved frames painted a dull gold and hung against royal-blue serge panels. Any notion that my female presence in the exhibit might be somehow overlooked was an impossibility.

Degas saw my expression. "Something wrong?"

"I sent along too many."

"It is a great number," confirmed Maman.

"Not at all," said Degas. "I put in ten. Monet nine like you." He lowered his voice. "We're setting the standard."

Pissarro's paintings, a humble five, hung to our left. Degas whispered, "Monet and I tried to limit Cézanne's submissions but Pissarro forbade bias against any member. I did manage to have him hung in the back room."

Degas' pictures depicted ballet dancers and laundresses. They weren't flattering but they were honest and inspired in me a sense of fellowship with the working class I'd not felt before. Pissarro's soothing landscapes reminded me of Corot's. I could have looked at them all day. Later, when we were introduced, and he took my hand, I understood that those hands were as intimate with the shovel as with the paintbrush.

The distant chatter sent up a shout, and Maman shot me a queasy look then flinched at the sound of mugs being pounded on tables and chanting egging someone on.

To the right of my paintings hung Claude Monet's. I stepped in front of his *Impression, Sunrise* and the lonely wonder of another day being born. Before I could register them, tears came. This was a man who knew how to appreciate a dawning sun over water and render not just the sight but the gather of feelings such a sight engendered. I thought: This is why I paint.

Degas toured us through the next room where I recognized Renoir's painting from the dreamlike night in Montmartre when I danced with Édouard under the flickering chandeliers. *Bal du Moulin de la Galette* was a cleaner version of events, of soft-cheeked women flushed with dancing rather than wine. Of couples pressed close to dance rather than for support. But I could hear those heavenly bells and taste the peculiar champagne, feel Édouard's grip on my waist. To think that was forever past... for a long moment I couldn't move.

In the second gallery Cézanne's strange visions swam and groped along the entire far wall, a grotesque parade repelling the eye. And then I saw the canvas that formed his centrepiece and let out an involuntary groan.

Degas sighed. "He means it as a tribute but, yes, it's unfortunate for Édouard."

"He feared being blamed for this exhibition. This will ensure it."

Maman clutched my arm. "Poor Édouard."

Crude figures, garish colours, a senseless composition, here hung a floating distortion of Édouard's most notorious painting. Cézanne even had the audacity to use the same title. *Olympia*.

"Can nothing be done? Surely we can ask Monsieur Cézanne to remove just this one."

"Pissarro would cancel the entire enterprise rather than compromise his principles." Degas smiled thinly. "*Our* principles."

We approached the work room, its loudness and coarse talk. I heard a voice proclaim over the din, "I have recently discovered the colour of air."

Gaping laughter.

"That's the stupidest thing I've—"

"Tell us, Claude, you cunt."

"We are expected somewhere within the half hour," said Maman.

I strained to hear the answer, and the voice said, "Violet," which elicited more jeering. But the air through which I walked looked somehow brighter and new to me.

There was a momentary hush as we entered. Men rose from chairs, hopped down from the edges of tables, straightened ties, brushed drink from their beards. Someone began a clumsy sputter of applause and I blushed. In my fancy dress and feathered hat I felt on display and kept close to Degas, who, preserving formalities, led us around for introductions.

Something ancient about his eyes, M. Pissarro was as elegant in manner and voice as his paintings had led me to imagine. Creases in his knobby wool jacket were noticeably darker than the sun-bleached rest. When I told him his paintings were soulful like those of my teacher Corot, then learned that we had both been Corot's student, a warmth passed between us that felt like friendship. He called my work "daring, original and heartfelt." Believing him incapable of duplicity, I was moved.

Renoir perched quietly in the corner, away from any grouping. Just as at the dance in Montmartre, he seemed content to observe gaiety rather than step into its midst. I wanted to tell him how his *Bal du Moulin de la Galette* brought back the best of memories, but with Maman beside me I cut short our conversation for fear he might mention it.

Cézanne resembled a poor farmer and true man of the people. His trousers were held up with a length of twine. Stains ringed the armpits of his shirt for his jacket was off and he hadn't bothered to put it on again. His dress, I then understood, was as purposeful as my own.

"Welcome, Madame and Mademoiselle," he said, stern-eyed and with a sharp nod, "to the greatest art exhibit on earth." This was said without humour.

"Thank you," I responded, and that was the extent of our exchange, for I could say nothing positive about his work and perhaps he felt the same about my own. Though I wished I was brave enough, for Édouard's sake, to ask if he'd consider removing his homage.

Stocky and muscular, Claude Monet had urgency about him, an impatience that seemed to roil under his skin. I had the feeling he resented Maman's and my presence, which had reduced their celebrations to polite murmurings.

I told him bluntly that standing in front of his *Impression, Sunrise* I'd found myself weeping. "I've studied and tried without success to copy your water. It's a marvel how you make it move or perhaps make the eye move, I can't figure which. You depict things the rest of us cannot. My friend Monsieur Manet is as envious as I."

He appeared disarmed by the praise and I moved on before he could respond, glad to have caught his attention. I'm not sure I liked the man, but that did not dim my respect for his talent.

On the carriage ride home, Maman, shaken by the whole affair and close to tears, bemoaned my involvement in the "ruffian" exhibit, convinced it would be my ruin. All I could think was that she was too late. I was already ruined.

THE EXHIBITION OPENED its doors to the public, but first to the critics, and Uncle Octave made sure Maman received every last damning review. In her humiliation and guilt, Maman made sure I heard them as well.

These madmen and one madder woman paint as if suffering seizures. One cannot make heads or tails of the work without taking ten paces back.

As in most notorious gangs, there's one woman in tow. She is Berthe Morisot and a curiosity indeed. For, in her case, a lady's life is maintained amidst the outpourings of a delirious mind.

Messieurs Monet—a more uncompromising Manet—Pissarro, Degas and Mlle. Morisot have declared war on beauty. Their paintings defy all that defines fine art and will soon be dismissed as such and forgotten.

Edma's and my former teacher, M. Guichard, was compelled to write his concerns to Maman.

Dear Madame Morisot,
That a young lady could destroy love letters reminding her of a painful liaison, I can grasp, such ashes as justifiable, but to destroy all efforts and aspirations of her artistic ambitions, that is madness! Even impiety.

As a painter and friend, here is my prescription: Escort your daughter to the Louvre twice weekly.

Sincerely, Joseph Guichard

One mean-spirited review proved insightful, despite itself. The critic Louis Leroy, writing for *Le Charivari* and inspired by Monet's *Impression Sunrise* denounced the exhibit as *a roomful of fuzzy impressions. These artists are all in need of spectacles to correct their eyesight and painting lessons to teach them form.* In an attempt at wit he retitled our show *The Exhibition of the Impressionists,* a term that captured something of the truth, perhaps even the essence of our process. I quite liked the sound of it. M. Pissarro did as well.

ÉDOUARD'S PREDICTIONS came true. *La Presse* referred to the group as "devotees of Manet." A cartoon on the cover of *Les Contemporains* under the title "King of the Impressionists" showed an unflattering caricature of Édouard sporting a crown and a paintbrush scepter.

Édouard had not been in contact since revealing his illness. I had made excuses to avoid his mother's gatherings, needing time to think before I spoke to him again, much less face his brother.

It was Eugène, not Édouard, who attended the opening of the Cooperative and sent along a note of congratulations and gushing praise for my work. A few days later I received a second note from him, this one filled with clipped reviews, but of a positive nature. Something I hadn't known existed. He must have gone out of his way to hunt them down in obscure avant-garde magazines. I showed Maman in hopes of relieving at least some of her distress.

Berthe Morisot has wit to the tips of her fingers, especially at their tips. What splendid artistic sensibility. You cannot find more graceful images handled with more delicacy and talent than The Cradle. *Here, the execution is in utter accord with the idea expressed.*

How can one expose an artistic refinement such as Mlle. Morisot's in the same location as Cézanne's The Bachelor's Dream? *She is a noteworthy artist whose work would enrich and warm any wall.*

There are four young men and a woman who stand out in this exhibit, each of whom for five or six years made the Salon jury tremble with fear and indignation. Denying such genius for so many years, the Salon jury has become more and more ridiculous, compromising itself before the public to the extent that there will soon be few men in France who can speak in its favour.

Zola wrote a short article extolling the exhibition's nerve and singling out a few pieces, *The Cradle* among them. I tracked down copies of the avant-garde magazines to send to Edma. She and I had stopped corresponding and this would be a way to thank her for her part in *The Cradle*'s success, however limited, so I had Maman include them in her next letter. It was also, of course, a matter of pride on my part that my sister read something that justified my life and my decisions.

On top of being blamed for our exhibition, Édouard was to enjoy none of last year's Salon celebrity. His watercolour was ignored and *The Railway* skewered. Its enigmatic quality infuriated. *Was this unintelligible painting depicting lunatics in an asylum?* asked *Le Vie Parisienne. Or a mother and child all dressed up and behind prison bars? Incarcerated for what? For killing that puppy in the mother's arms?*

Others lamented Édouard's sense, claiming him an artist capable of charming work but one who insisted on *bringing ruin upon himself by choosing to paint, with a lazy undisciplined hand, ridiculous and ignoble subject matter.*

I longed to write him with praise for *The Railway* and proclaiming my love, but like an addict pushing away his absinthe, held back.

The *exhibition moderne* did not result in a single sale. Not one. As a result the Cooperative was deeply in debt, debts which Degas and I were asked to take care of. Maman was incensed. "The arrogance and short-sightedness of those men. Edma warned me they were using you for your money." Still I talked her into allowing me to draw the fairly substantial sum from my inheritance.

From an ordinary viewpoint the exhibition was an unqualified debacle and yet I couldn't help but be glad to have taken part. Cézanne aside, all of those daring-to-try pieces were food for my ailing soul. Even ignoring the fact that the Salon was no longer an option, when the vote came as to whether the Société should repeat the same costly exercise next year, mine was a proud yes.

After weeks of deliberation, I finally sent Édouard a note. I had to force my hand to write the words: *Eugène is free to solicit me but you are the man to whom my soul is wedded.*

He wrote back immediately:

Berthe, I am relieved and heartbroken in the same breath.
My brother is a humble man who will support you in your artistic endeavours. You would not find another as devoted. You, my love, will have a husband who loves you, the freedom to paint, financial security and hopefully a child to love and name after his uncle. You will be my sister in appearance only. But I gladly sacrifice my own happiness so that yours be fulfilled as it should. Let us not be sad. I will always be by your side. Édouard

Maman began a ruse of flattery. "Did you know Eugène has a hand for gardening?" she asked me, apropos of nothing but morning greetings, and breakfast. "And that he's a voracious reader yet his eyes are very good still. He can read in the dimmest of light." Her desperation beyond transparent, in the next breath, her flattery graced me.

"He once told me you are the most intelligent and talented woman he has ever known. And I can tell he finds you handsome, even now, despite your age."

ONE EVENING, after Degas had escorted Maman and me to the Opera House, I invited him in for some hot milk. Unmarried and with no plans ever to be otherwise but alone, Degas barely tolerated the housekeeper that Maman and I had secured to cook and clean for him after we saw the state of his home. Awaiting our milk, I mentioned that I was considering marriage, secretly hoping he would discourage me.

"Absolutely you should," he said without hesitation, or conviction. "Now who is this fortunate man?"

I believed he knew about Édouard and me but was too much the gentleman to mention it. I was frank. "I'll be marrying Eugène Manet for practical purposes. Our two families have known each other a long time now."

He nodded. "Eugène will treat you like a queen. I'll be content knowing that. Think what artistic genius you may produce, combining the talents of a Manet with those of a Morisot."

I pressed his hand, holding back my tears, knowing how discomfited he would be.

"I was in love once," he said with sudden candour. "My mother had died the year before. I was fourteen."

"Just entering the arena."

"And my entrance was as awkward as it was earnest."

"And the woman?"

"She was my mother's younger sister. My unhappily married aunt. They looked and sounded very much alike." His expression was a surprising combination of shame and perplexed humour. He snorted and said, "Need I say, it did not begin well, and it ended worse."

I did not press my friend for details.

I MADE A POINT OF engaging Eugène at his mother's soirées. He was visibly nervous, as was I. We had crossed a line and the air we now breathed was charged with expectation and uncertainty. We were old friends but, strangely, one I knew little about, as I took the time to ask him about himself as well as listen to his answers. The more I listened, the more I realized that he was a cultivated man who owned some of his brother's wit. And that we had things in common. We liked to read novels—Édouard was not a reader—and shared a love of the country—Édouard hated the country—and a dislike of the sea. Unlike his brother, Eugène had supported my involvement in the Cooperative. Even after its spectacular failure, he believed it wise to continue with the group, as was my fervent hope, whereas Édouard believed it the end of my having a serious career.

Eugène acknowledged my independent nature and did not appear resentful of it. I recalled something Laure Reisener had once said—"If you want to be an artist, marry a man with no ambition of his own." In my case, Eugène did have one overriding ambition, and this was my happiness.

That season, our two families set off for Fécamp where we shared lodging, ate our meals together and took in the sights. At the last minute, Édouard had a change of plans and didn't join us.

On a hillside overlooking a laundress factory and its field of linen sheets blowing on ropelines, our smocks whipped by the wind, Eugène and I painted side by side as I had once imagined doing with Édouard. Eugène's medium was limited to watercolours but his eye was true and his brushwork sound. All that blustery day, overcast yet bright with a pearly blanket of light, shadows appeared and disappeared as land and sky danced and merged.

Above all else, I needed to speak plainly. "Édouard tells me you are thinking of asking me about marriage."

His hand halted before the canvas and he rocked back on his stool. I thought he might tip but he steadied himself. "I am."

"You understand that, at thirty-three, I may be too old to carry a child."

"That does not concern me."

His chest rose and fell as his breath quickened.

"I am selfish with my time and will not give up painting."

"I would never ask that of you."

"Painting will always come first. Ahead of social gatherings. Household duties. Even our own relations." I met his eye to see if he understood, as wind whipped the sleeves of his smock.

"Yes."

"I would like a place in the city and in the country."

"Of course."

I was running out of reasons to turn and run. But if I was to marry and share my life with him, I was determined ours be an honest, indeed a daringly honest, relationship. I knew the damage of secrets kept.

"You know that I'm in love with your brother Édouard."

"So he has told me."

I was too ashamed to look at him. "I am not spoiled." I wanted him to hear this from my lips. "But you, Eugène, deserve far better."

He went silent. I stared at my canvas, my cheeks seared with understanding. Who could blame him for packing his easel and paints. Leaving me to contemplate my future alone, struggling to make rent or living as an unwanted guest with Yves and Théo in the country.

Eugène touched my shoulder and launched a mix of emotions, their trajectories wild and unpredictable. My eyes welled, blurring the visible. His voice rattled and shook in the wind. "If I could be the husband of such an independent, complicated, talented, elegant and beautiful woman as yourself, well… it would honestly make me the happiest man in all of France."

Though perhaps I could never love him as he loved me, I fell in love with Eugène Manet a little that day, and a little more each day after.

OUR ENGAGEMENT WAS SHORT, the wedding small and unadorned. Edma found an excuse not to attend, though she sent her regards with *best wishes for an honest union*. This hurt beyond measure. I had invited her myself, explaining my decision and exactly what had transpired between Édouard and me. I even thanked her for trying to protect me from my own heartache but that *some lessons*, I wrote, *have to be lived*. Perhaps she believed I wasn't being honest and the marriage a sham in order to continue my clandestine affair with Édouard. If so, I understood her boycott. I had kept the truth from her once, so why would she trust me now? That was the end of all correspondence between us.

Tibby also didn't attend. He was away in England or the south of Spain spending his inheritance. Yves came up for Mirande and brought along her family. She was surprised at just how happy I was to see her. Missing Edma, I found comfort in her guileless support regarding my choice of husband. "He is shy and kind and clearly worships you," she said, never reluctant to share her opinions. "You, Berthe, will be in charge of this marriage and able to do just as you please. Just as you please."

The Reiseners were there. I asked Rosalie if she had been in touch with Edma of late.

Ever diplomatic, she told me, "Yes. She sounds very busy with the girls and a Fall Fair at the church. The Fair was long planned, I understand."

"The Fall Fair, yes. My engagement was exceedingly short."

"And when Edma commits to something, it's certain to get done."

I embraced her. "I'm glad you're here."

"I wouldn't miss it."

Marcello had shown up at my door a few weeks before the wedding, her servant laden with painting supplies. I had notified her of my engagement and told her that it had been her words that had given me the strength to go through with it. She insisted on painting a wedding portrait of me as a gift to my future husband. How could

I refuse? She also insisted on choosing my dress for her portrait, a pale sleeveless ball gown, and on arranging my hair and my pose. "Not Bia. Just Berthe," she said. "She is forceful enough on her own."

It was a flattering picture but a little too flattering. She had enhanced me, a jaded thirty-four-year-old bride-to-be, to look robust, busty and darkly sexual. We had two sittings only, for she had an opening in Portugal to attend. She'd not time to complete the background, for which she apologized profusely.

When Édouard saw the painting he laughed uproariously. I laughed right along. We both knew it had little to do with me. Eugène, though, cherished that portrait all his life. Marcello, I believe, had captured how I appeared to him in his romantic mind's eye.

During our sessions together Marcello encouraged me to continue to use my maiden name as my signature. "As a wife you must not lose your identity." A mistake, she said, that she had once made.

Before my marriage day, Édouard painted me one final time. Though the atmosphere was tender and not without melancholy, we were able to be playful. I boasted about and showed off my ring. He made jokes.

"I've told my brother how you like to sauce your goose."

"You've done no such thing."

"He snores so loudly his neighbours sold their adjoining *appartement* and moved."

"Liar."

"As a surprise for you, Degas is painting you a portrait of your betrothed."

"A surprise, you say?"

"Maman thinks you a bit of a snob..."

"It takes one to recognize one."

"...but that you'll make her son very happy and for this, she adores you."

"I can stand being adored."

"Well, good, because you will be adored by many Manets."

We did kiss but our lips did not linger. We embraced for a long time, silently, our chests rising and falling together, breathing each other in. I tried to memorize the shape of him under my hands, while his body was still strong and whole. There were no tears and nothing more to be said.

OVER THE ENSUING YEARS Édouard's gradual decline revealed itself in the lurch of his gait, a loss of balance, and jaundiced skin; even the whites of his eyes turned a dirty yellow. His moods grew extreme, marked by sudden violent outbursts, spells of obsessive painting that kept him from sleep, and a melancholy that chained him to his room. Painting was all he would speak about, and on this subject he remained coherent. It was terrible for Suzanne, who had her own health burdens and yet whose devotion never wavered. I'd once considered her a martyr, then a saint, before realizing that she simply loved him. Suzanne and I became close in our way, sisterly friends of the practical sort. She was by my side during my drawn-out labour with you, Julie, and helped care for me after, for there was much blood loss and I was unable to rise from bed for a fortnight. And I assisted Suzanne with our mother-in-law when she became bedridden. Together we suffered her lack of thanks, critiques of the soup or our rough handling, the cold *chaise de pot* against her paper-thin skin, her instructive finger jabbing the air after her speech failed her. Her sons she praised to the end and all three were by her side when she faded from this world.

Suzanne and I also worked in tandem during those final weeks in the rented house at Rueil when Édouard lay dying and friends came to pay their respects. Women, mostly, a steady stream of those he had painted and perhaps lain with and even loved for however brief a time. I was shocked by the sheer number, though Suzanne appeared unfazed. These women made me question all over again just how unique was the love he and I shared. But then, after becoming a mother, I realized that love is not quantifiable, nor is it finite, and to see it as so only diminishes one's capacity for it.

Suzanne thanked each woman for coming and for bringing flowers in glass vases for Édouard to paint, as per his wishes. Among the perfumed parade was she of the splendid gaze from *Le Déjeuner sur l'herbe*, *Olympia*, and *The Railway*, Victorine Meurent. Her flower offering was a champagne flute holding two overripe roses, one dark red, the other a blazing yellow. Meeting the common café singer brought up staggering pangs of jealousy. Not because of any carnal liaison with Édouard, but because it was she, not I, who inspired his best work. She kissed the grey skin of his forehead, stroked his hand and attempted to distract him from his face-distorting pain with a humourous anecdote about chasing her lover to America, and repeated the funny barks of English words she had struggled and failed with.

Only one distraction gave him respite from his agony. One might say from dying itself. He painted those flowers in their glass jars. Propped up in bed, a pillow supporting his elbow, his breath laboured as his eyes pursued the light, his hand produced one perfect little painting after another. Sixteen in all. Tender representations of his love for this world. I weep to think of it.

I'd all but forgotten that he once painted you, Julie, when you were three. In the garden at our house in Bougival. He wanted to paint you as you were, sitting next to the watering can and painstakingly filling it with torn bits of grass. You thought he was going to take the can away so you impishly sat on it. *Julie Manet Sitting on a Watering Can*, he named it. That portrait was never finished – he suffered blinding headaches that year. He insisted it was a poor likeness and wouldn't let me have it. But it is you. It is him seeing you seeing him, and therefore perfection.

Your father's and mine was a good decent marriage, I think. We confided in and comforted each other. We enjoyed gardening together, books and travel and a mostly peaceful house despite my moodiness. I'm afraid I let your father be the one to read to you, take you on walks and boat rides, oversee your lessons and even the dressmaker's designs—your papa's taste in women's clothes impeccable. Forgive me for putting painting first, but to go any length of time without was a kind of death for me. I know I too often expressed my love for you through my brush but it was a necessity.

Julie, I am very tired now but I want to say this: your Uncle Édouard taught me many things about art and passion. Your father taught me about loyalty, kindness and companionship. But it was your father who gave me the greatest gift of all. That is you, my precious jewel, my single and only perfection. You have been my biggest inspiration both in my work and in my days. Without you, life would have been nothing but incomplete, no matter how many sales or favourable reviews. Your Aunt Edma, as always, was right. There is no greater joy.

POSTSCRIPT

CORNÉLIE MARIE MORISOT died in December of 1876 after a protracted undiagnosed illness.

JULIE MANET was born in 1878 when Berthe was at the advanced maternal age of thirty-seven. Edgar Degas and Auguste Renoir were named as godfathers. Renoir painted Julie's portrait and one of Julie and Berthe. There are no known portraits of Julie or Berthe done by Degas. Degas played matchmaker to Julie Manet's marriage to Ernest Rouart, son of the Impressionist painter Henri Rouart. She was married at a double wedding. The other couple was Yves' youngest daughter (and Julie's best friend), Jeannie, and the poet Paul Valery.

ÉDOUARD MANET painted Berthe Morisot more than any other model. He won his first Salon medal in 1881, second place, for his *Portrait of Henri Rochefort*. And later that year, under the rule of Léon Gambetta, then head of a moderate government, Manet received the coveted Legion of Honour.

Almost twenty years to the day after he exhibited *Le Déjeuner sur l'herbe* at the Salon de Réfuses, in 1883, at the age of fifty-one, Édouard died of complications following a gangrenous leg amputation due to late-stage syphilis. Both Berthe and Suzanne were by his side. He was buried in the Cemetière de Passy. With Suzanne's help, Berthe organized a retrospective of his paintings, which was held across the street from his childhood home at the Académie des Beaux-Arts.

EUGÈNE MANET published his novel *Victims!* in 1877 to little acclaim. He devoted the rest of his life to his daughter and to supporting his wife's career. He died slowly over the winter and spring of 1892 of heart failure. He was fifty-nine.

BERTHE MORISOT died of influenza on February 28, 1895, which she contracted after nursing her daughter Julie back to health from the same ailment. She was fifty-four. She kept her commitment to the Société Anonyme Cooperative even after Renoir and Monet left in order to submit to the Salon. Of the original group only Pissarro, Degas and Morisot participated in all eight exhibitions. Each exhibit was a critical and monetary failure, but one that produced a new era and movement in painting that called itself Impressionism. Morisot would be described by critics, then and now, as being the most faithful to the thesis of the Impressionist School.

It was not until 1894, the year before her death, when her *Young Girl in a Ball Gown* was purchased by the state that she came to be held in equal esteem to her male colleagues. Her work is included in all major Impressionist exhibitions worldwide. The single largest collection of her work is displayed in the Marmottan Museum in the Passy district of Paris. The Marmottan is also home to Manet's *Berthe Morisot Reclining*. She lived her entire life in the 16th *arrondissement*, the District of Passy.

EDMA PONTILLON gave birth to her third and last child, a son, in 1878, and named him Edme, her father's middle name. She lived until she was eighty-one. Emotionally estranged from her sister, Edma Pontillon returned to Paris for Berthe Manet's funeral.

While in Paris, in the Passy cemetery near their family home, she arranged to have Eugène's remains moved from the Manet family crypt and buried, alongside Berthe, under an engraved slab which reads:

Eugène Manet
1834–1892

Berthe Morisot
widow of Eugène Manet
1841–1895

This gravestone was positioned below that of Édouard Manet's, a looming pedestal and bust of the great artist's likeness. Beneath his uncompromising gaze, now and forever fixed, Edma Pontillon laid her sister with the two men she loved, one above, one beside.

ACKNOWLEDGEMENTS

I want to thank, in the beginning: Lucy Bashford, Jen Fraser, Eve Joseph, Carol Matthews, Patricia Young, and especially Janice McCachen for showing me Paris and throwing open doors that would have remained closed. And to Brian Butler for his belief, and the cement.

I want to thank, in the middle: Lise Davidson, Bill Gaston, Sandy Mayzell, and Seán Virgo for their invaluable broad strokes.

And I want to thank, in the end: my agent John Pearce for his generous and brilliant editorial, my delightful, insightful and skilful editor, Deborah Willis, Kelsey Attard for seeing what others didn't and for answering my phone calls during the pandemic, and everyone at Freehand Books. Thank you Lilli Gaston for her research, and Josh Davidson for his tech savvy.

I am indebted to a number of sources in particular: Ross King, *The Judgement of Paris*. Anne Higonnet, *Berthe Morisot*. The Rouart Foundation, *Reasoned Audacity*. The Musée Marmottan Monet, *Berthe Morisot*. Giles Néret, *Manet*. Sue Roe, *the private lives of the impressionists*. Julie Manet, *The Diary of Julie Manet*.

I want to thank the Canada Council of the Arts and the British Columbia Arts Council, for being there.

Finally, to my beloved family, Bill, Lise, Connor, Vaughn and Millicent, who continue to raise the creative bar.